EVERYMAN,

I WILL GO WITH THEE,

AND BE THY GUIDE,

IN THY MOST NEED

TO GO BY THY SIDE

EVERYMAN'S POCKET CLASSICS

NEW YORK
STORIES

EDITED BY DIANA SECKER TESDELL

EVERYMAN'S POCKET CLASSICS
Alfred A. Knopf New York London Toronto

THIS IS A BORZOI BOOK
PUBLISHED BY ALFRED A. KNOPF

This selection by Diana Secker Tesdell first published in
Everyman's Library, 2011
Copyright © 2011 by Everyman's Library
A list of acknowledgments to copyright owners appears at the back
of this volume.
Fifth printing (US)

All rights reserved. Published in the United States by Alfred A. Knopf,
a division of Penguin Random House LLC, New York, and in
Canada by Penguin Random House of Canada Limited, Toronto.
Distributed by Penguin Random House LLC, New York. Published
in the United Kingdom by Everyman's Library, 50 Albemarle Street,
London W1S 4BD and distributed by Penguin Random House UK,
20 Vauxhall Bridge Road, London SW1V 2SA.

www.randomhouse.com/everymans
www.everymanslibrary.co.uk

ISBN: 978-0-307-59493-8 (US)
978-1-84159-607-5 (UK)

A CIP catalogue reference for this book is available from the
British Library

Typography by Peter B. Willberg

Typeset in the UK by AccComputing, North Barrow, Somerset
Printed and bound in Germany by GGP Media GmbH, Pössneck

NEW YORK STORIES

Contents

JACK KEROUAC

NEW YORK
NITE CLUB—

OUTSIDE, IN THE street, the sudden music which comes from the nitespot fills you with yearning for some intangible joy—and you feel that it can only be found within the smoky confines of the place. You leave the street and enter New York's night life—a sudden rush of festivity, not the wild dark festivity of Spain, but a cultured, toned festivity borne along by the nostalgic improvisations of a guitar, or the rich round moans of a Billie Holiday. There is the eternal smoke of cigarettes, the fine smell of bars ranged with colorful displays of bottles, gowned women, tuxedoed men, and those who reminisce, wrangle, and cry at the bar. You look down the bar—it is not like an ordinary bar, for there is something about the New York bars that no other bar can capture—and you see a gallery of faces, each as interesting as the other. Millions of dancing illusions cloud your eyes as you search into the eyes of these barflies—that one there looks a lot like a bookie, and the other much like an actor, and there is a high-priced harlot. Books and novels could be written about the lives of these rangy faces, these pouting velvet faces, these red lips, these dark mysterious faces, these jovial open-faced faces, these drunken dull-eyed faces. The bartender, looking a lot like a performer with the light of his brilliantly arrayed bar shining up to his face and softening it like footlights do, is mixing drinks. There is the hardness of the city in him— hardness, a certain look of hectic suspicion, a tinge of awed dismay, and an obviously false certainty that is helped along by the most mundane manipulation of a cigarette.

I remember once when I was quite childishly eating a hot fudge sundae at a fountain back home. It was raining, and I was as virile and masculine as anyone else in the place. But I was perched up on a stool and drooling in my fudge and cream like a child. I was self-conscious. Then in walked a fellow attired in soda pop clothes, a driver of the Coca-Cola trucks. He walked up to the cigarette counter with a preoccupied stride. The soda jerk recognized him:

"Howdy Joe. Just pull in?"

(Just pull in, I think. A truck driver, just pull in. Just pull in, the rain was slashing at his windshield. Just pull in, the hero. Wearing drivers' clothes, just pull in, and the rain.)

The truck driver looked carefully at his questioner, pulling out some money from his pocket and smoking knowingly on his cigarette. He answered, very curtly and with much competent authority, almost a scowl:

"Yeah."

(Oh boy, I sneer to myself. The great man, just pull in.)

I looked at him. He bought the pack of cigarettes, letting his last cigarette butt hang from his twisted mouth and spiral smoke up to his scowling eyes. He walked out, still preoccupied. A sort of false preoccupation designed to befuddle everyone with whom he communicated. Preoccupied with his paltry little truck universe, as if it were the only universe in the place. The big man, cigarette butt hanging from snarling mouth, Yeah, curtly scowling at the world, women and drink and trucks and the hell with anything and everything else.

Where is the naked unquestioning sincerity in this world today?

You buy yourself a Coke and take a table in an obscure corner. You light your cigarette and look around you. The music will soon begin—the little negro trumpeter is almost ready, but never quite begins. He holds the horn in his chubby black hands, with white fingernails, and he talks to friends and musicians around and below him. He smiles, and blows through his trumpet to emit a small round tone. Then he talks some more, jokes, maddeningly producing his horn to his mouth only to let it drop again in order to say something to the inevitable someone who is always around him. The music will never start, you say. And suddenly he starts playing on his trumpet.

O. HENRY

THE MAKING OF A NEW YORKER

BESIDES MANY THINGS, Raggles was a poet. He was called a tramp; but that was only an elliptical way of saying that he was a philosopher, an artist, a traveler, a naturalist, and a discoverer. But most of all he was a poet. In all his life he never wrote a line of verse; he lived his poetry. His Odyssey would have been a Limerick, had it been written. But, to linger with the primary proposition, Raggles was a poet.

Raggles's specialty, had he been driven to ink and paper, would have been sonnets to the cities. He studied cities as women study their reflections in mirrors; as children study the glue and sawdust of a dislocated doll; as the men who write about wild animals study the cages in the zoo. A city to Raggles was not merely a pile of bricks and mortar, peopled by a certain number of inhabitants; it was a thing with soul characteristic and distinct; an individual conglomeration of life, with its own peculiar essence, flavor, and feeling. Two thousand miles to the north and south, east and west, Raggles wandered in poetic fervor, taking the cities to his breast. He footed it on dusty roads, or sped magnificently in freight cars, counting time as of no account. And when he had found the heart of a city and listened to its secret confession, he strayed on, restless, to another. Fickle Raggles!—but perhaps he had not met the civic corporation that could engage and hold his critical fancy.

Through the ancient poets we have learned that the cities are feminine. So they were to poet Raggles; and his mind carried a concrete and clear conception of the figure that symbolized and typified each one that he had wooed.

Chicago seemed to swoop down upon him with a breezy suggestion of Mrs. Partington, plumes and patchouli, and to disturb his rest with a soaring and beautiful song of future promise. But Raggles would awake to a sense of shivering cold and a haunting impression of ideals lost in a depressing aura of potato salad and fish.

Thus Chicago affected him. Perhaps there is a vagueness and inaccuracy in the description; but that is Raggles's fault. He should have recorded his sensations in magazine poems.

Pittsburgh impressed him as the play of "Othello" performed in the Russian language in a railroad station by Dockstader's minstrels. A royal and generous lady this Pittsburgh, though—homely, hearty, with flushed face, washing the dishes in a silk dress and white kid slippers, and bidding Raggles sit before the roaring fireplace and drink champagne with his pigs' feet and fried potatoes.

New Orleans had simply gazed down upon him from a balcony. He could see her pensive, starry eyes and catch the flutter of her fan, and that was all. Only once he came face to face with her. It was at dawn, when she was flushing the red bricks of the banquette with a pail of water. She laughed and hummed a chansonette and filled Raggles's shoes with ice-cold water. Allons!

Boston construed herself to the poetic Raggles in an erratic and singular way. It seemed to him that he had drunk cold tea and that the city was a white, cold cloth that had been bound tightly around his brow to spur him to some unknown but tremendous mental effort. And, after all, he came to shovel snow for a livelihood; and the cloth, becoming wet, tightened its knots and could not be removed.

Indefinite and unintelligible ideas, you will say; but your disapprobation should be tempered with gratitude, for these are poets' fancies—and suppose you had come upon them in verse!

One day Raggles came and laid siege to the heart of the great city of Manhattan. She was the greatest of all; and he wanted to learn her note in the scale; to taste and appraise and classify and solve and label her and arrange her with the other cities that had given him up the secret of their individuality. And here we cease to be Raggles's translator and become his chronicler.

Raggles landed from a ferry-boat one morning and walked into the core of the town with the blasé air of a cosmopolite. He was dressed with care to play the rôle of an "unidentified man." No country, race, class, clique, union, party, clan, or bowling association could have claimed him. His clothing, which had been donated to him piece-meal by citizens of different height, but same number of inches around the heart, was not yet as uncomfortable to his figure as those specimens of raiment, self-measured, that are railroaded to you by trans-continental tailors with a suitcase, suspenders, silk handkerchief and pearl studs as a bonus. Without money —as a poet should be—but with the ardor of an astronomer discovering a new star in the chorus of the milky way, or a man who has seen ink suddenly flow from his fountain pen, Raggles wandered into the great city.

Late in the afternoon he drew out of the roar and commotion with a look of dumb terror on his countenance. He was defeated, puzzled, discomfited, frightened. Other cities had been to him as long primers to read; as country maidens quickly to fathom; as send-price-of-subscription-with-answer rebuses to solve; as oyster cocktails to swallow; but here was one as cold, glittering, serene, impossible as a four-carat diamond in a window to a lover outside fingering damply in his pocket his ribbon-counter salary.

The greetings of the other cities he had known—their homespun kindliness, their human gamut of rough charity, friendly curses, garrulous curiosity, and easily estimated credulity or indifference. This city of Manhattan gave him no clue; it was walled against him. Like a river of adamant it flowed past him in the streets. Never an eye was turned upon him; no voice spoke to him. His heart yearned for the clap of Pittsburgh's sooty hand on his shoulder; for Chicago's menacing but social yawp in his ear; for the pale and eleemosynary stare through the Bostonian eyeglass—even for the precipitate but unmalicious boot-toe of Louisville or St. Louis.

On Broadway Raggles, successful suitor of many cities, stood, bashful, like any country swain. For the first time he experienced the poignant humiliation of being ignored. And when he tried to reduce this brilliant, swiftly changing, ice-cold city to a formula he failed utterly. Poet though he was, it offered him no color similes, no points of comparison, no flaw in its polished facets, no handle by which he could hold it up and view its shape and structure, as he familiarly and often contemptuously had done with other towns. The houses were interminable ramparts loopholed for defense; the people were bright but bloodless specters passing in sinister and selfish array.

The thing that weighed heaviest on Raggles's soul and clogged his poet's fancy was the spirit of absolute egotism that seemed to saturate the people as toys are saturated with paint. Each one that he considered appeared a monster of abominable and insolent conceit. Humanity was gone from them; they were toddling idols of stone and varnish, worshiping themselves and greedy for though oblivious of worship from their fellow graven images. Frozen, cruel, implacable, impervious, cut to an identical pattern, they hurried on their ways like statues brought by some miracle to motion, while soul and feeling lay unaroused in the reluctant marble.

Gradually Raggles became conscious of certain types. One was an elderly gentleman with a snow-white, short beard, pink, unwrinkled face, and stony, sharp blue eyes, attired in the fashion of a gilded youth, who seemed to personify the city's wealth, ripeness and frigid unconcern. Another type was a woman, tall, beautiful, clear as a steel engraving, goddess-like, calm, clothed like the princesses of old, with eyes as coldly blue as the reflection of sunlight on a glacier. And another was a by-product of this town of marionettes— a broad, swaggering, grim, threateningly sedate fellow, with a jowl as large as a harvested wheat field, the complexion of a baptized infant, and the knuckles of a prize-fighter. This type leaned against cigar signs and viewed the world with frappéd contumely.

A poet is a sensitive creature, and Raggles soon shriveled in the bleak embrace of the undecipherable. The chill, sphinx-like, ironical, illegible, unnatural, ruthless expression of the city left him downcast and bewildered. Had it no heart? Better the woodpile, the scolding of vinegar-faced housewives at back doors, the kindly spleen of bartenders behind provincial free-lunch counters, the amiable truculence of rural constables, the kicks, arrests, and happy-go-lucky chances of the other vulgar, loud, crude cities than this freezing heartlessness.

Raggles summoned his courage and sought alms from the populace. Unheeding, regardless, they passed on without the wink of an eyelash to testify that they were conscious of his existence. And then he said to himself that this fair but pitiless city of Manhattan was without a soul; that its inhabitants were mannikins moved by wires and springs, and that he was alone in a great wilderness.

Raggles started to cross the street. There was a blast, a roar, a hissing and a crash as something struck him and hurled him over and over six yards from where he had been. As he was coming down like the stick of a rocket the earth and all the cities thereof turned to a fractured dream.

Raggles opened his eyes. First an odor made itself known to him—an odor of the earliest spring flowers of Paradise. And then a hand soft as a falling petal touched his brow. Bending over him was the woman clothed like the princess of old, with blue eyes, now soft and humid with human sympathy. Under his head on the pavement were silks and furs. With Raggles's hat in his hand and with his face pinker than ever from a vehement outburst of oratory against reckless driving, stood the elderly gentleman who personified the city's wealth and ripeness. From a nearby café hurried the by-product with the vast jowl and baby complexion, bearing a glass full of crimson fluid that suggested delightful possibilities.

"Drink dis, sport," said the by-product, holding the glass to Raggles's lips.

Hundreds of people huddled around in a moment, their faces wearing the deepest concern. Two flattering and gorgeous policemen got into the circle and pressed back the over-plus of Samaritans. An old lady in a black shawl spoke loudly of camphor; a newsboy slipped one of his papers beneath Raggles's elbow, where it lay on the muddy pavement. A brisk young man with a notebook was asking for names.

A bell clanged importantly, and the ambulance cleaned a lane through the crowd. A cool surgeon slipped into the midst of affairs.

"How do you feel, old man?" asked the surgeon, stooping easily to his task. The princess of silks and satins wiped a red drop or two from Raggles's brow with a fragrant cobweb.

"Me?" said Raggles, with a seraphic smile. "I feel fine."

He had found the heart of his new city.

In three days they let him leave his cot for the convalescent ward in the hospital. He had been in there an hour when the attendants heard sounds of conflict. Upon investigation they found that Raggles had assaulted and damaged a brother convalescent—a glowering transient whom a freight train collision had sent in to be patched up.

"What's all this about?" inquired the head nurse.

"He was runnin' down me town," said Raggles.

"What town?" asked the nurse.

"Noo York," said Raggles.

JOHN CHEEVER

O CITY OF
BROKEN DREAMS

WHEN THE TRAIN from Chicago left Albany and began to pound down the river valley toward New York, the Malloys, who had already experienced many phases of excitement, felt their breathing quicken, as if there were not enough air in the coach. They straightened their backs and raised their heads, searching for oxygen, like the crew of a doomed submarine. Their daughter, Mildred-Rose, took an enviable way out of the agitation. She fell asleep. Evarts Malloy wanted to get the suitcases down from the rack, but Alice, his wife, studied the timetable and said that it was too soon. She stared out of the window and saw the noble Hudson.

"Why do they call it the rind of America?" she asked her husband.

"The Rhine," Evarts said. "Not the rind."

"Oh."

They had left their home in Wentworth, Indiana, the day before, and in spite of the excitements of travel and their brilliant destination, they both wondered, now and then, if they had remembered to turn off the gas and extinguish the rubbish fire behind the barn. They were dressed, like the people you sometimes see in Times Square on Saturday nights, in clothing that had been saved for their flight. His light shoes had perhaps not been out of the back of the closet since his father's funeral or his brother's wedding. She was wearing her new gloves for the first time—the gloves she had been given for Christmas ten years ago. His tarnished collar pin and his initialed tie clip, with its gilt chain, his fancy socks, the rayon handkerchief in his breast pocket, and the carnation made of feathers in his lapel had all been husbanded in the top drawer of his bureau for years in the firm conviction that life would someday call him from Wentworth.

Alice Malloy had dark, stringy hair, and even her husband, who loved her more than he knew, was sometimes reminded by her lean face of a tenement doorway on a rainy day, for her countenance was long, vacant, and weakly lighted, a passage for the gentle transports and miseries of the poor. Evarts Malloy was very thin. He had worked as a bus driver and he stooped a little. Their child slept with her thumb in her mouth. Her hair was dark and her dirty face was lean, like her mother's. When a violent movement of the train roused her, she drew noisily at her thumb until she lost consciousness again. She had been unable to store up as much finery as her parents, since she was only five years old, but she wore a white fur coat. The matching hat and muff had been lost generations before; the skins of the coat were sere and worn, but as she slept, she stroked them, as if they had remarkable properties that assured her that all was well, all was well.

The conductor who came through the car taking tickets after Albany noticed the Malloys, and something about their appearance worried him. As he came back through the car, he stopped at their seat and talked with them, first about Mildred-Rose and then about their destination.

"You people going to New York for the first time?" he asked.

"Yes," Evarts said.

"Going down to see the sights?"

"Oh, no," Alice said. "We're going on business."

"Looking for a job?" the conductor asked.

"Oh, no," Alice said. "Tell him, Evarts."

"Well, it really isn't a job," Evarts said. "I'm not looking for a job, I mean. I mean, I sort of have a job." His manner was friendly and simple and he told his story enthusiastically, for the conductor was the first stranger to ask for it. "I was in the Army, you see, and then, when I got out of the Army, I went back home and began driving the bus again. I'm a night bus driver. But I didn't like it. I kept getting stomach aches, and it hurt my eyes, driving at night, so in my spare time, during the afternoons, I began to write this play. Now, out on Route 7, near Wentworth, where we live, there's this old woman named Mama Finelli, who has a gas station and a snake farm. She's a very salty and haunting old character, and so I decided to write this play about her. She has all these salty and haunting sayings. Well, I wrote this first act—and then Tracey Murchison, the producer, comes out from New York to give a lecture at the Women's Club about the problems of the theater. Well, Alice went to this lecture, and when he was complaining, when Murchison was complaining about the lack of young playwrights, Alice raises her hand and she tells Murchison that her husband is a young playwright and will he read his play. Didn't you, Alice?"

"Yes," Alice said.

"Well, he hems and haws," Evarts said. "Murchison hems and haws, but Alice pins him down, because all these other people are listening, and when he finishes his lecture, she goes right up on the platform and she gives him the play— she's got it in her pocketbook. Well, then she goes back to his hotel with him and she sits right beside him until he's read the play—the first act, that is. That's all I've written. Well in this play there's a part he wants for his wife, Madge Beatty, right off. I guess you know who Madge Beatty is. So you know what he does then? He sits right down and he

29

writes out a check for thirty-five dollars and he says for me and Alice to come to New York! So we take all our money out of the savings bank and we burn our bridges and here we are."

"Well, I guess there's lots of money in it," the conductor said. Then he wished the Malloys luck and walked away.

Evarts wanted to take the suitcases down at Poughkeepsie and again at Harmon, but Alice checked each place against the timetable and made him wait. Neither of them had seen New York before, and they watched its approaches greedily, for Wentworth was a dismal town and even the slums of Manhattan looked wonderful to them that afternoon. When the train plunged into the darkness beneath Park Avenue, Alice felt that she was surrounded by the inventions of giants and she roused Mildred-Rose and tied the little girl's bonnet with trembling fingers.

As the Malloys stepped from the train, Alice noticed that the paving, deep in the station, had a frosty glitter, and she wondered if diamonds had been ground into the concrete. She forbade Evarts to ask directions. "If they find out we're green, they'll fleece us," she whispered. They wandered through the marble waiting-room, following the noise of traffic and klaxons as if it were the bidding of life. Alice had studied a map of New York, and when they left the station, she knew which direction to take. They walked along Forty-second Street to Fifth Avenue. The faces that passed them seemed purposeful and intent, as if they all belonged to people who were pursuing the destinies of great industries. Evarts had never seen so many beautiful women, so many pleasant, young faces, promising an easy conquest. It was a winter afternoon, and the light in the city was clear and shaded with violet, just like the light on the fields around Wentworth.

Their destination, the Hotel Mentone, was on a side street west of Sixth Avenue. It was a dark place, with malodorous chambers, miserable food, and a lobby ceiling decorated with as much gilt and gesso as the Vatican chapels. It was a popular hotel among the old, it was attractive to the disreputable, and the Malloys had found the way there because the Mentone advertised on railroad-station hoardings all through the West. Many innocents had been there before them, and their sweetness and humility had triumphed over the apparent atmosphere of ruined splendor and petty vice and had left in all the public rooms a humble odor that reminded one of a country feed store on a winter afternoon. A bellboy took them to their room. As soon as he had gone, Alice examined the bath and pulled aside the window curtains. The window looked onto a brick wall, but when she raised it, she could hear the noise of traffic, and it sounded, as it had sounded in the station, like the irresistible and titanic voice of life itself.

The Malloys found their way, that afternoon, to the Broadway Automat. They shouted with pleasure at the magical coffee spigots and the glass doors that sprang open. "Tomorrow, I'm going to have the baked beans," Alice cried, "and the chicken pie the day after that and the fish cakes after that." When they had finished their supper, they went out into the street. Mildred-Rose walked between her parents, holding their callused hands. It was getting dark, and the lights of Broadway answered all their simple prayers. High in the air were large, brightly lighted pictures of bloody heroes, criminal lovers, monsters, and armed desperadoes. The names of movies and soft drinks, restaurants and cigarettes were written in a jumble of light, and in the distance they could see the pitiless winter afterglow beyond the Hudson River. The tall buildings in the east were lighted and

31

seemed to burn, as if fire had fallen onto their dark shapes. The air was full of music, and the light was brighter than day. They drifted with the crowd for hours.

Mildred-Rose got tired and began to cry, so at last her parents took her back to the Mentone. Alice had begun to undress her when someone knocked softly on the door.

"Come in," Evarts called.

A bellboy stood in the doorway. He had the figure of a boy, but his face was gray and lined. "I just wanted to see if you people were all right," he said. "I just wanted to see if maybe you wanted a little ginger ale or some ice water."

"Oh, no, thank you kindly," Alice said. "It was very nice of you to ask, though."

"You people just come to New York for the first time?" the bellboy asked. He closed the door behind him and sat on the arm of a chair.

"Yes," Evarts said. "We left Wentworth—that's in Indiana —yesterday on the nine-fifteen for South Bend. Then we went to Chicago. We had dinner in Chicago."

"I had the chicken pie," Alice said. "It was delicious." She slipped Mildred-Rose's nightgown over her head.

"Then we came to New York," Evarts said.

"What are you doing here?" the bellboy asked. "Anniversary?" He helped himself to a cigarette from a package on the bureau and slipped down into the chair.

"Oh, no," Evarts said. "We hit the jackpot."

"Our ship's come in," Alice said.

"A contest?" the bellboy asked. "Something like that?"

"Oh, no," Evarts said.

"You tell him, Evarts," Alice said.

"Yes," the bellboy said. "Tell me, Evarts."

"Well, you see," Evarts said, "it began like this." He sat down on the bed and lighted a cigarette. "I was in the Army,

32

you see, and then when I got out of the Army, I went back to Wentworth ..." He repeated to the bellboy the story he had told the conductor.

"Oh, you lucky, lucky kids!" the bellboy exclaimed when Evarts had finished. "Tracey Murchison! Madge Beatty! You lucky, lucky kids." He looked at the poorly furnished room. Alice was arranging Mildred-Rose on the sofa, where she would sleep. Evarts was sitting on the edge of the bed swinging his legs. "What you need now is a good agent," the bellboy said. He wrote a name and address on a piece of paper and gave it to Evarts. "The Hauser Agency is the biggest agency in the world," he said, "and Charlie Leavitt is the best man in the Hauser Agency. I want you to feel free to take your problems to Charlie, and if he asks who sent you, tell him Bitsey sent you." He went toward the door. "Good night, you lucky, lucky kids," he said. "Good night. Sweet dreams. Sweet dreams."

The Malloys were the hard-working children of an industrious generation, and they were up at half past six the next morning. They scrubbed their faces and their ears and brushed their teeth with soap. At seven o'clock, they started for the Automat. Evarts had not slept that night. The noise of traffic had kept him awake, and he had spent the small hours sitting at the window. His mouth felt scorched with tobacco smoke, and the loss of sleep had left him nervous. They were all surprised to find New York still sleeping. They were shocked. They had their breakfast and returned to the Mentone. Evarts called Tracey Murchison's office, but no one answered. He telephoned the office several times after that. At ten o'clock, a girl answered the phone. "Mr. Murchison will see you at three," she said. She hung up. Since there was nothing to do but wait, Evarts took his wife and daughter up Fifth Avenue. They stared in the store windows. At eleven

33

o'clock, when the doors of Radio City Music Hall opened, they went there.

This was a happy choice. They prowled the lounges and toilets for an hour before they took their seats, and when, during the stage show, an enormous samovar rose up out of the orchestra pit and debouched forty men in Cossack uniform singing "Dark Eyes," Alice and Mildred-Rose shouted with joy. The stage show, beneath its grandeur, seemed to conceal a simple and familiar intelligence, as if the drafts that stirred the miles of golden curtain had blown straight from Indiana. The performance left Alice and Mildred-Rose distracted with pleasure, and on the way back to the Mentone, Evarts had to lead them along the sidewalk to keep them from walking into hydrants. It was a quarter of three when they got back to the hotel. Evarts kissed his wife and child goodbye and started for Murchison's.

He got lost. He was afraid that he would be late. He began to run. He asked directions of a couple of policemen and finally reached the office building.

The front room of Murchison's office was dingy—intentionally dingy, Evarts hoped—but it was not inglorious, for there were many beautiful men and women there, waiting to see Mr. Murchison. None of them were sitting down, and they chatted together as if delighted by the delay that held them there. The receptionist led Evarts into a further office. This office was also crowded, but the atmosphere was of haste and trouble, as if the place were being besieged. Murchison was there and he greeted Evarts strenuously. "I've got your contracts right here," he said, and he handed Evarts a pen and pushed a stack of contracts toward him. "Now I want you to rush over and see Madge," Murchison said as soon as Evarts had signed the contracts. He looked at Evarts, plucked the feather carnation out of his lapel, and tossed it into a wastebasket. "Hurry, hurry, hurry," he said. "She's at 400 Park Avenue. She's crazy to see you. She's waiting now. I'll see you later tonight—I think Madge has something planned—but hurry."

Evarts rushed into the hall and rang impatiently for the elevator. As soon as he had left the building, he got lost and wandered into the fur district. A policeman directed him back to the Mentone. Alice and Mildred-Rose were waiting in the lobby, and he told them what had happened. "I'm on my way to see Madge Beatty now," he said. "I've got to hurry!" Bitsey, the bellboy, overheard this conversation. He dropped some bags he was carrying and joined the group. He told Evarts how to get to Park Avenue. Evarts kissed Alice and Mildred-Rose again. They waved goodbye as he ran out the door.

Evarts had seen so many movies of Park Avenue that he observed its breadth and bleakness with a sense of familiarity. He took an elevator to the Murchisons' apartment and was led by a maid into a pretty living-room. A fire was burning, and there were flowers on the mantel. He sprang to his feet when Madge Beatty came in. She was frail, animated, and golden, and her hoarse and accomplished voice made him feel naked. "I read your play, Evarts," she said, "and I loved it, I loved it, I loved it." She moved lightly around the room, talking now directly at him, now over her shoulder. She was not as young as she had first appeared to be, and in the light from the windows she looked almost wizened. "You're going to do more with my part when you write the second act, I hope," she said. "You're going to build it up and build it up and build it up."

"I'll do anything you want, Miss Beatty," Evarts said.

She sat down and folded her beautiful hands. Her feet were very big, Evarts noticed. Her shins were thin, and this made her feet seem very big. "Oh, we love your play, Evarts," she said. "We love it, we want it, we need it. Do you know how much we need it? We're in debt, Evarts, we're dreadfully in debt." She laid a hand on her breast and spoke in a whisper. "We owe one million nine hundred and sixty-five thousand dollars." She let the precious light flood her voice again. "But now I'm keeping you from writing your beautiful play," she said. "I'm keeping you from work, and I want you to go back and write and write and write, and I want you and your wife to come here any time after nine tonight and meet a few of our warmest friends."

Evarts asked the doorman how to get back to the Mentone, but he misunderstood the directions and got lost again. He walked around the East Side until he found a policeman, who directed him back to the hotel. It was so late when he returned that Mildred-Rose was crying with hunger. The three of them washed and went to the Automat and walked up and down Broadway until nearly nine. Then they went back to the hotel. Alice put on her evening dress, and she and Evarts kissed Mildred-Rose good night. In the lobby, they met Bitsey and told him where they were going. He promised to keep an eye on Mildred-Rose.

The walk over to the Murchisons' was longer than Evarts remembered. Alice's wrap was light. She was blue with cold when they reached the apartment building. They could hear in the distance, as they left the elevator, someone playing a piano and a woman singing "A kiss is but a kiss, a sigh is but a sigh . . ." A maid took their wraps, and Mr. Murchison greeted them from a farther door. Alice ruffled and arranged the cloth peony that hung from the front of her dress, and they went in.

The room was crowded, the lights were dim, the singer

was ending her song. There was a heady smell of animal skins and astringent perfume in the air. Mr. Murchison introduced the Malloys to a couple who stood near the door, and abandoned them. The couple turned their backs on the Malloys. Evarts was shy and quiet, but Alice was excited and began to speculate, in a whisper, about the identities of the people around the piano. She felt sure that they were all movie stars, and she was right.

The singer finished her song, got up from the piano, and walked away. There was a little applause and then a curious silence. Mr. Murchison asked another woman to sing. "I'm not going to go on after *her*," the woman said. The situation, whatever it was, had stopped conversation. Mr. Murchison asked several people to perform, but they all refused. "Perhaps Mrs. Malloy will sing for us," he said bitterly.

"All right," Alice said. She walked to the center of the room. She took a position and, folding her hands and holding them breast high, began to sing.

Alice's mother had taught her to sing whenever her host asked, and Alice had never violated any of her mother's teachings. As a child, she had taken singing lessons from Mrs. Bachman, an elderly widow who lived in Wentworth. She had sung in grammar-school assemblies and in high-school assemblies. On family holidays, there had always come a time, in the late afternoon, when she would be asked to sing; then she would rise from her place on the hard sofa near the stove or come from the kitchen, where she had been washing dishes, to sing the songs Mrs. Bachman had taught her.

The invitation that night had been so unexpected that Evarts had not had a chance to stop his wife. He had felt the bitterness in Murchison's voice, and he would have stopped her, but as soon as she began to sing, he didn't care. Her voice was well pitched, her figure was stern and touching, and she sang for those people in obedience to her mannerly heart. When he had overcome his own bewilderment, he noticed the respect and attention the Murchisons' guests were giving her music. Many of them had come from towns as small as Wentworth; they were good-hearted people, and the simple air, rendered in Alice's fearless voice, reminded them of their beginnings. None of them were whispering or smiling. Many of them had lowered their heads, and he saw a woman touch her eyes with a handkerchief. Alice had triumphed, he thought, and then he recognized the song as "Annie Laurie."

Years ago, when Mrs. Bachman had taught Alice the song, she had taught her to close it with a piece of business that brought her success as a child, as a girl, as a high-school senior, but that, even in the stuffy living-room in Wentworth, with its inexorable smells of poverty and cooking, had begun to tire and worry her family. She had been taught on the closing line, "Lay me doun and dee," to fall in a heap on the floor. She fell less precipitously now that she had got older, but she still fell, and Evarts could see that night, by her serene face, that a fall was in her plans. He considered going to her, embracing her, and whispering to her that the hotel was burning or that Mildred-Rose was sick. Instead, he turned his back.

Alice took a quick breath and attacked the last verse. Evarts had begun to sweat so freely that the brine got into his eyes. "I'll lay me doun and dee," he heard her sing; he heard the loud crash as she hit the floor; he heard the screams of helpless laughter, the tobacco coughs, and the oaths of a woman who laughed so hard she broke her pearl bib. The Murchisons' guests seemed bewitched. They wept, they shook, they stooped, they slapped one another on the back, and walked, like the demented, in circles. When Evarts faced the scene, Alice was sitting on the floor. He helped her to her feet. "Come, darling," he said. "Come." With his arm around her, he led her into the hall.

"Didn't they like my song?" she asked. She began to cry.

"It doesn't matter, my darling," Evarts said, "it doesn't matter, it doesn't matter." They got their wraps and walked back through the cold to the Mentone.

Bitsey was waiting for them in the corridor outside their room. He wanted to hear all about the party. Evarts sent Alice into the room and talked with the bellboy alone. He didn't feel like describing the party. "I don't think I want to have anything more to do with the Murchisons," he said. "I'm going to get a new producer."

"That's the boy, that's the boy," Bitsey said. "Now you're talking. But, first, I want you to go up to the Hauser Agency and see Charlie Leavitt!"

"All right," Evarts said. "All right, I'll go and see Charlie Leavitt."

Alice cried herself to sleep that night. Again, Evarts couldn't sleep. He sat in a chair by the window. He fell into a doze, a little before dawn, but not for long. At seven o'clock, he led his family off to the Automat.

Bitsey came up to the Malloys' room after breakfast. He was very excited. A columnist in one of the four-cent newspapers had reported Evarts' arrival in New York. A cabinet member and a Balkan king were mentioned in the same paragraph. Then the telephone began to ring. First, it was a man who wanted to sell Evarts a secondhand mink coat. Then a lawyer and a dry cleaner called, a dressmaker, a nursery school, several agencies, and a man who said he could get them a good apartment. Evarts said no to all these importunities, but in each case he had to argue before he could hang up. Bitsey had made a noon appointment for him with

Charlie Leavitt, and when it was time, he kissed Alice and Mildred-Rose and went down to the street.

The Hauser Agency was located in one of the buildings in Radio City. Now Evarts' business took him through the building's formidable doors as legitimately, he told himself, as anyone else. The Hauser offices were on the twenty-sixth floor. He didn't call his floor until the elevator had begun its ascent. "It's too late now," the operator said. "You got to tell me the number of the floor when you get in." This branded him as green to all the other people in the car, Evarts knew, and he blushed. He rode to the sixtieth floor and then back to the twenty-sixth. As he left the car, the elevator operator sneered.

At the end of a long corridor, there was a pair of bronze doors, fastened by a bifurcated eagle. Evarts turned the wings of the imperial bird and stepped into a lofty manor hall. The paneling on its walls was worm-pitted and white with rot. In the distance, behind a small glass window, he saw a woman wearing earphones. He walked over to her, told her his business, and was asked to sit down. He sat on a leather sofa and lighted a cigarette. The richness of the hall impressed him profoundly. Then he noticed that the sofa was covered with dust. So were the table, the magazines on it, the lamp, the bronze cast of Rodin's "Le Baiser"—everything in the vast room was covered with dust. He noticed at the same time the peculiar stillness of the hall. All the usual noises of an office were lacking. Into this stillness, from the distant earth, rose the recorded music from the skating rink, where a carillon played "Joy to the World! The Lord Is Come!" The magazines on the table beside the sofa were all five years old.

After a while, the receptionist pointed to a double door at the end of the hall, and Evarts walked there, timidly. The office on the other side of the door was smaller than the room he had just left but dimmer, richer, and more imposing, and in the distance he could still hear the music of the skating rink. A man was sitting at an antique desk. He stood as soon as he saw Evarts. "Welcome, Evarts, welcome to the Hauser Agency!" he shouted. "I hear you've got a hot property there, and Bitsey tells me you're through with Tracey Murchison. I haven't read your play, of course, but if Tracey wants it, I want it, and so does Sam Farley. I've got a producer for you, I've got a star for you, I've got a theater for you, and I think I've got a pre-production deal lined up. One hundred thou' on a four-hundred-thou' ceiling. Sit down, sit down."

Mr. Leavitt seemed either to be eating something or to be having trouble with his teeth, for at the end of every sentence he worked his lips noisily and thoughtfully, like a gourmet. He might have been eating something, since there were crumbs around his mouth. Or he might have been having trouble with his teeth, because the labial noises continued all through the interview. Mr. Leavitt wore a lot of gold. He had several rings, a gold identification bracelet, and a gold bracelet watch, and he carried a heavy gold cigarette case, set with jewels. The case was empty, and Evans furnished him with cigarettes as they talked.

"Now, I want you to go back to your hotel, Evarts," Mr. Leavitt shouted, "and I want you to take it easy. Charlie Leavitt is taking care of your property. I want you to promise me you won't worry. Now, I understand that you've signed a contract with Murchison. I'm going to declare that contract null and void, and my lawyer is going to declare that contract null and void, and if Murchison contests it, we'll drag him into court and have the judge declare that contract null and void. Before we go any further, though," he said, softening his voice, "I want you to sign these papers, which

41

will give me authority to represent you." He pressed some papers and a gold fountain pen on Evarts. "Just sign these papers," he said sadly, "and you'll make four hundred thousand dollars. Oh, you authors!" he exclaimed. "You lucky authors!"

As soon as Evarts had signed the papers, Mr. Leavitt's manner changed and he began to shout again. "The producer I've got for you is Sam Farley. The star is Susan Hewitt. Sam Farley is Tom Farley's brother. He's married to Clarissa Douglas and he's George Howland's uncle. Pat Levy's his brother-in-law and Mitch Kababian and Howie Brown are related to him on his mother's side. She was Lottie Mayes. They're a very close family. They're a great little team. When your show opens in Wilmington, Sam Farley, Tom Farley, Clarissa Douglas, George Howland, Pat Levy, Mitch Kababian, and Howie Brown are all right down there in that hotel writing your third act. When your show goes up to Baltimore, Sam Farley, Tom Farley, Clarissa Douglas, George Howland, Pat Levy, Mitch Kababian, and Howie Brown, they go up to Baltimore with it. And when your show opens up on Broadway with a high-class production, who's down there in the front row, rooting for you?" Mr. Leavitt had strained his voice, and he ended in a hoarse whisper, "Sam Farley, Tom Farley, George Howland, Clarissa Douglas, Pat Levy, Mitch Kababian, and Howie Brown.

"Now, I want you to go back to your hotel and have a good time," he shouted after he had cleared his throat. "I'll call you tomorrow and tell you when Sam Farley and Susan Hewitt can see you, and I'll telephone Hollywood now and tell Max Rayburn that he can have it for one hundred thou' on a four-hundred-thou' ceiling, and not one iota less." He patted Evarts on the back and steered him gently toward the door. "Have a good time, Evarts," he said.

As Evarts walked back through the hall, he noticed that the receptionist was eating a sandwich. She beckoned to him.

"You want to take a chance on a new Buick convertible?" she whispered. "Ten cents a chance."

"Oh, no, thank you," Evarts said.

"Fresh eggs?" she asked. "I bring them in from Jersey every morning."

"No, thank you," Evarts said.

Evarts hurried back through the crowds to the Mentone, where Alice, Mildred-Rose, and Bitsey were waiting. He described his interview with Leavitt to them. "When I get that four hundred thou'," he said, "I'm going to send some money to Mama Finelli." Then Alice remembered a lot of other people in Wentworth who needed money. By way of a celebration, they went to a spaghetti house that night instead of the Automat. After dinner, they went to Radio City Music Hall. Again, that night, Evarts was unable to sleep.

In Wentworth, Alice had been known as the practical member of the family. There was a good deal of jocularity on this score. She drew up the budget and managed the egg money, and it was often said that Evarts would have misplaced his head if it hadn't been for Alice. This business-like strain in her character led her to remind Evarts on the following day that he had not been working on his play. She took the situation in hand. "You just sit in the room," she said, "and write the play, and Mildred-Rose and I will walk up and down Fifth Avenue, so you can be alone."

Evarts tried to work, but the telephone began to ring again and he was interrupted regularly by jewelry salesmen, theatrical lawyers, and laundry services. At about eleven, he picked up the phone and heard a familiar and angry voice.

43

It was Murchison. "I brought you from Wentworth," he shouted, "and I made you what you are today. Now they tell me you breached my contract and double-crossed me with Sam Farley. I'm going to break you, I'm going to ruin you, I'm going to sue you, I'm—" Evarts hung up, and when the phone rang a minute later, he didn't answer it. He left a note for Alice, put on his hat, and walked up Fifth Avenue to the Hauser offices.

When he turned the bifurcated eagle of the double doors and stepped into the manor hall that morning, he found Mr. Leavitt there, in his shirt sleeves, sweeping the carpet. "Oh, good morning," Leavitt said. "Occupational therapy." He hid the broom and dustpan behind a velvet drape. "Come in, come in," he said, slipping into his jacket and leading Evarts toward the inner office. "This afternoon, you're going to meet Sam Farley and Susan Hewitt. You're one of the luckiest men in New York. Some men never see Sam Farley. Not even once in a lifetime—never hear his wit, never feel the force of his unique personality. And as for Susan Hewitt ..." He was speechless for a moment. He said the appointment was for three. "You're going to meet them in Sam Farley's lovely home," he said, and he gave Evarts the address.

Evarts tried to describe the telephone conversation with Murchison, but Leavitt cut him off. "I asked you one thing," he shouted. "I asked you not to worry. Is that too much? I ask you to talk with Sam Farley and take a look at Susan Hewitt and see if you think she's right for the part. Is that too much? Now, have a good time. Take in a newsreel. Go to the zoo. Go see Sam Farley at three o'clock." He patted Evarts on the back and pushed him toward the door.

Evarts ate lunch at the Mentone with Alice and Mildred-Rose. He had a headache. After lunch, they walked up and down Fifth Avenue, and when it got close to three, Alice

44

and Mildred-Rose walked with him to Sam Farley's house. It was an impressive building, faced with rough stone, like a Spanish prison. He kissed Mildred-Rose and Alice goodbye and rang the bell. A butler opened the door. Evarts could tell he was a butler because he wore striped pants. The butler led him upstairs to a drawing-room.

"I'm here to see Mr. Farley," Evarts said.

"I know," the butler said. "You're Evarts Malloy. You've got an appointment. But he won't keep it. He's stuck in a floating crap game in the Acme Garage, at a Hundred and Sixty-fourth Street, and he won't be back until tomorrow. Susan Hewitt's coming, though. You're supposed to see her. Oh, if you only knew what goes on in this place!" He lowered his voice to a whisper and brought his face close to Evarts'. "If these walls could only talk! There hasn't been any heat in this house since we came back from Hollywood and he hasn't paid me since the twenty-first of June. I wouldn't mind so much, but the son of a bitch never learned to let the water out of his bathtub. He takes a bath and leaves the dirty water standing there. To stagnate. On top of every-thing else, I cut my finger washing dishes yesterday." There was a dirty bandage on the butler's forefinger, and he began, hurriedly, to unwrap layer after layer of bloody gauze. "Look," he said, holding the wound to Evarts' face. "Cut right through to the bone. Yesterday you could see the bone. Blood. Blood all over everything. Took me half an hour to clean up. It's a miracle I didn't get an infection." He shook his head at this miracle. "When the mouse comes, I'll send her up." He wandered out of the room, trailing the length of bloody bandage after him.

Evarts' eyes were burning with fatigue. He was so tired that if he had rested his head against anything, he would have fallen asleep. He heard the doorbell ring and the butler greet Susan Hewitt. She ran up the stairs and into the drawing-room.

She was young, and she came into the room as if it were her home and she had just come back from school. She was light, her features were delicate and very small, and her fair hair was brushed simply and had begun to darken, of its own course, and was streaked softly with brown, like the grain in pine wood. "I'm so happy to meet you, Evarts," she said. "I want to tell you that I love your play." How she could have read his play, Evarts did not know, but he was too confused by her beauty to worry or to speak. His mouth was dry. It might have been the antic pace of the last days, it might have been his loss of sleep—he didn't know—but he felt as though he had fallen in love.

"You remind me of a girl I used to know," he said. "She worked in a lunch wagon outside South Bend. Never worked in a lunch wagon outside South Bend, did you?"

"No," she said.

"It isn't only that," he said. "You remind me of all of it. I mean the night drives. I used to be a night bus driver. That's what you remind me of. The stars, I mean, and the grade crossings, and the cattle lined up along the fences. And the girls in the lunch counters. They always looked so pretty. But you never worked in a lunch counter."

"No," she said.

"You can have my play," he said. "I mean, I think you're right for the part. Sam Farley can have the play. Everything."

"Thank you, Evarts," she said.

"Will you do me a favor?" he asked.

"What?"

"Oh, I know it's foolish," he said. He got up and walked around the room. "But there's nobody here, nobody will know about it. I hate to ask you."

46

"What do you want?"

"Will you let me lift you?" he said. "Just let me lift you. Just let me see how light you are."

"All right," she said. "Do you want me to take off my coat?"

"Yes, yes, yes," he said. "Take off your coat."

She stood. She let her coat fall to the sofa.

"Can I do it now?" he said.

"Yes."

He put his hands under her arms. He raised her off the floor and then put her down gently. "Oh, you're so light!" he shouted. "You're so light, you're so fragile, you don't weigh any more than a suitcase. Why, I could carry you, I could carry you anywhere, I could carry you from one end of New York to the other." He got his hat and coat and ran out of the house.

Evarts felt bewildered and exhausted when he returned to the Mentone. Bitsey was in the room with Mildred-Rose and Alice. He kept asking questions about Mama Finelli. He wanted to know where she lived and what her telephone number was. Evarts lost his temper at the bellboy and told him to go away. He lay down on the bed and fell asleep while Alice and Mildred-Rose were asking him questions. When he woke, an hour later, he felt much better. They went to the Automat and then to Radio City Music Hall, and they got to bed early, so that Evarts could work on his play in the morning. He couldn't sleep.

After breakfast, Alice and Mildred-Rose left Evarts alone in the room and he tried to work. He couldn't work, but it wasn't the telephone that troubled him that day. The difficulty that blocked his play was deep, and as he smoked and stared at the brick wall, he recognized it. He was in love with Susan Hewitt. This might have been an incentive to work, but he had left his creative strength in Indiana. He shut his eyes and tried to recall the strong, dissolute voice of Mama Finelli, but before he could realize a word, it would be lost in the noise from the street.

If there had been anything to set his memory free—a train whistle, a moment of silence, the smells of a barn—he might have been inspired. He paced the room, he smoked, he sniffed the sooty window curtains and stuffed his ears with toilet paper, but there seemed to be no way of recalling Indiana at the Mentone. He stayed near the desk all that day. He went without lunch. When his wife and child returned from Radio City Music Hall, where they had spent the afternoon, he told them he was going to take a walk. Oh, he thought as he left the hotel, if I could only hear the noise of a crow!

He strode up Fifth Avenue, holding his head high, trying to divine in the confusion of sound a voice that might lead him. He walked rapidly until he reached Radio City and could hear, in the distance, the music from the skating rink. Something stopped him. He lighted a cigarette. Then he heard someone calling him. "Behold the lordly moose, Evarts," a woman shouted. It was the hoarse, dissolute voice of Mama Finelli, and he thought that desire had deranged him until he turned and saw her, sitting on one of the benches, by a dry pool. "Behold the lordly moose, Evarts," she called, and she put her hands, spaced like antlers, above her head. This was the way she greeted everyone in Wentworth.

"Behold the lordly moose, Mama Finelli," Evarts shouted. He ran to her side and sat down. "Oh, Mama Finelli, I'm so glad to see you," he said. "You won't believe it, but I've been thinking about you all day. I've been wishing all day that I could talk with you." He turned to drink in her vulpine

48

features and her whiskery chin. "How did you ever get to New York, Mama Finelli?"

"Come up on a flying machine," she cried. "Come up on a flying machine today. Have a sandwich." She was eating some sandwiches from a paper bag.

"No, thanks," he said. "What do you think of New York?" he asked. "What do you think of that high building?"

"Well, I don't know," she said, but he could see that she did know and he could see her working her face into shape for a retort. "I guess there's just but the one, for if there hada been two, they'd of pollinated and bore!" She whooped with laughter and struck herself on the legs.

"What are you doing in New York, Mama Finelli? How did you happen to come here?"

"Well," she said, "man named Tracey Murchison calls me on the telephone long-distance and says for me to come up to New York and sue you for libel. Says you wrote a play about me and I can sue you for libel and git a lot of money and split it with him, fairly, he says, and then I don't have to run the gas station no more. So he wires me money for the flying-machine ticket and I come up here and I talk with him and I'm going to sue you for libel and split it with him, sixty-forty. That's what I'm going to do," she said.

Later that night, the Malloys returned to the marble waiting-room of Grand Central and Evarts began to search for a Chicago train. He found a Chicago train, bought some tickets, and they boarded a coach. It was a rainy night, and the dark, wet paving, deep in the station, did not glitter, but it was still Alice's belief that diamonds had been ground into it, and that was the way she would tell the story. They had picked up the lessons of travel rapidly, and they arranged themselves adroitly over several seats. After the train started, Alice made friends with a plain-spoken couple across the

49

aisle, who were traveling with a baby to Los Angeles. The woman had a brother there, who had written to her enthusiastically about the climate and the opportunities.

"Let's go to Los Angeles," Alice said to Evarts. "We still have a little money and we can buy tickets in Chicago and you can sell your play in Hollywood, where nobody's ever heard of Mama Finelli or any of the others."

Evarts said that he would make his decision in Chicago. He was weary and he fell asleep. Mildred-Rose put her thumb into her mouth, and soon both she and her mother had lost consciousness, too. Mildred-Rose stroked the sere skins of her coat and they told her that all was well, all was well.

The Malloys may have left the train in Chicago and gone back to Wentworth. It is not hard to imagine their homecoming, for they would be welcomed by their friends and relations, although their stories might not be believed. Or they may have changed, at Chicago, for a train to the West, and this, to tell the truth, is easier to imagine. One can see them playing hearts in the lounge car and eating cheese sandwiches in the railroad stations as they traveled through Kansas and Nebraska—over the mountains and on to the Coast.

SHIRLEY JACKSON

PILLAR OF SALT

FOR SOME REASON a tune was running through her head when she and her husband got on the train in New Hampshire for their trip to New York; they had not been to New York for nearly a year, but the tune was from farther back than that. It was from the days when she was fifteen or sixteen, and had never seen New York except in movies, when the city was made up, to her, of penthouses filled with Noël Coward people; when the height and speed and luxury and gaiety that made up a city like New York were confused inextricably with the dullness of being fifteen, and beauty unreachable and far in the movies.

"What *is* that tune?" she said to her husband, and hummed it. "It's from some old movie, I think."

"I know it," he said, and hummed it himself. "Can't remember the words."

He sat back comfortably. He had hung up their coats, put the suitcases on the rack, and had taken his magazine out. "I'll think of it sooner or later," he said.

She looked out the window first, tasting it almost secretly, savoring the extreme pleasure of being on a moving train with nothing to do for six hours but read and nap and go into the dining-car, going farther and farther every minute from the children, from the kitchen floor, with even the hills being incredibly left behind, changing into fields and trees too far away from home to be daily. "I love trains," she said, and her husband nodded sympathetically into his magazine.

Two weeks ahead, two unbelievable weeks, with all

arrangements made, no further planning to do, except perhaps what theaters or what restaurants. A friend with an apartment went on a convenient vacation, there was enough money in the bank to make a trip to New York compatible with new snow suits for the children; there was the smoothness of unopposed arrangements, once the initial obstacles had been overcome, as though when they had really made up their minds, nothing dared stop them. The baby's sore throat cleared up. The plumber came, finished his work in two days, and left. The dresses had been altered in time; the hardware store could be left safely, once they had found the excuse of looking over new city products. New York had not burned down, had not been quarantined, their friend had gone away according to schedule, and Brad had the keys to the apartment in his pocket. Everyone knew where to reach everyone else; there was a list of plays not to miss and a list of items to look out for in the stores—diapers, dress materials, fancy canned goods, tarnish-proof silverware boxes. And, finally, the train was there, performing its function, pacing through the afternoon, carrying them legally and with determination to New York.

Margaret looked curiously at her husband, inactive in the middle of the afternoon on a train, at the other fortunate people traveling, at the sunny country outside, looked again to make sure, and then opened her book. The tune was still in her head, she hummed it and heard her husband take it up softly as he turned a page in his magazine.

In the dining-car she ate roast beef, as she would have done in a restaurant at home, reluctant to change over too quickly to the new, tantalizing food of a vacation. She had ice cream for dessert but became uneasy over her coffee because they were due in New York in an hour and she still had to put on her coat and hat, relishing every gesture, and

Brad must take the suitcases down and put away the magazines. They stood at the end of the car for the interminable underground run, picking up their suitcases and putting them down again, moving restlessly inch by inch.

The station was a momentary shelter, moving visitors gradually into a world of people and sound and light to prepare them for the blasting reality of the street outside. She saw it for a minute from the sidewalk before she was in a taxi moving into the middle of it, and then they were bewilderingly caught and carried on uptown and whirled out on to another sidewalk and Brad paid the taxi driver and put his head back to look up at the apartment house. "This is it, all right," he said, as though he had doubted the driver's ability to find a number so simply given. Upstairs in the elevator, and the key fit the door. They had never seen their friend's apartment before, but it was reasonably familiar—a friend moving from New Hampshire to New York carries private pictures of a home not erasable in a few years, and the apartment had enough of home in it to settle Brad immediately in the right chair and comfort her with instinctive trust of the linen and blankets.

"This is home for two weeks," Brad said, and stretched. After the first few minutes they both went to the windows automatically; New York was below, as arranged, and the houses across the street were apartment houses filled with unknown people.

"It's wonderful," she said. There were cars down there, and people, and the noise was there. "I'm so happy," she said, and kissed her husband.

They went sight-seeing the first day; they had breakfast in an Automat and went to the top of the Empire State Building. "Got it all fixed up now," Brad said, at the top. "Wonder just where that plane hit."

They tried to peer down on all four sides, but were embarrassed about asking. "After all," she said reasonably, giggling in a corner, "if something of mine got broken I wouldn't want people poking around asking to see the pieces."

"If you owned the Empire State Building you wouldn't care," Brad said.

They traveled only in taxis the first few days, and one taxi had a door held on with a piece of string; they pointed to it and laughed silently at each other, and on about the third day, the taxi they were riding in got a flat tire on Broadway and they had to get out and find another.

"We've only got eleven days left," she said one day, and then, seemingly minutes later, "we've already been here six days."

They had got in touch with the friends they had expected to get in touch with, they were going to a Long Island summer home for a week end. "It looks pretty dreadful right now," their hostess said cheerfully over the phone, "and we're leaving in a week ourselves, but I'd never *forgive* you if you didn't see it *once* while you were here." The weather had been fair but cool, with a definite autumn awareness, and the clothes in the store windows were dark and already hinting at furs and velvets. She wore her coat every day, and suits most of the time. The light dresses she had brought were hanging in the closet in the apartment, and she was thinking now of getting a sweater in one of the big stores, something impractical for New Hampshire, but probably good for Long Island.

"I have to do some shopping, at least one day," she said to Brad, and he groaned.

"Don't ask me to carry packages," he said.

"You aren't up to a good day's shopping," she told him, "not after all this walking around you've been doing. Why don't you go to a movie or something?"

"I want to do some shopping myself," he said mysteriously. Perhaps he was talking about her Christmas present; she had thought vaguely of getting such things done in New York; the children would be pleased with novelties from the city, toys not seen in their home stores. At any rate she said, "You'll probably be able to get to your wholesalers at last."

They were on their way to visit another friend, who had found a place to live by a miracle and warned them consequently not to quarrel with the appearance of the building, or the stairs, or the neighborhood. All three were bad, and the stairs were three flights, narrow and dark, but there was a place to live at the top. Their friend had not been in New York long, but he lived by himself in two rooms, and had easily caught the mania for slim tables and low bookcases which made his rooms look too large for the furniture in some places, too cramped and uncomfortable in others.

"What a lovely place," she said when she came in, and then was sorry when her host said, "Some day this damn situation will let up and I'll be able to settle down in a really decent place."

There were other people there; they sat and talked companionably about the same subjects then current in New Hampshire, but they drank more than they would have at home and it left them strangely unaffected; their voices were louder and their words more extravagant; their gestures, on the other hand, were smaller, and they moved a finger where in New Hampshire they would have waved an arm. Margaret said frequently, "We're just staying here for a couple of weeks, on a vacation," and she said, "It's wonderful, so *exciting*," and she said, "We were *terribly* lucky; this friend went out of town just at the right. . . ."

Finally the room was very full and noisy, and she went into a corner near a window to catch her breath. The window

57

had been opened and shut all evening, depending on whether the person standing next to it had both hands free; and now it was shut, with the clear sky outside. Someone came and stood next to her, and she said, "Listen to the noise outside. It's as bad as it is inside."

He said, "In a neighborhood like this someone's always getting killed."

She frowned. "It sounds different than before. I mean, there's a different sound to it."

"Alcoholics," he said. "Drunks in the streets. Fighting going on across the way." He wandered away, carrying his drink.

She opened the window and leaned out, and there were people hanging out of the windows across the way shouting, and people standing in the street looking up and shouting, and from across the way she heard clearly, "Lady, lady." They must mean me, she thought, they're all looking this way. She leaned out farther and the voices shouted incoherently but somehow making an audible whole, "Lady, your house is on fire, lady, lady."

She closed the window firmly and turned around to the other people in the room, raising her voice a little. "Listen," she said, "they're saying the house is on fire." She was desperately afraid of their laughing at her, of looking like a fool while Brad across the room looked at her blushing. She said again, "The *house* is on *fire*," and added, "They say," for fear of sounding too vehement. The people nearest to her turned and someone said, "She says the house is on fire."

She wanted to get to Brad and couldn't see him; her host was not in sight either, and the people all around were strangers. They don't listen to me, she thought, I might as well not be here, and she went to the outside door and opened it. There was no smoke, no flame, but she was telling

58

herself, I might as well not be here, so she abandoned Brad in panic and ran without her hat and coat down the stairs, carrying a glass in one hand and a package of matches in the other. The stairs were insanely long, but they were clear and safe, and she opened the street door and ran out. A man caught her arm and said, "Everyone out of the house?" and she said, "No, Brad's still there." The fire engines swept around the corner, with people leaning out of the windows watching them, and the man holding her arm said, "It's down here," and left her. The fire was two houses away; they could see flames behind the top windows, and smoke against the night sky, but in ten minutes it was finished and the fire engines pulled away with an air of martyrdom for hauling out all their equipment to put out a ten-minute fire.

She went back upstairs slowly and with embarrassment, and found Brad and took him home.

"I was so frightened," she said to him when they were safely in bed, "I lost my head completely."

"You should have tried to find someone," he said.

"They wouldn't listen," she insisted. "I kept telling them and they wouldn't listen and then I thought I must have been mistaken. I had some idea of going down to see what was going on."

"Lucky it was no worse," Brad said sleepily.

"I felt trapped," she said. "High up in that old building with a fire; it's like a nightmare. And in a strange city."

"Well, it's all over now," Brad said.

The same faint feeling of insecurity tagged her the next day; she went shopping alone and Brad went off to see hardware, after all. She got on a bus to go downtown and the bus was too full to move when it came time for her to get out. Wedged standing in the aisle she said, "Out, please," and, "Excuse me," and by the time she was loose and near the door the bus had started again and she got off a stop beyond. "No one *listens* to me," she said to herself. "Maybe it's because I'm too polite." In the stores the prices were all too high and the sweaters looked disarmingly like New Hampshire ones. The toys for the children filled her with dismay; they were so obviously for New York children: hideous little parodies of adult life, cash registers, tiny pushcarts with imitation fruit, telephones that really worked (as if there weren't enough phones in New York that really worked), miniature milk bottles in a carrying case. "We get our milk from cows," Margaret told the salesgirl. "My children wouldn't know what these were." She was exaggerating, and felt guilty for a minute, but no one was around to catch her.

She had a picture of small children in the city dressed like their parents, following along with a miniature mechanical civilization, toy cash registers in larger and larger sizes that eased them into the real thing, millions of clattering jerking small imitations that prepared them nicely for taking over the large useless toys their parents lived by. She bought a pair of skis for her son, which she knew would be inadequate for the New Hampshire snow, and a wagon for her daughter inferior to the one Brad could make at home in an hour. Ignoring the toy mailboxes, the small phonographs with special small records, the kiddie cosmetics, she left the store and started home.

She was frankly afraid by now to take a bus; she stood on the corner and waited for a taxi. Glancing down at her feet, she saw a dime on the sidewalk and tried to pick it up, but there were too many people for her to bend down, and she was afraid to shove to make room for fear of being stared at. She put her foot on the dime and then saw a quarter near it, and a nickel. Someone dropped a pocketbook, she thought,

60

and put her other foot on the quarter, stepping quickly to make it look natural; then she saw another dime and another nickel, and a third dime in the gutter. People were passing her, back and forth, all the time, rushing, pushing against her, not looking at her, and she was afraid to get down and start gathering up the money. Other people saw it and went past, and she realized that no one was going to pick it up. They were all embarrassed, or in too much of a hurry, or too crowded. A taxi stopped to let someone off, and she hailed it. She lifted her feet off the dime and the quarter, and left them there when she got into the taxi. This taxi went slowly and bumped as it went; she had begun to notice that the gradual decay was not peculiar to the taxis. The buses were cracking open in unimportant seams, the leather seats broken and stained. The buildings were going, too—in one of the nicest stores there had been a great gaping hole in the tiled foyer, and you walked around it. Corners of the buildings seemed to be crumbling away into fine dust that drifted downward, the granite was eroding unnoticed. Every window she saw on her way uptown seemed to be broken; perhaps every street corner was peppered with small change. The people were moving faster than ever before; a girl in a red hat appeared at the upper side of the taxi window and was gone beyond the lower side before you could see the hat; store windows were so terribly bright because you only caught them for a fraction of a second. The people seemed hurled on in a frantic action that made every hour forty-five minutes long, every day nine hours, every year fourteen days. Food was so elusively fast, eaten in such a hurry, that you were always hungry, always speeding to a new meal with new people. Everything was imperceptibly quicker every minute. She stepped into the taxi on one side and stepped out the other side at her home; she pressed the fifth-floor button on the elevator and was coming down again, bathed and dressed and ready for dinner with Brad. They went out for dinner and were coming in again, hungry and hurrying to bed in order to get to breakfast with lunch beyond. They had been in New York nine days; tomorrow was Saturday and they were going to Long Island, coming home Sunday, and then Wednesday they were going home, really home. By the time she had thought of it they were on the train to Long Island; the train was broken, the seats torn and the floor dirty; one of the doors wouldn't open and the windows wouldn't shut. Passing through the outskirts of the city, she thought, It's as though everything were traveling so fast that the solid stuff couldn't stand it and were going to pieces under the strain, cornices blowing off and windows caving in. She knew she was afraid to say it truly, afraid to face the knowledge that it was a voluntary neck-breaking speed, a deliberate whirling faster and faster to end in destruction.

On Long Island, their hostess led them into a new piece of New York, a house filled with New York furniture as though on rubber bands, pulled this far, stretched taut, and ready to snap back to the city, to an apartment, as soon as the door was opened and the lease, fully paid, had expired. "We've had this place every year for simply ages," their hostess said. "Otherwise we couldn't have gotten it *possibly* this year."

"It's an awfully nice place," Brad said. "I'm surprised you don't live here all year round."

"Got to get back to the city *some* time," their hostess said, and laughed.

"Not much like New Hampshire," Brad said. He was beginning to be a little homesick, Margaret thought; he wants to yell, just once. Since the fire scare she was apprehensive about large groups of people gathering together; when friends began to drop in after dinner she waited for a while, telling herself they were on the ground floor, she could run right outside, all the windows were open; then she excused herself and went to bed. When Brad came to bed much later she woke up and he said irritably, "We've been playing anagrams. Such crazy people." She said sleepily, "Did you win?" and fell asleep before he told her.

The next morning she and Brad went for a walk while their host and hostess read the Sunday papers. "If you turn to the right outside the door," their hostess said encouragingly, "and walk about three blocks down, you'll come to our beach."

"What do they want with our beach?" their host said. "It's too damn cold to do anything down there."

"They can look at the *water*," their hostess said.

They walked down to the beach; at this time of year it was bare and windswept, yet still nodding hideously under traces of its summer plumage, as though it thought itself warmly inviting. There were occupied houses on the way there, for instance, and a lonely lunchstand was open, bravely advertising hot dogs and root beer. The man in the lunchstand watched them go by, his face cold and unsympathetic. They walked far past him, out of sight of houses, on to a stretch of gray pebbled sand that lay between the gray water on one side and the gray pebbled sand dunes on the other.

"Imagine going swimming here," she said with a shiver. The beach pleased her; it was oddly familiar and reassuring and at the same time that she realized this, the little tune came back to her, bringing a double recollection. The beach was the one where she had lived in imagination, writing for herself dreary love-broken stories where the heroine walked beside the wild waves; the little tune was the symbol of the golden world she escaped into to avoid the everyday dreariness that drove her into writing depressing stories about the beach. She laughed out loud and Brad said, "What on earth's so funny about this Godforsaken landscape?"

"I was just thinking how far away from the city it seems," she said falsely.

The sky and the water and the sand were gray enough to make it feel like late afternoon instead of midmorning; she was tired and wanted to go back, but Brad said suddenly, "Look at that," and she turned and saw a girl running down over the dunes, carrying her hat, and her hair flying behind her.

"Only way to get warm on a day like this," Brad remarked, but Margaret said, "She looks frightened."

The girl saw them and came toward them, slowing down as she approached them. She was eager to reach them but when she came within speaking distance the familiar embarrassment, the not wanting to look like a fool, made her hesitate and look from one to the other of them uncomfortably.

"Do you know where I can find a policeman?" she asked finally.

Brad looked up and down the bare rocky beach and said solemnly, "There don't seem to be any around. Is there something we can do?"

"I don't think so," the girl said. "I really need a policeman."

They go to the police for everything, Margaret thought, these people, these New York people, it's as though they had selected a section of the population to act as problem-solvers, and so no matter what they want they look for a policeman.

"Be glad to help you if we can," Brad said.

The girl hesitated again. "Well, if you *must* know," she said crossly, "there's a leg up there."

They waited politely for the girl to explain, but she only said, "Come *on*, then," and waved to them to follow her. She led them over the dunes to a spot near a small inlet, where the dunes gave way abruptly to an intruding head of water. A leg was lying on the sand near the water, and the girl gestured at it and said, "There," as though it were her own property and they had insisted on having a share.

They walked over to it and Brad bent down gingerly. "It's a leg all right," he said. It looked like part of a wax dummy, a death-white wax leg neatly cut off at top-thigh and again just above the ankle, bent comfortably at the knee and resting on the sand. "It's real," Brad said, his voice slightly different. "You're right about that policeman."

They walked together to the lunchstand and the man listened unenthusiastically while Brad called the police. When the police came they all walked out again to where the leg was lying and Brad gave the police their names and addresses, and then said, "Is it all right to go on home?"

"What the hell you want to hang around for?" the policeman inquired with heavy humor. "You waiting for the rest of him?"

They went back to their host and hostess, talking about the leg, and their host apologized, as though he had been guilty of a breach of taste in allowing his guests to come on a human leg; their hostess said with interest, "There was an arm washed up in Bensonhurst, I've been reading about it."

"One of these killings," the host said.

Upstairs Margaret said abruptly, "I suppose it starts to happen first in the suburbs," and when Brad said, "What starts to happen?" she said hysterically, "People starting to come apart."

In order to reassure their host and hostess about their minding the leg, they stayed until the last afternoon train to New York. Back in their apartment again it seemed to Margaret that the marble in the house lobby had begun to age a little; even in two days there were new perceptible cracks. The elevator seemed a little rusty, and there was a fine film of dust over everything in the apartment. They went to bed feeling uncomfortable, and the next morning Margaret said immediately, "I'm going to stay in today."

"You're not upset about yesterday, are you?"

"Not a bit," Margaret said. "I just want to stay in and rest."

After some discussion Brad decided to go off again by himself; he still had people it was important to see and places he must go in the few days they had left. After breakfast in the Automat Margaret came back alone to the apartment, carrying the mystery story she had bought on the way. She hung up her coat and hat and sat down by the window with the noise and the people far below, looking out at the sky where it was gray beyond the houses across the street.

I'm not going to worry about it, she said to herself, no sense thinking all the time about things like that, spoil your vacation and Brad's too. No sense worrying, people get ideas like that and then worry about them.

The nasty little tune was running through her head again, with its burden of suavity and expensive perfume. The houses across the street were silent and perhaps unoccupied at this time of day; she let her eyes move with the rhythm of the tune, from window to window along one floor. By gliding quickly across two windows, she could make one line of the tune fit one floor of windows, and then a quick breath and a drop down to the next floor; it had the same number of windows and the tune had the same number of beats, and then the next floor and the next. She stopped suddenly when it seemed to her that the windowsill she had just passed had soundlessly crumpled and fallen into fine sand; when she looked back it was there as before but then it seemed to be the windowsill above and to the right, and finally a corner of the roof.

No sense worrying, she told herself, forcing her eyes down to the street, stop thinking about things all the time. Looking down at the street for long made her dizzy and she stood up and went into the small bedroom of the apartment. She had made the bed before going out to breakfast, like any good housewife, but now she deliberately took it apart, stripping the blankets and sheets off one by one, and then she made it again, taking a long time over the corners and smoothing out every wrinkle. "*That*'s done," she said when she was through, and went back to the window. When she looked across the street the tune started again, window to window, sills dissolving and falling downward. She leaned forward and looked down at her own window, something she had never thought of before, down to the sill. It was partly eaten away; when she touched the stone a few crumbs rolled off and fell.

It was eleven o'clock; Brad was looking at blowtorches by now and would not be back before one, if even then. She thought of writing a letter home, but the impulse left her before she found paper and pen. Then it occurred to her that she might take a nap, a thing she had never done in the morning in her life, and she went in and lay down on the bed. Lying down, she felt the building shaking.

No sense worrying, she told herself again, as though it were a charm against witches, and got up and found her coat and hat and put them on. I'll just get some cigarettes and some letter paper, she thought, just run down to the corner. Panic caught her going down in the elevator; it went too fast, and when she stepped out in the lobby it was only the people standing around who kept her from running. As it was, she went quickly out of the building and into the street. For a minute she hesitated, wanting to go back. The cars were going past so rapidly, the people hurrying as always, but the panic of the elevator drove her on finally. She went to the corner, and, following the people flying along ahead, ran out into the street, to hear a horn almost overhead and a shout from behind her, and the noise of brakes. She ran blindly on and reached the other side where she stopped and looked around. The truck was going on its appointed way around the corner, the people going past on either side of her, parting to go around her where she stood.

No one even noticed me, she thought with reassurance, everyone who saw me has gone by long ago. She went into the drugstore ahead of her and asked the man for cigarettes; the apartment now seemed safer to her than the street— she could walk up the stairs. Coming out of the store and walking to the corner, she kept as close to the buildings as possible, refusing to give way to the rightful traffic coming out of the doorways. On the corner she looked carefully at the light; it was green, but it looked as though it were going to change. Always safer to wait, she thought, don't want to walk into another truck.

People pushed past her and some were caught in the middle of the street when the light changed. One woman, more cowardly than the rest, turned and ran back to the curb, but the others stood in the middle of the street, leaning forward and then backward according to the traffic moving past them on both sides. One got to the farther curb in a brief break in the line of cars, the others were a fraction of a second too late and waited. Then the light changed again and as the cars slowed down Margaret put a foot on the street to go, but a taxi swinging wildly around her corner frightened her back and she stood on the curb again. By the time the taxi had gone the light was due to change again and she thought, I can wait once more, no sense getting caught out in the middle. A man beside her tapped his foot impatiently for the light to change back; two girls came past her and walked out into the street a few steps to wait, moving back a little when cars came too close, talking busily all the time. I ought to stay right with them, Margaret thought, but then they moved back against her and the light changed and the man next to her charged into the street and the two girls in front waited a minute and then moved slowly on, still talking, and Margaret started to follow and then decided to wait. A crowd of people formed around her suddenly; they had come off a bus and were crossing here, and she had a sudden feeling of being jammed in the center and forced out into the street when all of them moved as one with the light changing, and she elbowed her way desperately out of the crowd and went off to lean against a building and wait. It seemed to her that people passing were beginning to look at her. What do they think of me, she wondered, and stood up straight as though she were waiting for someone. She looked at her watch and frowned, and then thought, What a fool I must look like, no one here ever saw me before, they all go by too fast. She went back to the curb again but the green light was just changing to red and she thought, I'll go back to the drugstore and have a coke, no sense going back to that apartment.

The man looked at her unsurprised in the drugstore and she sat and ordered a coke but suddenly as she was drinking it the panic caught her again and she thought of the people who had been with her when she first started to cross the street, blocks away by now, having tried and made perhaps a dozen lights while she had hesitated at the first; people by now a mile or so downtown, because they had been going steadily while she had been trying to gather her courage. She paid the man quickly, restrained an impulse to say that there was nothing wrong with the coke, she just had to get back, that was all, and she hurried down to the corner again.

The minute the light changes, she told herself firmly; there's no sense. The light changed before she was ready and in the minute before she collected herself traffic turning the corner overwhelmed her and she shrank back against the curb. She looked longingly at the cigar store on the opposite corner, with her apartment house beyond; she wondered, How do people ever manage to get there, and knew that by wondering, by admitting a doubt, she was lost. The light changed and she looked at it with hatred, a dumb thing, turning back and forth, back and forth, with no purpose and no meaning. Looking to either side of her slyly, to see if anyone were watching, she stepped quietly backward, one step, two, until she was well away from the curb. Back in the drugstore again she waited for some sign of recognition from the clerk and saw none; he regarded her with the same apathy as he had the first time. He gestured without interest at the telephone; he doesn't care, she thought, it doesn't matter to him who I call.

She had no time to feel like a fool, because they answered the phone immediately and agreeably and found him right away. When he answered the phone, his voice sounding surprised and matter-of-fact, she could only say miserably, "I'm in the drugstore on the corner. Come and get me."

"What's the matter?" He was not anxious to come.

"Please come and get me," she said into the black mouthpiece that might or might not tell him, "please come and get me, Brad. *Please*."

WILLA CATHER

PAUL'S CASE

IT WAS PAUL'S afternoon to appear before the faculty of
the Pittsburgh High School to account for his various mis-
demeanors. He had been suspended a week ago, and his
father had called at the Principal's office and confessed
his perplexity about his son. Paul entered the faculty room
suave and smiling. His clothes were a trifle outgrown, and
the tan velvet on the collar of his open overcoat was frayed
and worn; but for all that there was something of the dandy
about him, and he wore an opal pin in his neatly knotted
black four-in-hand, and a red carnation in his buttonhole.
This latter adornment the faculty somehow felt was not
properly significant of the contrite spirit befitting a boy
under the ban of suspension.

Paul was tall for his age and very thin, with high, cramped
shoulders and a narrow chest. His eyes were remarkable for
a certain hysterical brilliancy, and he continually used them
in a conscious, theatrical sort of way, peculiarly offensive in
a boy. The pupils were abnormally large, as though he were
addicted to belladonna, but there was a glassy glitter about
them which that drug does not produce.

When questioned by the Principal as to why he was there,
Paul stated, politely enough, that he wanted to come back
to school. This was a lie, but Paul was quite accustomed to
lying; found it, indeed, indispensable for overcoming
friction. His teachers were asked to state their respective
charges against him, which they did with such a rancor and

aggrievedness as evinced that this was not a usual case. Disorder and impertinence were among the offenses named, yet each of his instructors felt that it was scarcely possible to put into words the real cause of the trouble, which lay in a sort of hysterically defiant manner of the boy's; in the contempt which they all knew he felt for them, and which he seemingly made not the least effort to conceal. Once, when he had been making a synopsis of a paragraph at the blackboard, his English teacher had stepped to his side and attempted to guide his hand. Paul had started back with a shudder and thrust his hands violently behind him. The astonished woman could scarcely have been more hurt and embarrassed had he struck at her. The insult was so involuntary and definitely personal as to be unforgettable. In one way and another, he had made all his teachers, men and women alike, conscious of the same feeling of physical aversion. In one class he habitually sat with his hand shading his eyes; in another he always looked out of the window during the recitation; in another he made a running commentary on the lecture, with humorous intent.

His teachers felt this afternoon that his whole attitude was symbolized by his shrug and his flippantly red carnation flower, and they fell upon him without mercy, his English teacher leading the pack. He stood through it smiling, his pale lips parted over his white teeth. (His lips were continually twitching, and he had a habit of raising his eyebrows that was contemptuous and irritating to the last degree.) Older boys than Paul had broken down and shed tears under that ordeal, but his set smile did not once desert him, and his only sign of discomfort was the nervous trembling of the fingers that toyed with the buttons of his overcoat, and an occasional jerking of the other hand which held his hat. Paul was always smiling, always glancing about him, seeming to feel that people might be watching him and trying to detect something. This conscious expression, since it was as far as possible from boyish mirthfulness, was usually attributed to insolence or "smartness."

As the inquisition proceeded, one of his instructors repeated an impertinent remark of the boy's, and the Principal asked him whether he thought that a courteous speech to make to a woman. Paul shrugged his shoulders slightly and his eyebrows twitched.

"I don't know," he replied. "I didn't mean to be polite or impolite, either. I guess it's a sort of way I have, of saying things regardless."

The Principal asked him whether he didn't think that a way it would be well to get rid of. Paul grinned and said he guessed so. When he was told that he could go, he bowed gracefully and went out. His bow was like a repetition of the scandalous red carnation.

His teachers were in despair, and his drawing master voiced the feeling of them all when he declared there was something about the boy which none of them understood. He added: "I don't really believe that smile of his comes altogether from insolence; there's something sort of haunted about it. The boy is not strong, for one thing. There is something wrong about the fellow."

The drawing master had come to realize that, in looking at Paul, one saw only his white teeth and the forced animation of his eyes. One warm afternoon the boy had gone to sleep at his drawing-board, and his master had noted with amazement what a white, blue-veined face it was; drawn and wrinkled like an old man's about the eyes, the lips twitching even in his sleep.

His teachers left the building dissatisfied and unhappy; humiliated to have felt so vindictive toward a mere boy, to have uttered this feeling in cutting terms, and to have set each other on, as it were, in the gruesome game of intemperate reproach. One of them remembered having seen a miserable street cat set at bay by a ring of tormentors.

As for Paul, he ran down the hill whistling the Soldiers' Chorus from *Faust*, looking wildly behind him now and then to see whether some of his teachers were not there to witness his light-heartedness. As it was now late in the afternoon and Paul was on duty that evening as usher at Carnegie Hall, he decided that he would not go home to supper.

When he reached the concert hall the doors were not yet open. It was chilly outside, and he decided to go up into the picture gallery—always deserted at this hour—where there were some of Raffelli's gay studies of Paris streets and an airy blue Venetian scene or two that always exhilarated him. He was delighted to find no one in the gallery but the old guard, who sat in the corner, a newspaper on his knee, a black patch over one eye and the other closed. Paul possessed himself of the place and walked confidently up and down, whistling under his breath. After a while he sat down before a blue Rico and lost himself. When he bethought him to look at his watch, it was after seven o'clock, and he rose with a start and ran downstairs, making a face at Augustus Cæsar, peering out from the cast-room, and an evil gesture at the Venus of Milo as he passed her on the stairway.

When Paul reached the ushers' dressing-room half-a-dozen boys were there already, and he began excitedly to tumble into his uniform. It was one of the few that at all approached fitting, and Paul thought it very becoming—though he knew the tight, straight coat accentuated his narrow chest, about which he was exceedingly sensitive. He was always excited while he dressed, twanging all over to the tuning of the strings and the preliminary flourishes of the horns in the music-room; but tonight he seemed quite beside himself, and he teased and plagued the boys until, telling him that he was crazy, they put him down on the floor and sat on him.

Somewhat calmed by his suppression, Paul dashed out to the front of the house to seat the early comers. He was a model usher. Gracious and smiling he ran up and down the aisles. Nothing was too much trouble for him; he carried messages and brought programs as though it were his greatest pleasure in life, and all the people in his section thought him a charming boy, feeling that he remembered and admired them. As the house filled, he grew more and more vivacious and animated, and the color came to his cheeks and lips. It was very much as though this were a great reception and Paul were the host. Just as the musicians came out to take their places, his English teacher arrived with checks for the seats which a prominent manufacturer had taken for the season. She betrayed some embarrassment when she handed Paul the tickets, and a *hauteur* which subsequently made her feel very foolish. Paul was startled for a moment, and had the feeling of wanting to put her out; what business had she here among all these fine people and gay colors? He looked her over and decided that she was not appropriately dressed and must be a fool to sit downstairs in such togs. The tickets had probably been sent her out of kindness, he reflected, as he put down a seat for her, and she had about as much right to sit there as he had.

When the symphony began Paul sank into one of the rear seats with a long sigh of relief, and lost himself as he had done before the Rico. It was not that symphonies, as such, meant anything in particular to Paul, but the first sigh of the instruments seemed to free some hilarious spirit within him; something that struggled there like the Genius in the bottle found by the Arab fisherman. He felt a sudden zest of life; the lights danced before his eyes and the concert hall blazed into unimaginable splendor. When the soprano soloist came on, Paul forgot even the nastiness of his teacher's being there, and gave himself up to the peculiar intoxication such personages always had for him. The soloist chanced to be a German woman, by no means in her first youth, and the mother of many children; but she wore a satin gown and a tiara, and she had that indefinable air of achievement, that world-shine upon her, which always blinded Paul to any possible defects.

After a concert was over, Paul was often irritable and wretched until he got to sleep,—and tonight he was even more than usually restless. He had the feeling of not being able to let down; of its being impossible to give up this delicious excitement which was the only thing that could be called living at all. During the last number he withdrew and, after hastily changing his clothes in the dressing-room, slipped out to the side door where the singer's carriage stood. Here he began pacing rapidly up and down the walk, waiting to see her come out.

Over yonder the Schenley, in its vacant stretch, loomed big and square through the fine rain, the windows of its twelve stories glowing like those of a lighted cardboard house under a Christmas tree. All the actors and singers of any importance stayed there when they were in the city, and a number of the big manufacturers of the place lived there in the winter. Paul had often hung about the hotel, watching the people go in and out, longing to enter and leave schoolmasters and dull care behind him for ever.

At last the singer came out, accompanied by the conductor, who helped her into her carriage and closed the door with a cordial *auf wiedersehen*,—which set Paul to wondering whether she was not an old sweetheart of his. Paul followed the carriage over to the hotel, walking so rapidly as not to be far from the entrance when the singer alighted and disappeared behind the swinging glass doors which were opened by a negro in a tall hat and a long coat. In the moment that the door was ajar, it seemed to Paul that he, too, entered. He seemed to feel himself go after her up the steps, into the warm, lighted building, into an exotic, a tropical world of shiny, glistening surfaces and basking ease. He reflected upon the mysterious dishes that were brought into the dining-room, the green bottles in buckets of ice, as he had seen them in the supper party pictures of the Sunday supplement. A quick gust of wind brought the rain down with sudden vehemence, and Paul was startled to find that he was still outside in the slush of the gravel driveway; that his boots were letting in the water and his scanty overcoat was clinging wet about him; that the lights in front of the concert hall were out, and that the rain was driving in sheets between him and the orange glow of the windows above him. There it was, what he wanted—tangibly before him, like the fairy world of a Christmas pantomime; as the rain beat in his face, Paul wondered whether he were destined always to shiver in the black night outside, looking up at it.

He turned and walked reluctantly toward the car tracks. The end had to come sometime; his father in his night-clothes at the top of the stairs, explanations that did not explain, hastily improvised fictions that were forever tripping him up, his upstairs room and its horrible yellow wallpaper, the creaking bureau with the greasy plush collar box, and over his painted wooden bed the pictures of George Washington and John Calvin, and the framed motto, "Feed my Lambs," which had been worked in red worsted by his mother, whom Paul could not remember.

Half an hour later, Paul alighted from the Negley Avenue car and went slowly down one of the side streets off the main thoroughfare. It was a highly respectable street, where all the houses were exactly alike, and where business men of moderate means begot and reared large families of children, all of whom went to Sabbath-school and learned the shorter catechism, and were interested in arithmetic; all of whom were as exactly alike as their homes, and of a piece with the monotony in which they lived. Paul never went up Cordelia Street without a shudder of loathing. His home was next the house of the Cumberland minister. He approached it tonight with the nerveless sense of defeat, the hopeless feeling of sinking back forever into ugliness and commonness that he had always had when he came home. The moment he turned into Cordelia Street he felt the waters close above his head. After each of these orgies of living, he experienced all the physical depression which follows a debauch; the loathing of respectable beds, of common food, of a house permeated by kitchen odors; a shuddering repulsion for the flavorless, colorless mass of everyday existence, a morbid desire for cool things and soft lights and fresh flowers.

The nearer he approached the house, the more absolutely unequal Paul felt to the sight of it all; his ugly sleeping chamber; the cold bathroom with the grimy zinc tub, the cracked mirror, the dripping spiggots; his father, at the top of the stairs, his hairy legs sticking out from his nightshirt, his feet thrust into carpet slippers. He was so much later than usual that there would certainly be inquiries and reproaches. Paul stopped short before the door. He felt that he could not be accosted by his father tonight; that he could not toss again on that miserable bed. He would not go in. He would tell his father that he had no car fare, and it was raining so hard he had gone home with one of the boys and stayed all night.

Meanwhile, he was wet and cold. He went around to the back of the house and tried one of the basement windows, found it open, raised it cautiously, and scrambled down the cellar wall to the floor. There he stood, holding his breath, terrified by the noise he had made; but the floor above him was silent, and there was no creak on the stairs. He found a soap-box, and carried it over to the soft ring of light that streamed from the furnace door, and sat down. He was horribly afraid of rats, so he did not try to sleep, but sat looking distrustfully at the dark, still terrified lest he might have awakened his father. In such reactions, after one of the experiences which made days and nights out of the dreary blanks of the calendar, when his senses were deadened, Paul's head was always singularly clear. Suppose his father had heard him getting in at the window and had come down and shot him for a burglar? Then, again, suppose his father had come down, pistol in hand, and he had cried out in time to save himself, and his father had been horrified to think how nearly he had killed him? Then, again, suppose a day should come when his father would remember that night, and wish there had been no warning cry to stay his hand? With this last supposition Paul entertained himself until daybreak.

The following Sunday was fine; the sodden November chill was broken by the last flash of autumnal summer. In the morning Paul had to go to church and Sabbath-school, as always. On seasonable Sunday afternoons the burghers of Cordelia Street usually sat out on their front "stoops," and talked to their neighbors on the next stoop, or called to those across the street in neighborly fashion. The men sat placidly on gay cushions placed upon the steps that led down to the sidewalk, while the women, in their Sunday "waists," sat in rockers on the cramped porches, pretending to be greatly at their ease. The children played in the streets; there were so

81

many of them that the place resembled the recreation grounds of a kindergarten. The men on the steps—all in their shirt sleeves, their vests unbuttoned—sat with their legs well apart, their stomachs comfortably protruding, and talked of the prices of things, or told anecdotes of the sagacity of their various chiefs and overlords. They occasionally looked over the multitude of squabbling children, listened affectionately to their high-pitched, nasal voices, smiling to see their own proclivities reproduced in their offspring, and interspersed their legends of the iron kings with remarks about their sons' progress at school, their grades in arithmetic, and the amounts they had saved in their toy banks.

On this last Sunday of November, Paul sat all the afternoon on the lowest step of his "stoop," staring into the street, while his sisters, in their rockers, were talking to the minister's daughters next door about how many shirt-waists they had made in the last week, and how many waffles someone had eaten at the last church supper. When the weather was warm, and his father was in a particularly jovial frame of mind, the girls made lemonade, which was always brought out in a red-glass pitcher, ornamented with forget-me-nots in blue enamel. This the girls thought very fine, and the neighbors joked about the suspicious color of the pitcher.

Today Paul's father, on the top step, was talking to a young man who shifted a restless baby from knee to knee. He happened to be the young man who was daily held up to Paul as a model, and after whom it was his father's dearest hope that he would pattern. This young man was of a ruddy complexion, with a compressed, red mouth, and faded, near-sighted eyes, over which he wore thick spectacles, with gold bows that curved about his ears. He was clerk to one of the magnates of a great steel corporation, and was looked upon in Cordelia Street as a young man with a future. There was a story that, some five years ago—he was now barely twenty-six—he had been a trifle "dissipated," but in order to curb his appetites and save the loss of time and strength that a sowing of wild oats might have entailed, he had taken his chief's advice, oft reiterated to his employés, and at twenty-one had married the first woman whom he could persuade to share his fortunes. She happened to be an angular schoolmistress, much older than he, who also wore thick glasses, and who had now borne him four children, all near-sighted, like herself.

The young man was relating how his chief, now cruising in the Mediterranean, kept in touch with all the details of the business, arranging his office hours on his yacht just as though he were at home, and "knocking off work enough to keep two stenographers busy." His father told, in turn, the plan his corporation was considering, of putting in an electric railway plant at Cairo. Paul snapped his teeth; he had an awful apprehension that they might spoil it all before he got there. Yet he rather liked to hear these legends of the iron kings, that were told and retold on Sundays and holidays; these stories of palaces in Venice, yachts on the Mediterranean, and high play at Monte Carlo appealed to his fancy, and he was interested in the triumphs of cash boys who had become famous, though he had no mind for the cash-boy stage.

After supper was over, and he had helped to dry the dishes, Paul nervously asked his father whether he could go to George's to get some help in his geometry, and still more nervously asked for car fare. This latter request he had to repeat, as his father, on principle, did not like to hear requests for money, whether much or little. He asked Paul whether he could not go to some boy who lived nearer, and told him that he ought not to leave his school work until Sunday; but he gave him the dime. He was not a poor man, but he had a worthy ambition to come up in the world. His only reason for allowing Paul to usher was that he thought a boy ought to be earning a little.

Paul bounded upstairs, scrubbed the greasy odor of the dishwater from his hands with the ill-smelling soap he hated, and then shook over his fingers a few drops of violet water from the bottle he kept hidden in his drawer. He left the house with his geometry conspicuously under his arm, and the moment he got out of Cordelia Street and boarded a downtown car, he shook off the lethargy of two deadening days, and began to live again.

The leading juvenile of the permanent stock company which played at one of the downtown theaters was an acquaintance of Paul's, and the boy had been invited to drop in at the Sunday-night rehearsals whenever he could. For more than a year Paul had spent every available moment loitering about Charley Edwards's dressing-room. He had won a place among Edwards's following not only because the young actor, who could not afford to employ a dresser, often found him useful, but because he recognized in Paul something akin to what churchmen term "vocation."

It was at the theater and at Carnegie Hall that Paul really lived; the rest was but a sleep and a forgetting. This was Paul's fairy tale, and it had for him all the allurement of a secret love. The moment he inhaled the gassy, painty, dusty odor behind the scenes, he breathed like a prisoner set free, and felt within him the possibility of doing or saying splendid, brilliant things. The moment the cracked orchestra beat out the overture from *Martha*, or jerked at the serenade from *Rigoletto*, all stupid and ugly things slid from him, and his senses were deliciously, yet delicately fired.

Perhaps it was because, in Paul's world, the natural nearly

always wore the guise of ugliness, that a certain element of artificiality seemed to him necessary in beauty. Perhaps it was because his experience of life elsewhere was so full of Sabbath-school picnics, petty economies, wholesome advice as to how to succeed in life, and the unescapable odors of cooking, that he found this existence so alluring, these smartly-clad men and women so attractive, that he was so moved by these starry apple orchards that bloomed perennially under the limelight.

It would be difficult to put it strongly enough how convincingly the stage entrance of that theater was for Paul the actual portal of Romance. Certainly none of the company ever suspected it, least of all Charley Edwards. It was very like the old stories that used to float about London of fabulously rich Jews, who had subterranean halls, with palms, and fountains, and soft lamps and richly appareled women who never saw the disenchanting light of London day. So, in the midst of that smoke-palled city, enamored of figures and grimy toil, Paul had his secret temple, his wishing-carpet, his bit of blue-and-white Mediterranean shore bathed in perpetual sunshine.

Several of Paul's teachers had a theory that his imagination had been perverted by garish fiction; but the truth was, he scarcely ever read at all. The books at home were not such as would either tempt or corrupt a youthful mind, and as for reading the novels that some of his friends urged upon him— well, he got what he wanted much more quickly from music; any sort of music, from an orchestra to a barrel organ. He needed only the spark, the indescribable thrill that made his imagination master of his senses, and he could make plots and pictures enough of his own. It was equally true that he was not stage-struck—not, at any rate, in the usual acceptation of that expression. He had no desire to become an actor, any more than he had to become a musician. He felt no necessity to do any of these things; what he wanted was to see, to be in the atmosphere, float on the wave of it, to be carried out, blue league after blue league, away from everything.

After a night behind the scenes, Paul found the schoolroom more than ever repulsive; the bare floors and naked walls; the prosy men who never wore frock coats, or violets in their buttonholes; the women with their dull gowns, shrill voices, and pitiful seriousness about prepositions that govern the dative. He could not bear to have the other pupils think, for a moment, that he took these people seriously; he must convey to them that he considered it all trivial, and was there only by way of a joke, anyway. He had autograph pictures of all the members of the stock company which he showed his classmates, telling them the most incredible stories of his familiarity with these people, of his acquaintance with the soloists who came to Carnegie Hall, his suppers with them and the flowers he sent them. When these stories lost their effect, and his audience grew listless, he would bid all the boys goodbye, announcing that he was going to travel for awhile; going to Naples, to California, to Egypt. Then, next Monday, he would slip back, conscious and nervously smiling; his sister was ill, and he would have to defer his voyage until spring.

Matters went steadily worse with Paul at school. In the itch to let his instructors know how heartily he despised them, and how thoroughly he was appreciated elsewhere, he mentioned once or twice that he had no time to fool with theorems; adding—with a twitch of the eyebrows and a touch of that nervous bravado which so perplexed them— that he was helping the people down at the stock company; they were old friends of his.

The upshot of the matter was, that the Principal went to

Paul's father, and Paul was taken out of school and put to work. The manager at Carnegie Hall was told to get another usher in his stead; the doorkeeper at the theater was warned not to admit him to the house; and Charley Edwards remorsefully promised the boy's father not to see him again.

The members of the stock company were vastly amused when some of Paul's stories reached them—especially the women. They were hard-working women, most of them supporting indolent husbands or brothers, and they laughed rather bitterly at having stirred the boy to such fervid and florid inventions. They agreed with the faculty and with his father, that Paul's was a bad case.

The east-bound train was plowing through a January snow-storm; the dull dawn was beginning to show gray when the engine whistled a mile out of Newark. Paul started up from the seat where he had lain curled in uneasy slumber, rubbed the breath-misted window glass with his hand, and peered out. The snow was whirling in curling eddies above the white bottom lands, and the drifts lay already deep in the fields and along the fences, while here and there the long dead grass and dried weed stalks protruded black above it. Lights shone from the scattered houses, and a gang of laborers who stood beside the track waved their lanterns.

Paul had slept very little, and he felt grimy and uncomfortable. He had made the all-night journey in a day coach because he was afraid if he took a Pullman he might be seen by some Pittsburgh business man who had noticed him in Denny & Carson's office. When the whistle woke him, he clutched quickly at his breast pocket, glancing about him with an uncertain smile. But the little, clay-bespattered Italians were still sleeping, the slatternly women across the aisle were in open-mouthed oblivion, and even the crumby, crying babies were for the nonce stilled. Paul settled back to struggle with his impatience as best he could.

When he arrived at the Jersey City station, he hurried through his breakfast, manifestly ill at ease and keeping a sharp eye about him. After he reached the Twenty-third Street station, he consulted a cabman, and had himself driven to a men's furnishing establishment which was just opening for the day. He spent upward of two hours there, buying with endless reconsidering and great care. His new street suit he put on in the fitting-room; the frock coat and dress clothes he had bundled into the cab with his new shirts. Then he drove to a hatter's and a shoe house. His next errand was at Tiffany's, where he selected silver mounted brushes and a scarf-pin. He would not wait to have his silver marked, he said. Lastly, he stopped at a trunk shop on Broadway, and had his purchases packed into various traveling bags.

It was a little after one o'clock when he drove up to the Waldorf, and, after settling with the cabman, went into the office. He registered from Washington; said his mother and father had been abroad, and that he had come down to await the arrival of their steamer. He told his story plausibly and had no trouble, since he offered to pay for them in advance, in engaging his rooms; a sleeping-room, sitting-room and bath.

Not once, but a hundred times Paul had planned this entry into New York. He had gone over every detail of it with Charley Edwards, and in his scrap book at home there were pages of description about New York hotels, cut from the Sunday papers.

When he was shown to his sitting-room on the eighth floor, he saw at a glance that everything was as it should be; there was but one detail in his mental picture that the place did not realize, so he rang for the bellboy and sent him down for flowers. He moved about nervously until the boy returned, putting away his new linen and fingering it delightedly as he did so. When the flowers came, he put them hastily into water, and then tumbled into a hot bath. Presently he came out of his white bathroom, resplendent in his new silk underwear, and playing with the tassels of his red robe. The snow was whirling so fiercely outside his windows that he could scarcely see across the street; but within, the air was deliciously soft and fragrant. He put the violets and jonquils on the tabouret beside the couch, and threw himself down with a long sigh, covering himself with a Roman blanket. He was thoroughly tired; he had been in such haste, he had stood up to such a strain, covered so much ground in the last twenty-four hours, that he wanted to think how it had all come about. Lulled by the sound of the wind, the warm air, and the cool fragrance of the flowers, he sank into deep, drowsy retrospection.

It had been wonderfully simple; when they had shut him out of the theater and concert hall, when they had taken away his bone, the whole thing was virtually determined. The rest was a mere matter of opportunity. The only thing that at all surprised him was his own courage—for he realized well enough that he had always been tormented by fear, a sort of apprehensive dread that, of late years, as the meshes of the lies he had told closed about him, had been pulling the muscles of his body tighter and tighter. Until now, he could not remember a time when he had not been dreading something. Even when he was a little boy, it was always there—behind him, or before, or on either side. There had always been the shadowed corner, the dark place into which he dared not look, but from which something seemed always to be watching him—and Paul had done things that were not pretty to watch, he knew.

But now he had a curious sense of relief, as though he had at last thrown down the gauntlet to the thing in the corner.

Yet it was but a day since he had been sulking in the traces; but yesterday afternoon that he had been sent to the bank with Denny & Carson's deposit, as usual—but this time he was instructed to leave the book to be balanced. There was above two thousand dollars in checks, and nearly a thousand in the bank notes which he had taken from the book and quietly transferred to his pocket. At the bank he had made out a new deposit slip. His nerves had been steady enough to permit of his returning to the office, where he had finished his work and asked for a full day's holiday tomorrow, Saturday, giving a perfectly reasonable pretext. The bank book, he knew, would not be returned before Monday or Tuesday, and his father would be out of town for the next week. From the time he slipped the bank notes into his pocket until he boarded the night train for New York, he had not known a moment's hesitation.

How astonishingly easy it had all been; here he was, the thing done; and this time there would be no awakening, no figure at the top of the stairs. He watched the snowflakes whirling by his window until he fell asleep.

When he awoke, it was four o'clock in the afternoon. He bounded up with a start; one of his precious days gone already! He spent nearly an hour in dressing, watching every stage of his toilet carefully in the mirror. Everything was quite perfect; he was exactly the kind of boy he had always wanted to be.

When he went downstairs, Paul took a carriage and drove up Fifth Avenue toward the Park. The snow had somewhat abated; carriages and tradesmen's wagons were hurrying soundlessly to and fro in the winter twilight; boys in woollen mufflers were shoveling off the doorsteps; the avenue stages made fine spots of color against the white street. Here and there on the corners whole flower gardens blooming behind glass windows, against which the snowflakes stuck and melted; violets, roses, carnations, lilies of the valley—somehow vastly more lovely and alluring that they blossomed thus unnaturally in the snow. The Park itself was a wonderful stage winterpiece.

When he returned, the pause of the twilight had ceased, and the tune of the streets had changed. The snow was falling faster, lights streamed from the hotels that reared their many stories fearlessly up into the storm, defying the raging Atlantic winds. A long, black stream of carriages poured down the avenue, intersected here and there by other streams, tending horizontally. There were a score of cabs about the entrance of his hotel, and his driver had to wait. Boys in livery were running in and out of the awning stretched across the sidewalk, up and down the red velvet carpet laid from the door to the street. Above, about, within it all, was the rumble and roar, the hurry and toss of thousands of human beings as hot for pleasure as himself, and on every side of him towered the glaring affirmation of the omnipotence of wealth.

The boy set his teeth and drew his shoulders together in a spasm of realization; the plot of all dramas, the text of all romances, the nerve-stuff of all sensations was whirling about him like the snowflakes. He burnt like a faggot in a tempest.

When Paul came down to dinner, the music of the orchestra floated up the elevator shaft to greet him. As he stepped into the thronged corridor, he sank back into one of the chairs against the wall to get his breath. The lights, the chatter, the perfumes, the bewildering medley of color—he had, for a moment, the feeling of not being able to stand it. But only for a moment; these were his own people, he told himself. He went slowly about the corridors, through the writing-rooms, smoking-rooms, reception-rooms, as though he were exploring the chambers of an enchanted palace, built and peopled for him alone.

When he reached the dining-room he sat down at a table near a window. The flowers, the white linen, the many-colored wine glasses, the gay toilettes of the women, the low popping of corks, the undulating repetitions of the *Blue Danube* from the orchestra, all flooded Paul's dream with bewildering radiance. When the roseate tinge of his champagne was added—that cold, precious, bubbling stuff that creamed and foamed in his glass—Paul wondered that there were honest men in the world at all. This was what all the world was fighting for, he reflected; this was what all the struggle was about. He doubted the reality of his past. Had he ever known a place called Cordelia Street, a place where fagged-looking business men boarded the early car? Mere rivets in a machine they seemed to Paul,—sickening men, with combings of children's hair always hanging to their coats, and the smell of cooking in their clothes. Cordelia Street—Ah, that belonged to another time and country! Had he not always been thus, had he not sat here night after night, from as far back as he could remember, looking pensively over just such shimmering textures, and slowly twirling the stem of a glass like this one between his thumb and middle finger? He rather thought he had.

He was not in the least abashed or lonely. He had no especial desire to meet or to know any of these people; all he demanded was the right to look on and conjecture, to watch the pageant. The mere stage properties were all he contended for. Nor was he lonely later in the evening, in his loge at the Opera. He was entirely rid of his nervous misgivings, of his forced aggressiveness, of the imperative desire to show himself different from his surroundings. He felt now that his surroundings explained him. Nobody questioned the purple; he had only to wear it passively. He had only to glance down at his dress coat to reassure himself that here it would be impossible for anyone to humiliate him.

He found it hard to leave his beautiful sitting-room to go to bed that night, and sat long watching the raging storm from his turret window. When he went to sleep, it was with the lights turned on in his bedroom; partly because of his old timidity, and partly so that, if he should wake in the night, there would be no wretched moment of doubt, no horrible suspicion of yellow wallpaper, or of Washington and Calvin above his bed.

On Sunday morning the city was practically snowbound. Paul breakfasted late, and in the afternoon he fell in with a wild San Francisco boy, a freshman at Yale, who said he had run down for a "little flyer" over Sunday. The young man offered to show Paul the night side of the town, and the two boys went off together after dinner, not returning to the hotel until seven o'clock the next morning. They had started out in the confiding warmth of a champagne friendship, but their parting in the elevator was singularly cool. The freshman pulled himself together to make his train, and Paul went to bed. He awoke at two o'clock in the afternoon, very thirsty and dizzy, and rang for ice-water, coffee, and the Pittsburgh papers.

On the part of the hotel management, Paul excited no suspicion. There was this to be said for him, that he wore his spoils with dignity and in no way made himself conspicuous. His chief greediness lay in his ears and eyes, and his excesses were not offensive ones. His dearest pleasures were the gray winter twilights in his sitting-room; his quiet enjoyment of his flowers, his clothes, his wide divan, his cigarette and his

93

sense of power. He could not remember a time when he had felt so at peace with himself. The mere release from the necessity of petty lying, lying every day and every day, restored his self-respect. He had never lied for pleasure, even at school; but to make himself noticed and admired, to assert his difference from other Cordelia Street boys; and he felt a good deal more manly, more honest, even, now that he had no need for boastful pretensions, now that he could, as his actor friends used to say, "dress the part." It was characteristic that remorse did not occur to him. His golden days went by without a shadow, and he made each as perfect as he could.

On the eighth day after his arrival in New York, he found the whole affair exploited in the Pittsburgh papers, exploited with a wealth of detail which indicated that local news of a sensational nature was at a low ebb. The firm of Denny & Carson announced that the boy's father had refunded the full amount of his theft, and that they had no intention of prosecuting. The Cumberland minister had been interviewed, and expressed his hope of yet reclaiming the motherless lad, and Paul's Sabbath-school teacher declared that she would spare no effort to that end. The rumor had reached Pittsburgh that the boy had been seen in a New York hotel, and his father had gone East to find him and bring him home.

Paul had just come in to dress for dinner; he sank into a chair, weak in the knees, and clasped his head in his hands. It was to be worse than jail, even; the tepid waters of Cordelia Street were to close over him finally and forever. The gray monotony stretched before him in hopeless, unrelieved years; Sabbath-school, Young People's Meeting, the yellow-papered room, the damp dish-towels; it all rushed back upon him with sickening vividness. He had the old feeling that the orchestra had suddenly stopped, the sinking sensation that the play was over. The sweat broke out on his face, and he sprang to his feet, looked about him with his white, conscious smile, and winked at himself in the mirror. With something of the childish belief in miracles with which he had so often gone to class, all his lessons unlearned, Paul dressed and dashed whistling down the corridor to the elevator.

He had no sooner entered the dining-room and caught the measure of the music, than his remembrance was lightened by his old elastic power of claiming the moment, mounting with it, and finding it all sufficient. The glare and glitter about him, the mere scenic accessories had again, and for the last time, their old potency. He would show himself that he was game, he would finish the thing splendidly. He doubted, more than ever, the existence of Cordelia Street, and for the first time he drank his wine recklessly. Was he not, after all, one of these fortunate beings? Was he not still himself, and in his own place? He drummed a nervous accompaniment to the music and looked about him, telling himself over and over that it had paid.

He reflected drowsily, to the swell of the violin and the chill sweetness of his wine, that he might have done it more wisely. He might have caught an outbound steamer and been well out of their clutches before now. But the other side of the world had seemed too far away and too uncertain then; he could not have waited for it; his need had been too sharp. If he had to choose over again, he would do the same thing tomorrow. He looked affectionately about the dining-room, now gilded with a soft mist. Ah, it had paid indeed!

Paul was awakened next morning by a painful throbbing in his head and feet. He had thrown himself across the bed without undressing, and had slept with his shoes on. His limbs and hands were lead heavy, and his tongue and throat were parched. There came upon him one of those fateful attacks of clear-headedness that never occurred except when he was physically exhausted and his nerves hung loose. He lay still and closed his eyes and let the tide of realities wash over him.

His father was in New York; "stopping at some joint or other," he told himself. The memory of successive summers on the front stoop fell upon him like a weight of black water. He had not a hundred dollars left; and he knew now, more than ever, that money was everything, the wall that stood between all he loathed and all he wanted. The thing was winding itself up; he had thought of that on his first glorious day in New York, and had even provided a way to snap the thread. It lay on his dressing-table now; he had got it out last night when he came blindly up from dinner—but the shiny metal hurt his eyes, and he disliked the look of it, anyway.

He rose and moved about with a painful effort, succumbing now and again to attacks of nausea. It was the old depression exaggerated; all the world had become Cordelia Street. Yet somehow he was not afraid of anything, was absolutely calm; perhaps because he had looked into the dark corner at last, and knew. It was bad enough, what he saw there; but somehow not so bad as his long fear of it had been. He saw everything clearly now. He had a feeling that he had made the best of it, that he had lived the sort of life he was meant to live, and for half an hour he sat staring at the revolver. But he told himself that was not the way, so he went downstairs and took a cab to the ferry.

When Paul arrived at Newark, he got off the train and took another cab, directing the driver to follow the Pennsylvania tracks out of the town. The snow lay heavy on the roadways and had drifted deep in the open fields. Only here and there the dead grass or dried weed stalks projected, singularly black, above it. Once well into the country, Paul dismissed the carriage and walked, floundering along the tracks, his mind a medley of irrelevant things. He seemed to hold in his brain an actual picture of everything he had seen that morning. He remembered every feature of both his drivers, the toothless old woman from whom he had bought the red flowers in his coat, the agent from whom he had got his ticket, and all of his fellow passengers on the ferry. His mind, unable to cope with vital matters near at hand, worked feverishly and deftly at sorting and grouping these images. They made for him a part of the ugliness of the world, of the ache in his head, and the bitter burning on his tongue. He stooped and put a handful of snow into his mouth as he walked, but that, too, seemed hot. When he reached a little hillside, where the tracks ran through a cut some twenty feet below him, he stopped and sat down.

The carnations in his coat were drooping with the cold, he noticed; all their red glory over. It occurred to him that all the flowers he had seen in the show windows that first night must have gone the same way, long before this. It was only one splendid breath they had, in spite of their brave mockery at the winter outside the glass. It was a losing game in the end, it seemed, this revolt against the homilies by which the world is run. Paul took one of the blossoms carefully from his coat and scooped a little hole in the snow, where he covered it up. Then he dozed a while, from his weak condition, seeming insensible to the cold.

The sound of an approaching train woke him, and he started to his feet, remembering only his resolution, and afraid lest he should be too late. He stood watching the approaching locomotive, his teeth chattering, his lips drawn away from them in a frightened smile; once or twice he glanced nervously sidewise, as though he were being watched. When the right moment came, he jumped. As he fell, the folly of his haste occurred to him with merciless clearness, the vastness of what he had left undone. There flashed through his brain, clearer than ever before, the blue of Adriatic water, the yellow of Algerian sands.

He felt something strike his chest,—his body was being thrown swiftly through the air, on and on, immeasurably far and fast, while his limbs gently relaxed. Then, because the picture-making mechanism was crushed, the disturbing visions flashed into black, and Paul dropped back into the immense design of things.

TRUMAN CAPOTE

MASTER MISERY

HER HIGH HEELS, clacking across the marble foyer, made her think of ice cubes rattling in a glass, and the flowers, those autumn chrysanthemums in the urn at the entrance, if touched they would shatter, splinter, she was sure, into frozen dust; yet the house was warm, even somewhat overheated, but cold, and Sylvia shivered, but cold, like the snowy swollen wastes of the secretary's face: Miss Mozart, who dressed all in white, as though she were a nurse. Perhaps she really was; that, of course, could be the answer. Mr. Revercomb, you are mad, and this is your nurse; she thought about it for a moment; well, no. And now the butler brought her scarf. His beauty touched her: slender, so gentle, a Negro with freckled skin and reddish, unreflecting eyes. As he opened the door, Miss Mozart appeared, her starched uniform rustling dryly in the hall. "We hope you will return," she said, and handed Sylvia a sealed envelope. "Mr. Revercomb was most particularly pleased."

Outside, dusk was falling like blue flakes, and Sylvia walked crosstown along the November streets until she reached the lonely upper reaches of Fifth Avenue. It occurred to her then that she might walk home through the park: an act of defiance almost, for Henry and Estelle, always insistent upon their city wisdom, had said over and again, Sylvia, you have no idea how dangerous it is, walking in the park after dark; look what happened to Myrtle Calisher. This isn't Easton, honey. That was the other thing they said. And said. God, she was sick of it. Still, and aside from a few of the other typists at SnugFare, an underwear company for which she worked, who else in New York did she know? Oh, it would be all right if only she did not have to live with them, if she could afford somewhere a small room of her own; but there in that chintz-cramped apartment she sometimes felt she would choke them both. And why had she come to New York? For whatever reason, and it was indeed becoming vague, a principal cause of leaving Easton had been to rid herself of Henry and Estelle; or rather, their counterparts, though in point of fact Estelle was actually from Easton, a town north of Cincinnati. She and Sylvia had grown up together. The real trouble with Henry and Estelle was that they were so excruciatingly married. Namby-pamby, bootsytotsy, and everything had a name: the telephone was Tinkling Tillie, the sofa, Our Nelle, the bed, Big Bear; yes, and what about those His-Her towels, those He-She pillows? Enough to drive you loony. "Loony!" she said aloud, the quiet park erasing her voice. It was lovely now, and she was right to have walked here, with wind moving through the leaves, and globe lamps, freshly aglow, kindling the chalk drawings of children, pink birds, blue arrows, green hearts. But suddenly, like a pair of obscene words, there appeared on the path two boys: pimple-faced, grinning, they loomed in the dusk like menacing flames, and Sylvia, passing them, felt a burning all through her, quite as though she'd brushed fire. They turned and followed her past a deserted playground, one of them bump-bumping a stick along an iron fence, the other whistling: these two sounds accumulated around her like the gathering roar of an oncoming engine, and when one of the boys, with a laugh, called, "Hey, whatsa hurry?" her mouth twisted for breath. Don't, she thought, thinking to throw down her purse and run. At that moment, however, a man walking a dog came up a sidepath, and she followed at his heels to the exit. Wouldn't they feel gratified, Henry and Estelle, wouldn't they we-told-you-so if she were to tell them? and, what is more, Estelle would write it home and the next thing you knew it would be all over Easton that she'd been raped in Central Park. She spent the rest of the way home despising New York: anonymity, its virtuous terror; and the speaking drainpipe, all-night light, ceaseless footfall, subway corridor, numbered door (3C).

"Shh, honey," Estelle said, sidling out of the kitchen, "Bootsy's doing his homework." Sure enough, Henry, a law student at Columbia, was hunched over his books in the living-room, and Sylvia, at Estelle's request, took off her shoes before tiptoeing through. Once inside her room, she threw herself on the bed and put her hands over her eyes. Had today really happened? Miss Mozart and Mr. Revercomb, were they really in the tall house on Seventy-eighth Street?

"So, honey, what happened today?" Estelle had entered without knocking.

Sylvia sat up on her elbow. "Nothing. Except that I typed ninety-seven letters."

"About what, honey?" asked Estelle, using Sylvia's hairbrush.

"Oh, hell, what do you suppose? SnugFare, the shorts that safely support our leaders of Science and Industry."

"Gee, honey, don't sound so cross. I don't know what's wrong with you sometimes. You sound so cross. Ouch! Why don't you get a new brush? This one's just knotted with hair . . ."

"Mostly yours."

"What did you say?"

"Skip it."

"Oh, I thought you said something. Anyway, like I was saying, I wish you didn't have to go to that office and come home every day feeling cross and out of sorts. Personally, and I said this to Bootsy just last night and he agreed with me one hundred percent, I said, Bootsy, I think Sylvia ought to get married: a girl high-strung like that needs her tensions relaxed. There's no earthly reason why you shouldn't. I mean maybe you're not pretty in the ordinary sense, but you have beautiful eyes, and an intelligent, really sincere look. In fact you're the sort of girl any professional man would be lucky to get. And I should think you would want to . . . Look what a different person I am since I married Henry. Doesn't it make you lonesome seeing how happy we are? I'm here to tell you, honey, that there is nothing like lying in bed at night with a man's arms around you and . . ."

"Estelle! For Christ's sake!" Sylvia sat bolt upright in bed, anger on her cheeks like rouge. But after a moment she bit her lip and lowered her eyelids. "I'm sorry," she said, "I didn't mean to shout. Only I wish you wouldn't talk like that."

"It's all right," said Estelle, smiling in a dumb, puzzled way. Then she went over and gave Sylvia a kiss. "I understand, honey. It's just that you're plain worn out. And I'll bet you haven't had anything to eat either. Come on in the kitchen and I'll scramble you some eggs."

When Estelle set the eggs before her, Sylvia felt quite ashamed; after all, Estelle was trying to be nice; and so then, as though to make it all up, she said: "Something did happen today."

Estelle sat down across from her with a cup of coffee, and Sylvia went on: "I don't know how to tell about it. It's so very odd. But—well, I had lunch at the Automat today, and I had to share the table with these three men. I might as well have been invisible because they talked about the most personal things. One of the men said his girl friend was going to have a baby and he didn't know where he was going to get the money to do anything about it. So one of the other men asked him why didn't he sell something. He said he didn't have anything to sell. Whereupon the third man (he was rather delicate and didn't look as if he belonged with the others) said yes, there was something he could sell: *dreams*. Even I laughed, but the man shook his head and said very seriously: no, it was perfectly true, his wife's aunt, Miss Mozart, worked for a rich man who bought dreams, regular night-time dreams—from anybody. And he wrote down the man's name and address and gave it to his friend; but the man simply left it lying on the table. It was too crazy for him, he said."

"Me, too," Estelle put in a little righteously.

"I don't know," said Sylvia, lighting a cigarette. "But I couldn't get it out of my head. The name written on the paper was A. F. Revercomb and the address was on East Seventy-eighth Street. I only glanced at it for a moment, but it was ... I don't know, I couldn't seem to forget it. It was beginning to give me a headache. So I left the office early ..."

Slowly, and with emphasis, Estelle put down her coffee cup. "Honey, listen, you don't mean you went to see him, this Revercomb nut?"

"I didn't mean to," she said, immediately embarrassed. To try and tell about it she now realized was a mistake. Estelle had no imagination, she would never understand. So her eyes narrowed, the way they always did when she composed a lie. "And, as a matter of fact, I didn't," she said flatly. "I started to; but then I realized how silly it was, and went for a walk instead."

"That was sensible of you," said Estelle as she began stacking dishes in the kitchen sink. "Imagine what might have happened. Buying dreams! Whoever heard? Uh uh, honey, this sure isn't Easton."

Before retiring, Sylvia took a Seconal, something she seldom did; but she knew otherwise she would never rest, not with her mind so nimble and somersaulting; then, too, she felt a curious sadness, a sense of loss, as though she'd been the victim of some real or even moral theft, as though, in fact, the boys encountered in the park had snatched (abruptly she switched on the light) her purse. The envelope Miss Mozart had handed her: it was in the purse, and until now she had forgotten it. She tore it open. Inside there was a blue note folded around a bill; on the note there was written: *In payment of one dream, $5.* And now she believed it; it was true, and she had sold Mr. Revercomb a dream. Could it be really so simple as that? She laughed a little as she turned off the light again. If she were to sell a dream only twice a week, think of what she could do: a place somewhere all her own, she thought, deepening toward sleep; ease, like firelight, wavered over her, and there came the moment of twilit lantern slides, deeply deeper. His lips, his arms: telescoped, descending; and distastefully she kicked away the blanket. Were these cold man-arms the arms Estelle had spoken of? Mr. Revercomb's lips brushed her ear as he leaned far into her sleep. Tell me? he whispered.

It was a week before she saw him again, a Sunday afternoon in early December. She'd left the apartment intending to see a movie, but somehow, and as though it had happened without her knowledge, she found herself on Madison Avenue, two blocks from Mr. Revercomb's. It was a cold, silver-skied day, with winds sharp and catching as hollyhock; in store windows icicles of Christmas tinsel twinkled amid mounds of sequined snow: all to Sylvia's distress, for she hated holidays, those times when one is most alone. In one window she saw a spectacle which made her stop still. It was a life-sized, mechanical Santa Claus; slapping his stomach he rocked back and forth in a frenzy of electrical mirth. You could hear beyond the thick glass his squeaky uproarious laughter. The longer she watched the more evil he seemed, until, finally, with a shudder, she turned and made her way into the street of Mr. Revercomb's house. It was, from the outside, an ordinary town house, perhaps a trifle less polished, less imposing than some others, but relatively grand all the same. Winter-withered ivy writhed about the leaded windowpanes and trailed in octopus ropes over the door; at the sides of the door were two small stone lions with blind, chipped eyes. Sylvia took a breath, then rang the bell. Mr. Revercomb's pale and charming Negro recognized her with a courteous smile.

On the previous visit, the parlor in which she had awaited her audience with Mr. Revercomb had been empty except for herself. This time there were others present, women of several appearances, and an excessively nervous, gnat-eyed young man. Had this group been what it resembled, namely, patients in a doctor's anteroom, he would have seemed either an expectant father or a victim of St. Vitus. Sylvia was seated next to him, and his fidgety eyes unbuttoned her rapidly: whatever he saw apparently intrigued him very little, and Sylvia was grateful when he went back to his twitchy preoccupations. Gradually, though, she became conscious of how interested in her the assemblage seemed; in the dim, doubtful light of the plant-filled room their gazes were more rigid than the chairs upon which they sat; one woman was particularly relentless. Ordinarily, her face would have had a soft commonplace sweetness, but now, watching Sylvia, it was ugly with distrust, jealousy. As though trying to tame some creature which might suddenly spring full-fanged, she sat stroking a flea-bitten neck fur, her stare continuing its assault until the earthquake footstep of Miss Mozart was heard in the hall. Immediately, and like frightened students, the group, separating into their individual identities, came to attention. "You, Mr. Pocker," accused Miss Mozart, "you're next!" And Mr. Pocker, wringing his hands, jittering his eyes, followed after her. In the dusk-room the gathering settled again like sun motes.

It began then to rain; melting window reflections quivered on the walls, and Mr. Revercomb's young butler, seeping through the room, stirred a fire in the grate, set tea things upon a table. Sylvia, nearest the fire, felt drowsy with warmth and the noise of rain; her head tilted sideways, she closed her eyes, neither asleep nor really awake. For a long while only the crystal swingings of a clock scratched the polished silence of Mr. Revercomb's house. And then, abruptly, there was an enormous commotion in the hall, capsizing the room into a fury of sound: a bull-deep voice, vulgar as red, roared out: "Stop Oreilly? The ballet butler and who else?" The owner of this voice, a tub-shaped, brick-colored little man, shoved his way to the parlor threshold, where he stood drunkenly seesawing from foot to foot. "Well, well, well," he said, his gin-hoarse voice descending the scale, "and all these ladies before me? But Oreilly is a gentleman, Oreilly waits his turn."

"Not here, he doesn't," said Miss Mozart, stealing up behind him and seizing him sternly by the collar. His face went even redder and his eyes bubbled out: "You're choking me," he gasped, but Miss Mozart, whose green-pale hands were as strong as oak roots, jerked his tie still tighter, and propelled him toward the door, which presently slammed with shattering effect: a tea cup tinkled, and dry dahlia leaves tumbled from their heights. The lady with the fur slipped an aspirin into her mouth. "Dis*gusting*," she said, and the others, all except Sylvia, laughed delicately, admiringly, as Miss Mozart strode past dusting her hands.

It was raining thick and darkly when Sylvia left Mr. Rever-comb's. She looked around the desolate street for a taxi; there was nothing, however, and no one; yes, someone, the drunk man who had caused the disturbance. Like a lonely city child, he was leaning against a parked car and bouncing a rubber ball up and down. "Lookit, kid," he said to Sylvia, "lookit, I just found this ball. Do you suppose that means good luck?" Sylvia smiled at him; for all his bravado, she thought him rather harmless, and there was a quality in his face, some grinning sadness suggesting a clown minus makeup. Juggling his ball, he skipped along after her as she headed toward Madison Avenue. "I'll bet I made a fool of myself in there," he said. "When I do things like that I just want to sit down and cry." Standing so long in the rain seemed to have sobered him considerably. "But she ought not to have choked me that way; damn, she's too rough. I've known some rough women: my sister Berenice could brand the wildest bull; but that other one, she's the roughest of the lot. Mark Oreilly's word, she's going to end up in the electric chair," he said, and smacked his lips. "They've got no cause to treat me like that. It's every bit his fault anyhow. I didn't have an awful lot to begin with, but then he took it every bit, and now I've got *niente*, kid, *niente*."

"That's too bad," said Sylvia, though she did not know what she was being sympathetic about. "Are you a clown, Mr. Oreilly?"

"Was," he said.

By this time they had reached the avenue, but Sylvia did not even look for a taxi; she wanted to walk on in the rain with the man who had been a clown. "When I was a little girl I only liked clown dolls," she told him. "My room at home was like a circus."

"I've been other things besides a clown. I have sold insurance also."

"Oh?" said Sylvia, disappointed. "And what do you do now?"

Oreilly chuckled and threw his ball especially high; after the catch his head still remained tilted upward. "I watch the sky," he said. "There I am with my suitcase traveling through the blue. It's where you travel when you've got no place else to go. But what do I do on this planet? I have stolen, begged, and sold my dreams—all for purposes of whiskey. A man cannot travel in the blue without a bottle. Which brings us to a point: how'd you take it, baby, if I asked for the loan of a dollar?"

"I'd take it fine," Sylvia replied, and paused, uncertain of what she'd say next. They wandered along so slowly, the stiff rain enclosing them like an insulating pressure; it was as though she were walking with a childhood doll, one grown miraculous and capable; she reached and held his hand: dear clown traveling in the blue. "But I haven't got a dollar. All I've got is seventy cents."

"No hard feelings," said Oreilly. "But honest, is that the kind of money he's paying nowadays?"

Sylvia knew whom he meant. "No, no—as a matter of fact, I didn't sell him a dream." She made no attempt to explain; she didn't understand it herself. Confronting the graying invisibility of Mr. Revercomb (impeccable, exact as a scale, surrounded in a cologne of clinical odors; flat gray eyes planted like seed in the anonymity of his face and sealed within steel-dull lenses) she could not remember a dream, and so she told of two thieves who had chased her through the park and in and out among the swings of a playground. "Stop, he said for me to stop; there are dreams and dreams, he said, but that is not a real one, that is one you are making up. Now how do you suppose he knew that? So I told him another dream; it was about him, of how he held me in the night with balloons rising and moons falling all around. He said he was not interested in dreams concerning himself." Miss Mozart, who transcribed the dreams in shorthand, was told to call the next person. "I don't think I will go back there again," she said.

"You will," said Oreilly. "Look at me, even I go back, and he has long since finished with me, Master Misery."

"Master Misery? Why do you call him that?"

They had reached the corner where the maniacal Santa Claus rocked and bellowed. His laughter echoed in the rainy squeaking street, and a shadow of him swayed in the rainbow lights of the pavement. Oreilly, turning his back upon the Santa Claus, smiled and said: "I call him Master Misery on account of that's who he is. Master Misery. Only maybe you call him something else; anyway, he is the same fellow, and you must've known him. All mothers tell their kids about him: he lives in hollows of trees, he comes down chimneys late at night, he lurks in graveyards and you can hear his step in the attic. The sonofabitch, he is a thief and a threat: he will take everything you have and end by leaving you nothing, not even a dream. Boo!" he shouted, and laughed louder than Santa Claus. "Now do you know who he is?"

Sylvia nodded. "I know who he is. My family called him something else. But I can't remember what. It was so long ago."

"But you remember him?"

"Yes, I remember him."

"Then call him Master Misery," he said, and, bouncing his ball, walked away from her. "Master Misery," his voice trailed to a mere moth of sound, "Mas-ter Mis-er-y . . ."

It was hard to look at Estelle, for she was in front of a window, and the window was filled with windy sun, which hurt Sylvia's eyes, and the glass rattled, which hurt her head. Also, Estelle was lecturing. Her nasal voice sounded as though her throat were a depository for rusty blades. "I wish you could see yourself," she was saying. Or was that something she'd said a long while back? Never mind. "I don't know what's happened to you: I'll bet you don't weigh a hundred pounds, I can see every bone and vein, and your hair! you look like a poodle."

Sylvia passed a hand over her forehead. "What time is it, Estelle?"

"It's four," she said, interrupting herself long enough to look at her watch. "But where is your watch?"

"I sold it," said Sylvia, too tired to lie. It did not matter. She had sold so many things, including her beaver coat and gold mesh evening bag.

Estelle shook her head. "I give up, honey, I plain give up. And that was the watch your mother gave you for graduation. It's a shame," she said, and made an old-maid noise with her mouth, "a pity and a shame. I'll never understand why you left us. That is your business, I'm sure; only how could you have left us for this . . . this . . . ?"

"Dump," supplied Sylvia, using the word advisedly. It was a furnished room in the East Sixties between Second and Third Avenues. Large enough for a daybed and a splintery old bureau with a mirror like a cataracted eye, it had one window, which looked out on a vast vacant lot (you could hear the tough afternoon voices of desperate running boys) and in the distance, like an exclamation point for the skyline, there was the black smokestack of a factory. This smokestack occurred frequently in her dreams; it never failed to arouse Miss Mozart: "Phallic, phallic," she would mutter, glancing up from her shorthand. The floor of the room was a garbage pail of books begun but never finished, antique newspapers, even orange hulls, fruit cores, underwear, a spilled powder box.

Estelle kicked her way through this trash, and sat down on the daybed. "Honey, you don't know, but I've been worried crazy. I mean I've got pride and all that and if you don't like me, well, okay; but you've got no right to stay away like this and not let me hear from you in over a month. So today I said to Bootsy, Bootsy, I've got a feeling something terrible has happened to Sylvia. You can imagine how I felt when I called your office and they told me you hadn't worked there for the last four weeks. What happened, were you fired?"

"Yes, I was fired." Sylvia began to sit up. "Please, Estelle—I've got to get ready; I've got an appointment."

"Be still. You're not going anywhere till I know what's wrong. The landlady downstairs told me you were found sleepwalking . . ."

"What do you mean talking to her? Why are you spying on me?"

Estelle's eyes puckered, as though she were going to cry. She put her hand over Sylvia's and petted it gently. "Tell me, honey, is it because of a man?"

"It's because of a man, yes," said Sylvia, laughter at the edge of her voice.

"You should have come to me before," Estelle sighed. "I know about men. That is nothing for you to be ashamed of. A man can have a way with a woman that kind of makes her forget everything else. If Henry wasn't the fine upstanding potential lawyer that he is, why, I would still love him, and do things for him that before I knew what it was like to be with a man would have seemed shocking and horrible. But honey, this fellow you're mixed up with, he's taking advantage of you."

"It's not that kind of relationship," said Sylvia, getting up and locating a pair of stockings in the furor of her bureau drawers. "It hasn't got anything to do with love. Forget about it. In fact, go home and forget about me altogether."

Estelle looked at her narrowly. "You scare me, Sylvia; you really scare me." Sylvia laughed and went on getting dressed. "Do you remember a long time ago when I said you ought to get married?"

"Uh huh. And now you listen." Sylvia turned around; there was a row of hairpins spaced across her mouth; she extracted them one at a time all the while she talked. "You talk about getting married as though it were the answer absolute; very well, up to a point I agree. Sure, I want to be loved; who the hell doesn't? But even if I was willing to compromise, where is the man I'm going to marry? Believe me, he must've fallen down a manhole. I mean it seriously when I say there are no men in New York—and even if there were, how do you meet them? Every man I ever met here who seemed the slightest bit attractive was either married, too poor to get married, or queer. And anyway, this is no place to fall in love; this is where you ought to come when you want to get over being in love. Sure, I suppose I could marry somebody; but do I want that? Do I?"

Estelle shrugged. "Then what do you want?"

"More than is coming to me." She poked the last hairpin into place, and smoothed her eyebrows before the mirror. "I have an appointment, Estelle, and it is time for you to go now."

"I can't leave you like this," said Estelle, her hand waving helplessly around the room. "Sylvia, you were my childhood friend."

"That is just the point: we're not children any more; at least, I'm not. No, I want you to go home, and I don't want you to come here again. I just want you to forget about me."

Estelle fluttered at her eyes with a handkerchief, and by the time she reached the door she was weeping quite loudly. Sylvia could not afford remorse: having been mean, there was nothing to be but meaner. "Go on," she said, following Estelle into the hall, "and write home any damn nonsense about me you want to!" Letting out a wail that brought other roomers to their doors, Estelle fled down the stairs.

After this Sylvia went back into her room and sucked a piece of sugar to take the sour taste out of her mouth: it was her grandmother's remedy for bad tempers. Then she got down on her knees and pulled from under the bed a cigar box she kept hidden there. When you opened the box it played a homemade and somewhat disorganized version of "Oh How I Hate to Get Up in the Morning." Her brother had made the music-box and given it to her on her fourteenth birthday. Eating the sugar, she'd thought of her grandmother, and hearing the tune she thought of her brother; the rooms of the house where they had lived rotated before her, all dark and she like a light moving among them: up the stairs, down, out and through, spring sweet and lilac shadows in the air and the creaking of a porch swing. All gone, she thought, calling their names, and now I am absolutely alone. The music stopped. But it went on in her head; she could hear it bugling above the child-cries of the vacant lot. And it interfered with her reading. She was reading a little diary-like book she kept inside the box. In this book she wrote down the essentials of her dreams; they were endless now, and it was so hard to remember. Today she would tell Mr. Revercomb about the three blind children. He would like that. The prices he paid varied, and she was sure this was at least a ten-dollar dream. The cigar-box anthem followed her down the stairs and through the streets and she longed for it to go away.

In the store where the Santa Claus had been there was a new and equally unnerving exhibit. Even when she was late to Mr. Revercomb's, as now, Sylvia was compelled to pause by the window. A plaster girl with intense glass eyes sat astride a bicycle pedaling at the maddest pace; though its wheel spokes spun hypnotically, the bicycle of course never budged: all that effort and the poor girl going nowhere. It was a pitifully human situation, and one that Sylvia could so exactly identify with herself that she always felt a real pang. The music-box rewound in her head: the tune, her brother, the house, a high-school dance, the house, the tune! Couldn't Mr. Revercomb hear it? His penetrating gaze carried such dull suspicion. But he seemed pleased with her dream, and, when she left, Miss Mozart gave her an envelope containing ten dollars.

"I had a ten-dollar dream," she told Oreilly, and Oreilly, rubbing his hands together, said, "Fine! Fine! But that's just my luck, baby—you should've got here sooner 'cause I went and did a terrible thing. I walked into a liquor store up the street, snatched a quart and ran." Sylvia didn't believe him until he produced from his pinned-together overcoat a bottle of bourbon, already half gone. "You're going to get in trouble some day," she said, "and then what would happen to me? I don't know what I would do without you." Oreilly laughed and poured a shot of the whiskey into a water glass. They were sitting in an all-night cafeteria, a great glaring food depot alive with blue mirrors and raw murals. Although to Sylvia it seemed a sordid place, they met there frequently for dinner; but even if she could have afforded it she did not know where else they could go, for together they presented a curious aspect: a young girl and a doddering, drunken man. Even here people often stared at them; if they stared long enough, Oreilly would stiffen with dignity and say: "Hello, hot lips, I remember you from way back. Still working in the men's room?" But usually they were left to themselves, and sometimes they would sit talking until two and three in the morning.

"It's a good thing the rest of Master Misery's crowd don't know he gave you that ten bucks. One of them would say you stole the dream. I had that happen once. Eaten up, all of 'em, never saw such a bunch of sharks, worse than actors or clowns or business men. Crazy, if you think about it: you worry whether you're going to go to sleep, if you're going to have a dream, if you're going to remember the dream. Round and round. So you get a couple of bucks, so you rush to the nearest liquor store—or the nearest sleeping-pill machine. And first thing you know, you're roaming your way up outhouse alley. Why, baby, you know what it's like? It's just like life."

"No, Oreilly, that's what it isn't like. It hasn't anything to do with life. It has more to do with being dead. I feel as though everything were being taken from me, as though some thief were stealing me down to the bone. Oreilly, I tell you I haven't an ambition, and there used to be so much. I don't understand it and I don't know what to do."

He grinned. "And you say it isn't like life? Who understands life and who knows what to do?"

"Be serious," she said. "Be serious and put away that

whiskey and eat your soup before it gets stone cold." She lighted a cigarette, and the smoke, smarting her eyes, intensified her frown. "If only I knew what he wanted with those dreams, all typed and filed. What does he do with them? You're right when you say he is Master Misery. . . . He can't be simply some silly quack; it can't be so meaningless as that. But why does he want dreams? Help me, Oreilly, think, think: what does it mean?"

Squinting one eye, Oreilly poured himself another drink; the clown-like twist of his mouth hardened into a line of scholarly straightness. "That is a million-dollar question, kid. Why don't you ask something easy, like how to cure the common cold? Yes, kid, what does it mean? I have thought about it a good deal. I have thought about it in the process of making love to a woman, and I have thought about it in the middle of a poker game." He tossed the drink down his throat and shuddered. "Now a sound can start a dream; the noise of one car passing in the night can drop a hundred sleepers into the deep parts of themselves. It's funny to think of that one car racing through the dark, trailing so many dreams. Sex, a sudden change of light, a pickle, these are little keys that can open up our insides, too. But most dreams begin because there are furies inside of us that blow open all the doors. I don't believe in Jesus Christ, but I do believe in people's souls; and I figure it this way, baby: dreams are the mind of the soul and the secret truth about us. Now Master Misery, maybe he hasn't got a soul, so bit by bit he borrows yours, steals it like he would steal your dolls or the chicken wing off your plate. Hundreds of souls have passed through him and gone into a filing case."

"Oreilly, be serious," she said again, annoyed because she thought he was making more jokes. "And look, your soup is . . ." She stopped abruptly, startled by Oreilly's peculiar expression. He was looking toward the entrance. Three men were there, two policemen and a civilian wearing a clerk's cloth jacket. The clerk was pointing toward their table. Oreilly's eyes circled the room with trapped despair; he sighed then, and leaned back in his seat, ostentatiously pouring himself another drink. "Good evening, gentlemen," he said, when the official party confronted him, "will you join us for a drink?"

"You can't arrest him," cried Sylvia, "you can't arrest a clown!" She threw her ten-dollar bill at them, but the policemen did not pay any attention, and she began to pound the table. All the customers in the place were staring, and the manager came running up, wringing his hands. The police said for Oreilly to get to his feet. "Certainly," Oreilly said, "though I do think it shocking you have to trouble yourselves with such petty crimes as mine when everywhere there are master thieves afoot. For instance, this pretty child," he stepped between the officers and pointed to Sylvia, "she is the recent victim of a major theft: poor baby, she has had her soul stolen."

For two days following Oreilly's arrest Sylvia did not leave her room: sun on the window, then dark. By the third day she had run out of cigarettes, so she ventured as far as the corner delicatessen. She bought a package of cupcakes, a can of sardines, a newspaper and cigarettes. In all this time she'd not eaten and it was a light, delicious, sharpening sensation; but the climb back up the stairs, the relief of closing the door, these so exhausted her she could not quite make the daybed. She slid down to the floor and did not move until it was day again. She thought afterward that she'd been there about twenty minutes. Turning on the radio as loud as it would go, she dragged a chair up to the window and opened the newspaper on her lap: *Lana Denies, Russia Rejects, Miners Conciliate*: of all things this was saddest, that life goes on: if one leaves one's lover, life should stop for him, and if one disappears from the world, then the world should stop, too: and it never did. And that was the real reason for most people getting up in the morning: not because it would matter but because it wouldn't. But if Mr. Revercomb succeeded finally in collecting all the dreams out of every head, perhaps—the idea slipped, became entangled with radio and newspaper. *Falling Temperatures*. A snowstorm moving across Colorado, across the West, falling upon all the small towns, yellowing every light, filling every footfall, falling now and here: but how quickly it had come, the snowstorm: the roofs, the vacant lot, the distance deep in white and deepening, like sleep. She looked at the paper and she looked at the snow. But it must have been snowing all day. It could not have just started. There was no sound of traffic; in the swirling wastes of the vacant lot children circled a bonfire; a car, buried at the curb, winked its headlights: help! help! silent, like the heart's distress. She crumbled a cupcake and sprinkled it on the windowsill: north-birds would come to keep her company. And she left the window open for them; snow-wind scattered flakes that dissolved on the floor like April-fool jewels. *Presents Life Can Be Beautiful*: turn down that radio! The witch of the woods was tapping at her door: Yes, Mrs. Halloran, she said, and turned off the radio altogether. Snow-quiet, sleep-silent, only the fun-fire faraway songsinging of children; and the room was blue with cold, colder than the cold of fairy tales: lie down my heart among the igloo flowers of snow. Mr. Revercomb, why do you wait upon the threshold? Ah, do come inside, it is so cold out there.

But her moment of waking was warm and held. The

window was closed, and a man's arms were around her. He was singing to her, his voice gentle but jaunty: *cherryberry, moneyberry, happyberry pie, but the best old pie is a loveberry pie* . . .

"Oreilly, is it—is it really you?"

He squeezed her. "Baby's awake now. And how does she feel?"

"I had thought I was dead," she said, and happiness winged around inside her like a bird lamed but still flying. She tried to hug him and she was too weak. "I love you, Oreilly; you are my only friend and I was so frightened. I thought I would never see you again." She paused, remembering. "But why aren't you in jail?"

Oreilly's face got all tickled and pink. "I was never in jail," he said mysteriously. "But first, let's have something to eat. I brought some things up from the delicatessen this morning."

She had a sudden feeling of floating. "How long have you been here?"

"Since yesterday," he said, fussing around with bundles and paper plates. "You let me in yourself."

"That's impossible. I don't remember it at all."

"I know," he said, leaving it at that. "Here, drink your milk like a good kid and I'll tell you a real wicked story. Oh, it's wild," he promised, slapping his sides gladly and looking more than ever like a clown. "Well, like I said, I never was in jail and this bit of fortune came to me because there I was being hustled down the street by those bindlestiffs when who should I see come swinging along but the gorilla woman: you guessed it, Miss Mozart. Hi, I says to her, off to the barber shop for a shave? It's about time you were put under arrest, she says, and smiles at one of the cops. Do your duty, officer. Oh, I says to her, I'm not under arrest. Me, I'm just on my way to the station house to give them the lowdown on you, you dirty communist. You can imagine what sort of holler she set up then; she grabbed hold of me and the cops grabbed hold of her. Can't say I didn't warn them: careful, boys, I said, she's got hair on her chest. And she sure did lay about her. So I just sort of walked off down the street. Never have believed in standing around watching fistfights the way people do in this city."

Oreilly stayed with her in the room over the week end. It was like the most beautiful party Sylvia could remember; she'd never laughed so much, for one thing, and no one, certainly no one in her family, had ever made her feel so loved. Oreilly was a fine cook, and he fixed delicious dishes on the little electric stove; once he scooped snow off the windowsill and made sherbet flavored with strawberry syrup. By Sunday she was strong enough to dance. They turned on the radio and she danced until she fell to her knees, windless and laughing. "I'll never be afraid again," she said. "I hardly know what I was afraid of to begin with."

"The same things you'll be afraid of the next time," Oreilly told her quietly. "That is a quality of Master Misery: no one ever knows what he is—not even children, and they know mostly everything."

Sylvia went to the window; an arctic whiteness lay over the city, but the snow had stopped, and the night sky was as clear as ice: there, riding above the river, she saw the first star of evening. "I see the first star," she said, crossing her fingers.

"And what do you wish when you see the first star?"

"I wish to see another star," she said. "At least that is what I usually wish."

"But tonight?"

She sat down on the floor and leaned her head against his knee. "Tonight I wished that I could have back my dreams."

"Don't we all?" Oreilly said, stroking her hair. "But then what would you do? I mean what would you do if you could have them back?"

Sylvia was silent a moment; when she spoke her eyes were gravely distant. "I would go home," she said slowly. "And that is a terrible decision, for it would mean giving up most of my other dreams. But if Mr. Revercomb would let me have them back, then I would go home tomorrow."

Saying nothing, Oreilly went to the closet and brought back her coat. "But why?" she asked as he helped her on with it. "Never mind," he said, "just do what I tell you. We're going to pay Mr. Revercomb a call, and you're going to ask him to give you back your dreams. It's a chance."

Sylvia balked at the door. "Please, Oreilly, don't make me go. I can't, please, I'm afraid."

"I thought you said you'd never be afraid again."

But once in the street he hurried her so quickly against the wind she did not have time to be frightened. It was Sunday, stores were closed and the traffic lights seemed to wink only for them, for there were no moving cars along the snow-deep avenue. Sylvia even forgot where they were going, and chattered of trivial oddments: right here at this corner is where she'd seen Garbo, and over there, that is where the old woman was run over. Presently, however, she stopped, out of breath and overwhelmed with sudden realization. "I can't, Oreilly," she said, pulling back. "What can I say to him?"

"Make it like a business deal," said Oreilly. "Tell him straight out that you want your dreams, and if he'll give them to you you'll pay back all the money: on the installment plan, naturally. It's simple enough, kid. Why the hell couldn't he give them back? They are all right there in a filing case."

This speech was somehow convincing and, stamping her frozen feet, Sylvia went ahead with a certain courage. "That's the kid," he said. They separated on Third Avenue, Oreilly being of the opinion that Mr. Revercomb's immediate neighborhood was not for the moment precisely safe. He confined himself in a doorway, now and then lighting a match and singing aloud: *but the best old pie is a whiskeyberry pie!* Like a wolf, a long thin dog came padding over the moon-slats under the Elevated, and across the street there were the misty shapes of men ganged around a bar: the idea of maybe cadging a drink in there made him groggy.

Just as he had decided on perhaps trying something of the sort, Sylvia appeared. And she was in his arms before he knew that it was really her. "It can't be so bad, sweetheart," he said softly, holding her as best he could. "Don't cry, baby; it's too cold to cry: you'll chap your face." As she strangled for words, her crying evolved into a tremulous, unnatural laugh. The air was filled with the smoke of her laughter. "Do you know what he said?" she gasped. "Do you know what he said when I asked for my dreams?" Her head fell back, and her laughter rose and carried over the street like an abandoned, wildly colored kite. Oreilly had finally to shake her by the shoulders. "He said—I couldn't have them back because—because he'd used them all up."

She was silent then, her face smoothing into an expressionless calm. She put her arm through Oreilly's, and together they moved down the street; but it was as if they were friends pacing a platform, each waiting for the other's train, and when they reached the corner he cleared his throat and said: "I guess I'd better turn off here. It's as likely a spot as any."

Sylvia held on to his sleeve. "But where will you go, Oreilly?"

"Traveling in the blue," he said, trying a smile that didn't work out very well.

She opened her purse. "A man cannot travel in the blue without a bottle," she said, and, kissing him on the cheek, slipped five dollars in his pocket.

"Bless you, baby."

It did not matter that it was the last of her money, that now she would have to walk home, and alone. The pilings of snow were like the white waves of a white sea, and she rode upon them, carried by winds and tides of the moon. I do not know what I want, and perhaps I shall never know, but my only wish from every star will always be another star; and truly I am not afraid, she thought. Two boys came out of a bar and stared at her; in some park some long time ago she'd seen two boys and they might be the same. Truly I am not afraid, she thought, hearing their snowy footsteps following after her: and anyway, there was nothing left to steal.

EDITH WHARTON

A CUP OF
COLD WATER

I

IT WAS THREE O'CLOCK in the morning, and the cotillion was at its height, when Woburn left the overheated splendor of the Gildermere ballroom, and after a delay caused by the determination of the drowsy footman to give him a ready-made overcoat with an imitation astrakhan collar in place of his own unimpeachable Poole garment, found himself breasting the icy solitude of the Fifth Avenue. He was still smiling, as he emerged from the awning, at his insistence in claiming his own overcoat: it illustrated, humorously enough, the invincible force of habit. As he faced the wind, however, he discerned a providence in his persistency, for his coat was fur-lined, and he had a cold voyage before him on the morrow.

It had rained hard during the earlier part of the night, and the carriages waiting in triple line before the Gildermeres' door were still domed by shining umbrellas, while the electric lamps extending down the avenue blinked Narcissus-like at their watery images in the hollows of the sidewalk. A dry blast had come out of the north, with pledge of frost before daylight, and to Woburn's shivering fancy the pools in the pavement seemed already stiffening into ice. He turned up his coat collar and stepped out rapidly, his hands deep in his coat pockets.

As he walked he glanced curiously up at the ladder-like doorsteps which may well suggest to the future archaeologist that all the streets of New York were once canals; at the spectral tracery of the trees about St. Luke's, the fretted mass of the Cathedral, and the mean vista of the long side streets. The knowledge that he was perhaps looking at it all for the last time caused every detail to start out like a challenge to memory, and lit the brownstone house-fronts with the glamor of sword-barred Edens.

It was an odd impulse that had led him that night to the Gildermere ball; but the same change in his condition which made him stare wonderingly at the houses in the Fifth Avenue gave the thrill of an exploit to the tame business of ball-going. Who would have imagined, Woburn mused, that such a situation as his would possess the priceless quality of sharpening the blunt edge of habit?

It was certainly curious to reflect, as he leaned against the doorway of Mrs. Gildermere's ballroom, enveloped in the warm atmosphere of the accustomed, that twenty-four hours later the people brushing by him with looks of friendly recognition would start at the thought of having seen him and slur over the recollection of having taken his hand!

And the girl he had gone there to see: what would she think of him? He knew well enough that her trenchant classifications of life admitted no overlapping of good and evil, made no allowance for that incalculable interplay of motives that justifies the subtlest casuistry of compassion. Miss Talcott was too young to distinguish the intermediate tints of the moral spectrum; and her judgments were further simplified by a peculiar concreteness of mind. Her bringing-up had fostered this tendency and she was surrounded by people who focused life in the same way. To the girls in Miss Talcott's set, the attentions of a clever man who had to work for his living had the zest of a forbidden pleasure; but to marry such a man would be as unpardonable as to have one's carriage seen at the door of a cheap dressmaker. Poverty might make a man fascinating; but a settled income was the best evidence of stability of character. If there were anything in heredity, how could a nice girl trust a man whose parents had been careless enough to leave him unprovided for?

Neither Miss Talcott nor any of her friends could be charged with formulating these views; but they were implicit in the slope of every white shoulder and in the ripple of every yard of imported tulle dappling the foreground of Mrs. Gildermere's ballroom. The advantages of line and color in veiling the crudities of a creed are obvious to emotional minds; and besides, Woburn was conscious that it was to the cheerful materialism of their parents that the young girls he admired owed that fine distinction of outline in which their skillfully-rippled hair and skillfully-hung draperies co-operated with the slimness and erectness that came of participating in the most expensive sports, eating the most expensive food and breathing the most expensive air. Since the process which had produced them was so costly, how could they help being costly themselves? Woburn was too logical to expect to give no more for a piece of old Sèvres than for a bit of kitchen crockery; he had no faith in wonderful bargains, and believed that one got in life just what one was willing to pay for. He had no mind to dispute the taste of those who preferred the rustic simplicity of the earthen crock; but his own fancy inclined to the piece of *pâte tendre* which must be kept in a glass case and handled as delicately as a flower.

It was not merely by the external grace of these drawing-room ornaments that Woburn's sensibilities were charmed. His imagination was touched by the curious exoticism of view resulting from such conditions. He had always enjoyed listening to Miss Talcott even more than looking at her. Her ideas had the brilliant bloom and audacious irrelevance of those tropical orchids which strike root in air. Miss Talcott's opinions had no connection with the actual; her very materialism had the grace of artificiality. Woburn had been enchanted once by seeing her helpless before a smoking lamp: she had been obliged to ring for a servant because she did not know how to put it out.

Her supreme charm was the simplicity that comes of taking it for granted that people are born with carriages and country places: it never occurred to her that such congenital attributes could be matter for self-consciousness, and she had none of the *nouveau riche* prudery which classes poverty with the nude in art and is not sure how to behave in the presence of either.

The conditions of Woburn's own life had made him peculiarly susceptible to those forms of elegance which are the flower of ease. His father had lost a comfortable property through sheer inability to go over his agent's accounts; and this disaster, coming at the outset of Woburn's schooldays, had given a new bent to the family temperament. The father characteristically died when the effort of living might have made it possible to retrieve his fortunes; and Woburn's mother and sister, embittered by this final evasion, settled down to a vindictive war with circumstances. They were the kind of women who think that it lightens the burden of life to throw over the amenities, as a reduced housekeeper puts away her knick-knacks to make the dusting easier. They fought mean conditions meanly; but Woburn, in his resentment of their attitude, did not allow for the suffering which had brought it about: his own tendency was to overcome difficulties by conciliation rather than by conflict. Such surroundings threw into vivid relief the charming figure of Miss Talcott. Woburn instinctively associated poverty with bad food, ugly furniture, complaints, and recriminations: it was natural that he should be drawn toward the luminous atmosphere where life was a series of peaceful and good-humored acts, unimpeded by petty obstacles. To spend one's time in such society gave one the illusion of unlimited credit; and also, unhappily, created the need for it.

It was here in fact that Woburn's difficulties began. To marry Miss Talcott it was necessary to be a rich man: even to dine out in her set involved certain minor extravagances. Woburn had determined to marry her sooner or later; and in the meanwhile to be with her as much as possible.

As he stood leaning in the doorway of the Gildermere ballroom, watching her pass him in the waltz, he tried to remember how it had begun. First there had been the tailor's bill; the fur-lined overcoat with cuffs and collar of Alaska sable had alone cost more than he had spent on his clothes for two or three years previously. Then there were theater tickets; cab fares; florist's bills; tips to servants at the country houses where he went because he knew that she was invited; the *Omar Khayyám* bound by Sullivan that he sent her at Christmas; the contributions to her pet charities; the reckless purchases at fairs where she had a stall. His whole way of life had imperceptibly changed and his year's salary was gone before the second quarter was due.

He had invested the few thousand dollars which had been his portion of his father's shrunken estate: when his debts began to pile up, he took a flyer in stocks and after a few months of varying luck his little patrimony disappeared. Meanwhile his courtship was proceeding at an inverse ratio to his financial ventures. Miss Talcott was growing tender and he began to feel that the game was in his hands. The nearness of the goal exasperated him. She was not the girl to wait and he knew that it must be now or never. A friend lent him five thousand dollars on his personal note and he bought railway stocks on margin. They went up and he held them for a higher rise: they fluctuated, dragged, dropped below the level at which he had bought, and slowly continued their uninterrupted descent. His broker called for more margin; he could not respond and was sold out.

What followed came about quite naturally. For several years he had been cashier in a well-known banking-house. When the note he had given his friend became due it was obviously necessary to pay it and he used the firm's money for the purpose. To repay the money thus taken, he increased his debt to his employers and bought more stocks; and on these operations he made a profit of ten thousand dollars. Miss Talcott rode in the Park, and he bought a smart hack for seven hundred, paid off his tradesmen, and went on speculating with the remainder of his profits. He made a little more, but failed to take advantage of the market and lost all that he had staked, including the amount taken from the firm. He increased his overdraft by another ten thousand and lost that; he overdrew a farther sum and lost again. Suddenly he woke to the fact that he owed his employers fifty thousand dollars and that the partners were to make their semi-annual inspection in two days. He realized then that within forty-eight hours what he had called borrowing would become theft.

There was no time to be lost: he must clear out and start life over again somewhere else. The day that he reached this decision he was to have met Miss Talcott at dinner. He went to the dinner, but she did not appear: she had a headache, his hostess explained. Well, he was not to have a last look at her, after all; better so, perhaps. He took leave early and on his way home stopped at a florist's and sent her a bunch of violets. The next morning he got a little note from her: the violets had done her head so much good—she would tell him all about it that evening at the Gildermere ball. Woburn laughed and tossed the note into the fire. That evening he would be on board ship: the examination of the books was to take place the following morning at ten.

Woburn went down to the bank as usual; he did not want to do anything that might excite suspicion as to his plans, and from one or two questions which one of the partners had lately put to him he divined that he was being observed. At the bank the day passed uneventfully. He discharged his business with his accustomed care and went uptown at the usual hour.

In the first flush of his successful speculations he had set up bachelor lodgings, moved by the temptation to get away from the dismal atmosphere of home, from his mother's struggles with the cook and his sister's curiosity about his letters. He had been influenced also by the wish for surroundings more adapted to his tastes. He wanted to be able to give little teas, to which Miss Talcott might come with a married friend. She came once or twice and pronounced it all delightful: she thought it *so* nice to have only a few Whistler etchings on the walls and the simplest crushed levant for all one's books.

To these rooms Woburn returned on leaving the bank. His plans had taken definite shape. He had engaged passage on a steamer sailing for Halifax early the next morning; and there was nothing for him to do before going on board but to pack his clothes and tear up a few letters. He threw his clothes into a couple of portmanteaux, and when these had been called for by an expressman he emptied his pockets and counted up his ready money. He found that he possessed just fifty dollars and seventy-five cents; but his passage to Halifax was paid, and once there he could pawn his watch and rings.

This calculation completed, he unlocked his writing-table drawer and took out a handful of letters. They were notes from Miss Talcott. He read them over and threw them into the fire. On his table stood her photograph. He slipped it out of its frame and tossed it on top of the blazing letters. Having performed this rite, he got into his dress clothes and went to a small French restaurant to dine.

He had meant to go on board the steamer immediately after dinner; but a sudden vision of introspective hours in a silent cabin made him call for the evening paper and run his eye over the list of theaters. It would be as easy to go on board at midnight as now.

He selected a new vaudeville and listened to it with surprising freshness of interest; but toward eleven o'clock he again began to dread the approaching necessity of going down to the steamer. There was something peculiarly unnerving in the idea of spending the rest of the night in a stifling cabin jammed against the side of a wharf.

He left the theater and strolled across to the Fifth Avenue. It was now nearly midnight and a stream of carriages poured uptown from the opera and the theaters. As he stood on the corner watching the familiar spectacle it occurred to him that many of the people driving by him in smart broughams and C-spring landaus were on their way to the Gildermere ball. He remembered Miss Talcott's note of the morning and wondered if she were in one of the passing carriages; she had spoken so confidently of meeting him at the ball. What if he should go and take a last look at her? There was really nothing to prevent it. He was not likely to run across any member of the firm: in Miss Talcott's set his social standing was good for another ten hours at least. He smiled in anticipation of her surprise at seeing him, and then reflected with a start that she would not be surprised at all.

His meditations were cut short by a fall of sleety rain, and hailing a hansom he gave the driver Mrs. Gildermere's address.

As he drove up the avenue he looked about him like a traveler in a strange city. The buildings which had been so unobtrusively familiar stood out with sudden distinctness: he noticed a hundred details which had escaped his observation. The people on the sidewalks looked like strangers: he wondered where they were going and tried to picture the lives they led; but his own relation to life had been so suddenly reversed that he found it impossible to recover his mental perspective.

At one corner he saw a shabby man lurking in the shadow of the side street; as the hansom passed, a policeman ordered him to move on. Farther on, Woburn noticed a woman crouching on the doorstep of a handsome house. She had drawn a shawl over her head and was sunk in the apathy of despair or drink. A well-dressed couple paused to look at her. The electric globe at the corner lit up their faces, and Woburn saw the lady, who was young and pretty, turn away with a little grimace, drawing her companion after her.

The desire to see Miss Talcott had driven Woburn to the Gildermeres'; but once in the ballroom he made no effort to find her. The people about him seemed more like strangers than those he had passed in the street. He stood in the doorway, studying the petty maneuvers of the women and the resigned amenities of their partners. Was it possible that these were his friends? These mincing women, all paint and dye and whalebone, these apathetic men who looked as much alike as the figures that children cut out of a folded sheet of paper? Was it to live among such puppets that he had sold his soul? What had any of these people done that was noble, exceptional, distinguished? Who knew them by name even, except their tradesmen and the society reporters? Who were they, that they should sit in judgment on him?

The bald man with the globular stomach, who stood at Mrs. Gildermere's elbow surveying the dancers, was old Boylston, who had made his pile in wrecking railroads; the smooth chap with glazed eyes, at whom a pretty girl smiled up so confidingly, was Collerton, the political lawyer, who had been mixed up to his own advantage in an ugly lobbying transaction; near him stood Brice Lyndham, whose recent failure had ruined his friends and associates, but had not visibly affected the welfare of his large and expensive family. The slim fellow dancing with Miss Gildermere was Alec Vance, who lived on a salary of five thousand a year, but whose wife was such a good manager that they kept a brougham and victoria and always put in their season at Newport and their spring trip to Europe. The little ferret-faced youth in the corner was Regie Colby, who wrote the *Entre-Nous* paragraphs in the *Social Searchlight*: the women were charming to him and he got all the financial tips he wanted from their husbands and fathers.

And the women? Well, the women knew all about the men, and flattered them and married them and tried to catch them for their daughters. It was a domino-party at which the guests were forbidden to unmask, though they all saw through each other's disguises.

And these were the people who, within twenty-four hours, would be agreeing that they had always felt there was something wrong about Woburn! They would be extremely sorry for him, of course, poor devil; but there are certain standards, after all—what would society be without standards? His new friends, his future associates, were the suspicious-looking man whom the policeman had ordered to move on, and the drunken woman asleep on the doorstep. To these he was linked by the freemasonry of failure.

Miss Talcott passed him on Collerton's arm: she was giving him one of the smiles of which Woburn had fancied himself sole owner. Collerton was a sharp fellow; he must have made a lot in that last deal; probably she would marry him. How much did she know about the transaction? She was a shrewd girl and her father was in Wall Street. If Woburn's luck had turned the other way she might have married him instead; and if he had confessed his sin to her one evening, as they drove home from the opera in their new brougham, she would have said that really it was of no use to tell her, for she never *could* understand about business, but that she did entreat him in future to be nicer to Regie Colby. Even now, if he made a big strike somewhere, and came back in ten years with a beard and a steam yacht, they would all deny that anything had been proved against him, and Mrs. Collerton might blush and remind him of their friendship. Well—why not? Was not all morality based on a convention? What was the stanchest code of ethics but a trunk with a series of false bottoms? Now and then one had the illusion of getting down to absolute right or wrong, but it was only a false bottom—a removable hypothesis—with another false bottom underneath. There was no getting beyond the relative.

The cotillion had begun. Miss Talcott sat nearly opposite him: she was dancing with young Boylston and giving him a Woburn-Collerton smile. So young Boylston was in the syndicate too!

Presently Woburn was aware that she had forgotten young Boylston and was glancing absently about the room. She was looking for someone, and meant the someone to know it: he knew that *Lost-Chord* look in her eyes.

A new figure was being formed. The partners circled about the room and Miss Talcott's flying tulle drifted close to him as she passed. Then the favors were distributed; white skirts wavered across the floor like thistle-down on summer air; men rose from their seats and fresh couples filled the shining *parquet*.

Miss Talcott, after taking from the basket a Legion of Honor in red enamel, surveyed the room for a moment; then she made her way through the dancers and held out the favor to Woburn. He fastened it in his coat, and emerging from the crowd of men about the doorway, slipped his arm about her. Their eyes met; hers were serious and a little sad. How fine and slender she was! He noticed the little tendrils of hair about the pink convolution of her ear. Her waist was firm and yet elastic; she breathed calmly and regularly, as though dancing were her natural motion. She did not look at him again and neither of them spoke.

When the music ceased they paused near her chair. Her partner was waiting for her and Woburn left her with a bow.

He made his way downstairs and out of the house. He was glad that he had not spoken to Miss Talcott. There had been a healing power in their silence. All bitterness had gone from him and he thought of her now quite simply, as the girl he loved.

At Thirty-fifth Street he reflected that he had better jump into a car and go down to his steamer. Again there rose before him the repulsive vision of the dark cabin, with creaking noises overhead, and the cold wash of water against the pier: he thought he would stop in a café and take a drink. He turned into Broadway and entered a brightly-lit café; but when he had taken his whiskey and soda there seemed no reason for lingering. He had never been the kind of man who could escape difficulties in that way. Yet he was conscious that his will was weakening; that he did not mean to go down to the steamer just yet. What did he mean to do? He began to feel horribly tired and it occurred to him that a few hours' sleep in a decent bed would make a new man of him. Why not go on board the next morning at daylight?

He could not go back to his rooms, for on leaving the house he had taken the precaution of dropping his latch-key into his letter-box; but he was in a neighborhood of discreet hotels and he wandered on till he came to one which was known to offer a dispassionate hospitality to luggageless travelers in dress clothes.

II

He pushed upon the swinging door and found himself in a long corridor with a tessellated floor, at the end of which, in a brightly-lit enclosure of plate-glass and mahogany, the night-clerk dozed over a copy of the *Police Gazette*. The air in the corridor was rich in reminiscences of yesterday's dinners, and a bronzed radiator poured a wave of dry heat into Woburn's face.

The night-clerk, roused by the swinging of the door, sat watching Woburn's approach with the unexpectant eye of one who has full confidence in his capacity for digesting surprises. Not that there was anything surprising in Woburn's appearance; but the night-clerk's callers were given to such imaginative flights in explaining their luggageless arrival in the small hours of the morning, that he fared habitually on fictions which would have staggered a less experienced stomach. The night-clerk, whose unwrinkled bloom showed that he throve on this high-seasoned diet, had a fancy for classifying his applicants before they could frame their explanations.

"This one's been locked out," he said to himself as he mustered Woburn.

Having exercised his powers of divination with his accustomed accuracy he listened without stirring an eyelid to Woburn's statement; merely replying, when the latter asked the price of a room, "Two-fifty."

"Very well," said Woburn, pushing the money under the brass lattice, "I'll go up at once; and I want to be called at seven."

To this the night-clerk proffered no reply, but stretching out his hand to press an electric button, returned apathetically to the perusal of the *Police Gazette*. His summons was answered by the appearance of a man in shirt sleeves, whose rumpled head indicated that he had recently risen from some kind of makeshift repose; to him the night-clerk tossed a key, with the brief comment, "Ninety-seven"; and the man, after a sleepy glance at Woburn, turned on his heel and lounged toward the staircase at the back of the corridor.

Woburn followed and they climbed three flights in silence. At each landing Woburn glanced down the long passage-way lit by a lowered gas-jet, with a double line of boots before the doors, waiting, like yesterday's deeds, to carry their owners so many miles farther on the morrow's destined road. On the third landing the man paused, and after examining the number on the key, turned to the left, and slouching past three or four doors, finally unlocked one and preceded Woburn into a room lit only by the upward gleam of the electric globes in the street below.

The man felt in his pockets; then he turned to Woburn. "Got a match?" he asked.

Woburn politely offered him one, and he applied it to the gas-fixture which extended its jointed arm above an ash dressing-table with a blurred mirror fixed between two standards. Having performed this office with an air of detachment designed to make Woburn recognize it as an act of supererogation, he turned without a word and vanished down the passage-way.

Woburn, after an indifferent glance about the room, which seemed to afford the amount of luxury generally obtainable for two dollars and a half in a fashionable quarter of New York, locked the door and sat down at the ink-stained writing-table in the window. Far below him lay the pallidly-lit depths of the forsaken thoroughfare. Now and then he heard the jingle of a horse-car and the ring of hoofs on the freezing pavement, or saw the lonely figure of a policeman eclipsing the illumination of the plate-glass windows on the opposite side of the street. He sat thus for a long time, his elbows on the table, his chin between his hands, till at length the contemplation of the abandoned sidewalks, above which the electric globes kept Stylites-like vigil, became intolerable to him, and he drew down the window-shade, and lit the gas-fixture beside the dressing-table. Then he took a cigar from his case, and held it to the flame.

The passage from the stinging freshness of the night to the stale overheated atmosphere of the Haslemere Hotel had checked the preternaturally rapid working of his mind, and he was now scarcely conscious of thinking at all. His head was heavy, and he would have thrown himself on the bed had he not feared to oversleep the hour fixed for his departure. He thought it safest, instead, to seat himself once more by the table, in the most uncomfortable chair that he could find, and smoke one cigar after another till the first sign of dawn should give an excuse for action.

He had laid his watch on the table before him, and was gazing at the hour-hand, and trying to convince himself by so doing that he was still wide awake, when a noise in the adjoining room suddenly straightened him in his chair and banished all fear of sleep.

There was no mistaking the nature of the noise; it was that of a woman's sobs. The sobs were not loud, but the sound reached him distinctly through the frail door between the two rooms; it expressed an utter abandonment to grief; not the cloud-burst of some passing emotion, but the slow downpour of a whole heaven of sorrow.

Woburn sat listening. There was nothing else to be done; and at least his listening was a mute tribute to the trouble he was powerless to relieve. It roused, too, the drugged pulses of his own grief: he was touched by the chance propinquity of two alien sorrows in a great city throbbing with multifarious passions. It would have been more in keeping with the irony of life had he found himself next to a mother singing her child to sleep: there seemed a mute commiseration in the hand that had led him to such neighborhood.

Gradually the sobs subsided, with pauses betokening an effort at self-control. At last they died off softly, like the intermittent drops that end a day of rain.

"Poor soul," Woburn mused, "she's got the better of it for the time. I wonder what it's all about?"

At the same moment he heard another sound that made him jump to his feet. It was a very low sound, but in that nocturnal silence which gives distinctness to the faintest noises, Woburn knew at once that he had heard the click of a pistol.

"What is she up to now?" he asked himself, with his eye on the door between the two rooms; and the brightly-lit keyhole seemed to reply with a glance of intelligence. He turned out the gas and crept to the door, pressing his eye to the illuminated circle.

After a moment or two of adjustment, during which he seemed to himself to be breathing like a steam-engine, he discerned a room like his own, with the same dressing-table flanked by gas-fixtures, and the same table in the window. This table was directly in his line of vision; and beside it stood a woman with a small revolver in her hands. The lights being behind her, Woburn could only infer her youth from her slender silhouette and the nimbus of fair hair defining her head. Her dress seemed dark and simple, and on a chair under one of the gas-jets lay a jacket edged with cheap fur and a small traveling-bag. He could not see the other end of the room, but something in her manner told him that she was alone. At length she put the revolver down and took up a letter that lay on the table. She drew the letter from its envelope and read it over two or three times; then she put it back, sealing the envelope, and placing it conspicuously against the mirror of the dressing-table.

There was so grave a significance in this dumb-show that Woburn felt sure that her next act would be to return to the table and take up the revolver; but he had not reckoned on the vanity of woman. After putting the letter in place she still lingered at the mirror, standing a little sideways, so that he could now see her face, which was distinctly pretty, but of a small and unelastic mold, inadequate to the expression of the larger emotions. For some moments she continued to study herself with the expression of a child looking at a playmate who has been scolded; then she turned to the table and lifted the revolver to her forehead.

A sudden crash made her arm drop, and sent her darting backward to the opposite side of the room. Woburn had broken down the door, and stood torn and breathless in the breach.

"Oh!" she gasped, pressing closer to the wall.

"Don't be frightened," he said; "I saw what you were going to do and I had to stop you."

145

She looked at him for a moment in silence, and he saw the terrified flutter of her breast; then she said, "No one can stop me for long. And besides, what right have you—"

"Everyone has the right to prevent a crime," he returned, the sound of the last word sending the blood to his forehead.

"I deny it," she said passionately. "Everyone who has tried to live and failed has the right to die."

"Failed in what?"

"In everything!" she replied. They stood looking at each other in silence.

At length he advanced a few steps.

"You've no right to say you've failed," he said, "while you have breath to try again." He drew the revolver from her hand.

"Try again—try again? I tell you I've tried seventy times seven!"

"What have you tried?"

She looked at him with a certain dignity.

"I don't know," she said, "that you've any right to question me—or to be in this room at all—" and suddenly she burst into tears.

The discrepancy between her words and action struck the chord which, in a man's heart, always responds to the touch of feminine unreason. She dropped into the nearest chair, hiding her face in her hands, while Woburn watched the course of her weeping.

At last she lifted her head, looking up between drenched lashes.

"Please go away," she said in childish entreaty.

"How can I?" he returned. "It's impossible that I should leave you in this state. Trust me—let me help you. Tell me what has gone wrong, and let's see if there's no other way out of it."

146

Woburn had a voice full of sensitive inflections, and it was now trembling with profoundest pity. Its note seemed to reassure the girl, for she said, with a beginning of confidence in her own tones, "But I don't even know who you are."

Woburn was silent: the words startled him. He moved nearer to her and went on in the same quieting tone.

"I am a man who has suffered enough to want to help others. I don't want to know any more about you than will enable me to do what I can for you. I've probably seen more of life than you have, and if you're willing to tell me your troubles perhaps together we may find a way out of them."

She dried her eyes and glanced at the revolver.

"That's the only way out," she said.

"How do you know? Are you sure you've tried every other?"

"Perfectly sure. I've written and written, and humbled myself like a slave before him, and she won't even let him answer my letters. Oh, but you don't understand"—she broke off with a renewal of weeping.

"I begin to understand—you're sorry for something you've done?"

"Oh, I've never denied that—I've never denied that I was wicked."

"And you want the forgiveness of someone you care about?"

"My husband," she whispered.

"You've done something to displease your husband?"

"To displease him? I ran away with another man!" There was a dismal exultation in her tone, as though she were paying Woburn off for having underrated her offense.

She had certainly surprised him; at worst he had expected a quarrel over a rival, with a possible complication of mother-in-law. He wondered how such helpless little feet could have

147

taken so bold a step; then he remembered that there is no audacity like that of weakness.

He was wondering how to lead her to completer avowal when she added forlornly, "You see there's nothing else to do."

Woburn took a turn in the room. It was certainly a narrower strait than he had foreseen, and he hardly knew how to answer; but the first flow of confession had eased her, and she went on without farther persuasion.

"I don't know how I could ever have done it; I must have been downright crazy. I didn't care much for Joe when I married him—he wasn't exactly handsome, and girls think such a lot of that. But he just laid down and worshiped me, and I *was* getting fond of him in a way; only the life was so dull. I'd been used to a big city—I come from Detroit—and Hinksville is such a poky little place; that's where we lived; Joe is telegraph-operator on the railroad there. He'd have been in a much bigger place now, if he hadn't—well, after all, he behaved perfectly splendidly about *that*.

"I really was getting fond of him, and I believe I should have realized in time how good and noble and unselfish he was, if his mother hadn't been always sitting there and everlastingly telling me so. We learned in school about the Athenians hating some man who was always called just, and that's the way I felt about Joe. Whenever I did anything that wasn't quite right his mother would say how differently Joe would have done it. And she was forever telling me that Joe didn't approve of this and that and the other. When we were alone he approved of everything, but when his mother was round he'd sit quiet and let her say he didn't. I knew he'd let me have my way afterward, but somehow that didn't prevent my getting mad at the time.

"And then the evenings were so long, with Joe away, and

148

Mrs. Glenn (that's his mother) sitting there like an image knitting socks for the heathen. The only caller we ever had was the Baptist minister, and he never took any more notice of me than if I'd been a piece of furniture. I believe he was afraid to before Mrs. Glenn."

She paused breathlessly, and the tears in her eyes were now of anger.

"Well?" said Woburn gently.

"Well—then Arthur Hackett came along; he was traveling for a big publishing firm in Philadelphia. He was awfully handsome and as clever and sarcastic as anything. He used to lend me lots of novels and magazines, and tell me all about society life in New York. All the girls were after him, and Alice Sprague, whose father is the richest man in Hinksville, fell desperately in love with him and carried on like a fool; but he wouldn't take any notice of her. He never looked at anybody but me." Her face lit up with a reminiscent smile, and then clouded again. "I hate him now," she exclaimed, with a change of tone that startled Woburn. "I'd like to kill him—but he's killed me instead.

"Well, he bewitched me so I didn't know what I was doing; I was like somebody in a trance. When he wasn't there I didn't want to speak to anybody; I used to lie in bed half the day just to get away from folks; I hated Joe and Hinksville and everything else. When he came back the days went like a flash; we were together nearly all the time. I knew Joe's mother was spying on us, but I didn't care. And at last it seemed as if I couldn't let him go away again without me; so one evening he stopped at the back gate in a buggy, and we drove off together and caught the eastern express at River Bend. He promised to bring me to New York." She paused, and then added scornfully, "He didn't even do that!"

Woburn had returned to his seat and was watching her

attentively. It was curious to note how her passion was spending itself in words; he saw that she would never kill herself while she had anyone to talk to.

"That was five months ago," she continued, "and we traveled all through the southern states, and stayed a little while near Philadelphia, where his business is. He did things real stylishly at first. Then he was sent to Albany, and we stayed a week at the Delavan House. One afternoon I went out to do some shopping, and when I came back he was gone. He had taken his trunk with him, and hadn't left any address; but in my traveling-bag I found a fifty-dollar bill, with a slip of paper on which he had written, 'No use coming after me; I'm married.' We'd been together less than four months, and I never saw him again.

"At first I couldn't believe it. I stayed on, thinking it was a joke—or that he'd feel sorry for me and come back. But he never came and never wrote me a line. Then I began to hate him, and to see what a wicked fool I'd been to leave Joe. I was so lonesome—I thought I'd go crazy. And I kept thinking how good and patient Joe had been, and how badly I'd used him, and how lovely it would be to be back in the little parlor at Hinksville, even with Mrs. Glenn and the minister talking about free-will and predestination. So at last I wrote to Joe. I wrote him the humblest letters you ever read, one after another; but I never got any answer.

"Finally I found I'd spent all my money, so I sold my watch and my rings—Joe gave me a lovely turquoise ring when we were married—and came to New York. I felt ashamed to stay alone any longer in Albany; I was afraid that some of Arthur's friends, who had met me with him on the road, might come there and recognize me. After I got here I wrote to Susy Price, a great friend of mine who lives in Hinksville, and she answered at once, and told me just what I had expected—that Joe was ready to forgive me and crazy to have me back, but that his mother wouldn't let him stir a step or write me a line, and that she and the minister were at him all day long, telling him how bad I was and what a sin it would be to forgive me. I got Susy's letter two or three days ago, and after that I saw it was no use writing to Joe. He'll never dare go against his mother and she watches him like a cat. I suppose I deserve it—but he might have given me another chance! I know he would if he could only see me."

Her voice had dropped from anger to lamentation, and her tears again overflowed.

Woburn looked at her with the pity one feels for a child who is suddenly confronted with the result of some unpremeditated naughtiness.

"But why not go back to Hinksville," he suggested, "if your husband is ready to forgive you? You could go to your friend's house, and once your husband knows you are there you can easily persuade him to see you."

"Perhaps I could—Susy thinks I could. But I can't go back; I haven't got a cent left."

"But surely you can borrow money? Can't you ask your friend to forward you the amount of your fare?"

She shook her head.

"Susy ain't well off; she couldn't raise five dollars, and it costs twenty-five to get back to Hinksville. And besides, what would become of me while I waited for the money? They'll turn me out of here tomorrow; I haven't paid my last week's board, and I haven't got anything to give them; my bag's empty; I've pawned everything."

"And don't you know anyone here who would lend you the money?"

"No; not a soul. At least I do know one gentleman; he's a

friend of Arthur's, a Mr. Devine; he was staying at Rochester when we were there. I met him in the street the other day, and I didn't mean to speak to him, but he came up to me, and said he knew all about Arthur and how meanly he had behaved, and he wanted to know if he couldn't help me— I suppose he saw I was in trouble. He tried to persuade me to go and stay with his aunt, who has a lovely house right round here in Twenty-fourth Street; he must be very rich, for he offered to lend me as much money as I wanted."

"You didn't take it?"

"No," she returned; "I daresay he meant to be kind, but I didn't care to be beholden to any friend of Arthur's. He came here again yesterday, but I wouldn't see him, so he left a note giving me his aunt's address and saying she'd have a room ready for me at any time."

There was a long silence; she had dried her tears and sat looking at Woburn with eyes full of helpless reliance.

"Well," he said at length, "you did right not to take that man's money; but this isn't the only alternative," he added, pointing to the revolver.

"I don't know any other," she answered wearily. "I'm not smart enough to get employment; I can't make dresses or do typewriting, or any of the useful things they teach girls now; and besides, even if I could get work I couldn't stand the loneliness. I can never hold my head up again—I can't bear the disgrace. If I can't go back to Joe I'd rather be dead."

"And if you go back to Joe it will be all right?" Woburn suggested with a smile.

"Oh," she cried, her whole face alight, "if I could only go back to Joe!"

They were both silent again; Woburn sat with his hands in his pockets gazing at the floor. At length his silence seemed to rouse her to the unwontedness of the situation, and she rose from her seat, saying in a more constrained tone, "I don't know why I've told you all this."

"Because you believed that I would help you," Woburn answered, rising also; "and you were right; I'm going to send you home."

She colored vividly.

"You told me I was right not to take Mr. Devine's money," she faltered.

"Yes," he answered, "but did Mr. Devine want to send you home?"

"He wanted me to wait at his aunt's a little while first and then write to Joe again."

"I don't—I want you to start tomorrow morning; this morning, I mean. I'll take you to the station and buy your ticket, and your husband can send me back the money."

"Oh, I can't—I can't—you mustn't—" she stammered, reddening and paling. "Besides, they'll never let me leave here without paying."

"How much do you owe?"

"Fourteen dollars."

"Very well; I'll pay that for you; you can leave me your revolver as a pledge. But you must start by the first train; have you any idea at what time it leaves the Grand Central?"

"I think there's one at eight."

He glanced at his watch.

"In less than two hours, then; it's after six now."

She stood before him with fascinated eyes.

"You must have a very strong will," she said. "When you talk like that you make me feel as if I had to do everything you say."

"Well, you must," said Woburn lightly. "Man was made to be obeyed."

"Oh, you're not like other men," she returned; "I never

heard a voice like yours; it's so strong and kind. You must be a very good man; you remind me of Joe; I'm sure you've got just such a nature; and Joe is the best man I've ever seen."

Woburn made no reply, and she rambled on, with little pauses and fresh bursts of confidence.

"Joe's a real hero, you know; he did the most splendid thing you ever heard of. I think I began to tell you about it, but I didn't finish. I'll tell you now. It happened just after we were married; I was mad with him at the time, I'm afraid, but now I see how splendid he was. He'd been telegraph-operator at Hinksville for four years and was hoping that he'd get promoted to a bigger place; but he was afraid to ask for a raise. Well, I was very sick with a bad attack of pneumonia and one night the doctor said he wasn't sure whether he could pull me through. When they sent word to Joe at the telegraph office he couldn't stand being away from me another minute. There was a poor consumptive boy always hanging round the station; Joe had taught him how to operate, just to help him along; so he left him in the office and tore home for half an hour, knowing he could get back before the eastern express came along.

"He hadn't been gone five minutes when a freight-train ran off the rails about a mile up the track. It was a very still night, and the boy heard the smash and shouting, and knew something had happened. He couldn't tell what it was, but the minute he heard it he sent a message over the wires like a flash, and caught the eastern express just as it was pulling out of the station above Hinksville. If he'd hesitated a second, or made any mistake, the express would have come on, and the loss of life would have been fearful. The next day the Hinksville papers were full of Operator Glenn's presence of mind; they all said he'd be promoted. That was early in November and Joe didn't hear anything from the company till the first of January. Meanwhile the boy had gone home to his father's farm out in the country, and before Christmas he was dead. Well, on New Year's day Joe got a notice from the company saying that his pay was to be raised, and that he was to be promoted to a big junction near Detroit, in recognition of his presence of mind in stopping the eastern express. It was just what we'd both been pining for and I was nearly wild with joy; but I noticed Joe didn't say much. He just telegraphed for leave, and the next day he went right up to Detroit and told the directors there what had really happened. When he came back he told us they'd suspended him; I cried every night for a week, and even his mother said he was a fool. After that we just lived on at Hinksville, and six months later the company took him back; but I don't suppose they'll ever promote him now."

Her voice again trembled with facile emotion.

"Wasn't it beautiful of him? Ain't he a real hero?" she said. "And I'm sure you'd behave just like him; you'd be just as gentle about little things, and you'd never move an inch about big ones. You'd never do a mean action, but you'd be sorry for people who did; I can see it in your face; that's why I trusted you right off."

Woburn's eyes were fixed on the window; he hardly seemed to hear her. At length he walked across the room and pulled up the shade. The electric lights were dissolving in the gray alembic of the dawn. A milk-cart rattled down the street and, like a witch returning late from the Sabbath, a stray cat whisked into an area. So rose the appointed day.

Woburn turned back, drawing from his pocket the roll of bills which he had thrust there with so different a purpose. He counted them out, and handed her fifteen dollars.

"That will pay for your board, including your breakfast

this morning," he said. "We'll breakfast together presently if you like; and meanwhile suppose we sit down and watch the sunrise. I haven't seen it for years."

He pushed two chairs toward the window, and they sat down side by side. The light came gradually, with the icy reluctance of winter; at last a red disk pushed itself above the opposite house-tops and a long cold gleam slanted across their window. They did not talk much; there was a silencing awe in the spectacle.

Presently Woburn rose and looked again at his watch.

"I must go and cover up my dress coat," he said, "and you had better put on your hat and jacket. We shall have to be starting in half an hour."

As he turned away she laid her hand on his arm.

"You haven't even told me your name," she said.

"No," he answered; "but if you get safely back to Joe you can call me Providence."

"But how am I to send you the money?"

"Oh—well, I'll write you a line in a day or two and give you my address; I don't know myself what it will be; I'm a wanderer on the face of the earth."

"But you must have my name if you mean to write to me."

"Well, what is your name?"

"Ruby Glenn. And I think—I almost think you might send the letter right to Joe's—send it to the Hinksville station."

"Very well."

"You promise?"

"Of course I promise."

He went back into his room, thinking how appropriate it was that she should have an absurd name like Ruby. As he re-entered the room, where the gas sickened in the daylight, it seemed to him that he was returning to some forgotten land; he had passed, with the last few hours, into a wholly new phase of consciousness. He put on his fur coat, turning up the collar and crossing the lapels to hide his white tie. Then he put his cigar-case in his pocket, turned out the gas, and, picking up his hat and stick, walked back through the open doorway.

Ruby Glenn had obediently prepared herself for departure and was standing before the mirror, patting her curls into place. Her eyes were still red, but she had the happy look of a child that has outslept its grief. On the floor he noticed the tattered fragments of the letter which, a few hours earlier, he had seen her place before the mirror.

"Shall we go down now?" he asked.

"Very well," she assented; then, with a quick movement, she stepped close to him, and putting her hands on his shoulders lifted her face to his.

"I believe you're the best man I ever knew," she said, "the very best—except Joe."

She drew back blushing deeply, and unlocked the door which led into the passage-way. Woburn picked up her bag, which she had forgotten, and followed her out of the room. They passed a frowzy chambermaid, who stared at them with a yawn. Before the doors the row of boots still waited; there was a faint new aroma of coffee mingling with the smell of vanished dinners, and a fresh blast of heat had begun to tingle through the radiators.

In the unventilated coffee-room they found a waiter who had the melancholy air of being the last survivor of an exterminated race, and who reluctantly brought them some tea made with water which had not boiled, and a supply of stale rolls and staler butter. On this meager diet they fared in silence, Woburn occasionally glancing at his watch; at length he rose, telling his companion to go and pay her bill while he called a hansom. After all, there was no use in economizing his remaining dollars.

In a few moments she joined him under the portico of the hotel. The hansom stood waiting and he sprang in after her, calling to the driver to take them to the Forty-second Street station.

When they reached the station he found a seat for her and went to buy her ticket. There were several people ahead of him at the window, and when he had bought the ticket he found that it was time to put her in the train. She rose in answer to his glance, and together they walked down the long platform in the murky chill of the roofed-in air. He followed her into the railway carriage, making sure that she had her bag, and that the ticket was safe inside it; then he held out his hand, in its pearl-colored evening glove: he felt that the people in the other seats were staring at them.

"Goodbye," he said.

"Goodbye," she answered, flushing gratefully. "I'll never forget—never. And you *will* write, won't you? Promise."

"Of course, of course," he said, hastening from the carriage.

He retraced his way along the platform, passed through the dismal waiting-room and stepped out into the early sunshine. On the sidewalk outside the station he hesitated awhile; then he strolled slowly down Forty-second Street and, skirting the melancholy flank of the Reservoir, walked across Bryant Park. Finally he sat down on one of the benches near the Sixth Avenue and lit a cigar.

The signs of life were multiplying around him; he watched the cars roll by with their increasing freight of dingy toilers, the shop-girls hurrying to their work, the children trudging schoolward, their small vague noses red with cold, their satchels clasped in woolen-gloved hands. There is nothing very imposing in the first stirring of a great city's activities; it is a slow reluctant process, like the waking of a heavy sleeper; but to Woburn's mood the sight of that obscure renewal of humble duties was more moving than the spectacle of an army with banners.

He sat for a long time, smoking the last cigar in his case, and murmuring to himself a line from Hamlet—the saddest, he thought, in the play—

For every man hath business and desire.

Suddenly an unpremeditated movement made him feel the pressure of Ruby Glenn's revolver in his pocket; it was like a devil's touch on his arm, and he sprang up hastily. In his other pocket there were just four dollars and fifty cents; but that didn't matter now. He had no thought of flight.

For a few minutes he loitered vaguely about the park; then the cold drove him on again, and with the rapidity born of a sudden resolve he began to walk down the Fifth Avenue toward his lodgings. He brushed past a maid-servant who was washing the vestibule and ran upstairs to his room. A fire was burning in the grate and his books and photographs greeted him cheerfully from the walls; the tranquil air of the whole room seemed to take it for granted that he meant to have his bath and breakfast and go downtown as usual.

He threw off his coat and pulled the revolver out of his pocket; for some moments he held it curiously in his hand, bending over to examine it as Ruby Glenn had done; then he laid it in the top drawer of a small cabinet, and locking the drawer threw the key into the fire.

After that he went quietly about the usual business of his toilet. In taking off his dress coat he noticed the Legion of Honor which Miss Talcott had given him at the ball. He pulled it out of his buttonhole and tossed it into the fireplace. When he had finished dressing he saw with surprise that it was nearly ten o'clock. Ruby Glenn was already two hours nearer home.

Woburn stood looking about the room of which he had thought to take final leave the night before; among the ashes beneath the grate he caught sight of a little white heap which symbolized to his fancy the remains of his brief correspondence with Miss Talcott. He roused himself from this unseasonable musing and with a final glance at the familiar setting of his past, turned to face the future which the last hours had prepared for him.

He went downstairs and stepped our of doors, hastening down the street toward Broadway as though he were late for an appointment. Every now and then he encountered an acquaintance, whom he greeted with a nod and smile; he carried his head high, and shunned no man's recognition.

At length he reached the doors of a tall granite building honeycombed with windows. He mounted the steps of the portico, and passing through the double doors of plate-glass, crossed a vestibule floored with mosaic to another glass door on which was emblazoned the name of the firm.

This door he also opened, entering a large room with wainscotted subdivisions, behind which appeared the stooping shoulders of a row of clerks.

As Woburn crossed the threshold a gray-haired man emerged from an inner office at the opposite end of the room.

At sight of Woburn he stopped short.

"Mr. Woburn!" he exclaimed; then he stepped nearer and added in a low tone: "I was requested to tell you when you came that the members of the firm are waiting; will you step into the private office?"

BERNARD MALAMUD

THE MAGIC
BARREL

NOT LONG AGO there lived in uptown New York, in a small, almost meager room, though crowded with books, Leo Finkle, a rabbinical student at the Yeshiva University. Finkle, after six years of study, was to be ordained in June and had been advised by an acquaintance that he might find it easier to win himself a congregation if he were married. Since he had no present prospects of marriage, after two tormented days of turning it over in his mind, he called in Pinye Salzman, a marriage broker whose two-line advertisement he had read in the *Forward*.

The matchmaker appeared one night out of the dark fourth-floor hallway of the graystone rooming house where Finkle lived, grasping a black, strapped portfolio that had been worn thin with use. Salzman, who had been long in the business, was of slight but dignified build, wearing an old hat, and an overcoat too short and tight for him. He smelled frankly of fish, which he loved to eat, and although he was missing a few teeth, his presence was not displeasing, because of an amiable manner curiously contrasted with mournful eyes. His voice, his lips, his wisp of beard, his bony fingers were animated, but give him a moment of repose and his mild blue eyes revealed a depth of sadness, a characteristic that put Leo a little at ease although the situation, for him, was inherently tense.

He at once informed Salzman why he had asked him to come, explaining that but for his parents, who had married comparatively late in life, he was alone in the world. He had for six years devoted himself almost entirely to his studies, as a result of which, understandably, he had found himself without time for social life and the company of young women. Therefore he thought it the better part of trial and error—of embarrassing fumbling—to call in an experienced person to advise him on these matters. He remarked in passing that the function of the marriage broker was ancient and honorable, highly approved in the Jewish community, because it made practical the necessary without hindering joy. Moreover, his own parents had been brought together by a matchmaker. They had made, if not a financially profitable marriage—since neither had possessed any worldly goods to speak of—at least a successful one in the sense of their everlasting devotion to each other. Salzman listened in embarrassed surprise, sensing a sort of apology. Later, however, he experienced a glow of pride in his work, an emotion that had left him years ago, and he heartily approved of Finkle.

The two went to their business. Leo had led Salzman to the only clear place in the room, a table near a window that overlooked the lamp-lit city. He seated himself at the matchmaker's side but facing him, attempting by an act of will to suppress the unpleasant tickle in his throat. Salzman eagerly unstrapped his portfolio and removed a loose rubber band from a thin packet of much-handled cards. As he flipped through them, a gesture and sound that physically hurt Leo, the student pretended not to see and gazed steadfastly out the window. Although it was still February, winter was on its last legs, signs of which he had for the first time in years begun to notice. He now observed the round white moon, moving high in the sky through a cloud menagerie, and watched with half-open mouth as it penetrated a huge hen, and dropped out of her like an egg laying itself. Salzman, though pretending through eyeglasses he had just slipped on to be engaged in scanning the writing on the cards, stole occasional glances at the young man's distinguished face, noting with pleasure the long, severe scholar's nose, brown eyes heavy with learning, sensitive yet ascetic lips, and a certain almost hollow quality of the dark cheeks. He gazed around at shelves upon shelves of books and let out a soft, contented sigh.

When Leo's eyes fell upon the cards, he counted six spread out in Salzman's hand.

"So few?" he asked in disappointment.

"You wouldn't believe me how much cards I got in my office," Salzman replied. "The drawers are already filled to the top, so I keep them now in a barrel, but is every girl good for a new rabbi?"

Leo blushed at this, regretting all he had revealed of himself in a curriculum vitae he had sent to Salzman. He had thought it best to acquaint him with his strict standards and specifications but, in having done so, felt he had told the marriage broker more than was absolutely necessary.

He hesitantly inquired, "Do you keep photographs of your clients on file?"

"First comes family, amount of dowry, also what kind promises," Salzman replied, unbuttoning his tight coat and settling himself in the chair. "After comes pictures, rabbi."

"Call me Mr. Finkle. I'm not yet a rabbi."

Salzman said he would, but instead called him doctor, which he changed to rabbi when Leo was not listening too attentively.

Salzman adjusted his horn-rimmed spectacles, gently cleared his throat, and read in an eager voice the contents of the top card:

"Sophie P. Twenty-four years. Widow one year. No

children. Educated high school and two years college. Father promises eight thousand dollars. Has wonderful wholesale business. Also real estate. On the mother's side comes teachers, also one actor. Well known on Second Avenue."

Leo gazed up in surprise. "Did you say a widow?"

"A widow don't mean spoiled, rabbi. She lived with her husband maybe four months. He was a sick boy she made a mistake to marry him."

"Marrying a widow has never entered my mind."

"This is because you have no experience. A widow, especially if she is young and healthy like this girl, is a wonderful person to marry. She will be thankful to you the rest of her life. Believe me, if I was looking now for a bride, I would marry a widow."

Leo reflected, then shook his head.

Salzman hunched his shoulders in an almost imperceptible gesture of disappointment. He placed the card down on the wooden table and began to read another:

"Lily H. High-school teacher. Regular. Not a substitute. Has savings and new Dodge car. Lived in Paris one year. Father is successful dentist thirty-five years. Interested in professional man. Well-Americanized family. Wonderful opportunity.

"I know her personally," said Salzman. "I wish you could see this girl. She is a doll. Also very intelligent. All day you could talk to her about books and theayter and whatnot. She also knows current events."

"I don't believe you mentioned her age?"

"Her age?" Salzman said, raising his brows. "Her age is thirty-two years."

Leo said after a while, "I'm afraid that seems a little too old."

Salzman let out a laugh. "So how old are you, rabbi?"

"Twenty-seven."

"So what is the difference, tell me, between twenty-seven and thirty-two? My own wife is seven years older than me. So what did I suffer?—Nothing. If Rothschild's a daughter wants to marry you, would you say on account her age, no?"

"Yes," Leo said dryly.

Salzman shook off the no in the yes. "Five years don't mean a thing. I give you my word that when you will live with her for one week you will forget her age. What does it mean five years—that she lived more and knows more than somebody who is younger? On this girl, God bless her, years are not wasted. Each one that it comes makes better the bargain."

"What subject does she teach in high school?"

"Languages. If you heard the way she speaks French, you will think it is music. I am in the business twenty-five years, and I recommend her with my whole heart. Believe me, I know what I'm talking, rabbi."

"What's on the next card?" Leo said abruptly.

Salzman reluctantly turned up the third card:

"Ruth K. Nineteen years. Honor student. Father offers thirteen thousand cash to the right bridegroom. He is a medical doctor. Stomach specialist with marvelous practice. Brother-in-law owns own garment business. Particular people."

Salzman looked as if he had read his trump card.

"Did you say nineteen?" Leo asked with interest.

"On the dot."

"Is she attractive?" He blushed. "Pretty?"

Salzman kissed his fingertips. "A little doll. On this I give you my word. Let me call the father tonight and you will see what means pretty."

But Leo was troubled. "You're sure she's that young?"

"This I am positive. The father will show you the birth certificate."

"Are you positive there isn't something wrong with her?" Leo insisted.

"Who says there is wrong?"

"I don't understand why an American girl her age should go to a marriage broker."

A smile spread over Salzman's face.

"So for the same reason you went, she comes."

Leo flushed. "I am pressed for time."

Salzman, realizing he had been tactless, quickly explained. "The father came, not her. He wants she should have the best, so he looks around himself. When we will locate the right boy he will introduce him and encourage. This makes a better marriage than if a young girl without experience takes for herself. I don't have to tell you this."

"But don't you think this young girl believes in love?" Leo spoke uneasily.

Salzman was about to guffaw but caught himself and said soberly, "Love comes with the right person, not before."

Leo parted dry lips but did not speak. Noticing that Salzman had snatched a glance at the next card, he cleverly asked, "How is her health?"

"Perfect," Salzman said, breathing with difficulty. "Of course, she is a little lame on her right foot from an auto accident that it happened to her when she was twelve years, but nobody notices on account she is so brilliant and also beautiful."

Leo got up heavily and went to the window. He felt curiously bitter and upbraided himself for having called in the marriage broker. Finally, he shook his head.

"Why not?" Salzman persisted, the pitch of his voice rising.

"Because I detest stomach specialists."

"So what do you care what is his business? After you marry her do you need him? Who says he must come every Friday night in your house?"

Ashamed of the way the talk was going, Leo dismissed Salzman, who went home with heavy, melancholy eyes.

Though he had felt only relief at the marriage broker's departure, Leo was in low spirits the next day. He explained it as arising from Salzman's failure to produce a suitable bride for him. He did not care for his type of clientele. But when Leo found himself hesitating whether to seek out another matchmaker, one more polished than Pinye, he wondered if it could be—his protestations to the contrary, and although he honored his father and mother—that he did not, in essence, care for the matchmaking institution? This thought he quickly put out of mind yet found himself still upset. All day he ran around in the woods—missed an important appointment, forgot to give out his laundry, walked out of a Broadway cafeteria without paying and had to run back with the ticket in his hand; had even not recognized his land-lady in the street when she passed with a friend and courte-ously called out, "A good evening to you, Dr. Finkle." By nightfall, however, he had regained sufficient calm to sink his nose into a book and there found peace from his thoughts.

Almost at once there came a knock on the door. Before Leo could say enter, Salzman, commercial Cupid, was stand-ing in the room. His face was gray and meager, his expression hungry, and he looked as if he would expire on his feet. Yet the marriage broker managed, by some trick of the muscles, to display a broad smile.

"So good evening. I am invited?"

Leo nodded, disturbed to see him again, yet unwilling to ask the man to leave.

Beaming still, Salzman laid his portfolio on the table. "Rabbi, I got for you tonight good news."

"I've asked you not to call me rabbi. I'm still a student."

"Your worries are finished. I have for you a first-class bride."

"Leave me in peace concerning this subject." Leo pretended lack of interest.

"The world will dance at your wedding."

"Please, Mr. Salzman, no more."

"But first must come back my strength," Salzman said weakly. He fumbled with the portfolio straps and took out of the leather case an oily paper bag, from which he extracted a hard, seeded roll and a small smoked whitefish. With a quick motion of his hand he stripped the fish out of its skin and began ravenously to chew. "All day in a rush," he muttered.

Leo watched him eat.

"A sliced tomato you have maybe?" Salzman hesitantly inquired.

"No."

The marriage broker shut his eyes and ate. When he had finished he carefully cleaned up the crumbs and rolled up the remains of the fish, in the paper bag. His spectacled eyes roamed the room until he discovered, amid some piles of books, a one-burner gas stove. Lifting his hat he humbly asked, "A glass tea you got, rabbi?"

Conscience-stricken, Leo rose and brewed the tea. He served it with a chunk of lemon and two cubes of lump sugar, delighting Salzman.

After he had drunk his tea, Salzman's strength and good spirits were restored.

"So tell me, rabbi," he said amiably, "you considered some more the three clients I mentioned yesterday?"

"There was no need to consider."

"Why not?"

"None of them suits me."

"What then suits you?"

Leo let it pass because he could give only a confused answer.

Without waiting for a reply, Salzman asked, "You remember this girl I talked to you—the high-school teacher?"

"Age thirty-two?"

But, surprisingly, Salzman's face lit in a smile. "Age twenty-nine."

Leo shot him a look. "Reduced from thirty-two?"

"A mistake," Salzman avowed. "I talked today with the dentist. He took me to his safety deposit box and showed me the birth certificate. She was twenty-nine years last August. They made her a party in the mountains where she went for her vacation. When her father spoke to me the first time I forgot to write the age and I told you thirty-two, but now I remember this was different client, a widow."

"The same one you told me about, I thought she was twenty-four?"

"A different. Am I responsible that the world is filled with widows?"

"No, but I'm not interested in them, nor, for that matter, in school teachers."

Salzman pulled his clasped hands to his breast. Looking at the ceiling he devoutly exclaimed, "Yiddishe kinder, what can I say to somebody that he is not interested in high-school teachers? So what then you are interested?"

Leo flushed but controlled himself.

"In what else will you be interested," Salzman went on, "if you not interested in this fine girl that she speaks four languages and has personally in the bank ten thousand dollars? Also her father guarantees further twelve thousand.

171

Also she has a new car, wonderful clothes, talks on all subjects, and she will give you a first-class home and children. How near do we come in our life to paradise?"

"If she's so wonderful, why wasn't she married ten years ago?"

"Why?" said Salzman with a heavy laugh. "—Why? Because she is *partikiler*. This is why. She wants the *best*."

Leo was silent, amused at how he had entangled himself. But Salzman had aroused his interest in Lily H., and he began seriously to consider calling on her. When the marriage broker observed how intently Leo's mind was at work on the facts he had supplied, he felt certain they would soon come to an agreement.

Late Saturday afternoon, conscious of Salzman, Leo Finkle walked with Lily Hirschorn along Riverside Drive. He walked briskly and erectly, wearing with distinction the black fedora he had that morning taken with trepidation out of the dusty hat box on his closet shelf, and the heavy black Saturday coat he had thoroughly whisked clean. Leo also owned a walking stick, a present from a distant relative, but quickly put temptation aside and did not use it. Lily, petite and not unpretty, had on something signifying the approach of spring. She was au courant, animatedly, with all sorts of subjects, and he weighed her words and found her surprisingly sound—score another for Salzman, whom he uneasily sensed to be somewhere around, hiding perhaps high in a tree along the street, flashing the lady signals with a pocket mirror; or perhaps a cloven-hoofed Pan, piping nuptial ditties as he danced his invisible way before them, strewing wild buds on the walk and purple grapes in their path, symbolizing fruit of a union, though there was of course still none.

Lily startled Leo by remarking, "I was thinking of Mr. Salzman, a curious figure, wouldn't you say?"

Not certain what to answer, he nodded.

She bravely went on, blushing, "I for one am grateful for his introducing us. Aren't you?"

He courteously replied, "I am."

"I mean," she said with a little laugh—and it was all in good taste, or at least gave the effect of being not in bad— "do you mind that we came together so?"

He was not displeased with her honesty, recognizing that she meant to set the relationship aright, and understanding that it took a certain amount of experience in life, and courage, to want to do it quite that way. One had to have some sort of past to make that kind of beginning.

He said that he did not mind. Salzman's function was traditional and honorable—valuable for what it might achieve, which, he pointed out, was frequently nothing.

Lily agreed with a sigh. They walked on for a while and she said after a long silence, again with a nervous laugh, "Would you mind if I asked you something a little bit personal? Frankly, I find the subject fascinating." Although Leo shrugged, she went on half-embarrassedly, "How was it that you came to your calling? I mean, was it a sudden passionate inspiration?"

Leo, after a time, slowly replied, "I was always interested in the Law."

"You saw revealed in it the presence of the Highest?"

He nodded and changed the subject. "I understand that you spent a little time in Paris, Miss Hirschorn?"

"Oh, did Mr. Salzman tell you, Rabbi Finkle?" Leo winced but she went on, "It was ages ago and almost forgotten. I remember I had to return for my sister's wedding."

And Lily would not be put off. "When," she asked

in a slightly trembly voice, "did you become enamored of God?"

He stared at her. Then it came to him that she was talking about not Leo Finkle but a total stranger, some mystical figure, perhaps even passionate prophet that Salzman had dreamed up for her—no relation to the living or dead. Leo trembled with rage and weakness. The trickster had obviously sold her a bill of goods, just as he had him, who'd expected to become acquainted with a young lady of twenty-nine, only to behold, the moment he had laid eyes upon her strained and anxious face, a woman past thirty-five and aging rapidly. Only his self-control had kept him this long in her presence.

"I am not," he said gravely, "a talented religious person," and, in seeking words to go on, found himself possessed by shame and fear. "I think," he said in a strained manner, "that I came to God not because I loved Him but because I did not."

This confession he spoke harshly because its unexpectedness shook him.

Lily wilted. Leo saw a profusion of loaves of bread go flying like ducks high over his head, not unlike the winged loaves by which he had counted himself to sleep last night. Mercifully, then, it snowed, which he would not put past Salzman's machinations.

He was infuriated with the marriage broker and swore he would throw him out of the room the moment he reappeared. But Salzman did not come that night, and when Leo's anger had subsided, an unaccountable despair grew in its place. At first he thought this was caused by his disappointment in Lily, but before long it became evident that he had involved himself with Salzman without a true knowledge of his own intent. He gradually realized—with an emptiness that seized him with six hands—that he had called in the broker to find him a bride because he was incapable of doing it himself. This terrifying insight he had derived as a result of his meeting and conversation with Lily Hirschorn. Her probing questions had somehow irritated him into revealing—to himself more than her—the true nature of his relationship to God, and from that it had come upon him, with shocking force, that apart from his parents, he had never loved anyone. Or perhaps it went the other way, that he did not love God so well as he might, because he had not loved man. It seemed to Leo that his whole life stood starkly revealed and he saw himself for the first time as he truly was—unloved and loveless. This bitter but somehow not fully unexpected revelation brought him to a point of panic, controlled only by extraordinary effort. He covered his face with his hands and cried.

The week that followed was the worst of his life. He did not eat and lost weight. His beard darkened and grew ragged. He stopped attending seminars and almost never opened a book. He seriously considered leaving the Yeshiva, although he was deeply troubled at the thought of the loss of all his years of study—saw them like pages torn from a book, strewn over the city—and at the devastating effect of this decision upon his parents. But he had lived without knowledge of himself, and never in the Five Books and all the Commentaries—mea culpa—had the truth been revealed to him. He did not know where to turn, and in all this desolating loneliness there was no *to whom*, although he often thought of Lily but not once could bring himself to go downstairs and make the call. He became touchy and irritable, especially with his landlady, who asked him all manner of personal questions; on the other hand, sensing his own disagreeableness, he waylaid her on the stairs and apologized abjectly, until, mortified, she ran from him. Out of this, however, he drew the consolation that he was a Jew and that a Jew suffered. But gradually, as the long and terrible week drew to a close, he regained his composure and some idea of purpose in life: to go on as planned. Although he was imperfect, the ideal was not. As for his quest of a bride, the thought of continuing afflicted him with anxiety and heartburn, yet perhaps with this new knowledge of himself he would be more successful than in the past. Perhaps love would now come to him and a bride to that love. And for this sanctified seeking who needed a Salzman?

The marriage broker, a skeleton with haunted eyes, returned that very night. He looked, withal, the picture of frustrated expectancy—as if he had steadfastly waited the week at Miss Lily Hirschorn's side for a telephone call that never came.

Casually coughing, Salzman came immediately to the point: "So how did you like her?"

Leo's anger rose and he could not refrain from chiding the matchmaker. "Why did you lie to me, Salzman?"

Salzman's pale face went dead white, the world had snowed on him.

"Did you not state that she was twenty-nine?" Leo insisted.

"I give you my word—"

"She was thirty-five, if a day. *At least* thirty-five."

"Of this don't be too sure. Her father told me—"

"Never mind. The worst of it is that you lied to her."

"How did I lie to her, tell me?"

"You told her things about me that weren't true. You made me out to be more, consequently less than I am. She had in mind a totally different person, a sort of semi-mystical Wonder Rabbi."

"All I said, you was a religious man."

"I can imagine."

Salzman sighed. "This is my weakness that I have," he confessed. "My wife says to me I shouldn't be a salesman, but when I have two fine people that they would be wonderful to be married, I am so happy that I talk too much." He smiled wanly. "This is why Salzman is a poor man."

Leo's anger left him. "Well, Salzman, I'm afraid that's all."

The marriage broker fastened hungry eyes on him.

"You don't want anymore a bride?"

"I do," said Leo, "but I have decided to seek her in another way. I am no longer interested in an arranged marriage. To be frank, I now admit the necessity of premarital love. That is, I want to be in love with the one I marry."

"Love?" said Salzman, astounded. After a moment he remarked, "For us, our love is our life, not for the ladies. In the ghetto they—"

"I know, I know," said Leo. "I've thought of it often. Love, I have said to myself, should be a product of living and worship rather than its own end. Yet for myself I find it necessary to establish the level of my need and fulfill it."

Salzman shrugged but answered, "Listen, rabbi, if you want love, this I can find for you also. I have such beautiful clients that you will love them the minute your eyes will see them."

Leo smiled unhappily. "I'm afraid you don't understand."

But Salzman hastily unstrapped his portfolio and withdrew a manila packet from it.

"Pictures," he said, quickly laying the envelope on the table.

Leo called after him to take the pictures away, but as if on the wings of the wind, Salzman had disappeared.

March came. Leo had returned to his regular routine. Although he felt not quite himself yet—lacked energy—

he was making plans for a more active social life. Of course it would cost something, but he was an expert in cutting corners; and when there were no corners left he would make circles rounder. All the while Salzman's pictures had lain on the table, gathering dust. Occasionally as Leo sat studying, or enjoying a cup of tea, his eyes fell on the manila envelope, but he never opened it.

The days went by and no social life to speak of developed with a member of the opposite sex—it was difficult, given the circumstances of his situation. One morning Leo toiled up the stairs to his room and stared out the window at the city. Although the day was bright his view of it was dark. For some time he watched the people in the street below hurrying along and then turned with a heavy heart to his little room. On the table was the packet. With a sudden relentless gesture he tore it open. For a half hour he stood by the table in a state of excitement, examining the photographs of the ladies Salzman had included. Finally, with a deep sigh he put them down. There were six, of varying degrees of attractiveness, but look at them long enough and they all became Lily Hirschorn: all past their prime, all starved behind bright smiles, not a true personality in the lot. Life, despite their frantic yoohooings, had passed them by; they were pictures in a briefcase that stank of fish. After a while, however, as Leo attempted to return the photographs into the envelope, he found in it another, a snapshot of the type taken by a machine for a quarter. He gazed at it a moment and let out a low cry.

Her face deeply moved him. Why, he could at first not say. It gave him the impression of youth—spring flowers, yet age—a sense of having been used to the bone, wasted; this came from the eyes, which were hauntingly familiar, yet absolutely strange. He had a vivid impression that he had met her before, but try as he might he could not place her although he could almost recall her name, as if he had read it in her own handwriting. No, this couldn't be; he would have remembered her. It was not, he affirmed, that she had an extraordinary beauty—no, though her face was attractive enough; it was that *something* about her moved him. Feature for feature, even some of the ladies of the photographs could do better; but she leaped forth to his heart—had *lived*, or wanted to—more than just wanted, perhaps regretted how she had lived—had somehow deeply suffered: it could be seen in the depths of those reluctant eyes, and from the way the light enclosed and shone from her, and within her, opening realms of possibility: this was her own. Her he desired. His head ached and eyes narrowed with the intensity of his gazing, then as if an obscure fog had blown up in the mind, he experienced fear of her and was aware that he had received an impression, somehow, of evil. He shuddered, saying softly, It is thus with us all. Leo brewed some tea in a small pot and sat sipping it without sugar, to calm himself. But before he had finished drinking, again with excitement he examined the face and found it good: good for Leo Finkle. Only such a one could understand him and help him seek whatever he was seeking. She might, perhaps, love him. How she had happened to be among the discards in Salzman's barrel he could never guess, but he knew he must urgently go find her.

Leo rushed downstairs, grabbed up the Bronx telephone book, and searched for Salzman's home address. He was not listed, nor was his office. Neither was he in the Manhattan book. But Leo remembered having written down the address on a slip of paper after he had read Salzman's advertisement in the "personals" column of the *Forward*. He ran up to his room and tore through his papers, without luck. It was exasperating. Just when he needed the matchmaker he was nowhere to be found. Fortunately Leo remembered to look in his wallet. There on a card he found his name written and a Bronx address. No phone number was listed, the reason—Leo now recalled—he had originally communicated with Salzman by letter. He got on his coat, put a hat on over his skullcap, and hurried to the subway station. All the way to the far end of the Bronx he sat on the edge of his seat. He was more than once tempted to take out the picture and see if the girl's face was as he remembered, but he refrained, allowing the snapshot to remain in his inside coat pocket, content to have her so close. When the train pulled into the station he was waiting at the door and bolted out. He quickly located the street Salzman had advertised.

The building he sought was less than a block from the subway, but it was not an office building, nor even a loft, nor a store in which one could rent office space. It was a very old tenement house. Leo found Salzman's name in pencil on a soiled tag under the bell and climbed three dark flights to his apartment. When he knocked, the door was opened by a thin, asthmatic, gray-haired woman, in felt slippers.

"Yes?" she said, expecting nothing. She listened without listening. He could have sworn he had seen her, too, before but knew it was an illusion.

"Salzman—does he live here? Pinye Salzman," he said, "the matchmaker?"

She stared at him a long minute. "Of course."

He felt embarrassed. "Is he in?"

"No." Her mouth, though left open, offered nothing more.

"The matter is urgent. Can you tell me where his office is?"

"In the air." She pointed upward.

"You mean he has no office?" Leo asked.

"In his socks."

He peered into the apartment. It was sunless and dingy, one large room divided by a half-open curtain, beyond which he could see a sagging metal bed. The near side of the room was crowded with rickety chairs, old bureaus, a three-legged table, racks of cooking utensils, and all the apparatus of a kitchen. But there was no sign of Salzman or his magic barrel, probably also a figment of the imagination. An odor of frying fish made Leo weak to the knees.

"Where is he?" he insisted. "I've got to see your husband."

At length she answered, "So who knows where he is? Every time he thinks a new thought he runs to a different place. Go home, he will find you."

"Tell him Leo Finkle."

She gave no sign she had heard.

He walked downstairs, depressed.

But Salzman, breathless, stood waiting at his door.

Leo was astounded and overjoyed. "How did you get here before me?"

"I rushed."

"Come inside."

They entered. Leo fixed tea, and a sardine sandwich for Salzman. As they were drinking he reached behind him for the packet of pictures and handed them to the marriage broker.

Salzman put down his glass and said expectantly, "You found somebody you like?"

"Not among these."

The marriage broker turned away.

"Here is the one I want." Leo held forth the snapshot.

Salzman slipped on his glasses and took the picture into his trembling hand. He turned ghastly and let out a groan.

"What's the matter?" cried Leo.

"Excuse me. Was an accident this picture. She isn't for you."

Salzman frantically shoved the manila packet into his portfolio. He thrust the snapshot into his pocket and fled down the stairs.

Leo, after momentary paralysis, gave chase and cornered the marriage broker in the vestibule. The landlady made hysterical outcries but neither of them listened.

"Give me back the picture, Salzman."

"No." The pain in his eyes was terrible.

"Tell me who she is then."

"This I can't tell you. Excuse me."

He made to depart, but Leo, forgetting himself, seized the matchmaker by his tight coat and shook him frenziedly.

"Please," sighed Salzman. "*Please*."

Leo ashamedly let him go. "Tell me who she is," he begged. "It's very important for me to know."

"She is not for you. She is a wild one—wild, without shame. This is not a bride for a rabbi."

"What do you mean wild?"

"Like an animal. Like a dog. For her to be poor was a sin. This is why to me she is dead now."

"In God's name, what do you mean?"

"Her I can't introduce to you," Salzman cried.

"Why are you so excited?"

"Why, he asks," Salzman said, bursting into tears. "This is my baby, my Stella, she should burn in hell."

Leo hurried up to bed and hid under the covers. Under the cover he thought his life through. Although he soon fell asleep he could not sleep her out of his mind. He woke, beating his breast. Though he prayed to be rid of her, his prayers went unanswered. Through days of torment he endlessly struggled not to love her; fearing success, he escaped it. He then concluded to convert her to goodness, himself to God. The idea alternately nauseated and exalted him.

He perhaps did not know that he had come to a final decision until he encountered Salzman in a Broadway cafeteria. He was sitting alone at a rear table, sucking the bony remains of a fish. The marriage broker appeared haggard, and transparent to the point of vanishing.

Salzman looked up at first without recognizing him. Leo had grown a pointed beard and his eyes were weighted with wisdom.

"Salzman," he said, "love has at last come to my heart."

"Who can love from a picture?" mocked the marriage broker.

"It is not impossible."

"If you can love her, then you can love anybody. Let me show you some new clients that they just sent me their photographs. One is a little doll."

"Just her I want," Leo murmured.

"Don't be a fool, doctor. Don't bother with her."

"Put me in touch with her, Salzman," Leo said humbly. "Perhaps I can be of service."

Salzman had stopped eating and Leo understood with emotion that it was now arranged.

Leaving the cafeteria, he was, however, afflicted by a tormenting suspicion that Salzman had planned it all to happen this way.

Leo was informed by letter that she would meet him on a certain corner, and she was there one spring night, waiting under a street lamp. He appeared, carrying a small bouquet of violets and rosebuds. Stella stood by the lamppost, smoking. She wore white with red shoes, which fitted his expectations, although in a troubled moment he had imagined the dress red, and only the shoes white. She waited uneasily and shyly. From afar he saw that her eyes—clearly her father's—were filled with desperate innocence. He pictured, in her, his own redemption. Violins and lit candles revolved in the sky. Leo ran forward with flowers outthrust.

Around the corner, Salzman, leaning against a wall, chanted prayers for the dead.

DAMON RUNYAN

SOCIAL ERROR

WHEN MR. ZIEGFELD picks a doll, she is apt to be above the average when it comes to looks, for Mr. Ziegfeld is by no means a chump at picking dolls. But when Mr. Ziegfeld picks Miss Midgie Muldoon, he beats his own best record, or anyway ties it. I never see a better-looking doll in my life, although she is somewhat smaller than I like them. I like my dolls big enough to take a good hold on, and Miss Midgie Muldoon is only about knee-high to a Pomeranian. But she is very cute, and I do not blame Handsome Jack Maddigan for going daffy about her.

Now most any doll on Broadway will be very glad indeed to have Handsome Jack Maddigan give her a tumble, so it is very surprising to one and all when Miss Midgie Muldoon plays the chill for Handsome Jack, especially when you figure that Miss Midgie Muldoon is nothing but a chorus doll, while Handsome Jack is quite a high shot in this town. But one night in the Hot Box when Handsome Jack sends word to Miss Midgie Muldoon, by Miss Billy Perry, who is Dave the Dude's wife, that he will like to meet up with her, Miss Midgie Muldoon sends word back to Handsome Jack that she is not meeting up with tough guys.

Well, naturally this crack burns Handsome Jack up quite some. But Dave the Dude says never mind, and furthermore Dave says Miss Midgie Muldoon's crack serves Handsome Jack right for sitting around shooting off his mouth, and putting himself away as a tough guy, because if there is anything Dave hates it is a guy letting on he is tough, no matter how tough he really is, and Handsome Jack is certainly such a guy.

He is a big tall blond guy who comes up out of what they call Hell's Kitchen over on the West Side, and if he has a little more sense the chances are he will be as important a guy as Dave the Dude himself in time, instead of generally working for Dave, but Handsome Jack likes to wear very good clothes, and drink, and sit around a lot, and also do plenty of talking, and no matter how much dough he makes he never seems able to hold much of anything.

Personally, I never care to have any truck with Handsome Jack because he always strikes me as a guy who is a little too quick on the trigger to suit me, and I always figure the best you are going to get out of being around guys who are quick on the trigger is the worst of it, and so any time I see Handsome Jack I give him the back of my neck. But there are many people in this world such as Basil Valentine who love to be around these characters.

This Basil Valentine is a little guy who wears horn cheaters and writes articles for the magazines, and is personally a very nice little guy, and as harmless as a water snake, but he cannot have a whole lot of sense, or he will not be hanging out with Handsome Jack and other such characters.

If a guy hangs out with tough guys long enough he is apt to get to thinking maybe he is tough himself, and by and by other people may get the idea he is tough, and the first thing you know along comes some copper in plain clothes, such as Johnny Brannigan, of the strong-arm squad, and buffs him on the noggin with a blackjack just to see how tough he is. As I say, Basil Valentine is a very harmless guy, but after he is hanging out with Handsome Jack a while, I hear Basil talking very tough to a bus boy, and the chances are he is building himself up to talk tough to a waiter, and then maybe to a head waiter, and finally he may consider himself tough enough to talk tough to anybody.

I can show you many a guy who is supposed to be strictly legitimate sitting around with guys who are figured as tough guys, and why this is I do not know, but I am speaking to Waldo Winchester, the newspaper scribe, about the proposition one night, and Waldo Winchester, who is a half-smart guy in many respects, says it is what is called an underworld complex. Waldo Winchester says many legitimate people are much interested in the doings of tough guys, and consider them very romantic, and he says if I do not believe it look at all the junk the newspapers print making heroes out of tough guys.

Waldo Winchester says the underworld complex is a very common complex and that Basil Valentine has it, and so has Miss Harriet Mackyle, or she will not be all the time sticking her snoot into joints where tough guys hang out. This Miss Harriet Mackyle is one of these rich dolls who wears snaky-looking evening clothes, and has her hair cut like a boy's, with her ears sticking out, and is always around the night traps, generally with some guy with a little mustache, and a way of talking like an Englishman, and come to think of it I do see her in tough joints more than somewhat, saying hello to different parties such as nobody in their right minds will say hello to, including such as Red Henry, who is just back from Dannemora, after being away for quite a spell for taking things out of somebody's safe and blowing the safe open to take these things.

In fact, I see Miss Harriet Mackyle dancing one night in the Hearts and Flowers Club, which is a very tough joint indeed, and who is she dancing with but Red Henry, and when I ask Waldo Winchester what he makes of this proposition, he says it is part of the underworld complex he is talking about. He says Miss Harriet Mackyle probably thinks it smart to tell her swell friends she dances with a safe-blower, although personally if I am going to dance with a safe-blower at all, which does not seem likely, I will pick me out a nicer safe-blower than Red Henry, because he is such a guy as does not take a bath since he leaves Dannemora, and he is back from Dannemora for several months.

One party who does not seem to have much of Waldo Winchester's underworld complex as far as I can see is Miss Midgie Muldoon, because I never see her around any night traps except such as the Hot Box and the Sixteen Hundred Club, which are considered very nice places, and reasonably safe for anybody who does not get too far our of line, and Miss Midgie Muldoon is always with very legitimate guys such as Buddy Donaldson, the song writer, or Walter Gumble, who plays the trombone in Paul Whiteman's band, or maybe sometimes with Paul Hawley, the actor.

Furthermore, when she is around such places, Miss Midgie Muldoon minds her own business quite a bit, and always looks right past Handsome Jack Maddigan, which burns Jack up all the more. It is the first time Handsome Jack ever runs into a doll who does not seem excited about him, and he does not know what to make of such a situation.

Well, what happens but Dave the Dude comes to me one day and says to me like this: "Listen," Dave says, "this doll Miss Harriet Mackyle is one of my best customers for high-grade merchandise, and is as good as wheat in the bin, and she is asking a favor of me. She is giving a party Sunday night in her joint over on Park Avenue, and she wishes me to invite some of the mob, so go around and tell about a dozen guys to be there all dressed, and not get too fresh, because a big order of Scotch and champagne goes with the favor."

Now such a party is by no means unusual, although generally it is some swell guy who gives it rather than a doll, and he gets Broadway guys to be there to show his pals what a mixer he is. Waldo Winchester says it is to give color to things, though where the color comes in I do not know, for Broadway guys, such as will go to a party like this, are apt to just sit around and say nothing, and act very gentlemanly, because they figure they are on exhibition like freaks, and the only way you can get them to such parties in the first place is through some such connection as Miss Harriet Mackyle has with Dave the Dude.

Anyway, I go around and about and tell a lot of guys what Dave the Dude wishes them to do, and among others I tell Handsome Jack, who is tickled to death by the invitation, because if there is anything Jack loves more than anything else it is to be in a spot where he can show off some. Furthermore, Handsome Jack has a sneaking idea Miss Harriet Mackyle is red hot for him because she sometimes gives him the old eye when she sees him around the Sixteen Hundred Club, and other spots, but then she does the same thing to Big Nig, and a lot of other guys I can mention, because that is just naturally the way Miss Harriet Mackyle is. But of course I do not speak of this to Handsome Jack. Basil Valentine is with Jack when I invite him, so I tell Basil to come along, too, because I do not wish him to think I am a snob.

It turns out that Basil is one of the very first guys to show up Sunday night at Miss Harriet Mackyle's apartment, where I am already on hand to help get in the Scotch and champagne, and to make Miss Harriet Mackyle acquainted with such of the mob as I invite, although I find we are about lost in the shuffle of guys with little mustaches, and dolls in evening clothes that leave plenty of them sticking out here and there. It seems everybody on Broadway is there, as well as a lot of

Park Avenue, and Mr. Ziegfeld is especially well represented, and among his people I see Miss Midgie Muldoon, although I have to stand on tiptoe to see her on account of the guys with little mustaches around her, and their interest in Miss Midgie Muldoon proves that they are not such saps as they look, even if they do wear little mustaches.

It is a very large apartment, and the first thing I notice is a big green parrot swinging in the ring hung from the ceiling in a corner of what seems to be the main room, and the reason I notice this parrot is because it is letting out a squawk now and then, and yelling different words, such as Polly wants a cracker. There are also a lot of canary birds hung around the joint, so I judge Miss Harriet Mackyle loves animals, as well as peculiar people, such as she has for guests.

I am somewhat surprised to see Red Henry all dressed up in evening clothes moving around among the guests. I do not invite Red Henry, so I suppose Miss Harriet Mackyle invites him, or he hears rumors of the party, and just crashes in, but personally I consider it very bad taste on Red Henry's part to show himself in such a spot, and so does everybody else that knows him, although he seems to be minding his own business pretty well.

Finally when the serious drinking is under way, and a good time is being had by one and all, Miss Harriet Mackyle comes over to me and says to me like this: "Now tell me about your different friends, so I can tell my other guests. They will be thrilled to death meeting these bad characters."

"Well," I say, "you see the little guy over there staring at you as if you are a ghost, or some such? Well, he is nobody but Bad Basil Valentine, who will kill you as quick as you can say scat, and maybe quicker. He is undoubtedly the toughest guy here tonight, or anywhere else in this man's town for that matter. Yes, ma'am, Bad Basil Valentine is one dead tough mug," I say, "although he is harmless-looking at this time. Bad Basil kills many a guy in his day. In fact, Miss Mackyle," I say, "Bad Basil can scarcely sleep good any night he does not kill some guy."

"My goodness!" Miss Harriet Mackyle says, looking Basil over very carefully. "He does not look so bad at first glance, although now that I examine him closely I believe I do detect a sinister gleam in his eye."

Well, Miss Harriet Mackyle can hardly wait until she gets away from me, and the next I see of her she has Basil Valentine surrounded and is almost chewing his ear off as she gabs to him, and anybody can see that Basil is all pleasured up by this attention. In fact, Basil is snagged if ever I see a guy snagged, and personally I do not blame him, because Miss Harriet Mackyle may not look a million, but she has a couple, and you can see enough of her in her evening clothes to know that nothing about her is phony.

The party is going big along toward one o'clock when all of a sudden in comes Handsome Jack Maddigan with half a heat on, and in five minutes he is all over the joint, drinking everything that is offered him, and making a fast play for all the dolls, and talking very loud. He is sored up more than somewhat when he finds Miss Harriet Mackyle does not give him much of a tumble, because he figures she will be calling him on top the minute he blows in, but Miss Harriet Mackyle is too busy with Basil Valentine finding out from Basil how he knocks off six of Al Capone's mob out in Chicago one time when he is out there on a pleasure trip.

Well, while feeling sored up about Miss Harriet Mackyle passing him up for Basil Valentine, and not knowing how it comes Basil is in so stout with her, Handsome Jack bumps into Red Henry, and Red Henry makes some fresh crack to Jack about Basil moving in on him, which causes Handsome

Jack to hit Red Henry on the chin, and knock him half into the lap of Miss Midgie Muldoon, who is sitting in a chair with a lot of little mustaches around her.

Naturally this incident causes some excitement for a moment. But the way Miss Midgie Muldoon takes it is very surprising. She just sort of dusts Red Henry off her, and stands up no bigger than a demi-tasse, and looks Handsome Jack right in the eye very cool, and says: "Ah, a parlor tough guy." Then she walks away, leaving Handsome Jack with his mouth open, because he does not know up to this moment that Miss Midgie Muldoon is present.

Well, somebody heaves Red Henry out of the joint, and the party continues, but I see Handsome Jack wandering around looking very lonesome, and with not much speed left compared to what he brings in. Somehow I figure Handsome Jack is looking for Miss Midgie Muldoon, but she keeps off among the little mustaches, and finally Handsome Jack takes to belting the old grape right freely to get his zing back. He gets himself pretty well organized, and when he suddenly comes upon Miss Midgie Muldoon standing by herself for a moment, he is feeling very brisk indeed, and he says to her like this: "Hello, Beautiful, are you playing the hard-to-get for me?" But Miss Midgie Muldoon only looks him in the eye again and says: "Ah, the parlor tough guy! Go away, tough guy. I do not like tough guys."

Well, this is not so encouraging when you come to think of it, but Handsome Jack is a guy who will never be ruled off for not trying with the dolls, and he is just about to begin giving her a little more work, when all of a sudden a voice goes "Ha-ha-ha," and then it says: "Hello, you fool!"

Now of course it is nothing but the parrot talking, and it says again: "Ha-ha-ha. Hello, you fool!" Of course, the parrot, whose name turns out to be Polly, does not mean

Handsome Jack, but of course Handsome Jack does not know the parrot does not mean him, and naturally he feels very much insulted. Furthermore, he has plenty of champagne inside him. So all of a sudden he outs with the old equalizer and lets go at Polly, and the next minute there are green feathers flying all over the joint, and poor old Mister, or maybe Missus, Polly is stretched out as dead as a doornail, and maybe deader.

Well, I never see a doll carry on like Miss Harriet Mackyle does when she finds out her Polly is a goner, and what she says to Handsome Jack is really very cutting, and quite extensive, and the chances are Handsome Jack will finally haul off and smack Miss Harriet Mackyle in the snoot, only he realizes he is already guilty of a very grave social error in shooting the parrot, and he does not wish to make it any worse.

Anyway, Miss Midgie Muldoon is standing looking at Handsome Jack out of her great big round beautiful eyes with what Waldo Winchester, the scribe, afterward tells me is plenty of scorn, and it looks to me as if Handsome Jack feels worse about Miss Midgie Muldoon's looks than he does about what Miss Harriet Mackyle is saying to him. But Miss Midgie Muldoon never opens her mouth. She just keeps looking at him for quite a spell, and then finally walks away, and it looks to me as if she is ready to bust out crying any minute, maybe because she feels sorry for Polly.

Well, naturally Handsome Jack's error busts up the party, because Miss Harriet Mackyle does not wish to take any chances on Handsome Jack starting in to pot her canaries, so we all go away leaving Miss Harriet Mackyle weeping over what she can find of Polly, and Basil Valentine crying with her, which I consider very chummy of Basil, at that.

A couple of nights later Basil comes into Mindy's restaurant, where I happen to be sitting with Handsome Jack, and anybody can tell that Basil is much worried about something.

"Jack," he says, "Miss Harriet Mackyle is very, very, very angry about you shooting Polly. In fact, she hates you, because Polly is a family heirloom."

"Well," Jack says, "tell her I apologize, and will get her a new parrot as soon as I get the price. You know I am broke now. Tell her I am very sorry, although," Jack says, "her parrot has no right to call me a fool, and I leave this to everybody."

"Miss Harriet Mackyle is after me every day to shoot you, Jack," Basil says. "She thinks I am a very tough guy, and that I will shoot anybody on short notice, and she wishes me to shoot you. In fact, she is somewhat displeased because I do not shoot you when you shoot poor Polly, but of course I explain to her I do not have a gun at the moment. Now Miss Harriet Mackyle says if I do not shoot you she will not love me, and I greatly wish to have Miss Harriet Mackyle love me, because I am practically daffy about her. So," Basil says, "I am wondering how much you will take to hold still and let me shoot you, Jack?"

"Why," Handsome Jack says, very much astonished, "you must be screwy."

"Of course I do not mean to really shoot you, Jack," Basil says. "I mean to maybe shoot you with a blank cartridge, so Miss Harriet Mackyle will think I am shooting you sure enough, which will make her very grateful to me. I am thinking that maybe I can pay you one thousand five hundred dollars for such a job, although this sum represents nearly my life savings."

"Why," Handsome Jack says, "your proposition sounds very reasonable, at that. I am just wondering where I can get hold of a few bobs to send Miss Midgie Muldoon a bar pin, or some such, and see if I cannot round myself up with her.

196

She is still playing plenty of chill for me. You better make it two grand while you are about it."

Well, Basil Valentine finally agrees to pay the two grand. Furthermore, Basil promises to put the dough up in advance with Dave the Dude, or some other reliable party, as this is rather an unusual business deal, and naturally Handsome Jack wishes to have his interests fully protected.

Well, the thing comes off a few nights later in the Hot Box, and it is all pretty well laid out in advance. It is understood that Basil is to bring Miss Harriet Mackyle into the Hot Box after regular hours when there are not apt to be any too many people around, and to find Handsome Jack there. Basil is to out with a gun and take a crack at Handsome Jack, and Handsome Jack is to let on he is hit, and Basil is to get Miss Harriet Mackyle out of the joint in the confusion.

Handsome Jack promises to lay low a few weeks afterward so it will look as if he is dead, and Basil figures that in the meantime Miss Harriet Mackyle will be so grateful to him that she will love him very much indeed, and maybe marry him, which is really the big idea with Basil.

It is pretty generally known to one and all what is coming off, and quite a number of guys drift into the Hot Box during the night, including Dave the Dude, who seems to be getting quite a bang out of the situation. But who also bobs up very unexpectedly but Miss Midgie Muldoon with Buddy Donaldson, the song writer.

Handsome Jack is all upset by Miss Midgie Muldoon being there, but she never as much as looks at him. So Handsome Jack takes to drinking Scotch more than somewhat, and everybody commences to worry about whether he will hold still for Basil Valentine to shoot him, even with a blank cartridge. The Hot Box closes at three o'clock in the morning, and everybody is always turned out except the regulars.

So by three-thirty there are only about a dozen guys and dolls in the joint when in comes Basil Valentine and Miss Harriet Mackyle.

Handsome Jack happens to be standing with his back to the door and not far from the table where Miss Midgie Muldoon and this Buddy Donaldson are sitting when Basil and Miss Harriet Mackyle come in, and right away Basil sings out, his voice wobbling no little: "Handsome Jack Maddigan, your time has come!" At this Handsome Jack turns around, and there is Basil Valentine tugging a big rod out of the hind pocket of his pants.

The next thing anybody knows, there is a scream, and a doll's voice cries: "Jack! Look out, Jack!" and out of her seat and over to Handsome Jack Maddigan bounces Miss Midgie Muldoon, and just as Basil finally raises the rod and turns it on, Miss Midgie Muldoon plants herself right in front of Jack and stretches out her arms on either side of her as if to shield him.

Well, the gun goes bingo in Basil's hand, but instead of falling like he is supposed to do, Handsome Jack stands there with his mouth open looking at Miss Midgie Muldoon, not knowing what to make of her jumping between him and the gun, and it is a good thing he does not fall, at that, because he is able to catch Miss Midgie Muldoon as she starts to keel over. At first we think maybe it is only a faint, but she has on a low-neck dress, and across her left shoulder there slowly spreads a red smear, and what is this red smear but blood, and as Handsome Jack grabs her she says to him like this: "Hold me, dear, I am hurt."

Now this is most unexpected indeed, and is by no means a part of the play. Basil Valentine is standing by the door with the rod in his duke looking quite astonished, and making no move to get Miss Harriet Mackyle out of the joint as he is supposed to the minute he fires, and Miss Harriet Mackyle is letting out a few off-hand screams which are very piercing, and saying she never thinks that Basil will take her seriously and really plug anybody for her, although she also says she appreciates his thoughtfulness, at that.

You can see Basil is standing there wondering what goes wrong, when Dave the Dude, who is a fast thinker under all circumstances, takes a quick peek at Miss Midgie Muldoon, and then jumps across the room and nails Basil. "Why," Dave says to Basil, "you are nothing but a rascal. You mean to kill him after all. You do not shoot a blank, you throw a slug, and you get Miss Midgie Muldoon with it in the shoulder."

Well, Basil is a pretty sick-looking toad as Dave the Dude takes hold of him, and Miss Harriet Mackyle is putting on a few extra yips when Basil says: "My goodness, Dave," he says. "I never know this gun is really loaded. In fact, I forget all about getting a gun of my own until the last minute, and am looking around for one when Red Henry comes along and says he will lend me his. I explain to him how the whole proposition is a joke, and tell him I must have blanks, and he kindly takes the lead out of the cartridges in front of my own eyes and makes them blank."

"The chances are Red Henry works a quick change on you," Dave the Dude says. "Red Henry is very angry at Jack for hitting him on the chin."

Then Dave takes the rod out of Basil's hand and breaks it open, and sure enough there are enough real slugs in it to sink a rowboat and no blanks whatever, which surprises Basil Valentine no little.

"Now," Dave says, "get away from here before Jack realizes what happens, and keep out of sight until you hear from me, because if Miss Midgie Muldoon croaks it may cause some gossip. Furthermore," Dave says, "take this squawking doll with you."

Well, you can see that Dave the Dude is pretty much steamed up, and he remains steamed up until it comes out that Miss Midgie Muldoon is only a little bit shot, and is by no means in danger of dying. We take her over to the Polyclinic Hospital, and a guy there digs the bullet out of her shoulder, and we leave her there with Handsome Jack holding her tight in his arms, and swearing he will never be tough again, but will get her a nice little home on Basil Valentine's two grand, and find himself a job, and take no more part in his old life, all of which seems to sound fair enough.

It is a couple of years before we hear of Miss Harriet Mackyle again, and then she is Mrs. Basil Valentine, and is living in Naples over in Italy, and the people there are very much surprised because Mrs. Basil Valentine never lets Mr. Basil Valentine associate with guys over ten years old, and never lets him handle anything more dangerous than a niblick.

So this is about all there is to the story, except that when Handsome Jack Maddigan and Miss Midgie Muldoon stand up to be married by Father Leonard, Dave the Dude sizes them up for a minute, and then turns to me and says like this:

"Look," Dave says, "and tell me where does Miss Midgie Muldoon's shoulder come up to on Jack's left side."

"Well," I say, "her shoulder comes just up to Jack's heart."

"So you see," Dave says, "it is just as well for Jack she stops Basil's bullet, at that."

KATHERINE ANNE PORTER

THEFT

SHE HAD THE purse in her hand when she came in. Standing in the middle of the floor, holding her bathrobe around her and trailing a damp towel in one hand, she surveyed the immediate past and remembered everything clearly. Yes, she had opened the flap and spread it out on the bench after she had dried the purse with her handkerchief.

She had intended to take the Elevated, and naturally she looked in her purse to make certain she had the fare, and was pleased to find forty cents in the coin envelope. She was going to pay her own fare, too, even if Camilo did have the habit of seeing her up the steps and dropping a nickel in the machine before he gave the turnstile a little push and sent her through it with a bow. Camilo by a series of compromises had managed to make effective a fairly complete set of smaller courtesies, ignoring the larger and more troublesome ones. She had walked with him to the station in a pouring rain, because she knew he was almost as poor as she was, and when he insisted on a taxi, she was firm and said, "You know it simply will not do." He was wearing a new hat of a pretty biscuit shade, for it never occurred to him to buy anything of a practical color; he had put it on for the first time and the rain was spoiling it. She kept thinking, "But this is dreadful, where will he get another?" She compared it with Eddie's hats that always seemed to be precisely seven years old and as if they had been quite purposely left out in the rain, and yet they sat with a careless and incidental rightness on Eddie. But Camilo was far different; if he wore a shabby hat it would be merely shabby on him, and he would lose his spirits over it. If she had not feared Camilo would take it badly, for he insisted on the practice of his little ceremonies up to the point he had fixed for them, she would have said to him as they left Thora's house, "Do go home. I can surely reach the station by myself."

"It is written that we must be rained upon tonight," said Camilo, "so let it be together."

At the foot of the platform stairway she staggered slightly —they were both nicely set up on Thora's cocktails—and said: "At least, Camilo, do me the favor not to climb these stairs in your present state, since for you it is only a matter of coming down again at once, and you'll certainly break your neck."

He made three quick bows, he was Spanish, and leaped off through the rainy darkness. She stood watching him, for he was a very graceful young man, thinking that tomorrow morning he would gaze soberly at his spoiled hat and soggy shoes and possibly associate her with his misery. As she watched, he stopped at the far corner and took off his hat and hid it under his overcoat. She felt she had betrayed him by seeing, because he would have been humiliated if he thought she even suspected him of trying to save his hat.

Roger's voice sounded over her shoulder above the clang of the rain falling on the stairway shed, wanting to know what she was doing out in the rain at this time of night, and did she take herself for a duck? His long, imperturbable face was streaming with water, and he tapped a bulging spot on the breast of his buttoned-up overcoat: "Hat," he said. "Come on, let's take a taxi."

She settled back against Roger's arm which he laid around

her shoulders, and with the gesture they exchanged a glance full of long amiable associations, then she looked through the window at the rain changing the shapes of everything, and the colors. The taxi dodged in and out between the pillars of the Elevated, skidding slightly on every curve, and she said: "The more it skids the calmer I feel, so I really must be drunk."

"You must be," said Roger. "This bird is a homicidal maniac, and I could do with a cocktail myself this minute."

They waited on the traffic at Fortieth Street and Sixth Avenue, and three boys walked before the nose of the taxi. Under the globes of light they were cheerful scarecrows, all very thin and all wearing very seedy snappy-cut suits and gay neckties. They were not very sober either, and they stood for a moment wobbling in front of the car, and there was an argument going on among them. They leaned toward each other as if they were getting ready to sing, and the first one said: "When I get married it won't be jus' for getting married, I'm gonna marry for *love*, see?" and the second one said, "Aw, gwan and tell that stuff to *her*, why n't yuh?" and the third one gave a kind of hoot, and said, "Hell, dis guy? Wot the hell's he got?" and the first one said: "Aaah, shurrup yuh mush, I got plenty." Then they all squealed and scrambled across the street beating the first one on the back and pushing him around.

"Nuts," commented Roger, "pure nuts."

Two girls went skittering by in short transparent raincoats, one green, one red, their heads tucked against the drive of the rain. One of them was saying to the other, "Yes, I know all about *that*. But what about me? You're always so sorry for *him* . . ." and they ran on with their little pelican legs flashing back and forth.

The taxi backed up suddenly and leaped forward again,

and after a while Roger said: "I had a letter from Stella today, and she'll be home on the twenty-sixth, so I suppose she's made up her mind and it's all settled."

"I had a sort of letter today too," she said, "making up my mind for me. I think it is time for you and Stella to do something definite."

When the taxi stopped on the corner of West Fifty-third Street, Roger said, "I've just enough if you'll add ten cents," so she opened her purse and gave him a dime, and he said, "That's beautiful, that purse."

"It's a birthday present," she told him, "and I like it. How's your show coming?"

"Oh, still hanging on, I guess. I don't go near the place. Nothing sold yet. I mean to keep right on the way I'm going and they can take it or leave it. I'm through with the argument."

"It's absolutely a matter of holding out, isn't it?"

"Holding out's the tough part."

"Good night, Roger."

"Good night, you should take aspirin and push yourself into a tub of hot water, you look as though you're catching cold."

"I will."

With the purse under her arm she went upstairs, and on the first landing Bill heard her step and poked his head out with his hair tumbled and his eyes red, and he said: "For Christ's sake, come in and have a drink with me. I've had some bad news."

"You're perfectly sopping," said Bill, looking at her drenched feet. They had two drinks, while Bill told how the director had thrown his play out after the cast had been picked over twice, and had gone through three rehearsals. "I said to him, 'I didn't say it was a masterpiece, I said it would make a good show.' And he said, 'It just doesn't *play*, do you see? It needs a doctor.' So I'm stuck, absolutely stuck," said Bill, on the edge of weeping again. "I've been crying," he told her, "in my cups." And he went on to ask her if she realized his wife was ruining him with her extravagance. "I send her ten dollars every week of my unhappy life, and I don't really have to. She threatens to jail me if I don't, but she can't do it. God, let her try it after the way she treated me! She's no right to alimony and she knows it. She keeps on saying she's got to have it for the baby and I keep on sending it because I can't bear to see anybody suffer. So I'm way behind on the piano and the victrola, both—"

"Well, this is a pretty rug, anyhow," she said.

Bill stared at it and blew his nose. "I got it at Ricci's for ninety-five dollars," he said. "Ricci told me it once belonged to Marie Dressler, and cost fifteen hundred dollars, but there's a burnt place on it, under the divan. Can you beat that?"

"No," she said. She was thinking about her empty purse and that she could not possibly expect a check for her latest review for another three days, and her arrangement with the basement restaurant could not last much longer if she did not pay something on account. "It's no time to speak of it," she said, "but I've been hoping you would have by now that fifty dollars you promised for my scene in the third act. Even if it doesn't play. You were to pay me for the work anyhow out of your advance."

"Weeping Jesus," said Bill, "you, too?" He gave a loud sob, or hiccough, in his moist handkerchief. "Your stuff was no better than mine, after all. Think of that."

"But you got something for it," she said. "Seven hundred dollars."

Bill said, "Do me a favor, will you? Have another drink

207

and forget about it. I can't, you know I can't, I would if I could, but you know the fix I'm in."

"Let it go, then," she found herself saying almost in spite of herself. She had meant to be quite firm about it. They drank again without speaking, and she went to her apartment on the floor above.

There, she now remembered distinctly, she had taken the letter out of the purse before she spread the purse out to dry.

She had sat down and read the letter over again: but there were phrases that insisted on being read many times, they had a life of their own separate from the others, and when she tried to read past and around them, they moved with the movement of her eyes, and she could not escape them . . . "thinking about you more than I mean to . . . yes, I even talk about you . . . why were you so anxious to destroy . . . even if I could see you now I would not . . . not worth all this abominable . . . the end . . ."

Carefully she tore the letter into narrow strips and touched a lighted match to them in the coal grate.

Early the next morning she was in the bathtub when the janitress knocked and then came in, calling out that she wished to examine the radiators before she started the furnace going for the winter. After moving about the room for a few minutes, the janitress went out, closing the door very sharply.

She came out of the bathroom to get a cigarette from the package in the purse. The purse was gone. She dressed and made coffee, and sat by the window while she drank it. Certainly the janitress had taken the purse, and certainly it would be impossible to get it back without a great deal of ridiculous excitement. Then let it go. With this decision of her mind, there rose coincidentally in her blood a deep almost murderous anger. She set the cup carefully in the center of the table, and walked steadily downstairs, three long flights and a short hall and a steep short flight into the basement, where the janitress, her face streaked with coal dust, was shaking up the furnace. "Will you please give me back my purse? There isn't any money in it. It was a present, and I don't want to lose it."

The janitress turned without straightening up and peered at her with hot flickering eyes, a red light from the furnace reflected in them. "What do you mean, your purse?"

"The gold cloth purse you took from the wooden bench in my room," she said. "I must have it back."

"Before God I never laid eyes on your purse, and that's the holy truth," said the janitress.

"Oh, well then, keep it," she said, but in a very bitter voice; "keep it if you want it so much." And she walked away.

She remembered how she had never locked a door in her life, on some principle of rejection in her that made her uncomfortable in the ownership of things, and her paradoxical boast before the warnings of her friends, that she had never lost a penny by theft; and she had been pleased with the bleak humility of this concrete example designed to illustrate and justify a certain fixed, otherwise baseless and general faith which ordered the movements of her life without regard to her will in the matter.

In this moment she felt that she had been robbed of an enormous number of valuable things, whether material or intangible: things lost or broken by her own fault, things she had forgotten and left in houses when she moved: books borrowed from her and not returned, journeys she had planned and had not made, words she had waited to hear spoken to her and had not heard, and the words she had meant to answer with; bitter alternatives and intolerable substitutes worse than nothing, and yet inescapable: the long patient suffering of dying friendships and the dark inexplicable death of love—all that she had had, and all that she had missed, were lost together, and were twice lost in this landslide of remembered losses.

The janitress was following her upstairs with the purse in her hand and the same deep red fire flickering in her eyes. The janitress thrust the purse toward her while they were still a half dozen steps apart, and said: "Don't never tell on me. I musta been crazy. I get crazy in the head sometimes, I swear I do. My son can tell you."

She took the purse after a moment, and the janitress went on: "I got a niece who is going on seventeen, and she's a nice girl and I thought I'd give it to her. She needs a pretty purse. I musta been crazy; I thought maybe you wouldn't mind, you leave things around and don't seem to notice much."

She said: "I missed this because it was a present to me from someone . . ."

The janitress said: "He'd get you another if you lost this one. My niece is young and needs pretty things, we oughta give the young ones a chance. She's got young men after her maybe will want to marry her. She oughta have nice things. She needs them bad right now. You're a grown woman, you've had your chance, you ought to know how it is!"

She held the purse out to the janitress saying: "You don't know what you're talking about. Here, take it, I've changed my mind. I really don't want it."

The janitress looked up at her with hatred and said: "I don't want it either now. My niece is young and pretty, she don't need fixin' up to be pretty, she's young and pretty anyhow! I guess you need it worse than she does!"

"It wasn't really yours in the first place," she said, turning away. "You mustn't talk as if I had stolen it from you."

"It's not from me, it's from her you're stealing it," said the janitress, and went back downstairs.

She laid the purse on the table and sat down with the cup of chilled coffee, and thought: I was right not to be afraid of any thief but myself, who will end by leaving me nothing.

WILLIAM MAXWELL

THE THISTLES
IN SWEDEN

THE BROWNSTONE IS on Murray Hill, facing south. The year is 1950. We have the top floor-through, and our windows are not as tall as the windows on the lower floors. They are deeply recessed, and almost square, and have divided panes. I know that beauty is in the eye of the beholder and all that, but even so, these windows are romantic. The apartment could be in Leningrad or Innsbruck or Dresden (before the bombs fell on it) or Parma or any place we have never been to. When I come home at night, I look forward to the moment when I turn the corner and raise my eyes to those three lighted windows. Since I was a child, no place has been quite so much home to me. The front windows look out on Thirty-sixth Street, the back windows on an unpainted brick wall (the side of a house on Lexington Avenue) with no break in it on our floor, but on the floor below there is a single window with a potted plant, and when we raise our eyes we see the sky, so the room is neither dark nor prisonlike.

Since we are bothered by street noises, the sensible thing would be to use this room to sleep in, but it seems to want to be our living-room, and offers two irresistible arguments: (1) a Victorian white marble fireplace and (2) a stairway. If we have a fireplace it should be in the living-room, even though the chimney is blocked up, so we can't have a fire in it. (I spend a good deal of time unblocking it, in my mind.) The stairs are the only access to the roof for the whole building. There is, of course, nothing up there, but it looks as if we are in a house and you can go upstairs to bed, and this is very cozy: a house on the top floor of a brownstone walk-up. I draw the bolt and push the trapdoor up with my shoulder, and Margaret and I stand together, holding the cat, Floribunda, in our arms so she will not escape, and see the stars (when there are any) or the winking lights of an airplane, or sometimes a hallucinatory effect brought about by fog or very fine rain and mist—the lighted windows of midtown skyscrapers set in space, without any surrounding masonry. The living-room and the bedroom both have a door opening onto the outer hall, which, since we are on the top floor and nobody else in the building uses it, we regard as part of the apartment. We leave these doors open when we are at home, and the stair railing and the head of the stairs are blocked off with huge pieces of cardboard. The landlord says that this is a violation of the fire laws, but we cannot think of any other way to keep Floribunda from escaping down the stairs, and neither can he.

The living-room curtains are of heavy Swedish linen: life-sized thistles, printed in light blue and charcoal gray, on a white background. They are very beautiful (and so must the thistles in Sweden be) and they also have an emotional context; Margaret made them, and, when they did not hang properly, wept, and ripped them apart and remade them, and now they do hang properly. The bedroom curtains are of a soft ivory material, with seashells—cowries, scallops, sea urchins and sand dollars, turbinates, auriculae—drawn on them in brown indelible ink, with a flowpen. The bedroom floor is black, the walls are sandalwood, the woodwork is white. On the wall above the double bed is a mural in two sections—a hexagonal tower in an imaginary kingdom that resembles Persia. Children are flying kites from the roof. Inside the tower, another child is playing on a musical instrument that is cousin to the lute. The paperhanger hung the panels the wrong way, so the tower is even stranger architecturally than the artist intended. The parapet encloses outer instead of inner space—like a man talking to somebody who is standing behind him, facing the other way. And the fish-shaped kite, where is that being flown from? And by whom? Some other children are flying kites from the roof of the tower next to this one, perhaps, only there wasn't room to show it. (Lying in bed I often, in my mind, correct the paperhanger's mistake.) Next to the mural there is a projection made by a chimney that conducts sounds from the house next door. Or rather, a single sound: a baby crying in the night. The brownstone next door is not divided into apartments, and so much money has been spent on the outside (blue shutters, fresh paint, stucco, polished brass, etc.) that, for this neighborhood, the effect of chic is overdone. We assume there is a nurse, but nobody ever does anything when the baby cries, and the sound that comes through the wall is unbearably sad. (Unable to stand it any longer, Margaret gets up and goes through the brick chimney and picks the baby up and brings it back in our bedroom and rocks it.)

The double chest of drawers came from Macy's unfinished-furniture department, and Margaret gave it nine coats of enamel before she was satisfied with the way it looked. The black lacquered dining-table (we have two dining-tables and no dining-room) is used as a desk. Over it hangs a large engraving of the Spanish Steps, which, two years ago, in the summer of 1948, for a brief time belonged to us—flower stands, big umbrellas, Bernini fountain, English Tea Room, Keats museum, children with no conception of bedtime, everything. At night we drape our clothes over two cheap rush-bottom chairs, from Italy. The mahogany dressing-table, with an oval mirror in a lyre-shaped frame and turned legs such as one sees in English furniture of the late seventeenth century, came by express from the West Coast. The express company delivered it to the sidewalk in front of the building, and, notified by telephone that this was about to happen, I rushed home from the office to supervise the uncrating. As I stepped from the taxi, I saw the expressman with the mirror and half the lyre in his huge hands. He was looking at it thoughtfully. The rest of the dressing-table was ten feet away, by the entrance to the building. The break does not show unless you look closely. And most old furniture has been mended at one time or another.

When we were shown the apartment for the first time, the outgoing tenant let us in and stood by pleasantly while we tried to imagine what the place would look like if it were not so crowded with his furniture. It was hardly possible to take a step for oak tables and chests and sofas and armoires and armchairs. Those ancestral portraits and Italian landscapes in heavy gilt frames that there was no room for on the walls were leaning against the furniture. To get from one room to the next we had to step over pyramids of books and scientific journals. An inventory of the miscellaneous objects and musical instruments in the living-room would have taken days and been full of surprises. (Why did he keep that large soup tureen on the floor?) We thought at first he was packing, but he was not; this was the way he lived. If we had asked him to make a place in his life for us too, he would have. He was a very nice man. The disorder was dignified and somehow enviable, and the overfurnished apartment so remote from what went on down below in the street that it was like a cave deep in the forest.

Now it is underfurnished (we have just barely enough money to manage a small one-story house in the country and this apartment in town), instead, and all light and air. The living-room walls are a pale blue that changes according to the light and the time of day and the season of the year and the color of the sky. The walls are hardly there. The furniture is half old and half new, and there isn't much of it, considering the size of the room: a box couch, a cabinet with sliding doors, a small painted bookcase, an easy chair with its ottoman, a round fruitwood side-table with long, thin, spidery legs and a glass tray that fits over the top, the table and chairs we eat on, a lowboy that serves as a sideboard, another chair, a wobbly tea cart, and a canvas stool. The couch has a high wooden back, L-shaped, painted black, with a thin gold line. It was made for an old house in Dover, New Hampshire, and after I don't know how many generations found itself in Minneapolis. I first saw it in Margaret's mother's bedroom in Seattle, and now it is here. It took two big men and a lot of patient maneuvering to get it four times past the turning of the stairs. The shawl that is draped over the back and the large tin tray that serves as a coffee-table both came from Mexico—a country I do not regard as romantic, even though we have never been there. The lowboy made the trip from the West Coast with the dressing-table, and one of its Chippendale legs got broken in transit, or by that same impetuous expressman. I suppose it is a hundred and fifty or two hundred years old. The man in the furniture-repair shop, after considering the broken leg, asked if we wanted the lowboy refinished. I asked why, and he said, "Because it's been painted." We looked, and sure enough it had. "They did that sometimes," he said. "It's painted to simulate mahogany." I asked what was under the paint, and he picked up a chisel and took a delicate gouge out of the underside. This time it was his turn to be surprised. "It's mahogany," he announced. The lowboy was painted to simulate what it actually was, it looks like what it is, so we let it be.

The gateleg table we eat on has four legs instead of the usual six. When the sides are extended, it looks as if the cabinetmaker had been studying Euclid's geometry. Margaret found it in an antique shop in Putnam Valley, and asked me to come look at it. I got out of the car and went in and saw the table and knew I could not live without it. The antique dealer said the table had an interesting history that she wasn't free to tell us. (Was it a real Hepplewhite and not just in the style of? Was it stolen?) She was a very old woman and lived alone. The shop was lined with bookshelves, and the books on the shelves and lying around on the tables were so uncommon I had trouble keeping my hands off them. They were not for sale, the old woman said. They had belonged to her husband, and she was keeping them for her grandchildren; she herself read nothing but murder mysteries.

Margaret wanted the table, but she wanted also to talk about whether or not we could afford it. I can always afford what I dearly want—or rather, when I want something very much I would rather not think about whether or not we can afford it. As we drove away without the table, I said coldly, "We won't talk about it." As if she were the kind of wife she isn't. And we did talk about it, all the way home. The next day we were back, nobody had bought the table in the meantime, I wrote out a check for two hundred dollars, and the old woman gave us a big rag rug to wrap around the marvel so it wouldn't be damaged on the drive home. Also heavy twine to tie it with. But then I asked for a knife, and this upset her, to my astonishment. I looked carefully and saw that the expression in her faded blue eyes was terror: She thought I wanted a knife so I could murder her and make off with the table *and* the check. It is disquieting to have one's intentions so misjudged. (Am I a murderer? And is it usual for the murderer to ask for his weapon?) "A pair of scissors will do just as well," I said, and the color came back into her face.

The rug the table now stands on is only slightly larger than the table-top. It is threadbare, but we cannot find another like it. For some reason, it is the last yellowish beige rug ever made. People with no children have perfectionism to fall back on.

The space between the fireplace and the door to the kitchen is filled by shelves and a shallow cupboard. The tea cart is kept under the stairs. Then comes the door to the coat closet, the inside of which is painted a particularly beautiful shade of Chinese red, and the door to the hall. On the sliding-door cabinet (we have turned the corner now and are moving toward the windows) there is a pottery lamp with a wide perforated gray paper shade and such a long thin neck that it seems to be trying to turn into a crane. Also a record player that plays only 78s and has to be wound after every record. The oil painting over the couch is of a rock quarry in Maine, and we have discovered that it changes according to the time of day and the color of the sky. It is particularly alive after a snowfall.

Here we live, in our modest perfectionism, with two black cats. The one on the mantelpiece is Bastet, the Egyptian goddess of love and joy. The other is under the impression that she is our child. This is our fault, of course, not hers. Around her neck she wears a scarlet ribbon, or sometimes a turquoise ribbon, or a collar with little bells. Her toys dangle from the tea cart, her kitty litter is in a pan beside the bathtub, and she sleeps on the foot of our bed or curled against the back of Margaret's knees. When she is bored she asks us to remove a piece of the cardboard barricade so she can go tippeting down the stairs and pay a call on the landlord and his wife,

Mr. and Mrs. Holmes, who live in the garden apartment and have the rear half of the second floor, with an inside stairs, so they really do go upstairs to bed. The front part of the second floor is the pied-à-terre of the artist who designed the wallpaper mural of the children flying kites from a hexagonal tower in an imaginary kingdom that resembles Persia. It is through the artist's influence (Mr. Holmes is intimidated by her) that we managed to get our rent-controlled apartment, for which we pay a hundred and thirteen dollars and some odd cents. The landlord wishes we paid more, and Mr. and Mrs. Venable, who live under us, wish we'd get a larger rug for the living-room. Their bedroom is on the back, and Margaret's heels crossing the ceiling at night keep them awake. Also, in the early morning the Egyptian goddess leaves our bed and chases wooden spools and glass marbles from one end of the living-room to the other. The Venables have mentioned this subject of the larger rug to the landlord and he has mentioned it to us. We do nothing about it, except that Margaret puts the spools and marbles out of Floribunda's reach when we go to bed at night, and walks around in her stocking feet after ten o'clock. Some day, when we are kept awake by footsteps crossing our bedroom ceiling, hammering, furniture being moved, and other idiot noises, we will remember the Venables and wish we had been more considerate.

The Venables leave their door open too, and on our way up the stairs I look back over my shoulder and see chintz-covered chairs and Oriental rugs and the lamplight falling discreetly on an Early American this and an Old English that. (No children here, either; Mrs. Venable works in a decorator's shop.) Mrs. Pickering, third floor, keeps her door closed. She is a sweet-faced woman who smiles when we meet her on the stairs. She has a grown son and daughter who come to see her regularly, but her life isn't the same as when they were growing up and Mr. Pickering was alive. (Did she tell us this or have I invented it?) If we met her anywhere but on the stairs we would have racked our brains to find something to say to her. The Holmeses' furniture is nondescript but comfortable. Mrs. Holmes has lovely brown eyes and the voice that goes with them, and it is no wonder that Floribunda likes to sit on her lap. *He* wants everybody to be happy, which is not exactly the way to be happy yourself, and he isn't. If we all paid a little more rent, it would make him happier, but we don't feel like it, any of us.

I am happy because we are in town: I don't have to commute in bad weather. I can walk to the office. And after the theater we jump in a cab and are home in five minutes. I stand at the front window listening to the weather report. It is snowing in Westchester, and the driving conditions are very bad. In Thirty-sixth Street it is raining. The middle-aged man who lives on the top floor of the brownstone directly across from us is in the habit of posing at the window with a curtain partly wrapped around his naked body. He keeps guppies or goldfish in a lighted tank, spends the whole day in a kimono ironing, and at odd moments goes to the front window and acts out somebody's sexual dream. If I could only marry him off to the old woman who goes through the trash baskets on Lexington Avenue, talking to herself. What pleasure she would have in showing him the things she has brought home in her string bag—treasures whose value nobody else realizes. And what satisfaction to him it would be to wrap himself in a curtain just for her.

The view to the south is cut off by a big apartment building on Thirty-fifth Street. The only one. If it were not there (I spend a good deal of time demolishing it, with my bare hands) we would have the whole of the sky to look at. Because

I have not looked carefully enough at the expression in Margaret's eyes, I go on thinking that she is happy too. When I met her she was working in a publishing house. Shortly after we decided to get married she was offered a job with the *Partisan Review*. If she had taken it, it would have meant commuting with me or even commuting at different hours from when I did. When I was a little boy and came home from school and called out, "Is anybody home?" somebody nearly always was. I took it for granted that the same thing would be true when I married. We didn't talk about it, and should have. I didn't understand that in her mind it was the chance of a fulfilling experience. Because she saw that I could not even imagine her saying yes, she said no, and turned her attention to learning how to cook and keep house. If we had had children right away it would have been different; but then if we had had children we wouldn't have been living on the top floor of a brownstone on Thirty-sixth Street.

The days in town are long and empty for her. The telephone doesn't ring anything like as often as it does when we are in the country. There Hester Gale comes across the road to see how Margaret is, or because she is out of cake flour, and they have coffee together. Margaret sews with Olivia Bingham. There are conversations in the supermarket. And miles of woods to walk in. Old Mrs. Delano, whose front door on Thirty-sixth Street is ten feet west of ours, is no help whatever. Though she knows Margaret's Aunt Caroline, she doesn't know that Margaret is her niece, or even that she exists, probably, and Margaret has no intention of telling her. Any more than she has any intention of telling me that in this place where I am so happy she feels like a prisoner much of the time.

She is accustomed to space, to a part of the country where there is more room than people and buildings to occupy it.

In her childhood she woke up in the morning in a big house set on a wide lawn, with towering pine trees behind it, and a copper beech as big as two brownstones, and a snow-capped mountain that mysteriously comes and goes, like an idea in the mind. Every afternoon after school she went cantering through the trees on horseback. Now she is confined to two rooms—the kitchen cannot be called a room; it is hardly bigger than a handkerchief—and these two rooms are not enough. This is a secret she manages to keep from me so I can go on being happy.

There is another secret that cannot be kept from me because, with her head in a frame made by my head, arms, and shoulder, I know when she weeps. She weeps because her period was five days late and she thought something had happened that she now knows is not going to happen. The child is there, and could just as well as not decide to come to us, and doesn't, month after month. Instead, we consult one gynecologist after another, and take embarrassing tests (only they don't really embarrass me, they just seem unreal). And what the doctors do not tell us is why, when there is nothing wrong with either of us, nothing happens. Before we can have a child we must solve a riddle, like Oedipus and the Sphinx. On my forty-second birthday I go to the Spence-Chapin adoption service and explain our situation to a woman who listens attentively. I like her and feel that she understands how terribly much we want a child, and she shocks me by reaching across the desk and taking the application blank out of my hands: Forty-two is the age past which the agency will not consider giving out a child for adoption.

Meanwhile, Margaret herself has been adopted, by the Italian market under the El at Third Avenue and Thirty-fourth Street. Four or five whistling boys with white aprons wrapped around their skinny hips run it. They also appear to own it, but what could be more unlikely? Their faces light up when Margaret walks into the store. They drop what they are doing and come to greet her as if she were their older sister. And whatever she asks for, it turns out they have. Their meat is never tough, their vegetables are not tarnished and limp, their sole is just as good as the fish market's and nothing like as expensive. Now one boy, now another arrives at our door with a carton of groceries balanced on his head, having taken the stairs two steps at a time. Four flights are nothing to them. They are in business for the pure pleasure of it. They don't think or talk about love, they just do it. Or perhaps it isn't love but joy. But over what? Over the fact that they are alive and so are we?

It occurs to the landlord that the tenants could carry their garbage down to the street and then he wouldn't have to. I prepare for a scene, compose angry speeches in the bath. Everybody knows what landlords are like—only he isn't like that. He isn't even a landlord, strictly speaking. He has a good job with an actuarial firm. The building is a hobby. It was very run down when he bought it, and he has had the pleasure of fixing it up. We meet on the front sidewalk as I am on my way to work. Looking up at him—he is a very tall man—I announce that I will not carry our garbage down. Looking down at me, he says that if we don't feel like carrying our garbage down he will go on doing it. What an unsatisfactory man to quarrel with.

I come home from the office and find that Margaret has spent the afternoon drawing: a pewter coffeepot (Nantucket), a Venetian-glass goblet, a white china serving dish with a handle and a cover, two eggs, a lemon, apples, a rumpled napkin with a blue border. Or the view from the living-room all the way into the bedroom, through three doorways, involving the kind of foreshortened perspective Italian Renaissance artists were so fond of. Or the view from the bedroom windows (the apartment house on Thirty-fifth Street that I have so often taken down I now see is all right; it belongs there) in sepia wash. Or her own head and shoulders reflected in the dressing-table mirror. Or the goblet, the coffeepot, the lemon, a green pepper, and a brown luster bowl. The luster bowl has a chip in it, and so the old woman in the antique shop in Putnam Valley gave it to us for a dollar, after the table was safely stowed away in the backseat of the car. And some years later, her daughter, sitting next to me at a formal dinner party, said, "You're mistaken. Mother was absolutely fearless." She said it again, perceiving that I did not believe her. Somebody is mistaken, and it could just as well as not be me. Even though I looked quite carefully at the old woman's expression. In any case, there is something I didn't see. Her husband—the man whose books the old woman was unwilling to sell—committed suicide. "I was their only child, and had to deal with sadness all my life—sadness from within as well as from without." If the expression in the old woman's eyes was not terror, what was it?

Floribunda misses the country, and sits at the top of the living-room stairs, clawing at the trapdoor. She refuses to eat, is shedding. Her hairs are on everything. One night we take her across Park Avenue to the Morgan Library and push the big iron gate open like conspirators about to steal the forty-two-line Gutenberg Bible or the three folios of Redouté's roses. Floribunda leaps from Margaret's arms and runs across the sickly grass and climbs a small tree. Ecstatically she sharpens her claws on the bark. I know that we will be arrested, but it is worth it.

* * *

Neither the landlord and his wife, nor the artist and her husband, who is Dutch, nor Mrs. Pickering, nor the Venables ever entertain in their apartments, but we have a season of being sociable. We have the Fitzgeralds and Eileen Fitzgerald's father from Dublin for dinner. We celebrate Bastille Day with the Potters. We have Elinor Hinkley's mother to tea. She arrives at the head of the stairs, where she can see into the living-room, and exclaims—before she has even caught her breath—"What beautiful horizontal surfaces!" She is incapable of small talk. Instead, she describes the spiritual emanations of a row of huge granite boulders lining the driveway of her house on Martha's Vineyard. And other phenomena that cannot be described very easily, or that, when described, cannot be appreciated by someone who isn't half mad or a Theosophist.

Dean Wilson brings one intelligent, pretty girl after another to meet us. Like the woman in Isak Dinesen's story who sailed the seas looking for the perfect blue, he is looking for a flawless girl. Flawless in whose eyes is the question. And isn't flawlessness itself a serious flaw? "What a charming girl," we say afterward, and he looks in our faces and is not satisfied, and brings still another girl, including, finally, Ivy Sérurier, who is half English and half French. When she was seven years old her nurse took her every day to the Jardin du Luxembourg and there she ran after a hoop. She is attracted to all forms of occult knowledge, and things happen to her that do not happen to anyone who does not have a destiny. The light bulbs respond to her amazing stories by giving off a higher voltage. The expression on our faces is satisfactory. Dean brings her again, and again. He asks Margaret if she thinks they should get married, but he cannot quite bring himself to ask Ivy this question.

On a night when we are expecting Henry Coddington to

dinner, Hester and Nick Gale come up the stairs blithely at seven o'clock, having got the invitation wrong. Or perhaps it is our fault. There is plenty of food, and it turns out to be a pleasant evening. The guests get on well, but Henry must have thought we did not want to know why Louise left him and took their little girl, whom he idolizes—that we have insulated ourselves from his catastrophe by asking this couple from the country. Anyway, he never comes or calls again. But other people come. Melissa Lovejoy, from Montgomery, Alabama, comes for Sunday lunch, and her hilarious account of her skirmishes with her mother-in-law make the tears run down my cheeks. Melissa, who loves beautiful china, looks around the living-room and sees what no one else has ever seen or commented on—a Meissen plate on the other end of the mantelpiece from the Egyptian cat. It is white, with very small green grape leaves and a wide filigree border. Margaret's brother John had it in his rucksack when he made his way from Geneva to Bordeaux in May 1940. As easily as the plate could have got broken, so he could have ended up in a detention camp and then what? But they are both safe, intact, here in New York. He has his own place, on Lexington Avenue in the Fifties. On Christmas Eve he bends down and selects a present for Margaret and another for me from the pile under the tree at the foot of the stair.

On New Year's Eve, John and Dean and Ivy and Margaret and I sit down to dinner. The champagne cork hits the ceiling. Between courses we take turns getting up and going into the bedroom and waiting behind a closed door until a voice calls "Ready!" If you were a school of Italian painting or a color of the spectrum or a character from fiction, what school of Italian painting or color or character would you be? John is Dostoevski's Idiot, Margaret is lavender blue. Elinor Hinkley joins us for dessert. Just before midnight a couple from the U.N., whom Dean has invited, come up the stairs and an hour later on the dot they leave for another party. It is daylight when we push our chairs back. We have not left the table (except to go into the front room while the questions are being framed) all night long. With our heads out of the window, Margaret and I wait for them to emerge from the building and then we call down to them, "Happy New Year!" But softly, so as not to wake up the neighbors.

Margaret's Uncle James, who is not her uncle but her mother's first cousin, comes to dinner, bringing long-stemmed red roses. He confesses that he has been waiting for this invitation ever since we were married—eight or nine years—and he thoroughly enjoys himself, though he is dying of cancer of the throat. Faced with extinction, you can't just stand and scream; it isn't good manners. And men and women of that generation do not discuss their feelings. Anyway he doesn't. Instead he says, "I like your curtains, Margaret," and we are filled with remorse that we didn't ask him sooner. But still, he did come to dinner. And satisfied his curiosity about the way we live. And we were surprised to discover that we were fond of him—as the rabbit is surprised to discover that he is what was concealed in the magician's hat. *I am not the person you thought I was*, Uncle James as much as says, sitting back in the easy chair but not using the ottoman lest he look ill.

I realize that the air is full of cigarette smoke, and prop the trapdoor open with a couple of books—but only a crack. At eleven-thirty Uncle James rises and puts his coat on and says good night, and tromps down the stairs, waking the Venables, and Mrs. Pickering, and the artist and her husband, and Mr. and Mrs. Holmes. And we lock the doors and say what a nice evening it was, and empty the ashtrays, and carry the liquor glasses out to the kitchen, and suddenly perceive an emptiness, an absence. "Floribunda? . . . Pussy?" She is nowhere. She has slipped through the crack that I thought was too small for her to get through. Fur is deceptive, her bone structure is not what I thought it was, and perhaps cats have something in common with cigarette smoke. I have often seen her attenuate herself alarmingly. Outside, on the roof, I call softly, but no little black cat comes. In the night we both wake and talk about her. The bottom of the bed feels strange when we put our feet out and there is nothing there, no weight. When morning comes I dress and go up to the roof again, and make my way toward Park Avenue, stepping over two-foot-high tile walls and making my way around projections and feeling giddy when I peer down into back gardens.

Margaret, meanwhile, has dressed and gone down the stairs. She rings the Delanos' bell, and the Irish maid opens the door. "A little cat came in through my bedroom window last night and the mistress said to put her on the street, so I did." *On the street* . . . when she could so easily have put her back on the roof she came from! "Here, Puss, Puss, Puss . . . here, Puss!" Up Thirty-sixth Street and down Thirty-fifth. All her life she has known nothing but love, and she is so timid. How will she survive with no home? What will the poor creature do? We meet Rose Bernstein, who has just moved into town from our country road, and just as I am saying "On the street. Did you ever hear of anything so heartless?" there is a faint miaow. Floribunda heard us calling and was too frightened to answer. I find her hiding in an areaway. Margaret gathers her up in her arms and we say goodbye to Rose Bernstein, and, unable to believe our good fortune, take her home. Our love and joy.

* * *

In Chicago there is an adoption agency whose policy with respect to age is not so rigid as Spence-Chapin's. We pull strings. (Dean Wilson has a friend whose wife's mother is on the board.) Letters pass back and forth, and finally there we are, in Chicago, nervously waiting in the reception room. Miss Mattie Gessner is susceptible (or so I feel) to the masculine approach. It turns out that she voted for Truman too; and she doesn't reach across the desk and take the application from my hands. Instead she promises to help us. But it isn't as simple as the old song my mother used to sing: Today is not the day they give babies away with a half a pound of tay. The baby that is given to us for adoption must be the child of a couple reasonably like us—that is to say, a man and woman who, in the year 1952, would have a record player that plays only 78s and that you wind by hand; who draw seashells on their bedroom curtains and are made happy by a blocked-up fireplace and a stairway that leads nowhere. And this means we must wait God knows how long.

So we do wait, sometimes in rather odd places for a couple with no children. For example, by the carousel in Central Park. The plunging horses slowly come to a halt with their hoofs in midair. The children get off and more children climb up, take a firm grip on the pole, and look around for their mother or their nurse or their father, in the crowd standing in the open doorway. Slowly the cavalcade begins to move again, and I take the little boy in the plaid snowsuit, with half a pound of English Breakfast, and Margaret takes half a pound of Lipton's and the little girl with blue ribbons in her hair.

We start going to the country week ends. And then we go for the summer, taking suitcases full of clothes, boxes of unread books, drawing materials, the sewing machine, the typewriter. And in September all this is carried up four flights of stairs. And more: flowers, vegetables from the garden, plants we could not bear to have the frost put an end to, even though we know they will not live long in town. And one by one we take up our winter habits. When Saturday night comes around we put on our coats at ten o'clock and go out to buy the Sunday *Times* at the newspaper stand under the El. We rattle the door of the antique shop on Third Avenue that always has something interesting in the window but has never been known to be open at any hour of any day of the week. On three successive nights we go to *Ring Round the Moon*, *King Lear*, and *An Enemy of the People*, after which it seems strange to sit home reading a book. I am so in love with Adlai Stevenson's speeches that, though I am afraid of driving in ordinary traffic in New York City, I get the car out of the garage and we drive right down the center of 125th Street, in a torchlight parade, hemmed in by a flowing river of people, all of whom feel the way we do.

How many years did we live in that apartment on Thirty-sixth Street? From 1950 to—The mere dates are misleading, even if I could get them right, because time was not progressive or in sequence, it was one of Mrs. Hinkley's horizontal surfaces divided into squares. On one square an old woman waters a houseplant in the window of an otherwise blank wall. On another, Albertha, who is black, comes to clean. When she leaves, the apartment looks as if an angel had walked through it. She is the oldest of eleven children. And what she and Margaret say, over a cup of coffee, makes Margaret more able to deal with her solitary life. On another square, we go to the Huguenot Church on Sunday morning, expecting something new and strange, and instead the hymns are perfectly familiar to us from our Presbyterian childhoods:

In French they have become more elegant and rhetorical, and it occurs to me that they may not reach all the way to the ear of Heaven. But the old man who then mounts the stairs to the pulpit addresses Seigneur Dieu in a confident voice, as if they are extremely well acquainted, the two of them. On another square we go to Berlitz, and the instructor, a White Russian named Mikhael Miloradovitch, sits by blandly while Margaret and I say things to each other in French that we have managed not to say in English. I am upset when I discover that she prefers the country to the city. The discussion becomes heated, but because it is in French nothing comes of it. We go on living in the city. Until another summer comes and we fill the car, which is now nearly twenty years old, to the canvas top with our possessions; then, locking the doors of the apartment, we drive off to our other life. At which point the shine goes out of this one. The slipcovers fade and so do the seashells and thistles that are exposed to the direct light of the summer sun. Dust gathers on the books, the lampshades, the record player. In the middle of the night, a hand pries at the trapdoor and, finding it securely locked, tries somewhere else. The man out of Krafft-Ebing shows himself seductively to our blank windows. And the intense heat builds up to a violent thunderstorm. After which there is a spell of cooler weather. And a tragedy. For two days there has been no garbage outside Mrs. Pickering's door in the morning. She does not answer her telephone or the landlord's knocking, and she has not said she was going away. The first floor extends farther back than the rest of the house, and he is able to place a ladder on the roof of this extension. From the top of the ladder he stares into the third-floor bedroom at a terrible sight: Mrs. Pickering, sitting in a wing chair, naked. He thinks it is death he is staring at, but he is mistaken; she has had a stroke. He breaks the door down, and she is taken to the hospital in an ambulance. She does not die, but neither does she ever come back to this apartment. Passing her door on our way up the stairs, we are aware of the silence inside, and think uneasily of those two days and nights of helpless waiting. Along with the silence there is the sense of something malign, of trouble of a very serious kind that could spread all through the house. To ward it off, we draw closer to the other tenants, linger talking on the stairs, and speak to them in a more intimate tone of voice. We have the Holmeses and the Venables and the artist and her husband up for a drink. It doesn't do the trick. There *was* something behind Mrs. Pickering's door. My sister's only son turns up and, since we are in the country, we offer him the apartment to live in until he finds a job. He leads a life there that the books and furniture do not approve of. He brings girls home and makes love to them in our bed, under the very eyes of the children flying kites. He borrows fifty bucks from me, to eat on, and to get some shirts, so he won't look like a bum when he goes job hunting. He has a check coming from his previous job, in Florida, and will pay me back next week The check doesn't come, and he borrows some more money, and then some more, and it begins to mount up. Jobs that were as good as promised to him vanish into thin air, and meanwhile we are his sole means of support. I listen attentively to what I more and more suspect are inventions, but his footwork is fast, and what he says could be true; it just isn't what he said before, quite. My bones inform me that I am not the first person these excuses and appeals have been tried out on. He comes to my office to tell me that he has given up the idea of staying in New York and can I let him have the fare home, and I dial my sister's number in Evansville, Indiana, and hand the receiver to him and leave the room.

I give up smoking on one square, and on another I go

through all the variant pages of a book I have been writing for four and a half years and reduce it to a single pile of manuscript. This I put in a blue canvas duffel bag that can absentmindedly be left behind on the curbing when we drive off to the country at eleven o'clock of a spring night. At midnight, driving up the Taconic Parkway, I suddenly see in my mind's eye the backseat of the car: The blue duffel bag is not there. Nor, when we come to a stop in front of our house on Thirty-sixth Street at one o'clock in the morning, is it on the sidewalk where I left it. With a dry mouth I describe it to the desk sergeant in the police station, and he gets up and goes into the back room. "No, nothing," he calls. And then, as we are almost at the door, "Wait a minute."

On another square Margaret starts behaving in a way that is not at all like her. Sleepy at ten o'clock in the evening, and when I open my eyes in the morning she is already awake and looking at me. Her face is somehow different. Can it be that she is ... that we are going to ... that ... I study her when she is not aware that I am looking at her, and find in her behavior the answer to that riddle: If we are so longing for a child that we are willing to bring up somebody else's child—anybody's child whatever—then we may as well be allowed to have our own. Margaret comes home from the doctor bringing the news to me that I have not dared break to her.

After boning up on the subject, in a book, she shows me, on her finger, just how long the child in her womb now is. And it is growing larger, very slowly. And so is she. The child is safe inside her, and she is safe so long as she remains a prisoner in this top-floor apartment. The doctor has forbidden her to use the stairs. Everybody comes to see her, instead—including an emanation from the silent apartment two floors below. A black man, a stranger, suddenly appears at the top of the stairs. His intention, unclear but frightening, shows in his face, in his eyes. But the goddess Bastet is at work again, and the man comes on Albertha's day, and she, with a stream of such foulmouthed cursing as Margaret has never heard in her life, sends him running down the stairs. If he had come on a day that was not Albertha's day, when Margaret was there alone—But this holds true for everything, good or bad.

Margaret's face grows rounder, and she no longer has a secret that must be kept from me. The days while I am at the office are not lonely, and time is an unbroken landscape of daydreaming. When I get home at six o'clock, I creep in under the roof of the spell she is under, and am allowed into the daydream. But what shall we tell Miss Mattie Gessner when she comes to investigate the way we live?

The apartment, feeling our inattention, begins to withdraw from us sadly. And then something else unexpected happens. The landlord, having achieved perfection, having created the Peaceable Kingdom on Thirty-sixth Street, is restless and wants to begin all over again. "You'll be sorry," his wife tells him, stroking Floribunda's ear, and he is. But by that time they are living uptown, in a much less handsome house in the Nineties—a house that needs fixing from top to bottom. But it will never have any style, and it is filled with disagreeable tenants who do not pay their rent on time. On Thirty-sixth Street we have a new landlord, and in no time his hand is on everything. He hangs a cheap print of van Gogh's *The Drawbridge* in the downstairs foyer. We are obliged to take down the cardboard barricade and keep our doors closed. Hardly a day passes without some maddening new improvement. The artist is the first to go. Then we give notice; how is Margaret to carry the baby, the stroller, the package from the drugstore, etc., up four flights of stairs?

What better place can there be to bring up a child in? the marble fireplace asks, remembering the eighteen-eighties, when this was a one-family house and our top-floor living-room was the nursery. The stairway to the roof was devoted to the previous tenant (the man who lived in the midst of a monumental clutter) and says bitterly, in the night, when we are not awake to hear, *They seem as much a part of your life as the doors and windows, and then it turns out that they are not a part of your life at all. The moving men come and cart all the furniture away, and the people go down to the street, and that's the last you see of them. . . .*

What will the fireplace and the stairway to the roof say when they discover that they are about to be shut off forever from the front room? The landlord is planning to divide our apartment into two apartments and charge the same for each that he is now getting for the floor-through. For every evil under the sun there is a remedy or there is none. I soak the mural of the children flying kites, hoping to remove it intact and put it up somewhere in the house in the country. The paper tears no matter how gently I pull it loose from the wall, and comes off in little pieces, which end up in the wastebasket.

Now when I walk past that house I look up at the windows that could be in Leningrad or Innsbruck or Dresden or Parma, and I think of the stairway that led only to the trapdoor in the roof, and of the marble fireplace, the bathroom skylight, and the tiny kitchen, and of what school of Italian painting we would have been if we had been a school of Italian painting, and poor Mrs. Pickering sitting in her bedroom chair with her eyes wide open, waiting for help, and the rainy nights on Thirty-sixth Street, and the gray-and-blue thistles, the brown seashells, the Mills Brothers singing *Shine,*

238

little glowworm, glimmer, glimmer, and the guests who came the wrong night, the guest who was going to die and knew it, the sound of my typewriter, and of a paintbrush clinking in a glass of cloudy water, and Floribunda's adventure, and Margaret's empty days, and how it was settled that, although I wanted to put my head on her breast as I was falling asleep, she needed even more (at that point) to put her head on mine. And of our child's coming, at last, and the black cat who thought *she* was our child, and of the two friends who didn't after all get married, and the old woman who found one treasure after another in the trash baskets all up and down Lexington Avenue, and that other old woman, now dead, who was so driven by the need to describe the inner life of very large granite boulders. I think of how Miss Mattie Gessner's face fell and how she closed her notebook and became a stranger to us, who had been so deeply our friend. I think of the over-sexed ironer, and the Holmeses, and the Venables, and the stranger who meant nobody good and was frightened away by Albertha's cursing, and the hissing of the air brakes of the Lexington Avenue bus, and the curtains moving at the open window, and the baby crying on the other side of the wall. I think of that happy grocery store run by boys, and the horse-drawn flower cart that sometimes waited on the corner, and the sound of footsteps in the night, and the sudden no-sound that meant it was snowing, and I think of the unknown man or woman who found the blue duffel bag with the manuscript of my novel in it and took it to the police station, and the musical instrument (not a lute, but that's what the artist must have had in mind, only she no longer bothers to look at objects and draws what she remembers them as being like) played in the dark, over our sleeping bodies, while the children flew their kites, and I think if it is true that we are all in the hands of God, what a capacious hand it must be.

MAEVE BRENNAN

A SNOWY NIGHT ON WEST FORTY-NINTH STREET

IT SNOWED ALL NIGHT last night, and the dawn, which came not as a brightening but as a gray and silent awakening, showed the city vague and passive as a convalescent under light fields of snow that fell quickly and steadily from an expressionless heaven. This Broadway section where I live is all heights of roofs and all shapes of walls all going in different directions and reaching different heights, and there are times when the whole area seems to be a gigantic storehouse of stage flats and stage props that are stacked together as economically as possible and being put to use until something more substantial can be built, something that will last. At night, when the big Broadway lights go on, when the lights begin to run around high in the sky and up and down the sides of buildings, when rivers of lights start flowing along the edges of roofs, and wreaths and diadems begin sparkling from dark corners, and the windows of empty downtown offices begin streaming with watery reflections of brilliance, at that time, when Broadway lights up to make a night-time empire out of the tumbledown, makeshift daytime world, a powdery pink glow rises up and spreads over the whole area, a cloudy pink, an emanation, like a tent made of air and color. Broadway lights and Broadway night-time color make a glittering spectacle that throws all around it into darkness. The little side streets that live off Broadway also live in the shadow of Broadway, and there are times, looking from the windows of the hotel where I live at present, on West

Forty-ninth Street, when I think that my hotel and all of us here on this street are behind the world instead of in it. But tonight when I looked out of these windows just before going to dinner I saw a kaleidoscope out there, snow and lights whirling sky-high in a furious wind that seemed to have blown the Empire State Building clear out of the city, because it was not to be seen, although I had my usual good view of it this morning. It was a gray morning and the afternoon was gray, but tonight is very dark, and when I walked out of the hotel into the withering cold of this black-and-white night, West Forty-ninth Street seemed more than ever like an outpost, or a frontier street, or a one-street town that has been thrown together in excitement—a gold rush or an oil gush—and that will tumble into ruin when the excitement ends. This block, between Sixth and Seventh Avenues, exists only as a thoroughfare to Broadway, a small, narrow thoroughfare furnished with what was at hand—architectural remnants, architectural mistakes, and architectural experiments. The people who decided to put this street to use for the time that remains to it have behaved with the freedom of children playing in a junkyard. The houses and buildings are of all sizes, some thin and some fat, some ponderous and some small and humble, some that were built for grandeur at the turn of the century, like my hotel, which now has a neon sign hanging all down its fine, many-windowed front, and some that never could have been more than sheds, even if they are built out of cement. In the daytime and especially in the early morning, the street has a travel-stained look and an air of hardship, and then the two rows of ill-matched, ill-assorted houses make me think of a team of worn-out horses, collected from everywhere, that are being worked for all the life that is left in them and that will have to keep going until their legs give out. Nobody will care when this street comes down because nobody really lives here. It is a street of restaurants, bars, cheap hotels, rooming houses, garages, all-night coffee shops, quick-lunch counters, delicatessens, short-lived travel agencies, and sightseeing buses, and there are a quick dry-cleaning place, a liquor store, a Chinese laundry, a record shop, a dubious movie house, a young, imperturbable gypsy who shifts her fortune-telling parlor from one doorway to another up and down the street, and a souvenir shop. The people who work here have their homes as far away from the street as they can possibly get, and the hotels and rooming houses are simply hotels and rooming houses, with tenants for a night or a week or a month or an hour, although there are a few old faithfuls who moved in for a little while and stayed on and on until the years tamed them into permanent transients. The oldest houses on the street are four thin, retiring brownstones that still stand together on the north side, all of them with restaurants or bars on their ground floor. It was to one of these brownstone houses that I went for dinner tonight, to the Étoile de France. Above the restaurant all the floors of the house are abandoned, the windows staring blankly and the wall scarred, but the falling snow curtained the windows and shaped the roof so that the old house appeared once again as it did in its first snowstorm, when the street was new. I had walked along from the hotel, and I waited to cross over to the Étoile, but the cars were going wild, confined as they were to one uncertain lane by the mountains of snow piled up on both sides, and while I waited I looked back the length of the street. The bewildering snow gave the shabby street an air of melancholy that made it ageless, as it will someday appear in an old photograph. But it will have to be a very old photograph. The inquisitive and sympathetic eyes that will see this street again as I saw it tonight have not yet opened to look at anything in this world. It will have to be a very old photograph, deepened by time and by a regret that will have its source in the loss of all of New York as we know it now. Many trial cities, facsimiles of cities, will have been raised and torn down on Manhattan island before anybody begins to regret this version of West Forty-ninth Street, and perhaps the photograph will never be taken. But on the street level, Forty-ninth Street defied the snow, and business was garish as usual. The Étoile was very bright and cheerful when I walked in, but there were very few customers. There was only one man sitting, lounging sideways at the bar—an old Frenchman who comes in often at night, after having had his dinner at the Automat. Only three of the tables in the bar were occupied, and the big back room, the dining-room, was dim and deserted. The Étoile is a very plain place, with plain wooden chairs, very hard chairs, red-and-white-checked tablecloths, a stamped tin ceiling painted cream, and wall-paper decorated with pale, romantic nineteenth-century scenes. I sat at a table across from the bar, which has a long mirror behind it to reflect the bottles and glasses and the back of the bartender's head and the faces of the customers and the romantic wallpaper on the wall behind me. One waiter was still on duty—Robert—and he brought me a martini and took my order and went off to the kitchen in a hurry. I think the chef must have been making a fuss about getting away early on this stormy night when there were almost no customers and he was going to have trouble getting home. He lives in Long Island City. Mme. Jacquin, who owns the restaurant, had gone home, and her daughter, Mees Katie, was in charge, together with Leo, the bartender. Leo has been working here about fifteen years. He is Dutch, and I think he is in his late fifties, a few years younger than Mme. Jacquin. Mees Katie is about thirty. She has a singularly detached manner, as though she were only working at the Étoile while she waited for her chance to go to some place where she really wants to be, but she spends more and more time here, while her mother, who used to almost live in the place, often does not come in for days at a time. Mees Katie began coming in about five years ago to help during the luncheon hour, but now she is here every night as well. She leaves at ten o'clock, when the chef goes home, and after that Leo manages by himself. On good nights the bar is open until two in the morning, or even later.

Mees Katie was sitting as she always sits, facing toward the door, so that she could jump up when the customers came in. She often sits alone at the table for one by the street window, a huge window partly curtained in colorless gauze, and when there is a rush on, she stands in the arch that leads from the front room to the back and watches both rooms. She never sits at the bar. Tonight she was sitting beside a lady I have never seen at the Étoile before, a very wide, stout, elderly lady whose elaborate makeup—eyes, complexion, and mouth—looked as though it had been applied several days ago and then repaired here and there as patches of it wore off. Her hair was dyed gold and curled in tiny rings all over her head, and her face and neck were covered with a dark beige powder. Her face had spread so that it was very big, but her nose and mouth were quite small, and she had enormous brown eyes that had no light in them. She had put on a great deal of black mascara, and blue eyeshadow. The shadow had melted down into the corners of her eyes and settled into the wrinkles. She was all covered up in a closely fitted dark blue velvet dress that was cut into a ring around her neck and had long tight sleeves that strained at her arms every time she lifted her spoon to her mouth. She was eating pears in wine, and she ate very carefully, looking into the dish as she chose each morsel. When she wasn't attending to the pears, she watched the man sitting opposite Mees Katie, and she listened to him, and Mees Katie listened to him, and he listened to himself. His name is Michel, and he never stops talking. He has something to do with importing foreign movies, or with promoting them, and he is always busy. He is always on the run, going in all directions. He never finishes his dinner without jumping up from his chair at least once to dash into the back room, where the telephone is, to make a call, and it is always an urgent call. If the phone is busy, if there is someone ahead of him, he stands waiting impatiently in the arch between the two rooms, looking importantly about him, and when he has finally gotten into the telephone booth and put his call through, he keeps the door open until he is halfway through his conversation. His voice can be heard all over the restaurant until suddenly there is a little clatter as he shuts himself away with his secrets. He has a very high, harsh voice, and he twists each word so that only half of it sounds like English. Leo makes fun of him. Once, when Michel had pulled the phone booth door shut on himself, Leo called from the bar to Mees Katie, who was sitting at a table with some people, just as she was tonight, "Michel is talking with the weatherman again," and Mees Katie looked annoyed, although she smiled. She gets impatient with the Étoile, and with the people there, and especially with Michel, because he pesters her, but she has a kind heart, and she is always polite.

Michel always comes into the restaurant alone, looking for company, and once in a while when there is no acquaintance he can join for dinner he sits by himself. When he is alone, all his animation dies away and he looks old and tired. He has a very broad dark face, with loose wrinkles, furrows, running up and down it and overlapping its outline. His forehead is high, and he has kinky coal-black hair and a neat, thin mouth. When he sits at his table with nobody to talk to or to pay any attention to him, he looks deserted, as though he had been brought to the restaurant and left there by someone who had no intention of coming back to claim him. Alone, he is morose and dignified, as though humiliation had taken him unawares but had not found him unprepared. On nights like that, when he knows he is doomed to solitude, he stands at the bar with his drink, sweet vermouth, until his dinner is brought, and then he goes to his table and sits down very deliberately and shakes out his napkin very fussily. He places the napkin across his lap and folds it closely around him so that his jacket hangs free of it. He always wears a double-breasted suit, and a waistcoat. When the napkin is safely in place, he picks up his knife and fork and sounds all the food on his plate and looks severely at his green salad. Then he cuts off a piece of meat and places it in his mouth and begins to chew it. While he is chewing, his knife and fork lie on his plate, and his wrists rest against the edge of the table, with his hands limp, and he chews patiently, looking as proud and as indifferent as though he were facing a firing squad.

I think he must have had dinner alone tonight before I came in, and after dinner moved over to join Mees Katie and her acquaintance, the elderly painted lady. There was nothing, not even a glass of water, in front of Mees Katie and nothing in front of Michel, but the elderly lady's part of the tablecloth looked as though it had been thoroughly occupied by several different dishes before her pears in wine were brought. Mees Katie looked very tired. She has a lot of acquaintances, most of them inherited from her mother, and I suppose the elderly lady was one of them. Mees Katie has an attitude she falls into when she is being officially companionable. She sits with both elbows on the table, with her right hand placed flat against the side of her head and her left hand, with the fingers curled under, and turned down, supporting her chin. The right hand always holds her head up, while the left hand is ready to rise against her mouth, as though the polite attention she wants to give people calls for modesty from her, and for as complete a concealment of her own personality as she can manage. Tonight, as she listened wearily to Michel, her hand hid her mouth and her eyes were fixed on Michel's face. She is often bored, but as a rule she can escape from her entanglements by jumping up to greet a customer or to give an order to the waiter. There was no easy escape for her tonight—the Étoile might as well have been snowbound for all the coming and going there was. It was very quiet. Three men sitting at the last table in the bar were talking quietly, but the only voice really to be heard belonged to Michel, and Mees Katie kept her eyes fixed on him as though she feared she might fall asleep if she stopped watching him. She has extraordinary eyes, small slanted brown eyes that are filled with light, brilliant eyes of a transparent brown in which the color recedes, not growing darker but growing more intense, so that the point of truest color, the source of all that light, seems very far away, and perhaps it is for that reason that Mees Katie's expression always seems distant, no matter how close her face is as she bends down to answer a question or to whisper to some customer she knows well.

Suddenly the elderly lady finished her pears, and she laid down her spoon and smiled, a small, mild, accustomed smile of pleasure, and she turned to look at Mees Katie, and Mees Katie yawned and was shocked at herself.

"Oh, I am sorry, Michel!" she cried. "Excuse me, Mrs. Dolan, but I am so tired tonight."

Michel emerged from his monologue to see that he was

in danger of losing his audience, and he looked over at Leo and called excitedly for cognac, cognac all round.

"Oh, no no no, thank you, Michel," Mees Katie said. "No cognac for me, thank you very much."

But Mrs. Dolan was delighted. She removed her lips from the edge of her coffee cup, which she was holding with both hands, and for a minute she looked like the perky little person she must once have been, who knew that at the mention of a drink a girl brightens up. "Well, thank you very much," she said to Michel, who had begun to stare at her with alarm. "I believe I will." She had a very loud, rusty voice, and after regarding Michel with approval she turned to Mees Katie. "Have a drink," she said. "A little cognac will settle your stomach."

Mees Katie laughed in a horrified way. "Oh, my stomach is all right," she cried, and she called to Leo, "M. Leo, *deux cognacs, s'il vous plaît.*"

Mees Katie is tall and slender, and she moves very easily and quickly. She went to the bar and took the little tray with the two cognacs from Leo and handed it to Robert, who had come running from the end of the bar. Then she walked quickly away, through the bar and through the dim dining-room, and pushed open one of the doors leading to the kitchen and went in there and stayed a few minutes. When she returned she was very brisk in her beaver hat and her beaver-lined coat. She said good night to Michel, who had become very glum, and to Mrs. Dolan, and to the old Frenchman at the bar, and to me, and she motioned Leo to the end of the bar and spoke a few words privately to him as she pulled on her gloves, and off she went. As she talked with Leo she stood sideways to the bar, and looked through the window, and a minute later, watching through the window, I saw her go past, walking carefully on the dangerous sidewalk, with her hand up to hold her hat against the wind. She and her mother have an apartment where they have lived for many years, far over on the west side, near Tenth Avenue. Leo also watched her through the window, and when she disappeared he stayed where he was and continued to watch. There is a big open garage across the street that has pushed itself through the buildings and now is open at each end, making an arcade and therefore a vista—you can see a little section of the Forty-eighth Street scene from this window here, and the people walking along there, who almost never turn their heads to look over in this direction, seem very far away, and they seem to be walking faster and with more sense of direction than the passersby immediately outside the window. Tonight was so blurred and wild you could see nothing much except movements of struggle out there, but Leo continued to watch. The back of Leo's head is perfectly flat, and his skin is putty-colored, but more white than gray or beige. His features are thick and fleshy and very clearly defined, the nose a wide triangle, the upper lip a sharp bow. His eyes are small and blue, and his half smile, for he never smiles right out, is always accompanied by a deliberate glance in which suspicion and interest are equally mixed. Sometimes the interest becomes dislike. He is vain. He is slow-witted and not handsome, and he is past sixty and a bit fat, and yet he wears the pleased, secretive expression of a man who has always gotten along very well with women. After a while he abandoned his survey of the window and moved along to speak with the old Frenchman. They spoke in French. The Frenchman objects to hearing English spoken at the Étoile, and he becomes very irritable when English-speaking strangers try to strike up an acquaintance with him. The three men at the end of the room left their table and moved across to that end of the bar and called for

252

drinks. They were irresolute. They were marooned in the city for the night, and they had taken rooms at the Plymouth Hotel along the street, and they wanted to be entertained without becoming involved, and the evening was going flat on them. They had come to the Étoile for dinner because they often have lunch there and always imagined it to be a place where interesting people came at night—show people, artists and writers, people like that, or at least French people who would sit and stand around and talk excitedly as they did in the movies—but there was no one worth watching or listening to, and tomorrow night they will drive home to Larchmont with a disappointed feeling that they will translate as knowledge—New York City is just as dull as anywhere else when you have nothing to do.

Michel was still talking, but warily. The last thing he wanted was to be left alone with a strange woman, and he felt it was no compliment to him to be seen drinking with a Mrs. Dolan. He hadn't touched his cognac. She took a business-like sip from hers and set the glass back on the table. She had stopped listening to him, and now she was sizing him up. A smile kept coming and going on her face—it was her contribution to the conversation and her acknowledgment of it. But she was considering, or ruminating, and a little trick occurred to her. She smiled and put her finger against her lips as though Michel were a child who was talking too much. Michel stopped talking.

"Do you come here much?" Mrs. Dolan asked him. It wasn't much of a question, but it was too personal for poor Michel. He began to answer her, and then instead he jumped up and clapped his hands to the sides of his head. It is the gesture he makes when he remembers an urgent phone call, or when he has to run out of the restaurant on an urgent errand. Mrs. Dolan stopped smiling, but she showed no surprise or embarrassment. She simply looked at him. He had to run out on an urgent errand, but he would be back in ten minutes.

He always returned to the Étoile after these errands, but Mrs. Dolan didn't know that, and it was clear she did not believe him. She went on looking at him. In his excitement he knocked his chair back, and it fell against the edge of my table. He turned ungracefully and caught the chair and straightened it, using both hands. "Pardon, Madame," he said to me, gaily. He looked me in the eye and smiled at me. He was triumphant, or at least relieved, because he was managing to break away from Mrs. Dolan, and he was glad of the diversion, of the fallen chair, because it made his getaway seem easier, but he would have smiled anyway, challenging me or challenging anyone to ignore him. When he smiles, his dark, even teeth remain tightly closed because he must always remain on guard and must always show that he does not fear the snub he watches for. I said quickly, "It doesn't matter at all," and I was glad I did because, although he had already begun speaking to Mrs. Dolan again, he turned and nodded to me, and I knew I was forgiven for the sin I had not committed, of not recognizing him.

Then he bustled to the coatrack, beside where I was sitting, and began wrapping himself up in his warm clothes—his warm fur-collared overcoat and his fur hat and his big gloves. Mrs. Dolan watched him as indifferently as though he were a stranger who had chanced to share her table on a train journey, and, as she might in a train, she turned her head from him to look at the view, in this case the bar, Leo, the old Frenchman, and the three exiles from Larchmont. Leo had a dour expression on his face as he watched Michel, who looked happily back at him and then looked at Mrs.

Dolan and saw he had lost her attention. He called to her, "You will wait? You will be here? You will not run away?"

She looked at him stupidly, and I was surprised when she answered him. "I'm not going anywhere," she said in her dreadful voice.

Leo spoke up. "It is snowing out, Michel," he said.

Michel grinned at him. "Ten minutes!" he cried, and vanished.

"That Michel is a great joker, he thinks," Leo said.

"You call him a joker?" Mrs. Dolan said loudly. "Some joker, I'll say." But Leo ignored her, and she began rummaging in the huge leather handbag that was on the table beside her, propped against the wall. She took out a mirror and moved it about while she examined herself, her eyes, her mouth, and her earrings, and then she took out a dark red lipstick and smeared it thickly back and forth on her mouth, and afterward, while she was putting the lipstick away, she pressed her lips closely together. With her little finger, she rubbed the lipstick smooth, and tidied the corners of her mouth, and when she had finished she cleaned the color from her finger with her dinner napkin and took a tiny sip of her brandy, and glanced at Michel's brandy, which he had not touched. After that she sat gazing at the stained tablecloth, and from time to time she pursed her lips thoughtfully at something she saw there.

There are three young girls who have been coming to the Étoile for their Sunday dinner the last few months. They share an apartment on Forty-seventh, and they all work as secretaries. Lately one of them, Betty, has been dropping in alone, early in the evening, before ten o'clock. She never comes for dinner, and she never stays after Mees Katie has gone home. Betty is about five foot two, a brown-haired, blue-eyed, round-faced girl with a pretty figure and a pretty smile, who obviously enjoys being a friendly little child among the grown-ups. Her winter coat is dark green imitation fur, and she wears sweaters and skirts most of the time, schoolgirl clothes. She walks in timidly, as though she is not quite sure of her welcome, and then she sits up at the end of the bar and asks for a Perrier water and drinks it very slowly, making it last. She dreams of being an actress, but I think the part she dreams of playing is the part she plays as she sits up at the bar of the Étoile, and sips her Perrier and stares wonderingly all about her. The Étoile reminds her of a waterfront café she saw once in a movie that starred Jean Gabin and that I think has now been remade to include a very young unknown actress named Betty who sits at the bar with a Perrier stealing the show, although she has nothing to say and nothing to do except be herself, poor and alone and very young. She always puts down a dollar to pay for her Perrier, but Leo seldom takes the money, and if he does take it he gives her another Perrier on the house. Once or twice Betty has sat at Mees Katie's table and helped her listen to Michel. She finds Michel very entertaining. Tonight she walked in shortly after Michel ran out. She came in expectantly, almost laughing, walking out of the snowstorm as though she were walking into a party. She pulled off her scarf, shaking the snow from it, and as she began to unbutton her coat she looked around for Mees Katie. Leo had come to the end of the bar and was watching her, smiling.

"Where is everybody?" she cried. "Where's Mees Katie?" She sat up at the bar and Leo poured a Perrier for her.

"I'm celebrating, Leo," she said. "This is my very first snowstorm. The office let us off at three o'clock, and I walked round and round and round, all by myself, celebrating all by myself, and then I went home and made dinner, but I got so excited thinking about the snow I just had to come out again and thought I'd come here and see Mees Katie. I thought there'd be thousands of people here. Oh, I wish it would snow for weeks and weeks. I just can't bear for it to end. But after today I'm beginning to think New Yorkers never really enjoy themselves. Nobody seemed to be really enjoying the snow. I never saw such people. All they could think about was getting home. Wouldn't you think a storm like this would wake everybody up? But all it does is put them to sleep. Such people."

"It does not put me to sleep, Betty," Leo said in his deliberate way.

"I wish it would snow for a year," Betty said.

"It will take something warmer than a snowstorm to put me to sleep, Betty," Leo said.

Betty laughed self-consciously and looked at Mrs. Dolan.

"Michel is a bad boy tonight, Betty," Leo said, and he also looked at Mrs. Dolan. "He told this lady he'd be back in ten minutes and it has been twenty."

"Nearly half an hour," Mrs. Dolan said disgustedly. "Nearly half an hour."

"He'll be back," Betty said. "Michel always comes back, doesn't he, Leo?"

"Oh, yes, Michel comes back," Leo said, and he put his hand on Betty's arm and leaned far across the bar and began whispering in her ear, or tried to begin whispering in her ear, because at the touch of his face against her hair she pulled roughly away and looked at him with such distaste that he stepped back. Then he went to the cash register and opened the drawer and began looking in at the money and pretending to count it. He was furious. If she had spent ten years pondering a way to express disgust, she could not have found a better way. Even if they had been alone, Leo would never

257

have forgiven her, but the three lingering men were watching, and so was Mrs. Dolan.

Betty sat alone for a minute and then she took her Perrier and slipped down from her stool and walked over to Mrs. Dolan. Betty looked flustered, but she was smiling.

"May I sit down?" she asked Mrs. Dolan.

"Oh, please do," Mrs. Dolan said.

Betty sat down in Michel's chair, diagonally across from Mrs. Dolan. "Michel will be back soon," she said. "He always comes back."

"He left me sitting here like this," Mrs. Dolan said.

"Michel is really a sweet kind person when you get to know him," Betty said. "He's a darling, really."

Leo called out, "Miss Betty, you owe me sixty cents."

Betty looked over at him in surprise.

"You forgot to pay for your drink, little girl," he said, smiling, and he waved at Robert the waiter. Robert took Betty's dollar to the bar and brought her back her change. She had gotten very red.

"He needn't have shouted at me," she said to Mrs. Dolan. Mrs. Dolan said nothing.

Betty began talking. "This is the first big snow I've ever seen," she said. "I thought it would be like New Year's Eve here tonight, or something. When they first told us we were getting off early from the office I felt it was like a party or something, but then after I walked around a bit it seemed more like a disaster, and I kept wanting to get into the spirit of the thing. I felt very left out all day. I kept walking around."

When she fell silent, Mrs. Dolan still continued to watch her, but she said nothing. She had nothing to say, and nothing to give except her silence, and so she said nothing, and made no reply, and they sat without speaking until the silence they shared strengthened and expanded to enclose them both.

Not long ago I saw a photograph in the evening paper of a crowd of circus elephants gathered around a dying elephant, Flora, who had fallen and was lying on her side on the ground. The elephant closest to Flora was trying to revive her by blowing air into her open mouth with his trunk. The newspaper story said that all the elephants in the troupe took turns trying to save their dying comrade, and the story finished by saying, "This practice is instinctive among pachyderms."

But that practice, instinctive among pachyderms, that determination to win even a respite from death, is no more instinctive than the silence was that grew and turned into a lifeline between Betty and Mrs. Dolan, because their silence arose from a shame so deep that it was peace for them to sit in its silence, and to listen to this silence, which was only the silence of their own nature, of all they had in common. Mrs. Dolan's face grew ruminative, and Betty's profile suggested she was lost in recollections that were not unhappy.

Michel walked in, a snowman. He must have been standing out in the open, or walking, ever since he left the restaurant. He stood still just inside the door and banged the palms of his gloves together and sent a fond glance at Mrs. Dolan and at Betty, who had turned to watch him. Michel was very pleased with the entrance he had made, and he looked as though he would like to go out and come back in again.

"Don Juan, he thinks he is," Mrs. Dolan growled.

Michel moved to the coatrack and began unwrapping himself. He was very slow about it, and all the time he was pulling off his gloves, and unwinding his scarf, and shaking his fur hat, he faced the room as though he faced a full-length mirror, and he smiled, watching all of us, but not as he would watch the mirror. At last he stood revealed in his navy-blue-and-brown striped suit and his rings and his crinkly black hair and his bow tie, and he strolled back to his table and sat down beside Mrs. Dolan, and smiled sweetly at Betty, and picked up the cognac that had been waiting for him. When I left they were all ordering more drinks, and Mrs. Dolan had decided to switch to crème de menthe. The old Frenchman came out of his reverie and began looking unpleasantly at the three men who were chattering in English at the end of the bar, and I knew he was becoming happier. I paid my bill and left.

The self-service elevator at my hotel shivered piteously when I stepped into it, and hesitated before starting its painful ascent to the high floor where I live. That is as usual. The tiny, boxy elevator is as alien to this elegantly made hotel as the blue neon sign that winks on and off in front. A marble staircase winds all the way up through the heart of the building, and decorated windows over every stairwell still filter and color the light as they have done for more than sixty years. The fireplaces have all been blocked up long ago, but the rooms are very big and the ceilings are high and the walls shut out all sound. I looked again through the windows that give me my view of Broadway. Just below me, on Forty-eighth Street, on both sides of the street, a few small houses huddle together in the shadows, and from their low level other, newer walls rise higher and higher to the south and east, but tonight the big buildings, the giants that carry Manhattan's monumental broken skyline, were lost in fog. I could see only the little roofs below me and their neighbors immediately beyond, all of them under smooth snow that shaped them in the dark into separate triangles and squares and rectangles and slopes. The snow on Forty-eighth Street was rumpled, but there was no one in the street and the open parking lot was empty. To the right, Broadway was still lighted up as high as the sky, but the lights shone weakly, smothered in fog, except for the dazzling band of color that runs around the Latin Quarter, a few houses away from me. I pushed open the window. The cold air rushed in, but no noise. What sound there was was drugged, as though I were a hundred floors above the street instead of only eleven floors. The wind had died down, and the snow fell thickly, falling in large, calm flakes.

JAMES BALDWIN

SONNY'S BLUES

I READ ABOUT it in the paper, in the subway, on my way to work. I read it, and I couldn't believe it, and I read it again. Then perhaps I just stared at it, at the newsprint spelling out his name, spelling out the story. I stared at it in the swinging lights of the subway car, and in the faces and bodies of the people, and in my own face, trapped in the darkness which roared outside.

It was not to be believed and I kept telling myself that, as I walked from the subway station to the high school. And at the same time I couldn't doubt it. I was scared, scared for Sonny. He became real to me again. A great block of ice got settled in my belly and kept melting there slowly all day long, while I taught my classes algebra. It was a special kind of ice. It kept melting, sending trickles of ice water all up and down my veins, but it never got less. Sometimes it hardened and seemed to expand until I felt my guts were going to come spilling out or that I was going to choke or scream. This would always be at a moment when I was remembering some specific thing Sonny had once said or done.

When he was about as old as the boys in my classes his face had been bright and open, there was a lot of copper in it; and he'd had wonderfully direct brown eyes, and great gentleness and privacy. I wondered what he looked like now. He had been picked up, the evening before, in a raid on an apartment downtown, for peddling and using heroin.

I couldn't believe it: but what I mean by that is that I

265

couldn't find any room for it anywhere inside me. I had kept it outside me for a long time. I hadn't wanted to know. I had had suspicions, but I didn't name them, I kept putting them away. I told myself that Sonny was wild, but he wasn't crazy. And he'd always been a good boy, he hadn't ever turned hard or evil or disrespectful, the way kids can, so quick, so quick, especially in Harlem. I didn't want to believe that I'd ever see my brother going down, coming to nothing, all that light in his face gone out, in the condition I'd already seen so many others. Yet it had happened and here I was, talking about algebra to a lot of boys who might, every one of them for all I knew, be popping off needles every time they went to the head. Maybe it did more for them than algebra could.

I was sure that the first time Sonny had ever had horse, he couldn't have been much older than these boys were now. These boys, now, were living as we'd been living then, they were growing up with a rush and their heads bumped abruptly against the low ceiling of their actual possibilities. They were filled with rage. All they really knew were two darknesses, the darkness of their lives, which was now closing in on them, and the darkness of the movies, which had blinded them to that other darkness, and in which they now, vindictively, dreamed, at once more together than they were at any other time, and more alone.

When the last bell rang, the last class ended, I let out my breath. It seemed I'd been holding it for all that time. My clothes were wet—I may have looked as though I'd been sitting in a steam bath, all dressed up, all afternoon. I sat alone in the classroom a long time. I listened to the boys outside, downstairs, shouting and cursing and laughing. Their laughter struck me for perhaps the first time. It was not the joyous laughter which—God knows why—one associates with children. It was mocking and insular, its intent was to denigrate. It was disenchanted, and in this, also, lay the authority of their curses. Perhaps I was listening to them because I was thinking about my brother and in them I heard my brother. And myself.

One boy was whistling a tune, at once very complicated and very simple, it seemed to be pouring out of him as though he were a bird, and it sounded very cool and moving through all that harsh, bright air, only just holding its own through all those other sounds.

I stood up and walked over to the window and looked down into the courtyard. It was the beginning of the spring and the sap was rising in the boys. A teacher passed through them every now and again, quickly, as though he or she couldn't wait to get out of that courtyard, to get those boys out of their sight and off their minds. I started collecting my stuff. I thought I'd better get home and talk to Isabel.

The courtyard was almost deserted by the time I got downstairs. I saw this boy standing in the shadow of a door-way, looking just like Sonny. I almost called his name. Then I saw that it wasn't Sonny, but somebody we used to know, a boy from around our block. He'd been Sonny's friend. He'd never been mine, having been too young for me, and, any-way, I'd never liked him. And now, even though he was a grown-up man, he still hung around that block, still spent hours on the street corners, was always high and raggy. I used to run into him from time to time and he'd often work around to asking me for a quarter or fifty cents. He always had some real good excuse, too, and I always gave it to him, I don't know why.

But now, abruptly, I hated him. I couldn't stand the way he looked at me, partly like a dog, partly like a cunning child. I wanted to ask him what the hell he was doing in the school courtyard.

He sort of shuffled over to me, and he said, "I see you got the papers. So you already know about it."

"You mean about Sonny? Yes, I already know about it. How come they didn't get you?"

He grinned. It made him repulsive and it also brought to mind what he'd looked like as a kid. "I wasn't there. I stay away from them people."

"Good for you." I offered him a cigarette and I watched him though the smoke. "You come all the way down here just to tell me about Sonny?"

"That's right." He was sort of shaking his head and his eyes looked strange, as though they were about to cross. The bright sun deadened his damp dark brown skin and it made his eyes look yellow and showed up the dirt in his kinked hair. He smelled funky. I moved a little away from him and I said, "Well, thanks. But I already know about it and I got to get home."

"I'll walk you a little ways," he said. We started walking. There were a couple of kids still loitering in the courtyard and one of them said good night to me and looked strangely at the boy beside me.

"What're you going to do?" he asked me. "I mean, about Sonny?"

"Look. I haven't seen Sonny for over a year, I'm not sure I'm going to do anything. Anyway, what the hell *can* I do?"

"That's right," he said quickly, "ain't nothing you can do. Can't much help old Sonny no more, I guess."

It was what I was thinking and so it seemed to me he had no right to say it.

"I'm surprised at Sonny, though," he went on—he had a funny way of talking, he looked straight ahead as though he were talking to himself—"I thought Sonny was a smart boy, I thought he was too smart to get hung."

"I guess he thought so too," I said sharply, "and that's how he got hung. And now about you? You're pretty goddamn smart, I bet."

Then he looked directly at me, just for a minute. "I ain't smart," he said. "If I was smart, I'd have reached for a pistol a long time ago."

"Look. Don't tell *me* your sad story, if it was up to me, I'd give you one." Then I felt guilty—guilty, probably, for never having supposed that the poor bastard *had* a story of his own, much less a sad one, and I asked, quickly, "What's going to happen to him now?"

He didn't answer this. He was off by himself some place. "Funny thing," he said, and from his tone we might have been discussing the quickest way to get to Brooklyn, "when I saw the papers this morning, the first thing I asked myself was if I had anything to do with it. I felt sort of responsible."

I began to listen more carefully. The subway station was on the corner, just before us, and I stopped. He stopped, too. We were in front of a bar and he ducked slightly, peering in, but whoever he was looking for didn't seem to be there. The juke box was blasting away with something black and bouncy and I half watched the barmaid as she danced her way from the juke box to her place behind the bar. And I watched her face as she laughingly responded to something someone said to her, still keeping time to the music. When she smiled one saw the little girl, one sensed the doomed, still-struggling woman beneath the battered face of the semi-whore.

"I never *give* Sonny nothing," the boy said finally, "but a long time ago I come to school high and Sonny asked me how it felt." He paused, I couldn't bear to watch him, I watched the barmaid, and I listened to the music which seemed to be causing the pavement to shake. "I told him it felt great." The music stopped, the barmaid paused and watched the juke box until the music began again. "It did."

All this was carrying me some place I didn't want to go. I certainly didn't want to know how it felt. It filled everything, the people, the houses, the music, the dark, quicksilver barmaid, with menace; and this menace was their reality.

"What's going to happen to him now?" I asked again.

"They'll send him away some place and they'll try to cure him." He shook his head. "Maybe he'll even think he's kicked the habit. Then they'll let him loose"—he gestured, throwing his cigarette into the gutter. "That's all."

"What do you mean, that's *all*?"

But I knew what he meant.

"I *mean*, that's *all*." He turned his head and looked at me, pulling down the corners of his mouth. "Don't you know what I mean?" he asked, softly.

"How the hell *would* I know what you mean?" I almost whispered it, I don't know why.

"That's right," he said to the air, "how would *he* know what I mean?" He turned toward me again, patient and calm, and yet I somehow felt him shaking, shaking as though he were going to fall apart. I felt that ice in my guts again, the dread I'd felt all afternoon; and again I watched the barmaid, moving about the bar, washing glasses, and singing. "Listen. They'll let him out and then it'll just start all over again. That's what I mean."

"You mean—they'll let him out. And then he'll just start working his way back in again. You mean he'll never kick the habit. Is that what you mean?"

"That's right," he said, cheerfully. "*You* see what I mean."

"Tell me," I said at last, "why does he want to die? He must want to die, he's killing himself, why does he want to die?"

He looked at me in surprise. He licked his lips. "He don't

270

want to die. He wants to live. Don't nobody want to die, ever."

Then I wanted to ask him—too many things. He could not have answered, or if he had, I could not have borne the answers. I started walking. "Well, I guess it's none of my business."

"It's going to be rough on old Sonny," he said. We reached the subway station. "This is your station?" he asked. I nodded. I took one step down. "Damn!" he said, suddenly. I looked up at him. He grinned again. "Damn it if I didn't leave all my money home. You ain't got a dollar on you, have you? Just for a couple of days, is all."

All at once something inside gave and threatened to come pouring out of me. I didn't hate him any more. I felt that in another moment I'd start crying like a child.

"Sure," I said. "Don't sweat." I looked in my wallet and didn't have a dollar, I only had a five. "Here," I said. "That hold you?"

He didn't look at it—he didn't want to look at it. A terrible, closed look came over his face, as though he were keeping the number on the bill a secret from him and me. "Thanks," he said, and now he was dying to see me go. "Don't worry about Sonny. Maybe I'll write him or something."

"Sure," I said. "You do that. So long."

"Be seeing you," he said. I went on down the steps.

And I didn't write Sonny or send him anything for a long time. When I finally did, it was just after my little girl died, he wrote me back a letter which made me feel like a bastard.

Here's what he said:

> Dear brother,
> You don't know how much I needed to hear from you.
> I wanted to write you many a time but I dug how much

I must have hurt you and so I didn't write. But now I feel like a man who's been trying to climb up out of some deep, real deep and funky hole and just saw the sun up there, outside. I got to get outside.

I can't tell you much about how I got here. I mean I don't know how to tell you. I guess I was afraid of something or I was trying to escape from something and you know I have never been very strong in the head (smile). I'm glad Mama and Daddy are dead and can't see what's happened to their son and I swear if I'd known what I was doing I would never have hurt you so, you and a lot of other fine people who were nice to me and who believed in me.

I don't want you to think it had anything to do with me being a musician. It's more than that. Or maybe less than that. I can't get anything straight in my head down here and I try not to think about what's going to happen to me when I get outside again. Sometime I think I'm going to flip and *never* get outside and sometime I think I'll come straight back. I tell you one thing, though, I'd rather blow my brains out than go through this again. But that's what they all say, so they tell me. If I tell you when I'm coming to New York and if you could meet me, I sure would appreciate it. Give my love to Isabel and the kids and I was sure sorry to hear about little Gracie. I wish I could be like Mama and say the Lord's will be done, but I don't know it seems to me that trouble is the one thing that never does get stopped and I don't know what good it does to blame it on the Lord. But maybe it does some good if you believe it.

Your brother,
Sonny

Then I kept in constant touch with him and I sent him whatever I could and I went to meet him when he came back to New York. When I saw him many things I thought I had forgotten came flooding back to me. This was because I had begun, finally, to wonder about Sonny, about the life that Sonny lived inside. This life, whatever it was, had made him older and thinner and it had deepened the distant stillness in which he had always moved. He looked very unlike my baby brother. Yet, when he smiled, when we shook hands, the baby brother I'd never known looked out from the depths of his private life, like an animal waiting to be coaxed into the light.

"How you been keeping?" he asked me.

"All right. And you?"

"Just fine." He was smiling all over his face. "It's good to see you again."

"It's good to see you."

The seven years' difference in our ages lay between us like a chasm: I wondered if these years would ever operate between us as a bridge. I was remembering, and it made it hard to catch my breath, that I had been there when he was born; and I had heard the first words he had ever spoken. When he started to walk, he walked from our mother straight to me. I caught him just before he fell when he took the first steps he ever took in this world.

"How's Isabel?"

"Just fine. She's dying to see you."

"And the boys?"

"They're fine, too. They're anxious to see their uncle."

"Oh, come on. You know they don't remember me."

"Are you kidding? Of course they remember you."

He grinned again. We got into a taxi. We had a lot to say to each other, far too much to know how to begin.

As the taxi began to move, I asked, "You still want to go to India?"

He laughed. "You still remember that. Hell, no. This place is Indian enough for me."

"It used to belong to them," I said.

And he laughed again. "They damn sure knew what they were doing when they got rid of it."

Years ago, when he was around fourteen, he'd been all hipped on the idea of going to India. He read books about people sitting on rocks, naked, in all kinds of weather, but mostly bad, naturally, and walking barefoot through hot coals and arriving at wisdom. I used to say that it sounded to me as though they were getting away from wisdom as fast as they could. I think he sort of looked down on me for that.

"Do you mind," he asked, "if we have the driver drive alongside the park? On the west side—I haven't seen the city in so long."

"Of course not," I said. I was afraid that I might sound as though I were humoring him, but I hoped he wouldn't take it that way.

So we drove along, between the green of the park and the stony, lifeless elegance of hotels and apartment buildings, toward the vivid, killing streets of our childhood. These streets hadn't changed, though housing projects jutted up out of them now like rocks in the middle of a boiling sea. Most of the houses in which we had grown up had vanished, as had the stores from which we had stolen, the basements in which we had first tried sex, the rooftops from which we had hurled tin cans and bricks. But houses exactly like the houses of our past yet dominated the landscape, boys exactly like the boys we once had been found themselves smothering in these houses, came down into the streets for light and air and found themselves encircled by disaster. Some escaped the trap, most didn't. Those who got out always left something of themselves behind, as some animals amputate a leg and leave it in the trap. It might be said, perhaps, that I had escaped, after all, I was a school teacher; or that Sonny had, he hadn't lived in Harlem for years. Yet, as the cab moved uptown through streets which seemed, with a rush, to darken with dark people, and as I covertly studied Sonny's face, it came to me that what we both were seeking through our separate cab windows was that part of ourselves which had been left behind. It's always at the hour of trouble and confrontation that the missing member aches.

We hit 110th Street and started rolling up Lenox Avenue. And I'd known this avenue all my life, but it seemed to me again, as it had seemed on the day I'd first heard about Sonny's trouble, filled with a hidden menace which was its very breath of life.

"We almost there," said Sonny.

"Almost." We were both too nervous to say anything more.

We live in a housing project. It hasn't been up long. A few days after it was up it seemed uninhabitably new, now, of course, it's already rundown. It looks like a parody of the good, clean, faceless life—God knows the people who live in it do their best to make it a parody. The beat-looking grass lying around isn't enough to make their lives green, the hedges will never hold out the streets, and they know it. The big windows fool no one, they aren't big enough to make space out of no space. They don't bother with the windows, they watch the TV screen instead. The playground is most popular with the children who don't play at jacks, or skip rope, or roller skate, or swing, and they can be found in it after dark. We moved in partly because it's not too far from where I teach, and partly for the kids; but it's really just like the houses in which Sonny and I grew up. The same things happen, they'll have the same things to remember. The moment Sonny and I started into the house I had the feeling that I was simply bringing him back into the danger he had almost died trying to escape.

Sonny has never been talkative. So I don't know why I was sure he'd be dying to talk to me when supper was over the first night. Everything went fine, the oldest boy remembered him, and the youngest boy liked him, and Sonny had remembered to bring something for each of them; and Isabel, who is really much nicer than I am, more open and giving, had gone to a lot of trouble about dinner and was genuinely glad to see him. And she's always been able to tease Sonny in a way that I haven't. It was nice to see her face so vivid again and to hear her laugh and watch her make Sonny laugh. She wasn't, or, anyway, she didn't seem to be, at all uneasy or embarrassed. She chatted as though there were no subject which had to be avoided and she got Sonny past his first, faint stiffness. And thank God she was there, for I was filled with that icy dread again. Everything I did seemed awkward to me, and everything I said sounded freighted with hidden meaning. I was trying to remember everything I'd heard about dope addiction and I couldn't help watching Sonny for signs. I wasn't doing it out of malice. I was trying to find out something about my brother. I was dying to hear him tell me he was safe.

"Safe!" my father grunted, whenever Mama suggested trying to move to a neighborhood which might be safer for children. "Safe, hell! Ain't no place safe for kids, nor nobody."

He always went on like this, but he wasn't, ever, really as bad as he sounded, not even on week ends, when he got drunk. As a matter of fact, he was always on the lookout for "something a little better," but he died before he found it. He died suddenly, during a drunken week end in the middle of the war, when Sonny was fifteen. He and Sonny hadn't ever got on too well. And this was partly because Sonny was the apple of his father's eye. It was because he loved Sonny so much and was frightened for him, that he was always fighting with him. It doesn't do any good to fight with Sonny. Sonny just moves back, inside himself, where he can't be reached. But the principal reason that they never hit it off is that they were so much alike. Daddy was big and rough and loud-talking, just the opposite of Sonny, but they both had—that same privacy.

Mama tried to tell me something about this, just after Daddy died. I was home on leave from the army.

This was the last time I ever saw my mother alive. Just the same, this picture gets all mixed up in my mind with pictures I had of her when she was younger. The way I always see her is the way she used to be on a Sunday afternoon, say, when the old folks were talking after the big Sunday dinner. I always see her wearing pale blue. She'd be sitting on the sofa. And my father would be sitting in the easy chair, not far from her. And the living-room would be full of church folks and relatives. There they sit, in chairs all around the living-room, and the night is creeping up outside, but nobody knows it yet. You can see the darkness growing against the window-panes and you hear the street noises every now and again, or maybe the jangling beat of a tambourine from one of the churches close by, but it's real quiet in the room. For a moment nobody's talking, but every face looks darkening, like the sky outside. And my mother rocks a little from the waist, and my father's eyes are closed. Everyone is looking at something a child can't see. For a minute they've forgotten the children. Maybe a kid is lying on the rug, half asleep. Maybe somebody's got a kid in his lap and is absent-mindedly stroking the kid's head. Maybe there's a kid, quiet and big-eyed, curled up in a big chair in the corner. The silence, the darkness coming, and the darkness in the faces frightens the child obscurely. He hopes that the hand which strokes his forehead will never stop—will never die. He hopes that there will never come a time when the old folks won't be sitting around the living-room, talking about where they've come from, and what they've seen, and what's happened to them and their kinfolk.

But something deep and watchful in the child knows that this is bound to end, is already ending. In a moment someone will get up and turn on the light. Then the old folks will remember the children and they won't talk any more that day. And when light fills the room, the child is filled with darkness. He knows that every time this happens he's moved just a little closer to that darkness outside. The darkness outside is what the old folks have been talking about. It's what they've come from. It's what they endure. The child knows that they won't talk any more because if he knows too much about what's happened to *them*, he'll know too much too soon, about what's going to happen to *him*.

The last time I talked to my mother, I remember I was restless. I wanted to get out and see Isabel. We weren't married then and we had a lot to straighten out between us.

There Mama sat, in black, by the window. She was humming an old church song, *Lord, you brought me from a long ways off*. Sonny was out somewhere. Mama kept watching the streets.

"I don't know," she said, "if I'll ever see you again, after you go off from here. But I hope you'll remember the things I tried to teach you."

"Don't talk like that," I said, and smiled. "You'll be here a long time yet."

She smiled, too, but she said nothing. She was quiet for

278

a long time. And I said, "Mama, don't you worry about nothing. I'll be writing all the time, and you be getting the checks...."

"I want to talk to you about your brother," she said, suddenly. "If anything happens to me he ain't going to have nobody to look out for him."

"Mama," I said, "ain't nothing going to happen to you *or* Sonny. Sonny's all right. He's a good boy and he's got good sense."

"It ain't a question of his being a good boy," Mama said, "nor of his having good sense. It ain't only the bad ones, nor yet the dumb ones that gets sucked under." She stopped, looking at me. "Your Daddy once had a brother," she said, and she smiled in a way that made me feel she was in pain. "You didn't never know that, did you?"

"No," I said, "I never knew that," and I watched her face.

"Oh, yes," she said, "your Daddy had a brother." She looked out of the window again. "I know you never saw your Daddy cry. But *I* did—many a time, through all these years."

I asked her, "What happened to his brother? How come nobody's ever talked about him?"

This was the first time I ever saw my mother look old.

"His brother got killed," she said, "when he was just a little younger than you are now. I knew him. He was a fine boy. He was maybe a little full of the devil, but he didn't mean nobody no harm."

Then she stopped and the room was silent, exactly as it had sometimes been on those Sunday afternoons. Mama kept looking out into the streets.

"He used to have a job in the mill," she said, "and, like all young folks, he just liked to perform on Saturday nights. Saturday nights, him and your father would drift around to different places, go to dances and things like that, or just sit

279

around with people they knew, and your father's brother would sing, he had a fine voice, and play along with himself on his guitar. Well, this particular Saturday night, him and your father was coming home from some place, and they were both a little drunk and there was a moon that night, it was bright like day. Your father's brother was feeling kind of good, and he was whistling to himself, and he had his guitar slung over his shoulder. They was coming down a hill and beneath them was a road that turned off from the highway. Well, your father's brother, being always kind of frisky, decided to run down this hill, and he did, with that guitar banging and clanging behind him, and he ran across the road, and he was making water behind a tree. And your father was sort of amused at him and he was still coming down the hill, kind of slow. Then he heard a car motor and that same minute his brother stepped from behind the tree, into the road, in the moonlight. And he started to cross the road. And your father started to run down the hill, he says he don't know why. This car was full of white men. They was all drunk, and when they seen your father's brother they let out a great whoop and holler and they aimed the car straight at him. They was having fun, they just wanted to scare him, the way they do sometimes, you know. But they was drunk. And I guess the boy, being drunk, too, and scared, kind of lost his head. By the time he jumped it was too late. Your father says he heard his brother scream when the car rolled over him, and he heard the wood of that guitar when it give, and he heard them strings go flying, and he heard them white men shouting, and the car kept on a-going and it ain't stopped till this day. And, time your father got down the hill, his brother weren't nothing but blood and pulp."

Tears were gleaming on my mother's face. There wasn't anything I could say.

"He never mentioned it," she said, "because I never let him mention it before you children. Your Daddy was like a crazy man that night and for many a night thereafter. He says he never in his life seen anything as dark as that road after the lights of that car had gone away. Weren't nothing, weren't nobody on that road, just your Daddy and his brother and that busted guitar. Oh, yes. Your Daddy never did really get right again. Till the day he died he weren't sure but that every white man he saw was the man that killed his brother."

She stopped and took out her hankerchief and dried her eyes and looked at me.

"I ain't telling you all this," she said, "to make you scared or bitter or to make you hate nobody. I'm telling you this because you got a brother. And the world ain't changed."

I guess I didn't want to believe this. I guess she saw this in my face. She turned away from me, toward the window again, searching those streets.

"But I praise my Redeemer," she said at last, "that He called your Daddy home before me. I ain't saying it to throw no flowers at myself, but, I declare, it keeps me from feeling too cast down to know I helped your father get safely through this world. Your father always acted like he was the roughest, strongest man on earth. And everybody took him to be like that. But if he hadn't had *me* there—to see his tears!"

She was crying again. Still, I couldn't move. I said, "Lord, Lord, Mama, I didn't know it was like that."

"Oh, honey," she said, "there's a lot that you don't know. But you are going to find it out." She stood up from the window and came over to me. "You got to hold on to your brother," she said, "and don't let him fall, no matter what it looks like is happening to him and no matter how evil you gets with him. You going to be evil with him many a time. But don't you forget what I told you, you hear?"

"I won't forget," I said. "Don't you worry, I won't forget. I won't let nothing happen to Sonny."

My mother smiled as though she were amused at something she saw in my face. Then, "You may not be able to stop nothing from happening. But you got to let him know you's *there*."

Two days later I was married, and then I was gone. And I had a lot of things on my mind and I pretty well forgot my promise to Mama until I got shipped home on a special furlough for her funeral.

And, after the funeral, with just Sonny and me alone in the empty kitchen, I tried to find out something about him.

"What do you want to do?" I asked him.

"I'm going to be a musician," he said.

For he had graduated, in the time I had been away, from dancing to the juke box to finding out who was playing what, and what they were doing with it, and he had bought himself a set of drums.

"You mean, you want to be a drummer?" I somehow had the feeling that being a drummer might be all right for other people but not for my brother Sonny.

"I don't think," he said, looking at me very gravely, "that I'll ever be a good drummer. But I think I can play a piano."

I frowned. I'd never played the role of the older brother quite so seriously before, had scarcely ever, in fact, *asked* Sonny a damn thing. I sensed myself in the presence of something I didn't really know how to handle, didn't understand. So I made my frown a little deeper as I asked: "What kind of musician do you want to be?"

He grinned. "How many kinds do you think there are?"

"Be *serious*," I said.

He laughed, throwing his head back, and then looked at me. "I *am* serious."

"Well, then, for Christ's sake, stop kidding around and answer a serious question. I mean, do you want to be a concert pianist, you want to play classical music and all that, or—or what?" Long before I finished he was laughing again. "For Christ's *sake*, Sonny!"

He sobered, but with difficulty. "I'm sorry. But you sound so—*scared*!" and he was off again.

"Well, you may think it's funny now, baby, but it's not going to be so funny when you have to make your living at it, let me tell you *that*." I was furious because I knew he was laughing at me and I didn't know why.

"No," he said, very sober now, and afraid, perhaps, that he'd hurt me, "I don't want to be a classical pianist. That isn't what interests me. I mean"—he paused, looking hard at me, as though his eyes would help me to understand, and then gestured helplessly, as though perhaps his hand would help—"I mean, I'll have a lot of studying to do, and I'll have to study *everything*, but, I mean, I want to play *with*—jazz musicians." He stopped. "I want to play jazz," he said.

Well, the word had never before sounded as heavy, as real, as it sounded that afternoon in Sonny's mouth. I just looked at him and I was probably frowning a real frown by this time. I simply couldn't see why on earth he'd want to spend his time hanging around nightclubs, clowning around on bandstands, while people pushed each other around a dance floor. It seemed—beneath him, somehow. I had never thought about it before, had never been forced to, but I suppose I had always put jazz musicians in a class with what Daddy called "good-time people."

"Are you *serious*?"

"Hell, *yes*, I'm serious."

He looked more helpless than ever, and annoyed, and deeply hurt.

I suggested, helpfully: "You mean—like Louis Armstrong?"

His face closed as though I'd struck him. "No. I'm not talking about none of that old-time, down home crap."

"Well, look, Sonny, I'm sorry, don't get mad. I just don't altogether get it, that's all. Name somebody—you know, a jazz musician you admire."

"Bird."

"Who?"

"Bird! Charlie Parker! Don't they teach you nothing in the goddamn army?"

I lit a cigarette. I was surprised and then a little amused to discover that I was trembling. "I've been out of touch," I said. "You'll have to be patient with me. Now. Who's this Parker character?"

"He's just one of the greatest jazz musicians alive," said Sonny, sullenly, his hands in his pockets, his back to me. "Maybe *the* greatest," he added, bitterly, "that's probably why *you* never heard of him."

"All right," I said, "I'm ignorant. I'm sorry. I'll go out and buy all the cat's records right away, all right?"

"It don't," said Sonny, with dignity, "make any difference to me. I don't care what you listen to. Don't do me no favors."

I was beginning to realize that I'd never seen him so upset before. With another part of my mind I was thinking that this would probably turn out to be one of those things kids go through and that I shouldn't make it seem important by pushing it too hard. Still, I didn't think it would do any harm to ask: "Doesn't all this take a lot of time? Can you make a living at it?"

He turned back to me and half leaned, half sat, on the kitchen table. "Everything takes time," he said, "and—well, yes, sure, I can make a living at it. But what I don't seem to be able to make you understand is that it's the only thing I want to do."

"Well, Sonny," I said, gently, "you know people can't always do exactly what they *want* to do—"

"*No*, I don't know that," said Sonny, surprising me. "I think people *ought* to do what they want to do, what else are they alive for?"

"You getting to be a big boy," I said desperately, "it's time you started thinking about your future."

"I'm thinking about my future," said Sonny, grimly. "I think about it all the time."

I gave up. I decided, if he didn't change his mind, that we could always talk about it later. "In the meantime," I said, "you got to finish school." We had already decided that he'd have to move in with Isabel and her folks. I knew this wasn't the ideal arrangement because Isabel's folks are inclined to be dicty and they hadn't especially wanted Isabel to marry me. But I didn't know what else to do. "And we have to get you fixed up at Isabel's."

There was a long silence. He moved from the kitchen table to the window. "That's a terrible idea. You know it yourself."

"Do you have a *better* idea?"

He just walked up and down the kitchen for a minute. He was as tall as I was. He had started to shave. I suddenly had the feeling that I didn't know him at all.

He stopped at the kitchen table and picked up my cigarettes. Looking at me with a kind of mocking, amused defiance, he put one between his lips. "You mind?"

"You smoking already?"

He lit the cigarette and nodded, watching me through

the smoke. "I just wanted to see if I'd have the courage to smoke in front of you." He grinned and blew a great cloud of smoke to the ceiling. "It was easy." He looked at my face. "Come on, now. I bet you was smoking at my age, tell the truth."

I didn't say anything but the truth was on my face, and he laughed. But now there was something very strained in his laugh. "Sure. And I bet that ain't all you was doing."

He was frightening me a little. "Cut the crap," I said. "We already decided that you was going to go and live at Isabel's. Now what's got into you all of a sudden?"

"*You* decided it," he pointed out. "*I* didn't decide nothing." He stopped in front of me, leaning against the stove, arms loosely folded. "Look, brother. I don't want to stay in Harlem no more, I really don't." He was very earnest. He looked at me, then over toward the kitchen window. There was something in his eyes I'd never seen before, some thoughtfulness, some worry all his own. He rubbed the muscle of one arm. "It's time I was getting out of here."

"Where do you want to *go*, Sonny?"

"I want to join the army. Or the navy, I don't care. If I say I'm old enough, they'll believe me."

Then I got mad. It was because I was so scared. "You must be crazy. You goddamn fool, what the hell do you want to go and join the *army* for?"

"I just told you. To get out of Harlem."

"Sonny, you haven't even finished *school*. And if you really want to be a musician, how do you expect to study if you're in the *army*?"

He looked at me, trapped, and in anguish. "There's ways. I might be able to work out some kind of deal. Anyway, I'll have the G.I. Bill when I come out."

"*If* you come out." We stared at each other. "Sonny,

please. Be reasonable. I know the setup is far from perfect. But we got to do the best we can."

"I ain't learning nothing in school," he said. "Even when I go." He turned away from me and opened the window and threw his cigarette out into the narrow alley. I watched his back. "At least, I ain't learning nothing you'd want me to learn." He slammed the window so hard I thought the glass would fly out, and turned back to me. "And I'm sick of the stink of these garbage cans!"

"Sonny," I said, "I know how you feel. But if you don't finish school now, you're going to be sorry later that you didn't." I grabbed him by the shoulders. "And you only got another year. It ain't so bad. And I'll come back and I swear I'll help you do *whatever* you want to do. Just try to put up with it till I come back. Will you please do that? For me?"

He didn't answer and he wouldn't look at me.

"Sonny. You hear me?"

He pulled away. "I hear you. But you never hear any-thing *I* say."

I didn't know what to say to that. He looked out of the window and then back at me. "Okay," he said, and sighed. "I'll try."

Then I said, trying to cheer him up a little, "They got a piano at Isabel's. You can practice on it."

And as a matter of fact, it did cheer him up for a minute. "That's right," he said to himself. "I forgot that." His face relaxed a little. But the worry, the thoughtfulness, played on it still, the way shadows play on a face which is staring into the fire.

But I thought I'd never hear the end of that piano. At first, Isabel would write me, saying how nice it was that Sonny was so serious about his music and how, as soon as he came in from school, or wherever he had been when he was supposed to be at school, he went straight to that piano and stayed there until suppertime. And, after supper, he went back to that piano and stayed there until everybody went to bed. He was at the piano all day Saturday and all day Sunday. Then he bought a record player and started playing records. He'd play one record over and over again, all day long sometimes, and he'd improvise along with it on the piano. Or he'd play one section of the record, one chord, one change, one progression, then he'd do it on the piano. Then back to the record. Then back to the piano.

Well, I really don't know how they stood it. Isabel finally confessed that it wasn't like living with a person at all, it was like living with sound. And the sound didn't make any sense to her, didn't make any sense to any of them—naturally. They began, in a way, to be afflicted by this presence that was living in their home. It was as though Sonny were some sort of god, or monster. He moved in an atmosphere which wasn't like theirs at all. They fed him and he ate, he washed himself, he walked in and out of their door; he certainly wasn't nasty or unpleasant or rude, Sonny isn't any of those things; but it was as though he were all wrapped up in some cloud, some fire, some vision all his own; and there wasn't any way to reach him.

At the same time, he wasn't really a man yet, he was still a child, and they had to watch out for him in all kinds of ways. They certainly couldn't throw him out. Neither did they dare to make a great scene about that piano because even they dimly sensed, as I sensed, from so many thousands of miles away, that Sonny was at that piano playing for his life.

But he hadn't been going to school. One day a letter came from the school board and Isabel's mother got it—there had, apparently, been other letters but Sonny had torn them up.

This day, when Sonny came in, Isabel's mother showed him the letter and asked where he'd been spending his time. And she finally got it out of him that he'd been down in Greenwich Village, with musicians and other characters, in a white girl's apartment. And this scared her and she started to scream at him and what came up, once she began—though she denies it to this day—was what sacrifices they were making to give Sonny a decent home and how little he appreciated it.

Sonny didn't play the piano that day. By evening, Isabel's mother had calmed down but then there was the old man to deal with, and Isabel herself. Isabel says she did her best to be calm but she broke down and started crying. She says she just watched Sonny's face. She could tell, by watching him, what was happening with him. And what was happening was that they penetrated his cloud, they had reached him. Even if their fingers had been a thousand times more gentle than human fingers ever are, he could hardly help feeling that they had stripped him naked and were spitting on that nakedness. For he also had to see that his presence, that music, which was life or death to him, had been torture for them and that they had endured it, not at all for his sake, but only for mine. And Sonny couldn't take that. He can take it a little better today than he could then but he's still not very good at it and, frankly, I don't know anybody who is.

The silence of the next few days must have been louder than the sound of all the music ever played since time began. One morning, before she went to work, Isabel was in his room for something and she suddenly realized that all of his records were gone. And she knew for certain that he was gone. And he was. He went as far as the navy would carry him. He finally sent me a postcard from some place in Greece and that was the first I knew that Sonny was still alive. I didn't see him any more until we were both back in New York and the war had long been over.

He was a man by then, of course, but I wasn't willing to see it. He came by the house from time to time, but we fought almost every time we met. I didn't like the way he carried himself, loose and dreamlike all the time, and I didn't like his friends, and his music seemed to be merely an excuse for the life he led. It sounded just that weird and disordered.

Then we had a fight, a pretty awful fight, and I didn't see him for months. By and by I looked him up, where he was living, in a furnished room in the Village, and I tried to make it up. But there were lots of other people in the room and Sonny just lay on his bed, and he wouldn't come downstairs with me, and he treated these other people as though they were his family and I weren't. So I got mad and then he got mad, and then I told him that he might just as well be dead as live the way he was living. Then he stood up and he told me not to worry about him any more in life, that he *was* dead as far as I was concerned. Then he pushed me to the door and the other people looked on as though nothing were happening, and he slammed the door behind me. I stood in the hallway, staring at the door. I heard somebody laugh in the room and then the tears came to my eyes. I started down the steps, whistling to keep from crying, I kept whistling to myself, *You going to need me, baby, one of these cold, rainy days.*

I read about Sonny's trouble in the spring. Little Grace died in the fall. She was a beautiful little girl. But she only lived a little over two years. She died of polio and she suffered. She had a slight fever for a couple of days, but it didn't seem like anything and we just kept her in bed. And we would certainly have called the doctor, but the fever dropped, she seemed to be all right. So we thought it had just been a cold.

Then, one day, she was up, playing, Isabel was in the kitchen fixing lunch for the two boys when they'd come in from school, and she heard Grace fall down in the living-room. When you have a lot of children you don't always start running when one of them falls, unless they start screaming or something. And, this time, Grace was quiet. Yet, Isabel says that when she heard that *thump* and then that silence, something happened in her to make her afraid. And she ran to the living-room and there was little Grace on the floor, all twisted up, and the reason she hadn't screamed was that she couldn't get her breath. And when she did scream, it was the worst sound, Isabel says, that she'd ever heard in all her life, and she still hears it sometimes in her dreams. Isabel will sometimes wake me up with a low, moaning, strangled sound and I have to be quick to awaken her and hold her to me and where Isabel is weeping against me seems a mortal wound.

I think I may have written Sonny the very day that little Grace was buried. I was sitting in the living-room in the dark, by myself, and I suddenly thought of Sonny. My trouble made his real.

One Saturday afternoon, when Sonny had been living with us, or, anyway, been in our house, for nearly two weeks, I found myself wandering aimlessly about the living-room, drinking from a can of beer, and trying to work up the courage to search Sonny's room. He was out, he was usually out whenever I was home, and Isabel had taken the children to see their grandparents. Suddenly I was standing still in front of the living-room window, watching Seventh Avenue. The idea of searching Sonny's room made me still. I scarcely dared to admit to myself what I'd be searching for. I didn't know what I'd do if I found it. Or if I didn't.

On the sidewalk across from me, near the entrance to a bar-becue joint, some people were holding an old-fashioned revival meeting. The barbecue cook, wearing a dirty white apron, his conked hair reddish and metallic in the pale sun, and a cigarette between his lips, stood in the doorway, watch-ing them. Kids and older people paused in their errands and stood there, along with some older men and a couple of very tough-looking women who watched everything that hap-pened on the avenue, as though they owned it, or were maybe owned by it. Well, they were watching this, too. The revival was being carried on by three sisters in black, and a brother. All they had were their voices and their Bibles and a tambour-ine. The brother was testifying and while he testified two of the sisters stood together, seeming to say, amen, and the third sister walked around with the tambourine outstretched and a couple of people dropped coins into it. Then the brother's testimony ended and the sister who had been taking up the collection dumped the coins into her palm and transferred them to the pocket of her long black robe. Then she raised both hands, striking the tambourine against the air, and then against one hand, and she started to sing. And the two other sisters and the brother joined in.

It was strange, suddenly, to watch, though I had been seeing these street meetings all my life. So, of course, had everybody else down there. Yet, they paused and watched and listened and I stood still at the window. "'*Tis the old ship of Zion*," they sang, and the sister with the tambourine kept a steady, jangling beat, "*it has rescued many a thousand!*" Not a soul under the sound of their voices was hearing this song for the first time, not one of them had been rescued. Nor had they seen much in the way of rescue work being done around them. Neither did they especially believe in the holi-ness of the three sisters and the brother, they knew too much about them, knew where they lived, and how. The woman with the tambourine, whose voice dominated the air, whose face was bright with joy, was divided by very little from the woman who stood watching her, a cigarette between her heavy, chapped lips, her hair a cuckoo's nest, her face scarred and swollen from many beatings, and her black eyes glittering like coal. Perhaps they both knew this, which was why, when, as rarely, they addressed each other, they addressed each other as Sister. As the singing filled the air the watching, listening faces underwent a change, the eyes focusing on something within; the music seemed to soothe a poison out of them; and time seemed, nearly, to fall away from the sullen, belligerent, battered faces, as though they were fleeing back to their first condition, while dreaming of their last. The barbecue cook half shook his head and smiled, and dropped his cigarette and disappeared into his joint. A man fumbled in his pockets for change and stood holding it in his hand impatiently, as though he had just remembered a pressing appointment further up the avenue. He looked furious. Then I saw Sonny, standing on the edge of the crowd. He was carrying a wide, flat notebook with a green cover, and it made him look, from where I was standing, almost like a schoolboy. The coppery sun brought out the copper in his skin, he was very faintly smiling, standing very still. Then the singing stopped, the tambourine turned into a collection plate again. The furious man dropped in his coins and vanished, so did a couple of the women, and Sonny dropped some change in the plate, looking directly at the woman with a little smile. He started across the avenue, toward the house. He has a slow, loping walk, something like the way Harlem hipsters walk, only he's imposed on this his own half-beat. I had never really noticed it before.

I stayed at the window, both relieved and apprehensive.

As Sonny disappeared from my sight, they began singing again. And they were still singing when his key turned in the lock.

"Hey," he said.

"Hey, yourself. You want some beer?"

"No. Well, maybe." But he came up to the window and stood beside me, looking out. "What a warm voice," he said.

They were singing *If I could only hear my mother pray again!*

"Yes," I said, "and she can sure beat that tambourine."

"But what a terrible song," he said, and laughed. He dropped his notebook on the sofa and disappeared into the kitchen. "Where's Isabel and the kids?"

"I think they went to see their grandparents. You hungry?"

"No." He came back into the living-room with his can of beer. "You want to come some place with me tonight?"

I sensed, I don't know how, that I couldn't possibly say no. "Sure. Where?"

He sat down on the sofa and picked up his notebook and started leafing through it. "I'm going to sit in with some fellows in a joint in the Village."

"You mean, you're going to play, tonight?"

"That's right." He took a swallow of his beer and moved back to the window. He gave me a sidelong look. "If you can stand it."

"I'll try," I said.

He smiled to himself and we both watched as the meeting across the way broke up. The three sisters and the brother, heads bowed, were singing *God be with you till we meet again.* The faces around them were very quiet. Then the song ended. The small crowd dispersed. We watched the three women and the lone man walk slowly up the avenue.

"When she was singing before," said Sonny, abruptly, "her

voice reminded me for a minute of what heroin feels like sometimes—when it's in your veins. It makes you feel sort of warm and cool at the same time. And distant. And—and sure." He sipped his beer, very deliberately not looking at me. I watched his face. "It makes you feel—in control. Sometimes you've got to have that feeling."

"Do you?" I sat down slowly in the easy chair.

"Sometimes." He went to the sofa and picked up his notebook again. "Some people do."

"In order," I asked, "to play?" And my voice was very ugly, full of contempt and anger.

"Well"—he looked at me with great, troubled eyes, as though, in fact, he hoped his eyes would tell me things he could never otherwise say—"they *think* so. And *if* they think so—!"

"And what do *you* think?" I asked.

He sat on the sofa and put his can of beer on the floor. "I don't know," he said, and I couldn't be sure if he were answering my question or pursuing his thoughts. His face didn't tell me. "It's not so much to *play*. It's to *stand* it, to be able to make it at all. On any level." He frowned and smiled: "In order to keep from shaking to pieces."

"But these friends of yours," I said, "they seem to shake themselves to pieces pretty goddamn fast."

"Maybe." He played with the notebook. And something told me that I should curb my tongue, that Sonny was doing his best to talk, that I should listen. "But of course you only know the ones that've gone to pieces. Some don't—or at least they haven't *yet* and that's just about all *any* of us can say." He paused. "And then there are some who just live, really, in hell, and they know it and they see what's happening and they go right on. I don't know." He sighed, dropped the notebook, folded his arms. "Some guys, you can tell from the way

295

they play, they on something *all* the time. And you can see that, well, it makes something real for them. But of course," he picked up his beer from the floor and sipped it and put the can down again, "they *want* to, too, you've got to see that. Even some of them that say they don't—*some*, not all."

"And what about you?" I asked—I couldn't help it. "What about you? Do *you* want to?"

He stood up and walked to the window and remained silent for a long time. Then he sighed. "Me," he said. Then: "While I was downstairs before, on my way here, listening to that woman sing, it struck me all of a sudden how much suffering she must have had to go through—to sing like that. It's *repulsive* to think you have to suffer that much."

I said: "But there's no way not to suffer—is there, Sonny?"

"I believe not," he said and smiled, "but that's never stopped anyone from trying." He looked at me. "Has it?" I realized, with this mocking look, that there stood between us, forever, beyond the power of time or forgiveness, the fact that I had held silence—so long!—when he had needed human speech to help him. He turned back to the window. "No, there's no way not to suffer. But you try all kinds of ways to keep from drowning in it, to keep on top of it, and to make it seem—well, like *you*. Like you did something, all right, and now you're suffering for it. You know?" I said nothing. "Well you know," he said, impatiently, "why *do* people suffer? Maybe it's better to do something to give it a reason, *any* reason."

"But we just agreed," I said, "that there's no way not to suffer. Isn't it better, then, just to—take it?"

"But nobody just takes it," Sonny cried, "that's what I'm telling you! *Everybody* tries not to. You're just hung up on the *way* some people try—it's not *your* way!"

The hair on my face began to itch, my face felt wet. "That's not true," I said, "that's not true. I don't give a damn what other people do, I don't even care how they suffer. I just care how *you* suffer." And he looked at me. "Please believe me," I said, "I don't want to see you—die—trying not to suffer."

"I won't," he said, flatly, "die trying not to suffer. At least, not any faster than anybody else."

"But there's no need," I said, trying to laugh, "is there? in killing yourself."

I wanted to say more, but I couldn't. I wanted to talk about will power and how life could be—well, beautiful. I wanted to say that it was all within; but was it? or, rather, wasn't that exactly the trouble? And I wanted to promise that I would never fail him again. But it would all have sounded—empty words and lies.

So I made the promise to myself and prayed that I would keep it.

"It's terrible sometimes, inside," he said, "that's what's the trouble. You walk these streets, black and funky and cold, and there's not really a living ass to talk to, and there's nothing shaking, and there's no way of getting it out—that storm inside. You can't talk it and you can't make love with it, and when you finally try to get with it and play it, you realize *nobody's* listening. So *you've* got to listen. You got to find a way to listen."

And then he walked away from the window and sat on the sofa again, as though all the wind had suddenly been knocked out of him. "Sometimes you'll do *anything* to play, even cut your mother's throat." He laughed and looked at me. "Or your brother's." Then he sobered. "Or your own." Then: "Don't worry. I'm all right now and I think I'll *be* all right. But I can't forget—where I've been. I don't mean just the physical place I've been, I mean where I've *been*. And *what* I've been."

"What have you been, Sonny?" I asked.

He smiled—but sat sideways on the sofa, his elbow resting on the back, his fingers playing with his mouth and chin, not looking at me. "I've been something I didn't recognize, didn't know I could be. Didn't know anybody could be." He stopped, looking inward, looking helplessly young, looking old. "I'm not talking about it now because I feel *guilty* or anything like that—maybe it would be better if I did, I don't know. Anyway, I can't really talk about it. Not to you, not to anybody," and now he turned and faced me. "Sometimes, you know, and it was actually when I was most *out* of the world, I felt that I was in it, that I was *with* it, really, and I could play or I didn't really have to *play*, it just came out of me, it was there. And I don't know how I played, thinking about it now, but I know I did awful things, those times, sometimes, to people. Or it wasn't that I *did* anything to them—it was that they weren't real." He picked up the beer can; it was empty; he rolled it between his palms: "And other times—well, I needed a fix, I needed to find a place to lean, I needed to clear a space to *listen*—and I couldn't find it, and I—went crazy, I did terrible things to *me*, I was terrible *for* me." He began pressing the beer can between his hands, I watched the metal begin to give. It glittered, as he played with it, like a knife, and I was afraid he would cut himself, but I said nothing. "Oh well. I can never tell you. I was all by myself at the bottom of something, stinking and sweating and crying and shaking, and I smelled it, you know? *my* stink, and I thought I'd die if I couldn't get away from it and yet, all the same, I knew that everything I was doing was just locking me in with it. And I didn't know," he paused, still flattening the beer can, "I didn't know, I still *don't* know, something kept telling me that maybe it was good to smell your own stink, but I didn't think that *that* was what I'd

298

been trying to do—and—who can stand it?" and he abruptly dropped the ruined beer can, looking at me with a small, still smile, and then rose, walking to the window as though it were the lodestone rock. I watched his face, he watched the avenue. "I couldn't tell you when Mama died—but the reason I wanted to leave Harlem so bad was to get away from drugs. And then, when I ran away, that's what I was running from—really. When I came back, nothing had changed, *I* hadn't changed, I was just—older." And he stopped, drumming with his fingers on the windowpane. The sun had vanished, soon darkness would fall. I watched his face. "It can come again," he said, almost as though speaking to himself. Then he turned to me. "It can come again," he repeated. "I just want you to know that."

"All right," I said, at last. "So it can come again. All right."

He smiled, but the smile was sorrowful. "I had to try to tell you," he said.

"Yes," I said. "I understand that."

"You're my brother," he said, looking straight at me, and not smiling at all.

"Yes," I repeated, "yes. I understand that."

He turned back to the window, looking out. "All that hatred down there," he said, "all that hatred and misery and love. It's a wonder it doesn't blow the avenue apart."

We went to the only nightclub on a short, dark street, downtown. We squeezed through the narrow, chattering, jam-packed bar to the entrance of the big room, where the bandstand was. And we stood there for a moment, for the lights were very dim in this room and we couldn't see. Then, "Hello, boy," said a voice and an enormous black man, much older than Sonny or myself, erupted out of all that atmospheric lighting and put an arm around Sonny's shoulder. "I been sitting right here," he said, "waiting for you."

He had a big voice, too, and heads in the darkness turned toward us.

Sonny grinned and pulled a little away, and said, "Creole, this is my brother. I told you about him."

Creole shook my hand. "I'm glad to meet you, son," he said, and it was clear that he was glad to meet me *there*, for Sonny's sake. And he smiled, "You got a real musician in *your* family," and he took his arm from Sonny's shoulder and slapped him, lightly, affectionately, with the back of his hand.

"Well. Now I've heard it all," said a voice behind us. This was another musician, and a friend of Sonny's, a coal-black, cheerful-looking man, built close to the ground. He immediately began confiding to me, at the top of his lungs, the most terrible things about Sonny, his teeth gleaming like a lighthouse and his laugh coming up out of him like the beginning of an earthquake. And it turned out that everyone at the bar knew Sonny, or almost everyone; some were musicians, working there, or nearby, or not working, some were simply hangers-on, and some were there to hear Sonny play. I was introduced to all of them and they were all very polite to me. Yet, it was clear that, for them, I was only Sonny's brother. Here, I was in Sonny's world. Or, rather: his kingdom. Here, it was not even a question that his veins bore royal blood.

They were going to play soon and Creole installed me, by myself, at a table in a dark corner. Then I watched them, Creole, and the little black man, and Sonny, and the others, while they horsed around, standing just below the bandstand. The light from the bandstand spilled just a little short of them and, watching them laughing and gesturing and moving about, I had the feeling that they, nevertheless, were being most careful not to step into that circle of light too suddenly: that if they moved into the light too suddenly, without thinking, they would perish in flame. Then, while I watched, one of them, the small, black man, moved into the light and crossed the bandstand and started fooling around with his drums. Then—being funny and being, also, extremely ceremonious—Creole took Sonny by the arm and led him to the piano. A woman's voice called Sonny's name and a few hands started clapping. And Sonny, also being funny and being ceremonious, and so touched, I think, that he could have cried, but neither hiding it nor showing it, riding it like a man, grinned, and put both hands to his heart and bowed from the waist.

Creole then went to the bass fiddle and a lean, very bright-skinned brown man jumped up on the bandstand and picked up his horn. So there they were, and the atmosphere on the bandstand and in the room began to change and tighten. Someone stepped up to the microphone and announced them. Then there were all kinds of murmurs. Some people at the bar shushed others. The waitress ran around, frantically getting in the last orders, guys and chicks got closer to each other, and the lights on the bandstand, on the quartet, turned to a kind of indigo. Then they all looked different there. Creole looked about him for the last time, as though he were making certain that all his chickens were in the coop, and then he—jumped and struck the fiddle. And there they were.

All I know about music is that not many people ever really hear it. And even then, on the rare occasions when something opens within, and the music enters, what we mainly hear, or hear corroborated, are personal, private, vanishing evocations. But the man who creates the music is hearing something else, is dealing with the roar rising from the void and imposing order on it as it hits the air. What is evoked

301

in him, then, is of another order, more terrible because it has no words, and triumphant, too, for that same reason. And his triumph, when he triumphs, is ours. I just watched Sonny's face. His face was troubled, he was working hard, but he wasn't with it. And I had the feeling that, in a way, everyone on the bandstand was waiting for him, both waiting for him and pushing him along. But as I began to watch Creole, I realized that it was Creole who held them all back. He had them on a short rein. Up there, keeping the beat with his whole body, wailing on the fiddle, with his eyes half closed, he was listening to everything, but he was listening to Sonny. He was having a dialogue with Sonny. He wanted Sonny to leave the shoreline and strike out for the deep water. He was Sonny's witness that deep water and drowning were not the same thing—he had been there, and he knew. And he wanted Sonny to know. He was waiting for Sonny to do the things on the keys which would let Creole know that Sonny was in the water.

And, while Creole listened, Sonny moved, deep within, exactly like someone in torment. I had never before thought of how awful the relationship must be between the musician and his instrument. He has to fill it, this instrument, with the breath of life, his own. He has to make it do what he wants it to do. And a piano is just a piano. It's made out of so much wood and wires and little hammers and big ones, and ivory. While there's only so much you can do with it, the only way to find this out is to try; to try and make it do everything.

And Sonny hadn't been near a piano for over a year. And he wasn't on much better terms with his life, not the life that stretched before him now. He and the piano stammered, started one way, got scared, stopped; started another way, panicked, marked time, started again; then seemed to have

302

found a direction, panicked again, got stuck. And the face I saw on Sonny I'd never seen before. Everything had been burned out of it, and, at the same time, things usually hidden were being burned in, by the fire and fury of the battle which was occurring in him up there.

Yet, watching Creole's face as they neared the end of the first set, I had the feeling that something had happened, something I hadn't heard. Then they finished, there was scattered applause, and then, without an instant's warning, Creole started into something else, it was almost sardonic, it was *Am I Blue*. And, as though he commanded, Sonny began to play. Something began to happen. And Creole let out the reins. The dry, low, black man said something awful on the drums, Creole answered, and the drums talked back. Then the horn insisted, sweet and high, slightly detached perhaps, and Creole listened, commenting now and then, dry, and driving, beautiful and calm and old. Then they all came together again, and Sonny was part of the family again. I could tell this from his face. He seemed to have found, right there beneath his fingers, a damn brand-new piano. It seemed that he couldn't get over it. Then, for awhile, just being happy with Sonny, they seemed to be agreeing with him that brand-new pianos certainly were a gas.

Then Creole stepped forward to remind them that what they were playing was the blues. He hit something in all of them, he hit something in me, myself, and the music tightened and deepened, apprehension began to beat the air. Creole began to tell us what the blues were all about. They were not about anything very new. He and his boys up there were keeping it new, at the risk of ruin, destruction, madness, and death, in order to find new ways to make us listen. For, while the tale of how we suffer, and how we are delighted, and how we may triumph is never new, it always must be heard.

There isn't any other tale to tell, it's the only light we've got in all this darkness.

And this tale, according to that face, that body, those strong hands on those strings, has another aspect in every country, and a new depth in every generation. Listen, Creole seemed to be saying, listen. Now these are Sonny's blues. He made the little black man on the drums know it, and the bright, brown man on the horn. Creole wasn't trying any longer to get Sonny in the water. He was wishing him Godspeed. Then he stepped back, very slowly, filling the air with the immense suggestion that Sonny speak for himself.

Then they all gathered around Sonny and Sonny played. Every now and again one of them seemed to say, amen. Sonny's fingers filled the air with life, his life. But that life contained so many others. And Sonny went all the way back, he really began with the spare, flat statement of the opening phrase of the song. Then he began to make it his. It was very beautiful because it wasn't hurried and it was no longer a lament. I seemed to hear with what burning he had made it his, with what burning we had yet to make it ours, how we could cease lamenting. Freedom lurked around us and I understood, at last, that he could help us to be free if we would listen, that he would never be free until we did. Yet, there was no battle in his face now. I heard what he had gone through, and would continue to go through until he came to rest in earth. He had made it his: that long line, of which we knew only Mama and Daddy. And he was giving it back, as everything must be given back, so that, passing through death, it can live forever. I saw my mother's face again, and felt, for the first time, how the stones of the road she had walked on must have bruised her feet. I saw the moonlit road where my father's brother died. And it brought something else back to me, and carried me past it, I saw my little girl again and felt Isabel's tears again, and I felt my own tears begin to rise. And I was yet aware that this was only a moment, that the world waited outside, as hungry as a tiger, and that trouble stretched above us, longer than the sky.

Then it was over. Creole and Sonny let out their breath, both soaking wet, and grinning. There was a lot of applause and some of it was real. In the dark, the girl came by and I asked her to take drinks to the bandstand. There was a long pause, while they talked up there in the indigo light and after awhile I saw the girl put a Scotch and milk on top of the piano for Sonny. He didn't seem to notice it, but just before they started playing again, he sipped from it and looked toward me, and nodded. Then he put it back on top of the piano. For me, then, as they began to play again, it glowed and shook above my brother's head like the very cup of trembling.

JEAN STAFFORD

CHILDREN ARE BORED ON SUNDAY

THROUGH THE WIDE doorway between two of the painting galleries, Emma saw Alfred Eisenburg standing before "The Three Miracles of Zenobius," his lean, equine face ashen and sorrowing, his gaunt frame looking under-nourished, and dressed in a way that showed he was poorer this year than he had been last. Emma herself had been hunting for the Botticelli all afternoon, sidetracked first by a Mantegna she had forgotten, and then by a follower of Hieronymus Bosch, and distracted, in an English room as she was passing through, by the hot invective of two ladies who were lodged (so they bitterly reminded one another) in an outrageous and expensive mare's-nest at a hotel on Madison. Emma liked Alfred, and once, at a party in some other year, she had flirted with him slightly for seven or eight minutes. It had been spring, and even into that modern apartment, wherever it had been, while the cunning guests, on their guard and highly civilized, learnedly disputed on aesthetic and political subjects, the feeling of spring had boldly invaded, adding its nameless, sentimental sensations to all the others of the buffeted heart; one did not know and never had, even in the devouring raptures of adolescence, whether this was a feeling of tension or of solution—whether one flew or drowned.

In another year, she would have been pleased to run into Alfred here in the Metropolitan on a cold Sunday, when the galleries were thronged with out-of-towners and with people who dutifully did something self-educating on the day of rest. But this year she was hiding from just such people as Alfred Eisenburg, and she turned quickly to go back the way she had come, past the Constables and Raeburns. As she turned, she came face to face with Salvador Dali, whose sudden countenance, with its unlikely mustache and its histrionic eyes, familiar from the photographs in public places, momentarily stopped her dead, for she did not immediately recognize him and, still surprised by seeing Eisenburg, took him also to be someone she knew. She shuddered and then realized that he was merely famous, and she penetrated the heart of a guided tour and proceeded safely through the rooms until she came to the balcony that overlooks the medieval armor, and there she paused, watching two youths of high-school age examine the joints of an equestrian's shell.

She paused because she could not decide what to look at now that she had been denied the Botticelli. She wondered, rather crossly, why Alfred Eisenburg was looking at it and why, indeed, he was here at all. She feared that her afternoon, begun in such a burst of courage, would not be what it might have been; for this second's glimpse of him—who had no bearing on her life—might very well divert her from the pictures, not only because she was reminded of her ignorance of painting by the presence of someone who was (she assumed) versed in it but because her eyesight was now bound to be impaired by memory and conjecture, by the irrelevant mind-portraits of innumerable people who belonged to Eisenburg's milieu. And almost at once, as she had predicted, the air separating her from the schoolboys below was populated with the images of composers, of painters, of writers who pronounced judgments, in their individual argot, on Hindemith, Ernst, Sartre, on Beethoven, Rubens, Baudelaire, on Stalin and Freud and Kierkegaard, on Toynbee, Frazer,

Thoreau, Franco, Salazar, Roosevelt, Maimonides, Racine, Wallace, Picasso, Henry Luce, Monsignor Sheen, the Atomic Energy Commission, and the movie industry. And she saw herself moving, shaky with apprehensions and martinis, and with the belligerence of a child who feels himself laughed at, through the apartments of Alfred Eisenburg's friends, where the shelves were filled with everyone from Aristophanes to Ring Lardner, where the walls were hung with reproductions of Seurat, Titian, Vermeer, and Klee, and where the record cabinets began with Palestrina and ended with Copland.

These cocktail parties were a modus vivendi in themselves for which a new philosophy, a new ethic, and a new etiquette had had to be devised. They were neither work nor play, and yet they were not at all beside the point but were, on the contrary, quite indispensable to the spiritual life of the artists who went to them. It was possible for Emma to see these occasions objectively, after these many months of abstention from them, but it was still not possible to understand them, for they were so special a case, and so unlike any parties she had known at home. The gossip was different, for one thing, because it was stylized, creative (integrating the whole of the garrotted, absent friend), and all its details were precise and all its conceits were Jamesian, and all its practitioners sorrowfully saw themselves in the role of Pontius Pilate, that hero of the untoward circumstance. (It has to be done, though we don't want to do it; 'tis a pity she's a whore, when no one writes more intelligent verse than she.) There was, too, the matter of the drinks, which were much worse than those served by anyone else, and much more plentiful. They dispensed with the fripperies of olives in martinis and cherries in manhattans (God forbid! They had no sweet teeth), and half the time there was no ice, and when there was, it was as likely as not to be suspect shavings got from a bed for shad at the corner

311

fish store. Other species, so one heard, went off to dinner after cocktail parties certainly no later than half past eight, but no one ever left a party given by an Olympian until ten, at the earliest, and then groups went out together, stalling and squabbling at the door, angrily unable to come to a decision about where to eat, although they seldom ate once they got there but, with the greatest formality imaginable, ordered several rounds of cocktails, as if they had not had a drink in a month of Sundays. But the most surprising thing of all about these parties was that every now and again, in the middle of the urgent, general conversation, this cream of the enlightened was horribly curdled, and an argument would end, quite literally, in a bloody nose or a black eye. Emma was always astounded when this happened and continued to think that these outbursts did not arise out of hatred or jealousy but out of some quite unaccountable quirk, almost a reflex, almost something physical. She never quite believed her eyes—that is, was never altogether convinced that they were really beating one another up. It seemed, rather, that this was only a deliberate and perfectly honest demonstration of what might have happened often if they had not so diligently dedicated themselves to their intellects. Although she had seen them do it, she did not and could not believe that city people clipped each other's jaws, for, to Emma, urban equaled urbane, and ichor ran in these Augustans' veins.

As she looked down now from her balcony at the atrocious iron clothes below, it occurred to her that Alfred Eisenburg had been just such a first-generation metropolitan boy as these two who half knelt in lithe and eager attitudes to study the glittering splints of a knight's skirt. It was a kind of childhood she could not imagine and from the thought of which she turned away in secret, shameful pity. She had been really stunned when she first came to New York to find that almost no one she met had gluttonously read Dickens, as she had, beginning at the age of ten, and because she was only twenty when she arrived in the city and unacquainted with the varieties of cultural experience, she had acquired the idea, which she was never able to shake entirely loose, that these New York natives had been deprived of this and many other innocent pleasures because they had lived in apartments and not in two- or three-story houses. (In the early years in New York, she had known someone who had not heard a cat purr until he was twenty-five and went to a houseparty on Fire Island.) They had played hide-and-seek dodging behind ash cans instead of lilac bushes and in and out of the entries of apartment houses instead of up alleys densely lined with hollyhocks. But who was she to patronize and pity them? Her own childhood, rich as it seemed to her on reflection, had not equipped her to read, or to see, or to listen, as theirs had done; she envied them and despised them at the same time, and at the same time she feared and admired them. As their attitude implicitly accused her, before she beat her retreat, she never looked for meanings, she never saw the literary-historical symbolism of the cocktail party but went on, despite all testimony to the contrary, believing it to be an occasion for getting drunk. She never listened, their manner delicately explained, and when she talked she was always lamentably off key; often and often she had been stared at and had been told, "It's not the same thing at all."

Emma shuddered, scrutinizing this nature of hers, which they all had scorned, as if it were some harmless but sickening reptile. Noticing how cold the marble railing was under her hands, she felt that her self-blame was surely justified; she came to the Metropolitan Museum not to attend to the masterpieces but to remember cocktail parties where she had drunk too much and had seen Alfred Eisenburg, and to watch schoolboys, and to make experience out of the accidental contact of the palms of her hands with a cold bit of marble. What was there to do? One thing, anyhow, was clear and that was that today's excursion into the world had been premature; her solitude must continue for a while, and perhaps it would never end. If the sight of someone so peripheral, so uninvolving, as Alfred Eisenburg could scare her so badly, what would a cocktail party do? She almost fainted at the thought of it, she almost fell headlong, and the boys, abandoning the coat of mail, dizzied her by their progress toward an emblazoned tabard.

In so many words, she wasn't fit to be seen. Although she was no longer mutilated, she was still unkempt; her pretensions needed brushing; her ambiguities needed to be cleaned; her evasions would have to be completely overhauled before she could face again the terrifying learning of someone like Alfred Eisenburg, a learning whose components cohered into a central personality that was called "intellectual." She imagined that even the boys down there had opinions on everything political and artistic and metaphysical and scientific, and because she remained, in spite of all her opportunities, as green as grass, she was certain they had got their head start because they had grown up in apartments, where there was nothing else to do but educate themselves. This being an intellectual was not the same thing as dilettantism; it was a calling in itself. For example, Emma did not even know whether Eisenburg was a painter, a writer, a composer, a sculptor, or something entirely different. When, seeing him with the composers, she had thought he was one of them; when, the next time she met him, at a studio party, she decided he must be a painter; and when, on subsequent occasions, everything had pointed toward his being a writer, she had relied altogether on circumstantial evidence and not on anything he had said or done. There was no reason to suppose that he had not looked upon her as the same sort of variable and it made their anonymity to one another complete. Without the testimony of an impartial third person, neither she nor Eisenburg would ever know the other's actual trade. But his specialty did not matter, for his larger designation was that of "the intellectual," just as the man who confines his talents to the nose and throat is still a doctor. It was, in the light of this, all the more extraordinary that they had had that lightning-paced flirtation at a party.

Extraordinary, because Emma could not look upon herself as an intellectual. Her private antonym of this noun was "rube," and to her regret—the regret that had caused her finally to disappear from Alfred's group—she was not even a bona-fide rube. In her store clothes, so to speak, she was often taken for an intellectual, for she had, poor girl, gone to college and had never been quite the same since. She would not dare, for instance, go up to Eisenburg now and say that what she most liked in the Botticelli were the human and compassionate eyes of the centurions' horses, which reminded her of the eyes of her own Great-uncle Graham, whom she had adored as a child. Nor would she admit that she was delighted with a Crivelli Madonna because the peaches in the background looked exactly like marzipan, or that Goya's little red boy inspired in her only the pressing desire to go out immediately in search of a plump cat to stroke. While she knew that feelings like these were not really punishable, she had not perfected the art of tossing them off; she was no flirt. She was a bounty jumper in the war between Great-uncle Graham's farm and New York City, and liable to court-martial on one side and death on the other. Neither staunchly primitive nor confidently *au courant*, she rarely knew where she was at. And this was her Achilles' heel: her identity was always mistaken, and she was thought to be an intellectual who, however, had not made the grade. It was no use now to cry that she was not, that she was a simon-pure rube; not a soul would believe her. She knew, deeply and with horror, that she was thought merely stupid.

It was possible to be highly successful as a rube among the Olympians, and she had seen it done. Someone calling himself Nahum Mothersill had done it brilliantly, but she often wondered whether his name had not helped him, and, in fact, she had sometimes wondered whether that had been his real name. If she had been called, let us say, Hyacinth Derryberry, she believed she might have been able, as Mothersill had been, to ask who Ezra Pound was. (This struck her suddenly as a very important point; it was endearing, really, not to know who Pound was, but it was only embarrassing to know who he was but not to have read the "Cantos.") How different it would have been if education had not meddled with her rustic nature! Her education had never dissuaded her from her convictions, but certainly it had ruined the looks of her mind—painted the poor thing up until it looked like a mean, hypocritical, promiscuous malcontent, a craven and apologetic fancy woman. Thus she continued secretly to believe (but *never* to confess) that the apple Eve had eaten tasted exactly like those she had eaten when she was a child visiting on her Great-uncle Graham's farm, and that Newton's observation was no news in spite of all the hue and cry. Half the apples she had eaten had fallen out of the tree, whose branches she had shaken for this very purpose, and the Apple Experience included both the descent of the fruit and the consumption of it, and Eve and Newton and Emma understood one another perfectly in this particular of reality.

Emma started. The Metropolitan boys, who, however bright they were, would be boys, now caused some steely article of dress to clank, and she instantly quit the balcony, as if this unseemly noise would attract the crowd's attention and bring everyone, including Eisenburg, to see what had happened. She scuttered like a quarry through the sight-seers until she found an empty seat in front of Rembrandt's famous frump, "The Noble Slav"—it was this kind of thing, this fundamental apathy to most of Rembrandt, that made life in New York such hell for Emma—and there, upon the plum velours, she realized with surprise that Alfred Eisenburg's had been the last familiar face she had seen before she had closed the door of her tomb.

In September, it had been her custom to spend several hours of each day walking in a straight line, stopping only for traffic lights and outlaw taxicabs, in the hope that she would be tired enough to sleep at night. At five o'clock—and gradually it became more often four o'clock and then half past three—she would go into a bar, where, while she drank, she seemed to be reading the information offered by the *Sun* on "Where to Dine." Actually she had ceased to dine long since; every few days, with effort, she inserted thin wafers of food into her repelled mouth, flushing the frightful stuff down with enormous drafts of magical, purifying, fulfilling applejack diluted with tepid water from the tap. One weighty day, under a sky that grimly withheld the rain, as if to punish the whole city, she had started out from Ninetieth Street and had kept going down Madison and was thinking, as she passed the chancery of St. Patrick's, that it must be nearly time and that she needed only to turn east on Fiftieth Street to the New Weston, where the bar was cool, and dark to an almost absurd degree. And then she was hailed. She turned quickly, looking in all directions until she saw Eisenburg approaching, removing a gray pellet of gum from his mouth as he came. They were both remarkably shy and, at the time, she had thought they were so because this was the first time they had met since their brief and blameless flirtation. (How curious it was that she could scrape off the accretions of the months that had followed and could remember how she had felt on that spring night—as trembling, as expectant, as altogether young as if they had sat together underneath a blooming apple tree.) But now, knowing that her own embarrassment had come from something else, she thought that perhaps his had, too, and she connected his awkwardness on that September day with a report she had had, embedded in a bulletin on everyone, from her sole communicant, since her retreat, with the Olympian world. This informant had run into Alfred at a party and had said that he was having a very bad time of it with a divorce, with poverty, with a tempest that had carried off his job, and, at last, with a psychoanalyst, whose fees he could not possibly afford. Perhaps the nightmare had been well under way when they had met beside the chancery. Without alcohol and without the company of other people, they had had to be shy or their suffering would have shown in all its humiliating dishabille. Would it be true still if they should inescapably meet this afternoon in an Early Flemish room?

Suddenly, on this common level, in this state of social displacement, Emma wished to hunt for Alfred and urgently tell him that she hoped it had not been as bad for him as it had been for her. But naturally she was not so naïve, and she got up and went purposefully to look at two Holbeins. They pleased her, as Holbeins always did. The damage, though, was done, and she did not really see the pictures; Eisenburg's hypothetical suffering and her own real suffering blurred the clean lines and muddied the lucid colors. Between herself and the canvases swam the months of spreading, cancerous distrust, of anger that made her seasick, of grief that shook her like an influenza chill, of the physical afflictions by which the poor victimized spirit sought vainly to wreck the arrogantly healthy flesh.

Even that one glance at his face, seen from a distance through the lowing crowd, told her, now that she had repeated it to her mind's eye, that his cheeks were drawn and his skin was gray (no soap and water can ever clean away the grimy look of the sick at heart) and his stance was tired. She wanted them to go together to some hopelessly disreputable bar and to console one another in the most maudlin fashion over a lengthy succession of powerful drinks of whiskey, to compare their illnesses, to marry their invalid souls for these few hours of painful communion, and to babble with rapture that they were at last, for a little while, no longer alone. Only thus, as sick people, could they marry. In any other terms, it would be a *mésalliance*, doomed to divorce from the start, for rubes and intellectuals must stick to their own class. If only it could take place—this honeymoon of the cripples, this nuptial consummation of the abandoned— while drinking the delicious amber whiskey in a joint with a juke box, a stout barkeep, and a handful of tottering derelicts; if it could take place, would it be possible to prevent him from marring it all by talking of secondary matters? That is, of art and neurosis, art and politics, art and science, art and religion? Could he lay off the fashions of the day and leave his learning in his private entrepôt? Could he, that is, see the apple fall and not run madly to break the news to Newton and ask him what on earth it was all about? Could he, for her sake (for the sake of this pathetic rube all but weeping for her own pathos in the Metropolitan Museum), forget the whole dispute and, believing his eyes for a change, admit that the earth was flat?

It was useless for her now to try to see the paintings. She went, full of intentions, to the Van Eyck diptych and looked for a long time at the souls in Hell, kept there by the implacable, indifferent, and genderless angel who stood upon its closing mouth. She looked, in renewed astonishment, at Jo Davidson's pink, wrinkled, embalmed head of Jules Bache, which sat, a trinket on a fluted pedestal, before a Flemish tapestry. But she was really conscious of nothing but her desire to leave the museum in the company of Alfred Eisenburg, her cousin-german in the territory of despair.

So she had to give up, two hours before the closing time, although she had meant to stay until the end, and she made her way to the central stairs, which she descended slowly, in disappointment, enviously observing the people who were going up, carrying collapsible canvas stools on which they would sit, losing themselves in their contemplation of the pictures. Salvador Dali passed her, going quickly down. At the telephone booths, she hesitated, so sharply lonely that she almost looked for her address book, and she did take out a coin, but she put it back and pressed forlornly forward against the incoming tide. Suddenly, at the storm doors, she heard a whistle and she turned sharply, knowing that it would be Eisenburg, as, of course, it was, and he wore an incongruous smile upon his long, El Greco face. He took her hand and gravely asked her where she had been all this year and how she happened to be here, of all places, of all days. Emma replied distractedly, looking at his seedy clothes, his shaggy hair, the green cast of his white skin, his deep black eyes, in which all the feelings were disheveled, tattered, and held together only by the merest faith that change *had* to come. His hand was warm and her own seemed to cling to it and all their mutual necessity seemed centered here in their clasped hands. And there was no doubt about it; he had heard of her collapse and he saw in her face that she had heard of his. Their recognition of each other was instantaneous and absolute, for they cunningly saw that they were children and that, if they wished, they were free for the rest of this winter Sunday to play together, quite naked, quite innocent. "What a day it is! What a place!" said Alfred Eisenburg. "Can I buy you a drink, Emma? Have you time?"

She did not accept at once; she guardedly inquired where they could go from here, for it was an unlikely neighborhood for the sort of place she wanted. But they were *en rapport*, and he, wanting to avoid the grown-ups as much as she, said they would go across to Lexington. He needed a drink after an afternoon like this—didn't she? Oh, Lord, yes, she did, and she did not question what he meant by "an afternoon like this" but said that she would be delighted to go, even though they would have to walk on eggs all the way from the Museum to the place where the bottle was, the peace pipe on Lexington. Actually, there was nothing to fear; even if they had heard catcalls, or if someone had hooted at them, "Intellectual loves Rube!" they would have been impervious, for the heart carved in the bark of the apple tree would contain the names Emma and Alfred, and there were no perquisites to such a conjugation. To her own heart, which was shaped exactly like a valentine, there came a winglike palpitation, a delicate exigency, and all the fragrance of all the flowery springtime love affairs that ever were seemed waiting for them in the whiskey bottle. To mingle their pain, their handshake had promised them, was to produce a separate entity, like a child that could shift for itself, and they scrambled hastily toward this profound and pastoral experience.

JAY MCINERNEY

IT'S SIX A.M.
DO YOU KNOW
WHERE YOU ARE?

YOU ARE NOT the kind of guy who would be at a place like this at this time of the morning. But here you are, and you cannot say that the terrain is entirely unfamiliar, although the details are a little fuzzy. You are at a nightclub talking to a girl with a shaved head. The club is either the Bimbo Box or the Lizard Lounge. It might all come a little clearer if you could slip into the bathroom and do a little more Bolivian Marching Powder. Then again, it might not. There is a small voice inside of you insisting that this epidemic lack of clarity is the result of too much of that already, but you are not yet willing to listen to that voice. The night has already turned on that imperceptible pivot where two A.M. changes to six A.M. You know that moment has come and gone, though you are not yet willing to concede that you have crossed the line beyond which all is gratuitous damage and the palsy of unraveled nerve endings. Somewhere back there it was possible to cut your losses, but you rode past that moment on a comet trail of white powder and now are trying to hang on to the rush. Your brain at present is composed of brigades of tiny Bolivian soldiers. They are tired and muddy from their long march through the night. There are holes in their boots and they are hungry. They need to be fed. They need the Bolivian Marching Powder.

Something vaguely tribal about this scene—pendulous jewelry, face paint, ceremonial headgear and hairstyles. You feel that there is also a certain Latin theme, which is more than the fading buzz of marimbas in your brain.

You are leaning back against a post which may or may not be structural with regard to the building but nonetheless feels essential for the maintenance of an upright position. The bald girl is saying this used to be a good place to come before the assholes discovered it. You do not want to be talking to this bald girl, or even listening to her, which is all you're doing, but you don't have your barge pole handy, and just at the moment you don't want to test the powers of speech or locomotion.

How did you get here? It was your friend Tad Allagash who powered you in here, and now he has disappeared. Tad is the kind of guy who certainly would be at a place like this at this time of the morning. He is either your best self or your worst self, you're not sure which. Earlier in the evening it seemed clear that he was your best self. You started on the Upper East Side with Champagne and unlimited prospects, strictly observing the Allagash rule of perpetual motion: one drink per stop. Tad's mission in life is to have more fun than anyone else in New York City, and this involves a lot of moving around, since there is always the likelihood that you are missing something, that where you aren't is more fun than where you are. You are awed by this strict refusal to acknowledge any goal higher than the pursuit of pleasure. You want to be like that. You also think that he is shallow and dangerous. His friends are all rich and spoiled, like the cousin from Memphis you met earlier in the evening who refused to accompany you below Fourteenth Street because he said he didn't have a lowlife visa. This cousin had a girl friend with cheekbones to break your heart, and you knew she was the real thing when she never once acknowledged your presence. She possessed secrets—about islands, about horses—that you would never know.

You have traveled from the meticulous to the slime. The

girl with the shaved head has a scar tattooed on her scalp that looks like a long, sutured gash. You tell her it is very realistic. She takes this as a compliment and thanks you. You meant as opposed to romantic. "I could use one of those right over my heart," you say.

"You want I can give you the name of the guy did it. You'd be surprised how cheap." You don't tell her that nothing would surprise you now. Her voice, for instance, which is like the New Jersey state anthem played through an electric shaver.

The bald girl is emblematic of the problem. What the problem is is that for some reason you think you are going to meet the kind of girl who is not the kind of girl who would be at a place like this at this time of the morning. When you meet her you are going to tell her that what you really want is a house in the country with a garden. New York, the club scene, bald women—you're tired of all that. Your presence here is only a matter of conducting an experiment in limits, reminding yourself of what you aren't. You see yourself as the kind of guy who wakes up early on Sunday morning and steps out to pick up the *Times* and croissants. You take a cue from the Arts and Leisure section and decide to check out some exhibition—costumes of the Hapsburg Court at the Met, say, or Japanese lacquerware of the Muromachi period at the Asia Society. Maybe you will call that woman you met at the publishing party Friday night, the party you did not get sloppy drunk at, an editor at a famous publishing house even though she looks like a fashion model. See if she wants to check out the exhibition and maybe do an early dinner. You will wait until eleven A.M. to call her, because unlike you she may not be an early riser. She may have been out a little late, at a nightclub, say. It occurs to you that there is time for a couple sets of tennis before the museum. You wonder if she plays, but then, of course, she would.

When you meet the girl who wouldn't et cetera, you will tell her that you are slumming, visiting your own six A.M. Lower East Side of the soul on a lark, stepping nimbly between the piles of garbage to the marimba rhythms in your head.

On the other hand, any beautiful girl, specifically one with a full head of hair, would help you stave off this creeping sense of mortality. You remember the Bolivian Marching Powder and realize you're not down yet. First you have to get rid of this bald girl because of the bad things she is doing to your mood.

In the bathroom there are no doors on the stalls, which makes it tough to be discreet. But clearly you are not the only person here to take on fuel. Lots of sniffling going on. The windows in here are blacked over, and for this you are profoundly grateful.

Hup, two, three, four. The Bolivian soldiers are back on their feet, off and running in formation. Some of them are dancing, and you must do the same.

Just outside the door you spot her: tall, dark and alone, half hiding behind a pillar at the edge of the dance floor. You approach laterally, moving your stuff like a bad spade through the slalom of a synthesized conga rhythm. She jumps when you touch her shoulder.

"Dance?"

She looks at you as if you had just suggested instrumental rape. "I do not speak English," she says, after you ask again.

"Français?"

She shakes her head. Why is she looking at you that way, like there are tarantulas nesting in your eye sockets?

"You are by any chance from Bolivia? Or Peru?"

She is looking around for help now. Remembering a recent

encounter with a young heiress's bodyguard at Danceteria —or was it New Berlin?—you back off, hands raised over your head.

The Bolivian soldiers are still on their feet, but they have stopped singing their marching song. You realize that we are at a crucial juncture with regard to morale. What we need is a good pep talk from Tad Allagash, who is nowhere to be found. You try to imagine what he would say. *Back on the horse. Now we're* really *going to have some fun.* Something like that. You suddenly realize that he has already slipped out with some rich hose queen. He is back at her place on Fifth Ave., and they are doing some of her off-the-boat-quality drugs. They are scooping it out of tall Ming vases and snorting it off of each other's naked bodies. You hate Tad Allagash.

Go home. Cut your losses.

Stay. Go for it.

You are a republic of voices tonight. Unfortunately, the republic is Italy. All these voices are waving their arms and screaming at one another. There's an *ex cathedra* riff coming down from the Vatican: Repent. There's still time. *Your body is the temple of the Lord and you have defiled it.* It is, after all, Sunday morning, and as long as you have any brain cells left a resonant, patriarchal bass will echo down the marble vaults of your church-going childhood to remind you that this is the Lord's day. What you need is another overpriced drink to drown it out. But a search of pockets yields only a dollar bill and change. You paid ten to get in here. Panic gains on you.

You spot a girl at the edge of the dance floor who looks like your last chance for earthly salvation against the creeping judgment of the Sabbath. You know for a fact that if you go out into the morning alone, without even your sunglasses, which you have forgotten (because who, after all, plans on these travesties), that the harsh, angling light will turn you to flesh and bone. Mortality will pierce you through the retina. But there she is in her pegged pants, a kind of doo-wop retro ponytail pulled off to the side, great lungs, as eligible a candidate as you could hope to find this late in the game. The sexual equivalent of fast food.

She shrugs and nods when you ask her to dance. You like the way she moves, half-tempo, the oiled ellipses of her hips and shoulders. You get a little hip-and-ass contact. After the second song she says she's tired. She's on the edge of bolting when you ask her if she needs a little pick-me-up.

"You've got some blow?" she says.

"Monster," you say.

She takes your arm and leads you into the Ladies'. There's another guy in the stall beside yours so it's okay. After a couple of spoons she seems to like you just fine and you're feeling pretty likable yourself. A couple more. This girl is all nose. When she leans forward for the spoon, the front of her shirt falls open and you can't help wondering if this is her way of thanking you.

Oh yes.

"I love drugs," she says, as you march toward the bar.

"It's something we have in common," you say.

"Have you ever noticed how all the good words start with *D*? *D* and *L*."

You try to think about this. You're not sure what she's driving at. The Bolivians are singing their marching song but you can't quite make out the words.

"You know? Drugs. Delight. Decadence."

"Debauchery," you say, catching the tune now.

"Dexedrine."

"Delectable. Deranged. Debilitated."

"And *L*. Lush and luscious."

"Languorous."

"Lazy."

"Libidinous."

"What's that?" she says.

"Horny."

"Oh," she says and casts a long, arching look over your shoulder. Her eyes glaze in a way that reminds you precisely of the closing of a sand-blasted glass shower door. You can see that the game is over, though you're not sure which rule you broke. Possibly she finds *H* words offensive and is now scanning the dance floor for a man with a compatible vocabulary. You have more: *down* and *depressed, lost* and *lonely.* It's not that you are really going to miss this girl who thinks that *decadence* and *Dexedrine* are the high points of the language of the Kings James and Lear, but the touch of flesh, the sound of another human voice ... You know that there is a special purgatory waiting out there for you, a desperate half-sleep which is like a grease fire in the brainpan.

The girl half waves as she disappears into the crowd. There is no sign of the other girl, the girl who would not be here. There is no sign of Tad Allagash. The Bolivians are mutinous. You can't stop the voices.

Here you are again.

All messed up and no place to go.

It is worse even than you expected, stepping out into the morning. The light is like a mother's reproach. The sidewalk sparkles cruelly. Visibility unlimited. The downtown warehouses look serene and rested in this beveled light. A taxi passes uptown and you start to wave, then realize you have no money. The car stops. You jog over and lean in the window.

"I guess I'll walk after all."

"Asshole." The cabbie leaves rubber.

You start north, holding your hand over your eyes. A bum is sleeping on the sidewalk, swathed in garbage bags, and he lifts his head as you pass. "God bless you and forgive your sins," he says. You wait for the cadge, but that's all he says. You wish he hadn't said anything.

As you turn away, what is left of your olfactory equipment sends a message to your brain. The smell of fresh bread. Somewhere they are baking bread. You see bakery trucks loading in front of a loft building on the next block. You watch as bags of rolls are carried out onto the loading dock by a man with a tattooed forearm. This man is already at work, so that regular people will have fresh bread for their morning tables. The righteous people who sleep at night and eat eggs for breakfast. It is Sunday morning and you have not eaten since . . . when? Friday night. As you approach, the smell of the bread washes over you like a gentle rain. You inhale deeply, filling your lungs with it. Tears come to your eyes, and you are filled with such a rush of tenderness and pity that you stop beside a lamppost and hang on for support.

You remember another Sunday morning in your old apartment on Cornelia Street when you woke to the smell of bread from the bakery downstairs. There was the smell of bread every morning, but this is the one you remember. You turned to see your wife sleeping beside you. Her mouth was open and her hair fell down across the pillow to your shoulder. The tanned skin of her shoulder was the color of bread fresh from the oven. Slowly, and with a growing sense of exhilaration, you remembered who you were. You were the boy and she was the girl, your college sweetheart. You weren't famous yet, but you had the rent covered, you had your favorite restaurant where the waitresses knew your name and you could bring your own bottle of wine. It all seemed to be just as you had pictured it when you had discussed plans for marriage and New York. The apartment with the pressed tin ceiling, the claw-footed bath, the windows that didn't quite fit the frame. It seemed almost as if you had wished for that very place. You leaned against your wife's shoulder. Later you would get up quietly, taking care not to wake her, and go downstairs for croissants and the Sunday *Times*, but for a long time you lay there breathing in the mingled scents of bread, hair and skin. You were in no hurry to get up. You knew it was a moment you wanted to savor. You didn't know how soon it would be over, that within a year she would go back to Michigan to file for divorce.

You approach the man on the loading dock. He stops working and watches you. You feel that there is something wrong with the way your legs are moving.

"Bread." This is what you say to him. You meant to say something more, but this is as much as you can get out.

"What was your first clue?" he says. He is a man who has served his country, you think, a man with a family somewhere outside the city. Small children. Pets. A garden.

"Could I have some? A roll or something?"

"Get out of here."

The man is about your size, except for the belly, which you don't have. "I'll trade you my jacket," you say. It is one hundred percent raw silk from Paul Stuart. You take it off, show him the label.

"You're crazy," the man says. Then he looks back into the warehouse. He picks up a bag of hard rolls and throws them at your feet. You hand him the jacket. He checks the label, sniffs the jacket, then tries it on.

You tear the bag open and the smell of warm dough rushes over you. The first bite sticks in your throat and you almost gag. You will have to go slowly. You will have to learn everything all over again.

EDWIDGE DANTICAT

NEW YORK DAY WOMEN

TODAY, WALKING DOWN the street, I see my mother. She is strolling with a happy gait, her body thrust toward the DON'T WALK sign and the yellow taxicabs that make forty-five-degree turns on the corner of Madison and Fifty-seventh Street.

I have never seen her in this kind of neighborhood, peering into Chanel and Tiffany's and gawking at the jewels glowing in the Bulgari windows. My mother never shops outside of Brooklyn. She has never seen the advertising office where I work. She is afraid to take the subway, where you may meet those young black militant street preachers who curse black women for straightening their hair.

Yet, here she is, my mother, who I left at home that morning in her bathrobe, with pieces of newspapers twisted like rollers in her hair. My mother, who accuses me of random offenses as I dash out of the house.

Would you get up and give an old lady like me your subway seat? In this state of mind, I bet you don't even give up your seat to a pregnant lady.

My mother, who is often right about that. Sometimes I get up and give my seat. Other times, I don't. It all depends on how pregnant the woman is and whether or not she is with her boy friend or husband and whether or not *he* is sitting down.

As my mother stands in front of Carnegie Hall, one taxi driver yells to another, "What do you think this is, a dance floor?"

My mother waits patiently for this dispute to be settled before crossing the street.

In Haiti when you get hit by a car, the owner of the car gets out and kicks you for getting blood on his bumper.

My mother who laughs when she says this and shows a large gap in her mouth where she lost three more molars to the dentist last week. My mother, who at fifty-nine, says dentures are okay.

You can take them out when they bother you. I'll like them. I'll like them fine.

Will it feel empty when Papa kisses you?

Oh no, he doesn't kiss me that way anymore.

My mother, who watches the lottery drawing every night on channel 11 without ever having played the numbers.

A third of that money is all I would need. We would pay the mortgage, and your father could stop driving that taxi-cab all over Brooklyn.

I follow my mother, mesmerized by the many possibilities of her journey. Even in a flowered dress, she is lost in a sea of pinstripes and gray suits, high heels and elegant short skirts, Reebok sneakers, dashing from building to building.

My mother, who won't go out to dinner with anyone.

If they want to eat with me, let them come to my house, even if I boil water and give it to them.

My mother, who talks to herself when she peels the skin off poultry.

Fat, you know, and cholesterol. Fat and cholesterol killed your aunt Hermine.

My mother, who makes jam with dried grapefruit peel and then puts in cinnamon bark that I always think is cockroaches in the jam. My mother, whom I have always bought household appliances for, on her birthday. A nice rice cooker, a blender.

I trail the red orchids in her dress and the heavy faux leather bag on her shoulders. Realizing the ferocious pace of my pursuit, I stop against a wall to rest. My mother keeps on walking as though she owns the sidewalk under her feet.

As she heads toward the Plaza Hotel, a bicycle messenger swings so close to her that I want to dash forward and rescue her, but she stands dead in her tracks and lets him ride around her and then goes on.

My mother stops at a corner hot-dog stand and asks for something. The vendor hands her a can of soda that she slips into her bag. She stops by another vendor selling sundresses for seven dollars each. I can tell that she is looking at an African print dress, contemplating my size. I think to myself, Please Ma, don't buy it. It would be just another thing that I would bury in the garage or give to Goodwill.

Why should we give to Goodwill when there are so many people back home who need clothes? We save our clothes for the relatives in Haiti.

339

Twenty years we have been saving all kinds of things for the relatives in Haiti. I need the place in the garage for an exercise bike.

You are pretty enough to be a stewardess. Only dogs like bones.

This mother of mine, she stops at another hot-dog vendor's and buys a frankfurter that she eats on the street. I never knew that she ate frankfurters. With her blood pressure, she shouldn't eat anything with sodium. She has to be careful with her heart, this day woman.

I cannot just swallow salt. Salt is heavier than a hundred bags of shame.

She is slowing her pace, and now I am too close. If she turns around, she might see me. I let her walk into the park before I start to follow again.

My mother walks toward the sandbox in the middle of the park. There a woman is waiting with a child. The woman is wearing a leotard with biker's shorts and has small weights in her hands. The woman kisses the child goodbye and surrenders him to my mother; then she bolts off, running on the cemented stretches in the park.

The child given to my mother has frizzy blond hair. His hand slips into hers easily, like he's known her for a long time. When he raises his face to look at my mother, it is as though he is looking at the sky.

My mother gives this child the soda that she bought from the vendor on the street corner. The child's face lights up as she puts in a straw in the can for him. This seems to be a conspiracy just between the two of them.

My mother and the child sit and watch the other children play in the sandbox. The child pulls out a comic book from a knapsack with Big Bird on the back. My mother peers into his comic book. My mother, who taught herself to read as a little girl in Haiti from the books that her brothers brought home from school.

My mother, who has now lost six of her seven sisters in Ville Rose and has never had the strength to return for their funerals.

Many graves to kiss when I go back. Many graves to kiss.

She throws away the empty soda can when the child is done with it. I wait and watch from a corner until the woman in the leotard and biker's shorts returns, sweaty and breathless, an hour later. My mother gives the woman back her child and strolls farther into the park.

I turn around and start to walk out of the park before my mother can see me. My lunch hour is long since gone. I have to hurry back to work. I walk through a cluster of joggers, then race to a *Sweden Tours* bus. I stand behind the bus and take a peek at my mother in the park. She is standing in a circle, chatting with a group of women who are taking other people's children on an afternoon outing. They look like a Third World Parent-Teacher Association meeting.

I quickly jump into a cab heading back to the office. Would Ma have said hello had she been the one to see me first?

As the cab races away from the park, it occurs to me that perhaps one day I would chase an old woman down a street by mistake and that old woman would be somebody else's mother, who I would have mistaken for mine.

Day women come out when nobody expects them.

Tonight on the subway, I will get up and give my seat to a pregnant woman or a lady about Ma's age.

My mother, who stuffs thimbles in her mouth and then blows up her cheeks like Dizzy Gillespie while sewing yet another Raggedy Ann doll that she names Suzette after me.

I will have all these little Suzettes in case you never have any babies, which looks more and more like it is going to happen.

My mother who had me when she was thirty-three—*l'âge du Christ*—at the age that Christ died on the cross.

That's a blessing, believe you me, even if American doctors say by that time you can make retarded babies.

My mother, who sews lace collars on my company softball T-shirts when she does my laundry.

Why, you can't you look like a lady playing softball?

My mother, who never went to any of my Parent-Teacher Association meetings when I was in school.

You're so good anyway. What are they going to tell me? I don't want to make you ashamed of this day woman. Shame is heavier than a hundred bags of salt.

AMY HEMPEL

REFERENCE
#388475848-5

TO: PARKING VIOLATIONS BUREAU, New York City

I am writing in reference to the ticket I was issued today for "covering 'The Empire State'" on my license plate. I include two photographs I took this afternoon that show, front and back, that the words "The Empire State" *are* clearly visible. I noticed several cars on the same block featuring license plates on which these words were entirely covered by the frame provided by the car dealer, and I noticed that none of these cars had been ticketed, as mine had. I don't mean to appear insolent, but I am wondering if the ticket might have been issued by the young Hispanic guy I sometimes see patrolling the double-parked cars during the week? I ask because the other day my dog yanked the leash from my hand and ran to him and jumped up looking for a treat. He did not appear to be comfortable around dogs, and though mine is a friendly one, she's big, and maybe the guy was frightened for a moment? It happened as I was getting out of my car, so he would have known it was *my* car, is what I'm saying.

"The Empire State"—it occurred to me that this is a nickname. I mean, police officers do not put out an all-points bulletin in The Empire State, they put out an all-points bulletin in *New York*, which words are also clearly visible on my license plates. In fact, there is no information the government might require that is not visible on these plates. You could even say that the words "The Empire State" are *advertising*. They fit a standard definition: a paid announcement, a public notice in print to induce people to use something, the action of making that thing generally known, providing information of general interest. Close enough.

I have parked my car with the plates as they appear in the accompanying photos on New York City streets for five years, since I drove the car out of the dealership on the Island five years ago; it has never been a problem until now. (I bought the car without ever reading *Consumer Reports*. I checked with a friend who said the price I was quoted was a reasonable one, but that I should refuse the extended warranty the dealer was pushing. "I'm trying to do you a favor," the dealer said, pissed off.)

At the time I bought the car, I didn't know I would soon be back living in the city, and hardly ever needing it. I had thought I would stay the two-hour drive east. What is the saying?—"If you want to make God laugh, tell him your plans."

I haven't kept track of everything I'm supposed to do with the car, but your records will show that I paid the ticket for my expired registration the same week it was issued. I did better with the safety inspection, and FYI, I'm good through November.

It's not really about the money, the $75 the ticket would cost me. I wouldn't mind writing a check for that amount as a donation to a Police Athletic League, or a fund to help rebuild the city. I'm not like the guy at the film festival yesterday who asked the French director in the Q and A after his film was shown, "Are we going to get our money back?" I hadn't even wanted to see the film; before we went, I told my date what I did want to see, and he said, "They stole the idea from that other one, the one where they ate each other." And I said, "No, that was the plane crash; this is the two guys who had the mountain-climbing accident. It's a documentary." And he said, "What isn't?"

Then, after the French film, after the audience applauded for this *major piece of crap*, the date and I cut out and went to a place he had heard about in the East Village for tea. It turned out to be someone's exotic version of high tea, so instead of scones and clotted cream and cucumber sandwiches, we were each served a teaspoon of clear, rosemary-scented jelly with a single pomegranate seed inside! What came after that were these teensy cubes of polenta covered in grapefruit puree, all floating in a "bubble bath" of champagne. Then came a chocolate truffle the size of a tooth. The fellow and I were giddy. It was pouring outside, and when we left, after the tea ceremony, we didn't want to leave each other, so we walked another couple of blocks to see a second movie, one he wanted to see, and I didn't tell him I had already seen it because by that time I just wanted to sit next to him in the dark. "I wonder who that is singing," I whispered at one point in the sound track. He didn't know, but I did, from having read the credits the first time I saw the movie. "Kind of sounds like Dave Matthews," I said, knowing I was right. "Let's be sure to check at the end," I said. "I'd like to get it for you."

Music keeps you youthful. Like I'm not the target audience for the Verve, but this morning I put on that song that goes, "I'm a million different people from one day to the next— I can change, I can change . . ." and—what's my point? I was in a really good mood when I found the ticket on my windshield. Then how to get rid of the poison, like adrenaline, that flooded my system when I read what it was for?

There is a theory of healing based on animals in the wild. People have observed animals that barely escaped a predator, and they say these animals lie down and *shake*, and in so doing somehow release the trauma. Whereas human beings take it in; we don't work it out, so it lodges in us where it produces any number of nasty effects and symptoms. If you follow a kind of guided fantasy, supposedly you can locate a calm, still place inside you and practice visiting it over and over, and that's as far as I got with this theory. It's supposed to make you feel better.

Maybe I should sell the car. But there is something about being able to get in a car and *leave* when you want to, or need to, without waiting to get to a car rental agency if you even know where one is and if it is even open when you get there.

Like last week, after a guy grabbed my arm when I was running around the reservoir, when he was suddenly in front of me, coming from the trees on the south end of the track, and no one else was around just then and I couldn't swing around wide enough to get completely past him, and he grabbed my arm. I think it was my anger that made him finally release me, because that is what I felt, not fear, until I got back home with a sore throat from yelling at him to leave me the fuck alone. I was shaking like crazy, and it wouldn't stop, so I walked a block to where my car was parked, and I drove for a couple of hours toward the ocean. My right leg was bouncing on the accelerator from nerves for much of the way, but I stopped for coffee and when I started up again I steered with my knees, the way *real* drivers steer, with a cup of coffee in one hand, playing the radio with the other. So maybe I am a wild animal, shaking off the trauma of near-capture.

There were actually two men at the reservoir. And I thought it was odd that when the first one grabbed me, and I reflexively swung my free arm around to sock him in the chest, the other man didn't stop me. Because he could have. He watched, and listened to me yell, so I don't know what the deal was. But I think it was worth paying the insurance

348

and having to park the car and get this ticket to have the car there to use that day.

You could accuse me of trying to put a human face on this. And you would be correct. But is there anything wrong with that? Unless the ticket was issued by the guy my dog startled, I know it isn't personal. But I'm not a person who can take this ticket in stride with the kind of urbanity urbane people prize in each other. I feel I must question—and protest—this particular ticket.

I want what is fair. I don't want a fight. But the truth is, I'm shaking—right now, writing this letter. My hand is shaking while I write. It's saying what I can't say—this is the way I say it.

JUNOT DÍAZ

NEGOCIOS

MY FATHER, Ramón de las Casas, left Santo Domingo just before my fourth birthday. Papi had been planning to leave for months, hustling and borrowing from his friends, from anyone he could put the bite on. In the end it was just plain luck that got his visa processed when it did. The last of his luck on the Island, considering that Mami had recently discovered he was keeping with an overweight puta he had met while breaking up a fight on her street in Los Millonitos. Mami learned this from a friend of hers, a nurse and a neighbor of the puta. The nurse couldn't understand what Papi was doing loafing around her street when he was supposed to be on patrol.

The initial fights, with Mami throwing our silverware into wild orbits, lasted a week. After a fork pierced him in the cheek, Papi decided to move out, just until things cooled down. He took a small bag of clothes and broke out early in the morning. On his second night away from the house, with the puta asleep at his side, Papi had a dream that the money Mami's father had promised him was spiraling away in the wind like bright bright birds. The dream blew him out of bed like a gunshot. Are you okay? the puta asked and he shook his head. I think I have to go somewhere, he said. He borrowed a clean mustard-colored guayabera from a friend, put himself in a concho and paid our abuelo a visit.

Abuelo had his rocking-chair in his usual place, out on the sidewalk where he could see everyone and everything. He

353

had fashioned that chair as a thirtieth-birthday present to himself and twice had to replace the wicker screens that his ass and shoulders had worn out. If you were to walk down to the Duarte you would see that type of chair for sale everywhere. It was November, the mangoes were thudding from the trees. Despite his dim eyesight, Abuelo saw Papi coming the moment he stepped onto Sumner Welles. Abuelo sighed, he'd had it up to his cojones with this spat. Papi hiked up his pants and squatted down next to the rocking-chair.

I am here to talk to you about my life with your daughter, he said, removing his hat. I don't know what you've heard but I swear on my heart that none of it is true. All I want for your daughter and our children is to take them to the United States. I want a good life for them.

Abuelo searched his pockets for the cigarette he had just put away. The neighbors were gravitating toward the front of their houses to listen to the exchange. What about this other woman? Abuelo said finally, unable to find the cigarette tucked behind his ear.

It's true I went to her house, but that was a mistake. I did nothing to shame you, viejo. I know it wasn't a smart thing to do, but I didn't know the woman would lie like she did.

Is that what you said to Virta?

Yes, but she won't listen. She cares too much about what she hears from her friends. If you don't think I can do anything for your daughter then I won't ask to borrow that money.

Abuelo spit the taste of car exhaust and street dust from his mouth. He might have spit four or five times. The sun could have set twice on his deliberations but with his eyes quitting, his farm in Azua now dust and his familia in need, what could he really do?

Listen Ramón, he said, scratching his arm hairs. I believe you. But Virta, she hears the chisme on the street and you know how that is. Come home and be good to her. Don't yell. Don't hit the children. I'll tell her that you are leaving soon. That will help smooth things between the two of you.

Papi fetched his things from the puta's house and moved back in that night. Mami acted as if he were a troublesome visitor who had to be endured. She slept with the children and stayed out of the house as often as she could, visiting her relatives in other parts of the Capital. Many times Papi took hold of her arms and pushed her against the slumping walls of the house, thinking his touch would snap her from her brooding silence, but instead she slapped or kicked him. Why the hell do you do that? he demanded. Don't you know how soon I'm leaving?

Then go, she said.

You'll regret that.

She shrugged and said nothing else.

In a house as loud as ours, one woman's silence was a serious thing. Papi slouched about for a month, taking us to kung fu movies we couldn't understand and drilling into us how much we'd miss him. He'd hover around Mami while she checked our hair for lice, wanting to be nearby the instant she cracked and begged him to stay.

One night Abuelo handed Papi a cigar box stuffed with cash. The bills were new and smelled of ginger. Here it is. Make your children proud.

You'll see. He kissed the viejo's cheek and the next day had himself a ticket for a flight leaving in three days. He held the ticket in front of Mami's eyes. Do you see this?

She nodded tiredly and took up his hands. In their room, she already had his clothes packed and mended.

She didn't kiss him when he left. Instead she sent each of the children over to him. Say goodbye to your father. Tell him that you want him back soon.

When he tried to embrace her she grabbed his upper arms, her fingers like pincers. You had best remember where this money came from, she said, the last words they exchanged face-to-face for five years.

He arrived in Miami at four in the morning in a roaring poorly booked plane. He passed easily through customs, having brought nothing but some clothes, a towel, a bar of soap, a razor, his money and a box of Chiclets in his pocket. The ticket to Miami had saved him money but he intended to continue on to Nueva York as soon as he could. Nueva York was the city of jobs, the city that had first called the Cubanos and their cigar industry, then the Bootstrap Puerto Ricans and now him.

He had trouble finding his way out of the terminal. Everyone was speaking English and the signs were no help. He smoked half a pack of cigarettes while wandering around. When he finally exited the terminal, he rested his bag on the sidewalk and threw away the rest of the cigarettes. In the darkness he could see little of Northamerica. A vast stretch of cars, distant palms and a highway that reminded him of the Máximo Gómez. The air was not as hot as home and the city was well lit but he didn't feel as if he had crossed an ocean and a world. A cab driver in front of the terminal called to him in Spanish and threw his bag easily in the backseat of the cab. A new one, he said. The man was black, stooped and strong.

You got family here?

Not really.

How about an address?

Nope, Papi said. I'm here on my own. I got two hands and a heart as strong as a rock.

Right, the taxi driver said. He toured Papi through the

city, around Calle Ocho. Although the streets were empty and accordion gates stretched in front of store-fronts Papi recognized the prosperity in the buildings and in the tall operative lampposts. He indulged himself in the feeling that he was being shown his new digs to ensure that they met with his approval. Find a place to sleep here, the driver advised. And first thing tomorrow get yourself a job. Anything you can find.

I'm here to work.

Sure, said the driver. He dropped Papi off at a hotel and charged him five dollars for half an hour of service. Whatever you save on me will help you later. I hope you do well.

Papi offered the driver a tip but the driver was already pulling away, the dome atop his cab glowing, calling another fare. Shouldering his bag, Papi began to stroll, smelling the dust and the heat filtering up from the pressed rock of the streets. At first he considered saving money by sleeping outside on a bench but he was without guides and the inscrutability of the nearby signs unnerved him. What if there was a curfew? He knew that the slightest turn of fortune could dash him. How many before him had gotten this far only to get sent back for some stupid infraction? The sky was suddenly too high. He walked back the way he had come and went into the hotel, its spastic neon sign obtrusively jutting into the street. He had difficulty understanding the man at the desk, but finally the man wrote down the amount for a night's stay in block numbers. Room cuatro-cuatro, the man said. Papi had as much difficulty working the shower but finally was able to take a bath. It was the first bathroom he'd been in that hadn't curled the hair on his body. With the radio tuned in and incoherent, he trimmed his mustache. No photos exist of his mustache days but it is easily imagined. Within an hour he was asleep. He was twenty-four. He didn't dream about his familia and wouldn't for many years. He dreamed instead of gold coins, like the ones that had been salvaged from the many wrecks about our island, stacked high as sugar cane.

Even on his first disorienting morning, as an aged Latina snapped the sheets from the bed and emptied the one piece of scrap paper he'd thrown in the trash can, Papi pushed himself through the sit-ups and push-ups that kept him kicking ass until his forties.

You should try these, he told the Latina. They make work a lot easier.

If you had a job, she said, you wouldn't need exercise.

He stored the clothes he had worn the day before in his canvas shoulder bag and assembled a new outfit. He used his fingers and water to flatten out the worst of the wrinkles. During the years he'd lived with Mami, he'd washed and ironed his own clothes. These things were a man's job, he liked to say, proud of his own upkeep. Razor creases on his pants and resplendent white shirts were his trademarks. His generation had, after all, been weaned on the sartorial lunacy of the Jefe, who had owned just under ten thousand ties on the eve of his assassination. Dressed as he was, trim and serious, Papi looked foreign but not mojado.

That first day he chanced on a share in an apartment with three Guatemalans and his first job washing dishes at a Cuban sandwich shop. Once an old gringo diner of the hamburger-and-soda variety, the shop now filled with Óyeme's and the aroma of lechón. Sandwich pressers clamped down methodically behind the front counter. The man reading the newspaper in the back told Papi he could start right away and gave him two white ankle-length aprons. Wash these every day, he said. We stay clean around here.

Two of Papi's flatmates were brothers, Stefan and Tomás Hernández. Stefan was older than Tomás by twenty years. Both had families back home. Cataracts were slowly obscuring Stefan's eyes; the disease had cost him half a finger and his last job. He now swept floors and cleaned up vomit at the train station. This is a lot safer, he told my father. Working at a fábrica will kill you long before any tíguere will. Stefan had a passion for the track and would read the forms, despite his brother's warnings that he was ruining what was left of his eyes, by bringing his face down to the type. The tip of his nose was often capped in ink.

Eulalio was the third apartment-mate. He had the largest room to himself and owned the rusted-out Duster that brought them to work every morning. He'd been in the States close to two years and when he met Papi he spoke to him in English. When Papi didn't answer, Eulalio switched to Spanish. You're going to have to practice if you expect to get anywhere. How much English do you know?

None, Papi said after a moment.

Eulalio shook his head. Papi met Eulalio last and liked him least.

Papi slept in the living-room, first on a carpet whose fraying threads kept sticking to his shaved head, and then on a mattress he salvaged from a neighbor. He worked two long shifts a day at the shop and had two four-hour breaks in between. On one of the breaks he slept at home and on the other he would handwash his aprons in the shop's sink and then nap in the storage-room while the aprons dried, amidst the towers of El Pico coffee cans and sacks of bread. Sometimes he read the Western dreadfuls he was fond of—he could read one in about an hour. If it was too hot or he was bored by his book, he walked the neighborhoods, amazed at streets unblocked by sewage and the orderliness of the cars and houses. He was impressed with the transplanted Latinas, who had been transformed by good diets and beauty products unimagined back home. They were beautiful but unfriendly women. He would touch a finger to his beret and stop, hoping to slip in a comment or two, but these women would walk right on by, grimacing.

He wasn't discouraged. He began joining Eulalio on his nightly jaunts to the bars. Papi would have gladly shared a drink with the Devil rather than go out alone. The Hernández brothers weren't much for the outings; they were hoarders, though occasionally they cut loose, blinding themselves on tequila and beers. The brothers would stumble home late, stepping on Papi, howling about some morena who had spurned them to their faces.

Eulalio and Papi went out two, three nights a week, drinking rum and stalking. Whenever he could, Papi let Eulalio do the buying. Eulalio liked to talk about the finca he had come from, a large plantation near the center of his country. I fell in love with the daughter of the owner and she fell in love with me. Me, a peon. Can you believe that? I would fuck her on her own mother's bed, in sight of the Holy Mother and her crucified Son. I tried to make her take down that cross but she wouldn't hear of it. She loved it that way. She was the one who lent me the money to come here. Can you believe that? One of these days, when I got a little money on the side I'm going to send for her.

It was the same story, seasoned differently, every night. Papi said little, believed less. He watched the women who were always with other men. After an hour or two, Papi would pay his bill and leave. Even though the weather was cool, he didn't need a jacket and liked to push through the breeze in short-sleeved shirts. He'd walk the mile home, talking to anyone who would let him. Occasionally drunkards would stop at his Spanish and invite him to a house where men and women were drinking and dancing. He liked those parties far better than the face-offs at the bars. It was with these strangers that he practiced his fledgling English, away from Eulalio's gleeful criticisms.

At the apartment, he'd lie down on his mattress, stretching out his limbs to fill it as much as he could. He abstained from thoughts of home, from thoughts of his two bellicose sons and the wife he had nicknamed Melao. He told himself, Think only of today and tomorrow. Whenever he felt weak, he'd take from under the couch the road map he bought at a gas station and trace his fingers up the coast, enunciating the city names slowly, trying to copy the awful crunch of sounds that was English. The northern coast of our island was visible on the bottom right-hand corner of the map.

He left Miami in the winter. He'd lost his job and gained a new one but neither paid enough and the cost of the living-room floor was too great. Besides, Papi had figured out from a few calculations and from talking to the gringa downstairs (who now understood him) that Eulalio wasn't paying culo for rent. Which explained why he had so many fine clothes and didn't work nearly as much as the rest. When Papi showed the figures to the Hernández brothers, written on the border of a newspaper, they were indifferent. He's the one with the car, they said, Stefan blinking at the numbers. Besides, who wants to start trouble here? We'll all be moving on anyway.

But this isn't right, Papi said. I'm living like a dog for this shit.

What can you do? Tomás said. Life smacks everybody around.

We'll see about that.

There are two stories about what happened next, one from

Papi, one from Mami: either Papi left peacefully with a suit-case filled with Eulalio's best clothes or he beat the man first, and then took a bus and the suitcase to Virginia.

Papi logged most of the miles after Virginia on foot. He could have afforded another bus ticket but that would have bitten into the rent money he had so diligently saved on the advice of many a veteran immigrant. To be homeless in Nueva York was to court the worst sort of disaster. Better to walk 380 miles than to arrive completely broke. He stored his savings in a fake alligator change purse sewn into the seam of his boxer shorts. Though the purse blistered his thigh, it was in a place no thief would search.

He walked in his bad shoes, froze and learned to distin-guish different cars by the sounds of their motors. The cold wasn't as much a bother as his bags were. His arms ached from carrying them, especially the meat of his biceps. Twice he hitched rides from truckers who took pity on the shiver-ing man and just outside of Delaware a K-car stopped him on the side of I-95.

These men were federal marshals. Papi recognized them immediately as police; he knew the type. He studied their car and considered running into the woods behind him. His visa had expired five weeks earlier and if caught, he'd go home in chains. He'd heard plenty of tales about the North-american police from other illegals, how they liked to beat you before they turned you over to la migra and how some-times they just took your money and tossed you out toothless on an abandoned road. For some reason, perhaps the whip-ping cold, perhaps stupidity, Papi stayed where he was, shuffling and sniffing. A window rolled down on the car. Papi went over and looked in on two sleepy blancos.

You need a ride?

Jes, Papi said.

The men squeezed together and Papi slipped into the front seat. Ten miles passed before he could feel his ass again. When the chill and the roar of passing cars finally left him, he realized that a fragile-looking man, handcuffed and shackled, sat in the backseat. The small man wept quietly.

How far you going? the driver asked.

New York, he said, carefully omitting the Nueva and the Yol.

We ain't going that far but you can ride with us to Trenton if you like. Where the hell you from pal?

Miami.

Miami. Miami's kind of far from here. The other man looked at the driver. Are you a musician or something?

Jes, Papi said. I play the accordion.

That excited the man in the middle. Shit, my old man played the accordion but he was a Polack like me. I didn't know you spiks played it too. What kind of polkas do you like?

Polkas?

Jesus, Will, the driver said. They don't play polkas in Cuba.

They drove on, slowing only to unfold their badges at the tolls. Papi sat still and listened to the man crying in the back. What is wrong? Papi asked. Maybe sick?

The driver snorted. Him sick? We're the ones who are about to puke.

What's your name? the Polack asked.

Ramón.

Ramón, meet Scott Carlson Porter, murderer.

Murderer?

Many many murders. Mucho murders.

He's been crying since we left Georgia, the driver

explained. He hasn't stopped. Not once. The little pussy cries even when we're eating. He's driving us nuts.

We thought maybe having another person inside with us would shut him up—the man next to Papi shook his head—but I guess not.

The marshals dropped Papi off in Trenton. He was so relieved not to be in jail that he didn't mind walking the four hours it took to summon the nerve to put his thumb out again.

His first year in Nueva York he lived in Washington Heights, in a roachy flat above what's now the Tres Marías restaurant. As soon as he secured his apartment and two jobs, one cleaning offices and the other washing dishes, he started writing home. In the first letter he folded four twenty-dollar bills. The trickles of money he sent back were not premeditated like those sent by his other friends, calculated from what he needed to survive; these were arbitrary sums that often left him broke and borrowing until the next payday.

The first year he worked nineteen-, twenty-hour days, seven days a week. Out in the cold he coughed explosively, feeling as if his lungs were tearing open from the force of his exhales and in the kitchens the heat from the ovens sent pain corkscrewing into his head. He wrote home sporadically. Mami forgave him for what he had done and told him who else had left the barrio, via coffin or plane ticket. Papi's replies were scribbled on whatever he could find, usually the thin cardboard of tissue boxes or pages from the bill books at work. He was so tired from working that he misspelled almost everything and had to bite his lip to stay awake. He promised her and the children tickets soon. The pictures he received from Mami were shared with his friends at work and then forgotten in his wallet, lost between old lottery slips.

The weather was no good. He was sick often but was able to work through it and succeeded in saving up enough money to start looking for a wife to marry. It was the old routine, the oldest of the postwar maromas. Find a citizen, get married, wait, and then divorce her. The routine was well practiced and expensive and riddled with swindlers.

A friend of his at work put him in touch with a portly balding blanco named el General. They met at a bar. El General had to eat two plates of greasy onion rings before he talked business. Look here friend, el General said. You pay me fifty bills and I bring you a woman that's interested. Whatever the two of you decide is up to you. All I care is that I get paid and that the women I bring are for real. You get no refunds if you can't work something out with her.

Why the hell don't I just go out looking for myself?

Sure, you can do that. He patted vegetable oil on Papi's hand. But I'm the one who takes the risk of running into Immigration. If you don't mind that then you can go out looking anywhere you want.

Even to Papi fifty bucks wasn't exorbitant but he was reluctant to part with it. He had no problem buying rounds at the bar or picking up a new belt when the colors and the moment suited him but this was different. He didn't want to deal with any more change. Don't get me wrong: it wasn't that he was having fun. No, he'd been robbed twice already, his ribs beaten until they were bruised. He often drank too much and went home to his room, and there he'd fume, spinning, angry at the stupidity that had brought him to this freezing hell of a country, angry that a man his age had to masturbate when he had a wife, and angry at the blinkered existence his jobs and the city imposed on him. He never had time to sleep, let alone to go to a concert or the museums that filled entire sections of the newspapers. And the roaches.

The roaches were so bold in his flat that turning on the lights did not startle them. They waved their three-inch antennas as if to say, Hey puto, turn that shit off. He spent five minutes stepping on their carapaced bodies and shaking them from his mattress before dropping into his cot and still the roaches crawled on him at night. No, he wasn't having fun but he also wasn't ready to start bringing his family over. Getting legal would place his hand firmly on that first rung. He wasn't so sure he could face us so soon. He asked his friends, most of whom were in worse financial shape than he was, for advice.

They assumed he was reluctant because of the money. Don't be a pendejo, hombre. Give fulano his money and that's it. Maybe you make good, maybe you don't. That's the way it is. They built these barrios out of bad luck and you got to get used to that.

He met el General across from the Boricua Cafeteria and handed him the money. A day later the man gave him a name: Flor de Oro. That isn't her real name of course, el General assured Papi. I like to keep things historical.

They met at the cafeteria. Each of them had an empanada and a glass of soda. Flor was business-like, about fifty. Her gray hair coiled in a bun on top of her head. She smoked while Papi talked, her hands speckled like the shell of an egg.

Are you Dominican? Papi asked.

No.

You must be Cuban then.

One thousand dollars and you'll be too busy being an American to care where I'm from.

That seems like a lot of money. Do you think once I become a citizen I could make money marrying people?

I don't know.

Papi threw two dollars down on the counter and stood. How much then? How much do you have?

366

I work so much that sitting here is like having a week's vacation. Still I only have six hundred.

Find two hundred more and we got a deal.

Papi brought her the money the next day stuffed in a wrinkled paper bag and in return was given a pink receipt. When do we get started? he asked.

Next week. I have to start on the paperwork right away.

He pinned the receipt over his bed and before he went to sleep, he checked behind it to be sure no roaches lurked. His friends were excited and the boss at the cleaning job took them out for drinks and appetizers in Harlem, where their Spanish drew more looks than their frumpy clothes. Their excitement was not his; he felt as if he'd moved too precipitously. A week later, Papi went to see the friend who had recommended el General.

I still haven't gotten a call, he explained. The friend was scrubbing down a counter.

You will. The friend didn't look up. A week later Papi lay in bed, drunk, alone, knowing full well that he'd been robbed.

He lost the cleaning job shortly thereafter for punching the friend off a ladder. He lost his apartment and had to move in with a familia and found another job frying wings and rice at a Chinese take-out joint. Before he left his flat, he wrote an account of what had happened to him on the pink receipt and left it on the wall as a warning to whatever fool came next to take his place. Ten cuidado, he wrote. These people are worse than sharks.

He sent no money home for close to six months. Mami's letters would be read and folded and tucked into his well-used bags.

Papi met her on the morning before Christmas, in a laundry, while folding his pants and knotting his damp socks. She was short, had daggers of black hair pointing down in front of her ears and lent him her iron. She was originally from La Romana, but like so many Dominicans had eventually moved to the Capital.

I go back there about once a year, she told Papi. Usually around Pascua to see my parents and my sister.

I haven't been home in a long long time. I'm still trying to get the money together.

It will happen, believe me. It took me years before I could go back my first time.

Papi found out she'd been in the States for six years, a citizen. Her English was excellent. While he packed his things in his nylon bag, he considered asking her to the party. A friend had invited him to a house in Corona, Queens, where fellow Dominicans were celebrating la Noche Buena together. He knew from a past party that up in Queens the food, dancing and single women came in heaps.

Four children were trying to pry open the plate at the top of a dryer to reach the coin mechanism underneath. My fucking quarter is stuck, a kid was shouting. In the corner, a student, still in medical greens, was trying to read a magazine and not be noticed but as soon as the kids were tired of the machine, they descended on him, pulling at his magazine and pushing their hands into his pockets. He began to shove back.

Hey, Papi said. The kids threw him the finger and ran outside. Fuck all spiks! they shrieked.

Niggers, the medical student muttered. Papi pulled the drawstring shut on his bag and decided against asking her. He knew the rule: Strange is the woman who goes strange places with a complete stranger. Instead, Papi asked her if he could practice his English on her one day. I really need to practice, he said. And I'd be willing to pay you for your time.

368

She laughed. Don't be ridiculous. Stop by when you can. She wrote her number and address in crooked letters.

Papi squinted at the paper. You don't live around here?

No but my cousin does. I can give you her number if you want.

No, this will be fine.

He had a grand time at the party and actually avoided the rum and the six-packs he liked to down. He sat with two older women and their husbands, a plate of food on his lap (potato salad, pieces of roast chicken, a stack of tostones, half an avocado and a tiny splattering of mondongo out of politeness to the woman who'd brought it) and talked about his days in Santo Domingo. It was a lucid enjoyable night that would stick out in his memory like a spike. He swaggered home around one o'clock, bearing a plastic bag loaded with food and a loaf of telera under his arm. He gave the bread to the shivering man sleeping in the hallway of his building.

When he called Nilda a few days later he found out from a young girl who spoke in politely spaced words that she was at work. Papi left his name and called back that night. Nilda answered.

Ramón, you should have called me yesterday. It was a good day to start since neither of us had work.

I wanted to let you celebrate the holiday with your family.

Family? she clucked. I only have a daughter here. What are you doing now? Maybe you want to come over.

I wouldn't want to intrude, he said because he was a sly one, you had to admit that.

She owned the top floor of a house on a bleak quiet street in Brooklyn. The house was clean, with cheap bubbled linoleum covering the floors. Nilda's taste struck Ramón as low-class. She threw together styles and colors the way a child might throw together paint or clay. A bright orange plaster elephant reared up from the center of a low glass table. A tapestry of a herd of mustangs hung opposite vinyl cutouts of African singers. Fake plants relaxed in each room. Her daughter Milagros was excruciatingly polite and seemed to have an endless supply of dresses more fit for quinceañeras than everyday life. She wore thick plastic glasses and sat in front of the television when Papi visited, one skinny leg crossed over the other. Nilda had a well-stocked kitchen and Papi cooked for her, his stockpile of Cantonese and Cuban recipes inexhaustible. His ropa vieja was his best dish and he was glad to see he had surprised her. I should have you in my kitchen, she said.

She liked to talk about the restaurant she owned and her last husband, who had a habit of hitting her and expecting that all his friends be fed for free. Nilda wasted hours of their study time caught between the leaves of tome-sized photo albums, showing Papi each stage of Milagros's development as if the girl were an exotic bug. He did not mention his own familia. Two weeks into his English lessons, Papi kissed Nilda. They were sitting on the plastic-covered sofa, in the next room a game show was on the TV, and his lips were greasy from Nilda's pollo guisado.

I think you better leave, she said.

You mean now?

Yes, now.

He drew on his windbreaker as slowly as he could, expecting her to recant. She held open the door and shut it quickly after him. He cursed her the entire train ride back into Manhattan. The next day at work, he told his co-workers that she was insane and had a snake coiled up in her heart. I should've known, he said bitterly. A week later he was back at her house, grating coconuts and talking in English. He tried again and again she had him leave.

Each time he kissed her she threw him out. It was a cold winter and he didn't have much of a coat. Nobody bought coats then, Papi told me, because nobody was expecting to stay that long. So I kept going back and any chance I got I kissed her. She would tense up and tell me to leave, like I'd hit her. So I would kiss her again and she'd say, Oh, I really think you better leave now. She was a crazy lady. I kept it up and one day she kissed me back. Finally. By then I knew every maldito train in the city and I had this big wool coat and two pairs of gloves. I looked like an Eskimo. Like an American.

Within a month Papi moved out of his apartment into her house in Brooklyn. They were married in March.

Although he wore a ring, Papi didn't act the part of the husband. He lived in Nilda's house, shared her bed, paid no rent, ate her food, talked to Milagros when the TV was broken and set up his weight bench in the cellar. He regained his health and liked to show Nilda how his triceps and biceps could gather in prominent knots with a twist of his arm. He bought his shirts in size medium so he could fill them out.

He worked two jobs close to her house. The first soldering at a radiator shop, plugging holes mostly, the other as a cook at a Chinese restaurant. The owners of the restaurant were Chinese-Cubans; they cooked a better arroz negro than pork fried rice and loved to spend the quiet hours between lunch and dinner slapping dominos with Papi and the other help on top of huge drums of shortening. One day, while adding up his totals, Papi told these men about his familia in Santo Domingo.

The chief cook, a man so skinny they called him Needle, soured. You can't forget your familia like that. Didn't they support you to send you here?

371

I'm not forgetting them, Papi said defensively. Right now is just not a good time for me to send for them. You should see my bills.

What bills?

Papi thought a moment. Electricity. That's very expensive. My house has eighty-eight light bulbs.

What kind of house are you living in?

Very big. An antique house needs a lot of bulbs, you know.

Come mierda. Nobody has that many light bulbs in their house.

You better do more playing and less talking or I'm going to have to take all your money.

These harangues must not have bothered his conscience much because that year he sent no money.

Nilda learned about Papi's other familia from a chain of friends that reached back across the Caribe. It was inevitable. She was upset and Papi had to deliver some of his most polished performances to convince her that he no longer cared about us. He'd been fortunate in that when Mami reached back across a similar chain of immigrants to locate Papi in the north, he'd told her to direct her letters to the restaurant he was working at and not to Nilda's home.

As with most of the immigrants around them, Nilda was usually at work. The couple saw each other mostly in the evenings. Nilda not only had her restaurant, where she served a spectacular and popular sancocho with wedges of cold avocado, but she also pushed her tailoring on the customers. If a man had a torn work shirt or a pant cuff soiled in machine oil, she'd tell him to bring it by, that she'd take care of it, cheap. She had a loud voice and could draw the attention of the entire eatery to a shabby article of clothing and few, under the combined gaze of their peers, could resist her. She brought the clothes home in a garbage bag and spent her time off sewing and listening to the radio, getting up only to bring Ramón a beer or change the channel for him. When she had to bring money home from the register, her skills at secreting it away were uncanny. She kept nothing but coins in her purse and switched her hiding place each trip. Usually she lined her bra with twenty-dollar bills as if each cup was a nest but Papi was amazed at her other ploys. After a crazy day of mashing platanos and serving the workers, she sealed nearly nine hundred dollars in twenties and fifties in a sandwich bag and then forced the bag into the mouth of a Malta bottle. She put a straw in there and sipped on it on her way home. She never lost a brown penny in the time she and Papi were together. If she wasn't too tired she liked to have him guess where she was hiding the money and with each wrong guess he'd remove a piece of her clothing until the cache was found.

Papi's best friend at this time, and Nilda's neighbor, was Jorge Carretas Lugones, or Jo-Jo as he was commonly known in the barrio. Jo-Jo was a five-foot-tall Puerto Rican whose light skin was stippled with moles and whose blue eyes were the color of larimar. On the street, he wore a pava, angled in the style of the past, carried a pen and all the local lotteries in his shirt pockets, and would have struck anyone as a hustler. Jo-Jo owned two hot-dog carts and co-owned a grocery store that was very prosperous. It had once been a tired place with rotting wood and cracked tiles but with his two brothers he'd pulled the porquería out and rebuilt it over the four months of one winter, while driving a taxi and working as a translator and letter-writer for a local patrón. The years of doubling the price on toilet paper, soap and diapers to pay the loan sharks were over. The coffin refrigerators lining one wall were new, as were the bright green lottery machine and the revolving racks of junk food at the end of each short shelf. He was disdainful of anyone who had a regular crowd of parasites loafing about their stores, discussing the taste of yuca and their last lays. And though this neighborhood was rough (not as bad as his old barrio in San Juan where he had seen all his best friends lose fingers in machete fights), Jo-Jo didn't need to put a grate over his store. The local kids left him alone and instead terrorized a Pakistani family down the street. The family owned an Asian grocery store that looked like a holding cell, windows behind steel mesh, door reinforced with steel plates.

Jo-Jo and Papi met at the local bar regularly. Papi was the man who knew the right times to laugh and when he did, everyone around him joined in. He was always reading newspapers and sometimes books and seemed to know many things. Jo-Jo saw in Papi another brother, a man from a luckless past needing a little direction. Jo-Jo had already rehabilitated two of his siblings, who were on their way to owning their own stores.

Now that you have a place and papers, Jo-Jo told Papi, you need to use these things to your advantage. You have some time, you don't have to break your ass paying the rent, so use it. Save some money and buy yourself a little business. I'll sell you one of my hot-dog carts cheap if you want. You can see they're making steady plata. Then you get your familia over here and buy yourself a nice house and start branching out. That's the American way.

Papi wanted a negocio of his own, that was his dream, but he balked at starting at the bottom, selling hot dogs. While most of the men around him were two-times broke, he had seen a few, fresh off the boat, shake the water from their backs and jump right into the lowest branches of the American establishment. That leap was what he envisioned for himself, not some slow upward crawl through the mud. What it would be and when it would come, he did not know.

I'm looking for the right investment, he told Jo-Jo. I'm not a food man.

What sort of man are you then? Jo-Jo demanded. You Dominicans got restaurants in your blood.

I know, Papi said, but I am not a food man.

Worse, Jo-Jo spouted a hard line on loyalty to familia which troubled Papi. Each scenario his friend proposed ended with Papi's familia living safely within his sight, showering him with love. Papi had difficulty separating the two threads of his friend's beliefs, that of negocios and that of familia, and in the end the two became impossibly intertwined.

With the hum of his new life Papi should have found it easy to bury the memory of us but neither his conscience, nor the letters from home that found him wherever he went, would allow it. Mami's letters, as regular as the months themselves, were corrosive slaps in the face. It was now a one-sided correspondence, with Papi reading and not mailing anything back. He opened the letters wincing in anticipation. Mami detailed how his children were suffering, how his littlest boy was so anemic people thought he was a corpse come back to life; she told him about his oldest son, playing in the barrio, tearing open his feet and exchanging blows with his so-called friends. Mami refused to talk about her condition. She called Papi a desgraciado and a puto of the highest order for abandoning them, a traitor worm, an eater of pubic lice, a cockless, ball-less cabrón. He showed Jo-Jo the letters, often at drunken bitter moments, and Jo-Jo would shake his head, waving for two more beers. You, my compadre, have done too many things wrong. If you keep this up, your life will spring apart.

What in the world can I do? What does this woman want from me? I've been sending her money. Does she want me to starve up here?

You and I know what you have to do. That's all I can say, otherwise I'd be wasting my breath.

Papi was lost. He would take long perilous night walks home from his jobs, sometimes arriving with his knuckles scuffed and his clothes disheveled. His and Nilda's child was born in the spring, a son, also named Ramón, cause for fiesta but there was no celebration among his friends. Too many of them knew. Nilda could sense that something was wrong, that a part of him was detained elsewhere but each time she brought it up Papi told her it was nothing, always nothing.

With a regularity that proved instructional, Jo-Jo had Papi drive him to Kennedy to meet one or the other of the relatives Jo-Jo had sponsored to come to the States to make it big. Despite his prosperity, Jo-Jo could not drive and did not own a car. Papi would borrow Nilda's Chevy station wagon and would fight the traffic for an hour to reach the airport. Depending on the season, Jo-Jo would bring either a number of coats or a cooler of beverages taken from his shelves— a rare treat since Jo-Jo's cardinal rule was that one should never prey on one's own stock. At the terminal, Papi would stand back, his hands pressed in his pockets, his beret plugged on tight, while Jo-Jo surged forward to greet his familia. Papi's English was good now, his clothes better. Jo-Jo would enter a berserk frenzy when his relatives stumbled through the arrival gate, dazed and grinning, bearing cardboard boxes and canvas bags. There would be crying and abrazos. Jo-Jo would introduce Ramón as a brother and Ramón would be dragged into the circle of crying people. It was a simple matter for Ramón to rearrange the faces of the arrivals and see his wife and his children there.

He began again to send money to his familia on the Island. Nilda noticed that he began to borrow from her for his tobacco and to play the lotteries. Why do you need my money? she complained. Isn't that the reason you're working? We have a baby to look after. There are bills to pay.

One of my children died, he said. I have to pay for the wake and the funeral. So leave me alone.

Why didn't you tell me?

He put his hands over his face but when he removed them she was still staring skeptically.

Which one? she demanded. His hand swung clumsily. She fell down and neither of them said a word.

Papi landed a union job with Reynolds Aluminum in West New York that paid triple what he was making at the radiator shop. It was nearly a two-hour commute, followed by a day of tendon-ripping labor, but he was willing—the money and the benefits were exceptional. It was the first time he had moved outside the umbra of his fellow immigrants. The racism was pronounced. The two fights he had were reported to the bosses and they put him on probation. He worked through that period, got a raise and the highest performance rating in his department and the shittiest schedule in the entire fábrica. The whites were always dumping their bad shifts on him and on his friend Chuito. Guess what, they'd say, clapping them on the back. I need a little time with my kids this week. I know you wouldn't mind taking this or that day for me.

No, my friend, Papi would say. I wouldn't mind. Once Chuito complained to the bosses and was written up for detracting *from the familial spirit of the department*. Both men knew better than to speak up again.

On a normal day Papi was too exhausted to visit with Jo-Jo. He'd enjoy his dinner and then settle down to watch Tom and Jerry, who delighted him with their violence. Nilda, watch this, he'd scream and she'd dutifully appear, needles in mouth, baby in her arms. Papi would laugh so loud that Milagros upstairs would join in without even seeing what had occurred. Oh, that's wonderful, he'd say. Would you look at that! They're *killing* each other!

One day, he skipped his dinner and a night in front of the TV to drive south with Chuito into New Jersey to a small town outside of Perth Amboy. Chuito's Gremlin pulled into a neighborhood under construction. Huge craters had been gouged in the earth and towering ziggurats of tan bricks stood ready to be organized into buildings. New pipes were being laid by the mile and the air was tart with the smell of chemicals. It was a cool night. The men wandered around the pits and the sleeping trucks.

I have a friend who is doing the hiring for this place, Chuito said.

Construction?

No. When this neighborhood goes up they'll need superintendents to watch over things. Keep the hot water running, stop a leaking faucet, put new tile in the bathroom. For that you get a salary and free rent. That's the kind of job worth having. The towns nearby are quiet, lots of good gringos. Listen Ramón, I can get you a job here if you like. It would be a good place to move. Out of the city, safety. I'll put your name at the top of the list and when this place is done you'll have a nice easy job.

This sounds better than a dream.

Forget dreams. This is real, compadre.

The two men inspected the site for about an hour and then headed back toward Brooklyn. Papi was silent. A plan was forming. Here was the place to move his familia if it came from the Island. Quiet and close to his job. Most important, the neighborhood would not know him or the wife he had in the States. When he reached home that night he said nothing to Nilda about where he had been. He didn't care that she was suspicious and that she yelled at him about his muddy shoes.

Papi continued to send money home and in Jo-Jo's lockbox he was saving a tidy sum for plane tickets. And then one morning, when the sun had taken hold of the entire house and the sky seemed too thin and blue to hold a cloud, Nilda said, I want to go to the Island this year.

Are you serious?

I want to see my viejos.

What about the baby?

He's never gone, has he?

No.

Then he should see his patria. I think it's important.

I agree, he said. He tapped a pen on the wrinkled place mat. This sounds like you're serious.

I think I am.

Maybe I'll go with you.

If you say so. She had reason to doubt him; he was real good at planning but real bad at doing. And she didn't stop doubting him either, until he was on the plane next to her, rifling anxiously through the catalogs, the vomit bag and the safety instructions.

He was in Santo Domingo for five days. He stayed at Nilda's familia's house on the western edge of the city. It was painted bright orange with an outhouse slumped nearby and a pig pushing around in a pen. Homero and Josefa, tíos of Nilda, drove home with them from the airport in a cab and gave them the "bedroom." The couple slept in the other room, the "living-room."

Are you going to see them? Nilda asked that first night. They were both listening to their stomachs struggling to

379

digest the heaping meal of yuca and hígado they had eaten. Outside, the roosters were pestering each other.

Maybe, he said. If I get the time.

I know that's the only reason you're here.

What's wrong with a man seeing his familia? If you had to see your first husband for some reason, I'd let you, wouldn't I?

Does she know about me?

Of course she knows about you. Not like it matters now. She's out of the picture completely.

She didn't answer him. He listened to his heart beating, and began to sense its slick contours.

On the plane, he'd been confident. He'd talked to the vieja near the aisle, telling her how excited he was. It is always good to return home, she said tremulously. I come back anytime I can, which isn't so much anymore. Things aren't good.

Seeing the country he'd been born in, seeing his people in charge of everything, he was unprepared for it. The air whooshed out of his lungs. For nearly four years he'd not spoken his Spanish loudly in front of the Northamericans and now he was hearing it bellowed and flung from every mouth.

His pores opened, dousing him as he hadn't been doused in years. An awful heat was on the city and the red dust dried out his throat and clogged his nose. The poverty—the unwashed children pointing sullenly at his new shoes, the familias slouching in hovels—was familiar and stifling.

He felt like a tourist, riding a guagua to Boca Chica and having his and Nilda's photograph taken in front of the Alcázar de Colón. He was obliged to eat two or three times a day at various friends of Nilda's familia; he was, after all, the new successful husband from the North. He watched Josefa pluck a chicken, the wet plumage caking her hands and plastering the floor, and remembered the many times he'd done the same, up in Santiago, his first home, where he no longer belonged.

He tried to see his familia but each time he set his mind to it, his resolve scattered like leaves before a hurricane wind. Instead he saw his old friends on the force and drank six bottles of Brugal in three days. Finally, on the fourth day of his visit, he borrowed the nicest clothes he could find and folded two hundred dollars into his pocket. He took a guagua down Sumner Welles, as Calle XXI had been renamed, and cruised into the heart of his old barrio. Colmados on every block and billboards plastering every exposed wall or board. The children chased each other with hunks of cinder block from nearby buildings—a few threw rocks at the guagua, the loud pings jerking the passengers upright. The progress of the guagua was frustratingly slow, each stop seemed spaced four feet from the last. Finally, he disembarked, walking two blocks to the corner of XXI and Tunti. The air must have seemed thin then, and the sun like a fire in his hair, sending trickles of sweat down his face. He must have seen people he knew. Jayson sitting glumly at his colmado, a soldier turned grocer. Chicho, gnawing at a chicken bone, at his feet a row of newly shined shoes. Maybe Papi stopped there and couldn't go on, maybe he went as far as the house, which hadn't been painted since his departure. Maybe he even stopped at our house and stood there, waiting for his children out front to recognize him.

In the end, he never visited us. If Mami heard from her friends that he was in the city, with his other wife, she never told us about it. His absence was a seamless thing to me. And if a strange man approached me during my play and stared down at me and my brother, perhaps asking our names, I don't remember it now.

*   *   *

381

Papi returned home and had trouble resuming his routine. He took a couple of sick days, the first three ever, and spent the time in front of the television and at the bar. Twice he turned down negocios from Jo-Jo. The first ended in utter failure, cost Jo-Jo "the gold in his teeth," but the other, the FOB clothing store on Smith Street, with the bargain basement buys, the enormous bins of factory seconds and a huge layaway shelf, pulled in the money in bags. Papi had recommended the location to Jo-Jo, having heard about the vacancy from Chuito, who was still living in Perth Amboy. London Terrace Apartments had not yet opened.

After work Papi and Chuito caroused in the bars on Smith and Elm Streets and every few nights Papi stayed over in Perth Amboy. Nilda had continued to put on weight after the birth of the third Ramón and while Papi favored heavy women, he didn't favor obesity and wasn't inclined to go home. Who needs a woman like you? he told her. The couple began to fight on a regular schedule. Locks were changed, doors were broken, slaps were exchanged but week ends and an occasional week day night were still spent together.

In the dead of summer, when the potato-scented fumes from the diesel forklifts were choking the warehouses, Papi was helping another man shove a crate into position when he felt a twinge about midway up his spine. Hey asshole, keep pushing, the other man grunted. Pulling his work shirt out of his Dickies, Papi twisted to the right, then to the left and that was it, something snapped. He fell to his knees. The pain was so intense, shooting through him like fireballs from Roman candles, that he vomited on the concrete floor of the warehouse. His co-workers moved him to the lunch-room. For two hours he tried repeatedly to walk and failed. Chuito came down from his division, concerned for his friend but also worried that this unscheduled break would piss off his boss. How are you? he asked.

Not so good. You have to get me out of here.

You know I can't leave.

Then call me a cab. Just get me home. Like anyone wounded, he thought home could save him.

Chuito called him the taxi; none of the other employees took time to help him walk out.

Nilda put him in bed and had a cousin manage the restaurant. Jesú, he moaned to her. I should've slowed down a little. Just a little bit longer and I would've been home with you. Do you know that? A couple of hours more.

She went down to the botánica for a poultice and then down to the bodega for aspirin. Let's see how well the old magic works, she said, smearing the poultice onto his back.

For two days he couldn't move, not even his head. He ate very little, strictly soups she concocted. More than once he fell asleep and woke up to find Nilda out, shopping for medicinal teas, and Milagros over him, a grave owl in her large glasses. Mi hija, he said. I feel like I'm dying.

You won't die, she said.

And what if I do?

Then Mama will be alone.

He closed his eyes and prayed that she would be gone and when he opened them, she was and Nilda was coming in through the door with another remedy, steaming on a battered tray.

He was able to sit up and call in sick by himself on the fourth day. He told the morning-shift manager that he couldn't move too well. I think I stay in bed, he said. The manager told him to come in so he could receive a medical furlough. Papi had Milagros find the name of a lawyer in the phone book. He was thinking lawsuit. He had dreams, fantastic dreams of gold rings and a spacious house with caged tropical birds in its rooms, a house awash with sea winds. The woman lawyer he contacted only worked divorces but she gave him the name of her brother.

Nilda wasn't optimistic about his plan. Do you think the gringo will part with his money like that? The reason they're so pale is because they're terrified of not having any plata. Have you even spoken to the man you were helping? He's probably going to be a witness for the company so that he won't lose his job the same way you're going to lose yours. That maricón will probably get a raise for it, too.

I'm not an illegal, he said. I'm protected.

I think it's better if you let it drop.

He called Chuito to sound him out. Chuito wasn't optimistic either. The boss knows what you're trying to yank. He no like it, compadre. He say you better get back to work or you're quitted.

His courage failing, Papi started pricing a consultation with an independent doctor. Very likely, his father's foot was hopping about in his mind. His father, José Edilio, the loud-mouthed ball-breaking vagrant who had never married Papi's mother but nevertheless had given her nine children, had attempted a similar stunt when he worked in a hotel kitchen in Río Piedras. José had accidentally dropped a tin of stewed tomatoes on his foot. Two small bones broke but instead of seeing a doctor, José kept working, limping around the kitchen. Every day at work, he'd smile at his fellow workers and say, I guess it's time to take care of that foot. Then he'd smash another can on it, figuring the worse it was, the more money he'd get when he finally showed the bosses. It saddened and shamed Papi to hear of this while he was growing up. The old man was rumored to have wandered the barrio he lived in, trying to find someone who would take a bat to the foot. For the old man that foot was an investment, an heirloom he cherished and burnished, until half of it had to be amputated because the infection was so bad.

After another week and with no calls from the lawyers, Papi saw the company doctor. His spine felt as if there were broken glass inside of it but he was given only three weeks of medical leave. Ignoring the instructions on the medication, he swallowed ten pills a day for the pain. He got better. When he returned to the job he could work and that was enough. The bosses were unanimous, however, in voting down Papi's next raise. They demoted him to the rotating shift he'd been on during the first days of the job.

Instead of taking his licks, he blamed it on Nilda. Puta, was what he took to calling her. They fought with renewed vigor; the orange elephant was knocked over and lost a tusk. She kicked him out twice but after probationary weeks at Jo-Jo's allowed him to return. He saw less of his son, avoiding all of the daily routines that fed and maintained the infant. The third Ramón was a handsome child who roamed the house restlessly, tilted forward and at full speed, as if he were a top that had been sent spinning. Papi was good at playing with the baby, pulling him by his foot across the floor and tickling his sides, but as soon as the third Ramón started to fuss, playtime was over. Nilda, come and tend to this, he'd say.

The third Ramón resembled Papi's other sons and on occasion he'd say, Yunior, don't do that. If Nilda heard these slips she would explode. Maldito, she'd cry, picking up the child and retreating with Milagros into the bedroom. Papi didn't screw up too often but he was never certain how many times he'd called the third Ramón with the second son Ramón in mind.

With his back killing him and his life with Nilda headed

down the toilet, Papi began more and more to regard his departure as inevitable. His first familia was the logical destination. He began to see them as his saviors, as a regenerative force that could redeem his fortunes. He said as much to Jo-Jo. Now you're finally talking sense, panín, Jo-Jo said. Chuito's imminent departure from the warehouse also emboldened Ramón to act. London Terrace Apartments, delayed because of a rumor that it had been built on a chemical dump site, had finally opened.

Jo-Jo was only able to promise Papi half the money he needed. Jo-Jo was still throwing away money on his failed negocio and needed a little time to recover. Papi took this as a betrayal and said so to their friends. He talks a big game but when you're at the final inning, you get nada. Although these accusations filtered back to Jo-Jo and wounded him, he still loaned Papi the money without comment. That's how Jo-Jo was. Papi worked for the rest of it, more months than he expected. Chuito reserved him an apartment and together they began filling the place with furniture. He started taking a shirt or two with him to work, which he then sent to the apartment. Sometimes he'd cram socks in his pockets or put on two pairs of underwear. He was smuggling himself out of Nilda's life.

What's happening to your clothes? she asked one night.

It's that damn cleaners, he said. That bobo keeps losing my things. I'm going to have to have a word with him as soon as I get a day off.

Do you want me to go?

I can handle this. He's a very nasty guy.

The next morning she caught him cramming two guayaberas in his lunch pail. I'm sending these to be cleaned, he explained.

Let me do them.

You're too busy. It's easier this way.

He wasn't very smooth about it.

They spoke only when necessary.

Years later Nilda and I would speak, after he had left us for good, after her children had moved out of the house. Milagros had children of her own and their pictures crowded on tables and walls. Nilda's son loaded baggage at JFK. I picked up the picture of him with his girl friend. We were brothers all right, though his face respected symmetry.

We sat in the kitchen, in that same house, and listened to the occasional pop of a rubber ball being batted down the wide channel between the building fronts. My mother had given me her address (Give my regards to the puta, she'd said) and I'd taken three trains to reach her, walked blocks with her address written on my palm.

I'm Ramón's son, I'd said.

Hijo, I know who you are.

She fixed café con leche and offered me a Goya cracker. No thanks, I said, no longer as willing to ask her questions or even to be sitting there. Anger has a way of returning. I looked down at my feet and saw that the linoleum was worn and filthy. Her hair was white and cut close to her small head. We sat and drank and finally talked, two strangers reliving an event—a whirlwind, a comet, a war—we'd both seen but from different faraway angles.

He left in the morning, she explained quietly. I knew something was wrong because he was lying in bed, not doing anything but stroking my hair, which was very long back then. I was a Pentecostal. Usually he didn't lay around in bed. As soon as he was awake he was showered and dressed and gone. He had that sort of energy. But when he got up he just stood over little Ramón. Are you okay? I asked him and he said he was just fine. I wasn't going to fight with him about it so I went right back to sleep. The dream I had is one I still think about. I was young and it was my birthday and I was eating a plate of quail's eggs and all of them were for me. A silly dream really. When I woke up I saw that the rest of his things were gone.

She cracked her knuckles slowly. I thought that I would never stop hurting. I knew then what it must have been like for your mother. You should tell her that.

We talked until it got dark and then I got up. Outside the local kids were gathered in squads, stalking in and out of the lucid clouds produced by the street lamps. She suggested I go to her restaurant but when I got there and stared through my reflection in the glass at the people inside, all of them versions of people I already knew, I decided to go home.

December. He had left in December. The company had given him a two-week vacation, which Nilda knew nothing about. He drank a cup of black café in the kitchen and left it washed and drying in the caddy. I doubt if he was crying or even anxious. He lit a cigarette, tossed the match on the kitchen table and headed out into the angular winds that were blowing long and cold from the south. He ignored the convoys of empty cabs that prowled the streets and walked down Atlantic. There were less furniture and antique shops then. He smoked cigarette after cigarette and killed his pack within the hour. He bought a carton at a stand, knowing how expensive they would be abroad.

The first subway station on Bond would have taken him to the airport and I like to think that he grabbed that first train, instead of what was more likely true, that he had gone out to Chuito's first, before flying south to get us.

ACKNOWLEDGMENTS

JAMES BALDWIN: "Sonny's Blues" © 1957 by James Baldwin was originally published in *Partisan Review.* Copyright renewed. Collected in *Going to Meet the Man,* published by Vintage Books. Reprinted by arrangement with the James Baldwin Estate.

MAEVE BRENNAN: "A Snowy Night on West Forty-Ninth Street" by Maeve Brennan. Copyright © 2000 by The Estate of Maeve Brennan from *The Rose Garden: Short Stories.* Reprinted by permission of Counterpoint.

TRUMAN CAPOTE: "Master Misery" from *The Complete Stories* by Truman Capote. Used by permission of Random House, Inc.

JOHN CHEEVER: "O City of Broken Dreams" from *The Stories of John Cheever* by John Cheever, copyright © 1978 by John Cheever. Used by permission of Alfred A. Knopt, a division of Random House, Inc. "O City of Broken Dreams" from *The Stories of John Cheever,* published by Jonathan Cape. Reprinted by permission of The Random House Group Ltd.

EDWIDGE DANTICAT: "New York Day Women" from *Krik? Krak!,* copyright © 1995 by Edwidge Danticat, reprinted by permission of Soho Press Inc. All rights reserved.

JUNOT DÍAZ: "Negocios" from *Drown* by Junot Díaz, copyright © 1996 by Junot Díaz. Used by permission of Riverhead Books, an imprint of Penguin Group (USA). "Negocios" from *Drown* by Junot Díaz. Used by permission of Faber and Faber Limited.